Cousin Hazel,

You were a word
wonderful person.
Thank you for everything.
Happy reading!
Love, Emma Austen

The Xavier Mosaic

Prince Asyrias

by
Emma Austen

Artwork by C. Kilby

Copyright © 2012 by Emma Austen

All rights reserved.

No part of this publication may be reproduced, distributed, or transmitted in any form or by any means, including photocopying, recording, or other electronic or mechanical methods, without the prior written permission of the author, except in the case of brief quotations embodied in critical reviews and certain other noncommercial uses permitted by copyright law.

Library of Congress Control Number: 2012900019

ISBN-10: 146811526X
ISBN-13: 978-1468115260

Printed in the United States of America
First edition, April 2012

Dividers courtesy of "Designed to a T"
www.designedtoat.com

http://www.xaviermosaic.com

for Abbi, for all of her patience and enthusiasm.

also for Ms. Burgess, who taught me the power of words.

Once upon a time, in a land without a god,

there lived a handsome Prince.

That handsome Prince married a beautiful Princess,

and together they had a son.

The Prince's father died and he became King,

Princess became Queen,

their son a Prince.

Then the handsome King sent a sorcerer to fry,

while his Queen screamed and shrieked.

Eight years later, the Prince would die.

The fairytale unraveled

Prologue

The mosaics' eyes haunted Morana, even in her own room. The result of her husband's sickness—his strange art, his prophetic claims, his obsession with unreal visions manifested in the mosaics he created, darkening the light of every window in the palace. The Queen-Mother could not escape it, the glass artwork her late husband had left behind. King Cedric's dragons watched her—dragons of red, blue, green, loomed like specters around every turn, their spiteful gazes staring, staring deep into her soul. Even there, locked in the safety of her own chambers, she was aware of the mosaic across the hall, facing her doors: a blue dragon, whose feminine smirk was lit by wintry light.

Outside, in the enchanted city around them – Larasca's proud capital, Joanissia – the people would not feel the bite of winter. Peasants, merchants, scholars, and noblemen alike were all blessed with the capital's unusual warmth, which remained even when snow blanketed the land. Inside the palace, this was not the case. Morana Xavier had to clench her teeth to keep them from chattering, wrapping her fur cape tighter around her shoulders even as she sat at her own vanity. It took too long to regain her composure.

The fire in the hearth made the room somewhat bearable. She had no intention of leaving that warmed space that day, not for needy subjects, Councilmen, or the boy King himself. However, this proved too much to hope for. The hardened Captain of the Guard came to her that morning, as he had every morning, to remind her of her duty.

"A guest has arrived in the throne room," said Art.

The woman did not turn from her vanity. The former Queen looked only at her reflection, her fingers moving from the hem of her cape to trace the glass brooch tied about her neck. She noticed its glow, catching the light, shimmering against her pale skin. The gift retained its splendor, though its giver had expired.

"I do not wish to go there today, nor anywhere else," she said. "Send him away."

Art stayed, though he uncomfortably shifted beneath her doorway.

"He won't allow that, Your Majesty."

Sudden agitation turned Morana from the mirror, for years of power had dulled her temper's restraints.

"And who so thinks they can command a Queen?"

His expression was easily read. He, like all of his men, had had his head shaved to make it such. So at once, she saw uncertainty change the captain's stoic face. His emerald gaze strayed from her as rough fingertips tapped his armor plates, creating the music for his unrest.

"I…can't dismiss him, Your Highness."

"And why not?" she snapped.

The man paused, his tap ceasing as frustration hardened his features. Yet, he seemed nervous, shaken by recent events. An unnerving emotion, when seen upon a man who usually held little natural expression.

"My men answer to him," he explained. "I have reason to believe it's witchcraft."

Her previous resolve was forgotten. All at once, she could feel the cold seep through the thick lining of her dress, a foreboding all-too familiar slithering beneath her skin. Through practice, she hid her anxiety. She rose from her chair.

"Fine, then. I will see the reason for your nonsense."

She forced herself to leave her chambers to venture through the frozen halls of the castle, subject again to the knowing eyes of the palace mosaics. However, they now seemed less oppressive—for the glazed eyes of the castle guards were far more chilling. She was now certain of this visitor's identity. Unwelcome as he was, that guest would not allow her to ignore his presence.

Soon enough, Art opened the grand double-doors of the palace throne room. She at once saw the cloaked man who stood beside her throne, whose withered hand lingered near its silk. Though the torchlight illuminated the scarlet cloth on which he stood, it could not penetrate the dark shadow of his hood. His long, gnarled beard soiled the floor. Yet despite these grotesque features, it was his smirk that sickened her most.

His cracked lips curled back, revealing a tongue that flickered behind rotten teeth—allowed the wheeze of his stale breath.

She spat his name like a curse.

"Jaska."

The hooded man hardly moved away from her throne, impervious to her scowl. His deliberate smile only broadened as he wrapped an arm about him, bowing to his foreign-born leader.

"My beautiful Storma," he purred, his back creaking as he lifted himself. "It is always such an honor to behold that infamous sapphire gaze. You, Larasca's beautiful Queen—"

A pause, as if he knew her sneer before he saw it. It was enough that he chose to remind her of her ethnicity, which even now made her suspect in these lands—to remark on her diminished authority was to smear dirt in the wound. Her irritation served to deepen his pleasure.

"My apologies, I had forgotten. Your sister has usurped your title; you are only Queen-Mother, now."

Morana glimpsed Art's anxious retreat towards the open entry, though her glare stopped his exit. Even so, the Captain offered no assistance when the creature came upon her, clawed fingers reaching for the white glass of her pendant.

"Ah, Cedric's brooch: the fabled gift to his blushing bride. What a lovely adornment, to mark the day of his passing…"

Repulsed, Morana smacked his hand from her chest.

"What do you want?"

Her assault could not dismay him. Hoarse laughter shook his body, forcing him to curl his fingers about the arm of the throne for its support.

"After ten years, I assumed a woman of such sweet semblance could forgive a previous intrusion. My words then were for your benefit, my Queen."

"I doubt that," she said.

Jaska's grin grew, despite the weight of his whiskers.

"I will not hold such action against you. Perhaps the Storma find it difficult to allow warmth into such narrow eyes."

Rage threatened to overwhelm her. Clenched fists shook at her sides, barely concealed by the folds of her silver gown. She wished to strike him, but feared that decaying skin would be left upon her palm.

"I'll call my guards," she warned.

His chuckle negated her spite.

"I doubt that would do you much good. They are a

little…unresponsive."

She clenched her teeth in frustration, attempting to keep her already suffering composure. Jaska was unconcerned. The haggard man moved from her, retreating mere steps along the crimson rug. Raising a tawny hand, he gestured towards the entryway.

"Why so angry, Your Highness? I've brought you a gift."

At once, the oak doors were flung open. Two expressionless guards entered the room, armor plates creaking as they dragged their prisoner across stone tiles. In their tactless grip was a young man, who screamed and cursed like a commoner. But they were not swayed, for they seemed to hear nothing. They thrust him upon the ground in one motion, impassive to his cry.

"I present a troublesome trespasser," Jaska said, chuckling, "plucked from the city before he could cause you trouble."

Morana had thought no presence could take her eyes from that unwelcome creature. However, it took only a glimpse of the bewildered youth to transfix her gaze. His short hair was as black as hers, a trait all but nonexistent in homogenous Larasca. Though he had a grown man's build, his face seemed somehow young, still full of pride and arrogance. He was free of stubble, and despite his curses, attractive. Yet, one trait kept her gaze. His eyes were hers—their shape, their intensity, their sapphire glow.

The captive watched her with similar bewilderment, mouth agape as he tried to form words.

"This has to be some kind of joke," he stammered. "Nikolai must have put you up to this…"

Suddenly, he seemed to forget himself. Head hung over the ground, his shoulders shook with laughter. Though his face was hidden by the shadow of his locks, she could see the madness of his smile.

"Very funny, you prick!" he called, laughter growing. "You can come out now! Gloat like the arrogant bastard that you are!"

Jaska's grin did not waver. He only watched, amused by the faltering sanity of his young captive.

"My child, Nikolai isn't here." With sinister pleasure, he raised a yellowed nail towards the Queen-Mother. "It's she you must answer to, now."

Despite his paleness, she could see blood drain from the young man's face. His narrow eyes widened as he stared up at her, choking on his own tongue. Morana turned her fury on Jaska. She would demand an explanation; however, no sooner had she opened her mouth than she heard the captive's whisper.

"You do look like him."

Her gaze fell upon him. He appeared somehow subdued, by his own will. His eyes were set on the crimson rug beneath him, dark hair shrouding his face. He offered no elaboration.

Irritated, she at last stepped from the throne's platform.

"Who?" she asked. "To whom could you possibly be referring?"

She was answered by a quiet, bitter laugh.

"Asyrias."

The very word chilled her blood to ice. The nails of one hand began to dig into her palm, paining her with their force, yet she could not feel it. She could only stare at the man who still knelt upon the rug.

"Where did you hear that name?"

"Who doesn't remember your son's name, Morana?" Jaska asked. "It was remarkably cruel of you to name him after a ruined country."

Her skin crawled with fury, her muscles tightened to knots. Within her was an inexplicable anger, for her son was long dead, all but forgotten.

His name shouldn't have continued to hold such power. It shouldn't have inspired such hatred.

"My son is dead," she said, something threatening in her cold tone. "What gives a commoner the right to speak of him? Just who do you think you are?"

The youth merely smiled.

"Proof of otherwise."

His voice betrayed no emotion, no matter how she searched for it. Instead, she sought to meet his eyes, if only to know the depth of his insolence—but even as she knelt before him, jerking his chin up with a harsh grip, she could decipher nothing from his sly gaze.

Cruelty hardened her features.

"Who are you?" she demanded.

He said nothing. As he averted his eyes, a clever smile curled his lips. The look, his silence: both wrung her nerves, upsetting the balance of her unstable nature. Unable to control her anger, she turned his face with a strike.

"Answer when I speak to you!"

His cheek turned red where it had met her hand, proof of his pain. Even then, he ignored it. The youth's continuing smile was a testament to his amusement, for he remained unafraid.

"My Queen would never show such weakness," he said.

She could have screamed. Again she turned upon Jaska, enraged enough by the boy's nature to shriek.

"Don't just leave me some lunatic! Tell me who this boy is!"

Jaska's smile showed no pity. His cloak's tattered ends dragged along the scarlet trail as he turned from her, becoming the only sound of his ghostly exit. Bewitched guards heaved the doors shut, trapping Morana with his tribute.

Somewhere near the throne, she heard the Captain clear his throat.

"Shall I pursue him?"

Morana found it difficult to form words. Her blood boiled, in spite of the frost. As she stared at the prisoner, irate, she noticed familiarity in more than his eyes. He had a strong, Larascan jaw to go with otherwise smooth features, his dark hair tending to fall over his eyes in its stubborn way. The way he stared up at her, such insolent expectance in his gaze— everything, everything about him echoed that child she despised.

"Your Highness, should I—"

"Gather your men, Art," she said, coolly. "I want this boy locked up."

Art paused, clearly surprised by the sudden command.

"They may still be—"

"Do it!" she shrieked.

With a sudden slam, the doors closed behind the platform. At last, the Queen-Mother was alone with her prisoner. The man looked up, perhaps disturbed by this development, but even then showed no fear. He would not be broken.

This would be dealt with.

That morning, as she had every morning, she had placed a flat, black diamond into the secret fold of her dress's yoke. It was a powerful artifact, which still tingled with the enticing presence of the man who had last owned it. In its warmth, there was the power necessary to tame the boy.

The youth drew back from her, as if sensing this danger, knowing it.

"An Avdotian Diamond," he whispered.

Not even the Councilmen knew of its existence. It was too peculiar that a stranger would understand what it was so quickly, even giving it a name. Yet, she would not let it distract her. She knelt before him, pushing the gem's point beneath his chin.

"You know of it," she said. "Then you know what it's for."

Light rose from the gem in serpentine streams, slithering into his every crevice. The life in his eyes began to fade, replaced by a dull, listless stare. She heard a haunting whisper fill the air, detached from her, though it was her own. Coaxed by this sound, tangled lights danced for the sorcerer's words.

At last, she lowered the black diamond. Its support gone, his head hung limp.

"Who are you, boy?"

He did not lift his head.

"They call me Ariel," he said.

"And how do you know of these diamonds?"

For an instant, she glimpsed his dry smile. She grew tense, ready to weave the spell again; however, it proved only a shadow. His eyes remained empty, and his face vacant of all expression.

"How I know of them is not important," he said. "What you are doing with them now is all that is relevant, in these years."

Her slight comfort in the spell was now overshadowed by suspicion. She again was certain she had told no one of these diamonds, aside from a band of soldiers she had recently sent to foreign territory. He was a spy, or a madman, or both.

"What are you muttering?"

He responded as vacantly as before.

"You are using a Larascan military Rank to retrieve the missing diamonds from your home country. Do you not think that will raise questions?"

This intimate knowledge of her most clandestine scheme made her nervous, agitated. Moreover, the charm the sorcerer had taught her should have left him entirely impassive, only able to answer simple inquiry. This youth was defiant even of his unnatural binds.

She thrust the diamond to his throat, jerking his chin up to her.

"That's none of your concern," she snapped.

The gaze she met betrayed nothing. He remained expressionless, seemingly under her control. She was forced to regain her composure. Slowly, she pulled the gemstone from his neck.

"How do you know of my son?"

He said nothing.

Too soon, the echoes of heavy footsteps called her attention to the corridor beyond the grand entry. Despite his silence, she was forced to forget her frustration. She rose quickly to her feet, concealing the diamond within the secret fold of her gown.

His voice came without warning.

"I know him because he lives here," he said. "This is his home."

The doors burst open, parted by five armored guards. They rushed into the room, taking Ariel in their bruising grips. He didn't move. He could not. But even as they removed him from her presence, his words remained, rendering her as motionless as he. For the first time in ten years, she was forced to recall her son's face—she was forced to recall his father's.

As the Captain went to close the double doors, he was stopped. A new man had appeared, more unwelcome than the last. His young visage defied the icy air, maintaining its virtuous glow; his blonde hair still freshly brushed, and green eyes bright as day. She longed for the Captain to slam the doors on that pristine face. However, Art gave in to her nephew's whim;

he left with his men.

"Morana, what's going on?" Attlas asked, doe-eyed with bewilderment. "You have to tell me something, you just condemned a man!"

Morana was silent, too preoccupied with her own thoughts. The woman tried not to see his eyes, or recall her husband's. She wished they weren't one and the same.

"I'm your King, Morana, you have an obligation! I've let you boss me around for too long; I'll not endure it!"

She could not shake her anger. His every word evoked memories of a blackened past, more nightmare than truth. Her fingers curled tighter around her glass pendant, tighter. All the while, its ribbon had begun to loosen about her neck.

"Get out," she whispered.

Attlas' ferocity melted into trepidation, as though he sensed the danger of her mood. In his concern, he reached towards her, as Cedric had.

"Morana…"

Her ribbon snapped. All at once, the sound of shattering glass was drowned by her resonant shriek.

"GET OUT!"

The young King vanished into the corridor, escaping the assault. She did not notice. Queen Morana was left staring at Cedric's brooch—white shards upon a crimson path.

Part I:

Betrayal

Chapter I

*P*ain pulsed through her body, seizing every part of her. Nothing tangible existed. Sound and color had blurred, thoughts too scattered to form. Everywhere, through muffled sounds, she heard screams.

A single voice reached her, untainted. It seemed feminine, yet it rasped with a man's rancor.

"Did you honestly think you could defeat me with pawns?"

Black began to taint the swirl of colors before her, though her vision began to settle. Through the haze, she saw the glint of her friend's golden locks. His back was to her. When the pain worsened, she tried to scream for him, praying that he could somehow stop it. The boy would not turn.

The darkness began to worsen, lacing through her vision like a spider's web. Before the final moments, she saw another figure, gazing only at her—a man with eyes of amethyst.

His voice came to her: a low, reassuring comfort. He said only one thing.

"Wait, Rina."

With the last pain, the darkness was complete.

Something woke her, though the haze of sound took time to sort itself out. A clinking came to her, followed by sloshing and the rumble of men's laughter. All the while, there was another sound. At first, it was only a murmur in her ear. Then, it was a voice.

"Rina..."

At once, she jerked her head off the table. Brown locks fell about her in waves, confusing her with the tickle of loose strands. Around her, life in the tavern went on, oblivious to her and the man whose breath heated her neck.

"Richard," she squeaked, scrambling to her feet. "I wasn't asleep, I was—"

This time, the man wouldn't hear her lie. He raised his hand, stopping her words.

"I assume Alastor made another of his late-night visits."

The short man did not hide the detestation that accompanied his words. His arms were crossed, head shaking – a usual stance. But despite his weary gaze, its green hue showed no cruelty towards her. Only her employer could stand amidst liquor's stench and appear so calm. The irritation that creased his brow was not for her, she decided, but for her mentioned friend.

For Alastor's sake, she tried not to be defensive. Hands clasped behind a loose skirt, she scanned her reflection in a puddle below.

"N-no, it's...this corset," she explained. "I'm just not used to it yet, especially not wearing it over clothing, so sometimes I can't breathe..."

It was a wretched lie. Even in murky water she could see how the strain of it changed her face, tightening her jaw and lips. Still, she knew it was fatigue that caused the blue of her eyes to dull.

"Even if he had come, he's just lonely, being on his own now. We both miss the orphanage…"

Richard's sigh was enough to drown the men's drunken laughter. His patience with her never ran deep. Despite her weariness, she soon remembered the reason for her tight garb.

Time to work.

With a short bow, Rina stumbled to grab her platter and return to her duties. Yet, Richard snatched her wrist.

"Damn it, Rina, hold still for three seconds," he snapped.

His calloused grip scathed her, and she cringed as she turned. At once, she was forced to confront Richard's frustration. Though shadowed by his gray, bushy brows, his eyes were windows to his constant exasperation. Unsettled, Rina forced a smile.

"What is it?"

To her relief, her wrist dropped. Averting her sight from his scowl, she wrung her hand atop the rim of her plate, trying to ignore the amused glances of the other tavern girls as they giggled behind her back. She knew she wasn't a strong soul, or even a brave one. She wished the others wouldn't mock her for it.

Rina didn't see her boss reach into his belt-bag. It was only when he revealed the small rock, metal coat glistening in the torchlight, that she almost forgot her insecurity.

"An aclara?" she asked, stunned.

He held a symbol of their city in his hands, pristine and glistening in its glory. That seemingly simple stone, unimpressive in both size and appearance, represented all she had ever known. Beneath its coarse exterior was the origin of miracles—even the sight of it left her speechless.

"This is yours," said Richard, his words accompanied by the glimmer of an approving smile. "Duke Baldric's chosen you to be the fourth Pillar."

Whatever she might have said no longer mattered. She could not pry her hand from her mouth. For years the orphan had watched the conclusion of the Lucadian festival from the sidelines, admiring the Pillars for their beauty and their part in the Blessing—the mysterious ceremony that protected their town from what lurked in the Great Forest.

Once a year, four woman would be chosen to represent the virtues of humanity, protecting their given aclara until it came time for the artifact to be surrendered to the sacred fire. Four men – the Defenders – would stand watch over them, to ensure no cruel force could interfere with the ritual. For that day, those men and women were the most honored of all Lucadia's people. Never once had Rina believed she would be one of them.

Richard was none too pleased with her silent daze, which was an unfortunately common state for the young woman. Still, his usual annoyance soon gave way to a duller, drained appearance. He placed a hand on her shoulder, a light shake bringing her from her trance.

"Rina, you're as scatter-brained as they come. I've seen cattle with more wit. But..." The man paused, again fighting a more pleasant expression. "I have to say, of all the things you've managed, this makes me most proud."

The girl barely managed to respond.

"Why me?"

The other maidens the Duke chose were the most striking, beautiful young maidens in all of Lucadia. She wasn't. Barely sixteen years of age, Rina was barely considered a woman, and had never been more than plain in her own mind. No matter how gaudy her tavern garb, that wouldn't change.

"Don't ask me," he said, shrugging.

Richard shook his head, pressing the aclara into her free hand. Even as she accepted it, shyness could not allow her to look him in the eye.

"Look, it doesn't matter why," he went on. "Duke said you had to be there—you and that no-good friend of yours. My sis and I will be there, so put on a happy face."

Her head shot up at the mention of her former caretaker.

"Gwen's coming?" she asked.

Naturally, he betrayed no sentimental love in his face. He decided to straighten the table beside them, pushing in chairs and stacking grimy plates.

"'Course," he said, grunting as he took the platter from her shaking hand. "Whole orphanage was a blubbering mess when you left. Gwen would never sleep again if she didn't take them to see you."

Her silent protest meant little; she was still forced to watch while he cleared her table. Even so, she felt herself smiling.

"I hoped they would miss me…"

He nodded, grunting when he dropped the loaded tray back onto the table. Somewhere behind them, glass shattered, the sound nearly drowned by raucous laughter. Richard cursed, grabbing a soiled rag from his belt. But when Rina moved to help, he held up his hand.

"Get out of here," he snapped. "You smell enough like this dump."

She would have argued, if she had that strength, as she was embarrassed to be ending her shift so early. However, no sooner had she opened her mouth than he had left, without a word. Rina could only bow her head in resignation.

"Thank you, Sir," she sighed.

Rina didn't want to leave; she was incapable of braving the streets alone. But he left her with little choice. Cautiously, she maneuvered the tightly packed tables towards the entry, wary of customers' curious stares. Probing looks were even more common from her fellow workers, who giggled as she passed.

"Look, it's little Rina!" Sarah laughed, looking up from her place among the men of a more boisterous table, "Leaving early again?"

She smiled at the blonde, hiding the aclara behind her skirt. Rina said nothing in reply. Swiftly, she tried to disappear from her comrades' sights. As the door neared, her grip only tightened on the coarse rock, as though that alone could give her the courage to keep going.

It's not a mistake, she tried to tell herself. *Duke Baldric really asked for me.*

Her hand was barely wrapped about the door's handle before she heard another crash, too close to ignore. When she looked at her feet, she saw the shattered remains of one of Richard's glass mugs, scattered in a pool of murky liquid.

"Hey, wench! Clean that up!"

Rina didn't recognize the voice or its robust owner, who smirked at her from a nearby table. Even so, she soon found herself kneeling in the puddle, a familiar rag drawn from her side. The action was so habitual that she no longer needed to think.

"Yes, Sir," she said.

Again, she saw herself in that puddle. She saw her long hair fall limp over her shoulders, making her face seem ever thinner, and her pale arms still appeared too scrawny for her work. Yet, her uniform was beginning to look small on her, her bosom forced into its bind.

She liked little about her appearance. Try as she may, she couldn't understand the Duke's decision to give her such an honor. As the rag grew sodden with the frothy liquid, she did her best to ignore all she saw.

Her thoughts were stopped by a sudden splash, the sole of black boots splattering liquor on her arm.

"Well, would you look at that—I thought even *you* would stop working on a day like the festival."

Even before she looked, she knew his voice. Her childhood friend was now so tall she had to crane her head to see him, though he appeared as thin as the day they had met. His crooked smile, too, had not changed: it seemed radiant, and drew as much attention as the gleam of his sandy-blonde locks.

He laughed when he saw her expression, crossing his arms.

"As much as I like you gawking at me, we have an appointment."

With that, Alastor hoisted her up by the back of her corset, paying no mind to her shout. Bewildered, she stuttered a response.

"W-we?"

Before she could protest, the youth jerked the sopping rag from her grasp.

"That's right," he said, smirking. "You didn't think I'd let you have all the fun?"

He wrung the towel carelessly, not flinching when the brown liquid spilled back onto the floor. When she grabbed for it, he held it out of reach.

"You know those guys that stand behind the 'Pillars,' right? The Defenders, or whatnot." He chuckled at her pout, responding by draping the soaked rag over her shoulder. "I'm one of them. I can look at your pretty behind all I want."

Even as the rag dripped cold liquor down her back, her face grew warm. She tried to look away, clutching the aclara tighter as she searched for words.

"You should have waited for me to come," she said, biting the inside of her lip. "Richard still doesn't like you much."

"Well, Richard isn't looking now, is he?"

Clearly, he thought little of her hesitation. His green eyes swept the room just once before he heaved open the doors, letting sunlight penetrate the stale air. With a smile, he gestured her out.

"After you, my lady."

Too accustomed to flickering torchlight, Rina had to shield her eyes from even the dim light of evening. She needed a moment to collect her wits. However, that moment was too long for Alastor. He seized her aclara and held the rock high above her, as if examining it against the sun's rays.

"So this is what it looks like…"

Rina's befuddlement turned to shock: she jumped for the rock, futilely pursuing when her friend evaded her.

"Alastor! Please!"

He only laughed.

"Gotta catch me, Ri."

The doors slammed behind them.

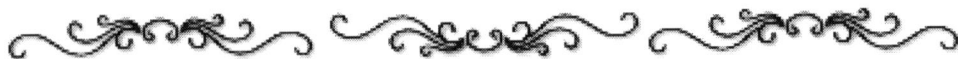

All around them, festival life raged on. Fire-jugglers dazzled people in the streets, blowing pillars of flames high into the blue-gray sky. Merchants hollered similar lies over one another, promising better items for less gold and claiming impossible miracles. All the while, children frolicked across cobblestone paths, tired parents trailing behind. Her wrist in Alastor's clutches, Rina felt much like those parents, dragged along strange routes to an unspoken destination.

"Come on, pick up the pace," Alastor laughed, jerking her onward once again. "I thought you were excited about this so-called 'honor.'"

As she stumbled forward, Rina tightened her hold on her reclaimed rock.

"Sorry, I just don't know where we're going…"

The Great Forest loomed far in the distance, intimidating as it always was. Yet, Rina found herself worrying less about it than she usually did. Its vengeful spirits were far away, now. The festival lights would keep them at bay.

The double-doors to the blacksmith's shops were thrown open as they passed, two young boys stumbling onto the road with laughter. Naturally, the stout blacksmith followed right behind them—red-faced and shouting.

"Little porkers!" he bellowed.

They didn't pass fast enough, for in that moment, Rina met the man's gaze. She hurried to look from his beady eyes; however, she saw another emotion change his face. The very sight of her seemed to unnerve him, as his teeth clenched while the color left his face. Alarmed by this, she tried to call to him as Alastor jerked her past.

"Sorry for getting in the way, Sir!"

The blacksmith thought little of her apology. The double doors slammed shut.

Alastor glanced over his shoulder to her, briefly stopping their pace.

"You need to stop apologizing to everyone. No one really cares."

She must have nodded, even smiled, despite her shaken thoughts. Her friend shrugged, reaffirming his grip on her wrist.

"Come on, then."

In the distance, she heard the growing sound of dog's bark. This wasn't unusual for Lucadia; many farmers brought their dogs into the city. Still, the sound troubled her. No matter how they maneuvered the narrow street, the sound grew closer. With every step she heard its echo, as if it pursued the scent of her fear.

"Alastor, do you hear that?" she whispered.

"Hear what?"

Suddenly, a great weight forced her to the ground, wrenching her from Alastor's grasp. The aclara clattered onto the street. Rina cried out, fighting to stand, but padded feet held her shoulders against the cobblestone. A low growl resonated in her ears, tightening her throat with fear. Alastor was as frozen as she—frozen by the unseen eyes of the beast that pinned her.

"Down, Rajj!"

The deep voice was unfamiliar to her ears. However, no sooner had it come than the creature was jerked off her body, snarling with fury. She gasped to re-inflate her starved lungs. When she managed to turn over, she froze again at the sight before her.

A young man stared down at her, so unlike any she had ever seen. His hair was a thick, deep brown – so nearly black that light couldn't illuminate it – that curled subtly about his neck. Though his eyes were green, a feature shared by many Larascans, they were pale enough to be gray. They appeared shadowed, haunted by time. Still, she found their strangeness so beautiful that she forgot the rabid beast he struggled to restrain.

"Are you all right, *Segnora?*" he asked.

Hearing this, she knew he was foreign. And yet he did not seem malignant or ugly, as foreigners were always described—only different. She remained silent, for her still-pounding heart rendered speech impossible. In her silence, she saw the wolf etched upon the breast of his long, worn tunic that she had seen many times before. She stared with disbelief.

A Stag?

Though the possibility was far-fetched, the emblem she saw left her without doubt: the foreigner was a trainee for the Larascan army.

With a sudden snarl, the mongrel snapped its teeth at her nose, if only to remind her of its presence. She jerked back, muscles tightening in renewed fear. This time, she was forced to see the beast that attacked her. Its fur was blacker than its captor's hair, and stood twice the size of the average stray. Yet it was its eyes that held her—eyes redder than blood.

"I apologize for Rajj," he rushed, dragging the creature back by a rusty collar. "He's trained to hunt deer, not women. He's never acted like this before."

She managed to pull herself to her feet, more by terror than will. As she grabbed her fallen artifact, she even kept a smile for her savior's benefit.

"I'm fine, he…barely scratched me."

It was then Alastor pressed past her, new anger possessing him. His fists were clenched, trembling at his waist, as he tried futilely to intimidate the foreigner.

"You let that thing go on purpose," he snapped.

In spite of his carefree attitude, Alastor was not usually one for open confrontation. The fact that he spoke so harshly now was out of character, and worried her greatly. She felt nervous when she saw the Stag return his cold look, accepting the challenge.

"No, I did not," he said. "But I don't think I saw you trying to fight him off."

"Please, both of you…"

Her words were soft, though cracked, attempting to soothe the young men while keeping attention away from herself. Always, she kept a wary eye on the snarling dog.

"I'm fine now," she said. "Please don't fight."

Her concern was real, for Alastor would be unable to act on any threats he made. He was physically much too thin, due mostly to recently-added height, and hadn't won one fight since he stopped sucking his thumb. His opponent, on the other hand, was clearly trained in how to use the sword at his hip. In muscle alone, the foreigner was likely twice her friend's weight. However, despite her concern, her attention was soon captured by another sound. She heard a voice resonate through the narrow street, its tremor one of great power.

"I told you not to bring those diamonds into this city, General!"

Further down the street, beyond the Stag, she saw the Duke Baldric standing in the street and away from his black carriage, which was tended to by footmen not far off. She knew him by his silken shirt and unnaturally dark hair, perfectly brushed back from his brow. His handsome face was red, strained from shouting at the bald, armored man who stood so calmly beside an open wagon.

"As the Queen's chosen Rank, we can go wherever we please," the man replied, thin lips curling into a sneer.

"You say that to me after I let you stay in *my* castle?! After you ate at *my* table?!"

The General smirked.

"You offered. Why should I rob my men of a free meal?"

Rina had never known Baldric Alexander to be a violent man. Although she had only seen him during nights of the Blessing, he had always appeared collected, calm and powerful. Yet when the Duke heard these words, true anger changed him. He drew his sword with dangerous swiftness, and sneered at a man twice his weight.

Rina gasped, afraid enough to cover her face; however, his attack was stopped by the hand of a golden-haired woman, as richly dressed as he, grasping his trembling fist with surprising calm.

"Let him be, Baldric," the woman said, "he only wants to enjoy our city. They're only diamonds; you have many of your own." The woman released his hand, shaking her head in blatant disapproval. "I swear, love, sometimes you take this festival of yours so seriously…"

It had been many years since Rina had seen Raquel Alexander. And yet, time had not touched her. Her golden tresses were still arranged perfectly atop her head, held off her neck by diamond pins that glistened even in twilight. Her eyes glistened like emeralds – narrowed though they were by irritation – and her skin was pale; her posture was without flaw, crowned by an aura of perfection. Despite this, Rina now noticed Raquel's strange resemblance to someone much closer to her. For an instant, she thought she saw Alastor in the Duchess' tried smile.

Strange…

Baldric did not seem pleased by his wife's presence. Even so, he slowly lowered his weapon.

"Those are cursed jewels, Lance," he growled, each word deliberately spoken. "And I'll not have them tainting festival grounds!"

Their argument continued, each speaking loud enough to drown out the other. Raquel grew exasperated, and she gripped her husband's shoulder in an attempt to draw him away from the scene. Rina tried to hear more, but her attention was shifted once more by a sudden, icy feeling. At once, she saw the Duke's eldest daughter appear by his carriage, arms crossed in apparent boredom.

A couple years younger than Rina, Heather Alexander stood tall for her age, her massive gown unflattering on her awkward frame. Unlike her mother, her hair was not golden, yet not quite brown. It fell limp about her shoulders, lifeless as her scarce smile. But she was not smiling now. Rina soon realized that the sensation she felt – the dark, foreboding feeling that tightened her gut – came from Lady Heather's cold stare. Rina looked about swiftly, hoping to find the real object of the girl's distaste. There was none. Heather's glare was for her.

With haste, Rina focused again on the young men at her side.

"Oh yeah? You think you can just drag around your rabid dog and act like you own the place?!"

"For the last time, this is not *my* dog!"

It appeared Alastor and the Stag had not improved their relations since Rina had last spoken. Both were poised to attack, the foreigner's free hand on his sword, and Alastor's nails digging into his palms. The feral dog appeared calmest; his crimson glare remained only on Rina, observing in silence. This alone was enough to keep her quiet.

"I know you let that dog go on purpose!" Alastor declared.

The Stag visibly grit his teeth in frustration.

"How many times must I say this? I did not…"

Something changed in his expression, then. As he trailed off, he began to scrutinize Alastor with a new look. There was recognition in his pale eyes.

"I've seen you before," the foreigner remarked.

Rina looked to her friend in surprise, in time to see his body go rigid.

"What are you talking about?" the boy asked. "I've never met you."

"I didn't say I met you, I said I saw you."

She saw the foreigner's hand shift towards an empty space on his belt, in some sort of recollection. Beside her, Alastor was utterly silent, hiding something behind a wary gaze.

Rina was reminded of the coarse rock clenched within her palm. Its reaffirmed presence seemed to urge her voice, trying to coax the slightest sound past her lips—anything to relieve Alastor of that scrutiny.

Please...

No sound would come. Insecure silence, her habit, rendered her a statue beside her friend. Great was her relief when a strident voice caused them to turn.

"Hey, Tallk!"

At first, she mistook this for the foreigner's name. However, she saw how he tensed when he heard it, hand clamping tight around his sword. She knew she had to be mistaken.

The youth who said it soon appeared: a young boy with a malicious smile, sporting the same garb as the Stag. Though not pretty, his face disfigured by a prominently crooked nose, he was Larascan from every angle: light-brown hair with green eyes flecked by hazel. Yet, she somehow trusted him less than his foreign comrade.

He approached the group with vigor unappreciated by the young man he called to. Even the dog, once too preoccupied with Rina's presence, turned to snap at the boy's trousers. Its master did nothing to restrain him.

"What do you want, Colin?" he spat.

Colin's initial enthusiasm was curbed by the mongrel's presence. Still, he would not be deterred. Casting a side-glance towards the duo, he addressed his fellow Stag in a haughty voice.

"General wants you back by the cart. He says Tallks should be more mindful of their….responsibilities."

Even as Colin spoke, the foreigner's eyes searched Alastor. Rina could see how the scrutiny made him squirm. However, when the word came again – Tallk – the scrutinizer finally looked away. His hold on the beast's leash tightened, and for an instant, his visage was as ferocious as the creature he restrained.

"He doesn't think keeping track of his deranged dog is enough?"

The younger Stag's response came with little more than a yawn.

"Someone's gotta watch the gold. Everyone else is too good for that sorta thing."

At once, she saw anger in the foreigner's handsome features. It was written on his brow, and in the veins raised in his worn hands. Rina could only watch, helpless, ignorant. She didn't know who to defend, or whether involvement was even necessary. Naturally, her thoughts were wasted. Alastor gripped her wrist then, pulling her from the scene with muttered words.

"Let's just go."

As her worn sandals caught on cobblestones, she found herself looking back on the Stags, hoping to catch the outcome of their dispute. The two had already started in the opposite direction.

"Don't you think we should say…something?" she asked.

"It's not our problem."

Alastor's reply came far swifter than it should have. When she looked up to him, she found it impossible to keep his gaze. Again she glanced to the Stags, still eager to attain closure. She saw the foreigner glance over his shoulder only once, betraying his passing suspicion.

Rina was jerked around the corner, into the unsuspecting crowd; he was gone.

The festival went on there just as it had before, undisturbed. They passed fire-breathers and dancers, who continued to twist and jump to the music of the crowd's cries. Puppeteers orchestrated children's laughter. The quarrels nearby had no part in their lives. Yet, Rina remained shaken by what she had witnessed. She knew cruelty when she saw it. As long as its echo rang in her ears, she could take no joy in festivities. Alastor's touch no longer held the assurance it once had. This feeling crept into her voice as she stepped from a child's path.

"Why the rush? Why did we have to leave?"

Even then, he seemed hesitant to respond. Forgetting subtlety, his grip on her tightened. They pushed through another crowd. Still, he wouldn't look back at her.

"He was a jerk. Why else?"

She cringed at this, aclara clenched tighter.

"Alastor, that doesn't answer anything! We could have said something! That boy was being cruel to him!"

Rina was more frustrated with her own silence than she was with his behavior. She felt now that she should have done something for the foreigner, after his selfless aid. The dog could have killed her, and probably him in the process. Yet, he had stepped in, without any hesitation. However, it was clear Alastor didn't share her gratitude.

His eyes continued to avoid hers, offering her neither answer nor comfort. It was only when they had left the crowd behind them that he was willing to speak.

"Look, Rina," he said, looking anywhere but at her. "I've kind of...seen him before."

She took the opportunity to free her wrist of his clutches. Wary, she looked up at him in the near-darkness. She thought she saw mischief in his countenance.

"What do you mean?" she asked.

After a moment's hesitation, he reached into his pouch. Out came a leather bag, strung by a modest rope. However, when it shook, there was a clink of precious metal.

A cold dread drained the color from her face.

"Where did you get that, Alastor?"

Over the course of their life, she had learned to put blind confidence in her friend. It was a matter of survival, more than faith. As long as she trusted him, she had a friend. Still, there were times that confidence felt misplaced. Seeing him then, his satisfied expression twisting his lips as he rubbed the leather between his fingers, she felt that faltering trust begin to slip away.

"The soldiers are rolling in gold, Ri," he said, "You know they won't miss it."

He tousled her hair, smiling his crooked smile.

"Think of it this way: you won't have to work for weeks."

Shock silenced her. Yet, Alastor took no notice of her trembling. He looked about in disinterest, until he turned away from her completely.

He instead watched a far-off commotion, either enthralled by it or repulsed by her look. She wanted to tell him *something*. She wanted to, she would have, were her tongue not so dry and useless in her mouth.

"Alastor….why…?"

He took no notice. Already, his sights flickered elsewhere, and his hand slithered back into his pocket. He was silent. Before she could muster the courage to speak again, she too saw the sight that so bewitched her friend.

Through the crowd, she saw curling fire. It stretched high above the people, painting the landscape with its flickering shadow. Two young women, barely clad in golden clothes, danced within the bonfire's orange light. Flames teased their bronze skin; their raven hair flowed in streams. They seemed very similar in looks, aside from height – both even had the same black chain tattooed around their slender forearms. Rina had never seen such exotic beauty. No Lucadian woman could dance as they did, hips alive, ribs moving as smoothly as their limbs. Their laughter was as much music as the poignant pulse of the pounding drums.

Forgotten was Alastor's confession. Before she realized it, they were standing before the dark-skinned women, among a crowd of awed people. All watched as the women swayed and shifted with the music, twisting and stretching like charmed snakes. The women blended with the flickering flames, moving as they did, a mere shadow of them. Rina was lost in the sight.

Suddenly, one stopped. Though Rina had first thought her nearly indistinguishable from her partner, she saw now that her face was of more striking beauty, and that her tattooed arm was also bound by a beautiful bracelet—a snake, wrapped about her bronze skin.

While her partner continued dancing undisturbed, this woman set her dark eyes upon the crowd. Taller, she seemed at first to overlook everyone as her scarlet skirt settled back against her thighs. She seemed to search the faces, looking for something. A smile graced her thin lips, that unreadable gaze ever searching. And then, it settled on Rina. The girl stared, entranced by it.

The dancer's voice came without warning, a tone as silky as her movements.

"You must be one of the chosen maidens."

This quick recognition seemed impossible. Yet, the dark-skinned woman clearly spoke to her.

"That is their…rock, is it not?"

Rina realized she spoke of the aclara, clearly visible in the lax grip at her side. Even in twilight, the stone's crevices somehow caught the light as well as the attention of all who stood around her. The girl grew pale, becoming aware of these looks. Her tongue was again weighted by self-consciousness.

She heard Alastor's voice in her ear before she could regain her composure, a chuckle to his hushed words.

"Looks like the Kala girl likes you."

Kala. It came from the name of that sandy country behind the southern mountains, the strange Akalin. At once, she realized she had never seen an Akalinian woman before this night. But when she should have been fascinated, she could think only of her embarrassment—and the redder she became, the more the woman smiled. Before Rina could protest, she felt a hot grip slither about her wrist.

"You can dance, can you not…?"

All at once, Rina was caught between the foreign dancers, so near to the flames that they licked her skirt. She was too startled to protest, horrified as she heard the faceless spectators begin to laugh. The other woman was holding her waist, gently shifting Rina to move this way and that, stepping and stepping to the beat of the sturdy drum. She was twisted and turned, tossed smoothly between both fluid dancers, the woman who first pulled her in smiling with such amusement Rina was left bewildered.

"She is a natural, R'ta; don't you believe so?"

The woman of smaller stature, whose shorter, wilder hair did not sway as easily as her partner's, laughed in response. Rina soon found herself pulled back to this performer with a sudden tug of her skirt.

"I know not, dear Sh'ka. She has a face like our deceased A'vra, but her footing is a shame…"

Her aclara was gone. Rina realized it much too slowly; she almost tripped as she was tossed again, her sandal again loosening some cobblestone from its place. But her anxiety was quelled when she saw her stone again—in Sh'ka's hands.

"What a pretty little artifact," said the Kala, smiling far too broadly.

At last, Rina found her voice. She stumbled forward again, out of R'ta's grip, to reclaim her lost property.

"Please, give it back…"

Sh'ka's lips curled with feline pleasure. Rina's attempts to snatch back her possession were thwarted by the woman's bends and bounds, the sound of laughter entwining so densely with her partner's that Rina thought she would suffocate in it. She awkwardly chased her around the fire, forced to follow the flickering shadow of her tormentor at the expense of her own dignity. She tripped and shouted, whining and pleading, to no avail.

Abruptly, her face met with Sh'ka's breast in the most embarrassing collision Rina had ever endured. She heard a chorus of laughter begin, loud and boisterous. Even the Kala laughed, taking Rina's wrist and twirling her away.

"Isn't she wonderful?" she asked the crowd.

Rina was not so amused. She stared intensely at the ground beneath her, her face vibrantly red. She wanted nothing more than to be away from these people, out of their sights. She wanted to return to the straw cot in the back of Richard's tavern and hide under her quilt, waiting for day to come again.

"Now, why the long face?"

The woman tugged her back towards her. With a glance, Rina saw the sly smile on her red-painted lips.

"Have I kept this from you too long?"

She displayed the aclara in an open hand.

"There. All better, *Guriya*."

She couldn't have been any happier. Rina quickly accepted her aclara, scurrying back to stand at Alastor's side. People around her continued to clap; one man gave her a solid slap on the back of her corset.

"Great show, girly!"

Her smile only weakened, the grip on her aclara growing protectively tighter. The foreign drummers began a new beat, and the laughing women began a new dance. Feeling her embarrassment begin to lessen, Rina glanced towards her friend, who still grinned broadly in his amusement.

"You could have helped," she offered, voice still very weak.

He replied with a laugh.

"Oh, lighten up, Ri. Looked like you were having the time of your life out ther—"

Alastor paused abruptly, a new sound loud enough to alert them both. He craned his head far back, to see what was coming up the street. Rina heard it too: the sound of clinking chain mail and wagon wheels bouncing over the cobblestones.

"Pigshit pigshit pigshit…"

Her friend grabbed her wrist somewhere during those curses, pulling her away from the flames. Too soon, they were running down the streets again, Alastor practically leaping over whatever came into his path and Rina stumbling into it soon after.

"Why are we running?!" she cried.

"Why did the Kala call you a Guriyash?!" Alastor called back, half-laughing, half-terrified.

She knew he was avoiding the question, but by this time, Rina had decided she did not want the answer. She was now more confused by his question than she was of their situation, far too accustomed to his strange antics.

"She called me a doll," she called, "Not a Guriyash…"

He cast back the strangest look she had ever seen, stopping in his tracks. One brow raised, he looked her over again.

"Did you hear her right?"

She nodded.

"*Guriya* is just another word for doll…isn't it?"

Alastor's green eyes examined her more thoroughly, baffled. The intense scrutiny caused her body to tense, and she began to rethink her own words. Her friend soon sighed. The noise that had started their rush was gone now, and a new stretch of the festival lay ahead of them. Tsking in disapproval, her friend soon began down that path without her.

"Where are you going now?" she called, running to catch up.

"To our preparation tent," he replied with a shrug. "Did you already forget what you got that rock for? We have to be pure for the Blessing, or whatnot…"

Her cheeks grew hot, embarrassed to have forgotten. Rina was quickly at his side again, kneading her hands over the strange stone she had been given. Even so, she found her mind wandering back to the foreign women. They seemed familiar to her, now. Somehow, she already knew their dance. The steady pounding of the drums had effortlessly engrained itself into her mind, as if she needed only the brief sound to recall the memory of many other listenings.

She brushed these thoughts away.

Sh'ka grew bored with her dance far too quickly. Though the crowd still hollered for her, her inner fire had died out. Ignorant cheers could only amuse her so long. As soon as the firelight dimmed, the Kala grasped her partner's wrist and bowed, forcing R'ta into the same form.

"Thank you for your patronage," she said, smiling in her deep, humble sort of bow, "but I would not want to be tired for performance tonight. Many apologies, my friends."

The thick Akalinian accent that embellished her words was entirely for show, but her guests knew no different. The men cheered wildly for the poor foreign girls, tossing coins at her bare feet. It took only a bit more shooing to fully dismiss the simple folk, but Sh'ka was pleased with their obedience. It seemed the less clothing a woman wore, the easier Larascan crowds were to control. It made her existence a rather satisfying one.

"I suppose it is about time they run home," said her partner, "Their wives won't go much longer without tracking them down."

R'ta's voice was always something of a burden on her ears, with the unnatural way it would climb to the top of its pitch before descending again, sort of rounding itself off at the conclusion of the sentence. It made listening to her taxing, the journey of inflections more difficult than what the girl actually meant. Of course, Sh'ka said nothing of this annoyance; it was better to tend to the appearance of friendship than to start the tiring task of fixing one.

"You were wonderful tonight, Sh'ka," she went on, grinning when Sh'ka glanced in her direction, "Especially with that one girl, the one with the bouncing breasts in that uncomfortable looking top. Was she the one that 'Heather' wanted you to swipe from? She looked like her: brown hair, bug-eyes and all."

Sh'ka lifted another fallen coin from the ground, slipping it into the pouch at her waist.

"I would like you to stop listening in on my business deals, R'ta. It makes me wonder why I should bother telling you anything at all."

"It is not like I had to try very hard to hear you," R'ta replied hastily, already braiding her tangled hair over one shoulder. "The Princess or whatever she is came while we were dressing, remember? Our tents are quite near now—"

"Separated by the horses' trough. I did not think you could hear whispers over stallions' snorting."

R'ta was stumped by this remark, and Sh'ka appreciated the subsequent period of frustrated silence. However, she was obligated by that appearance of friendship to speak.

"No matter. I forgive you."

A coin's cool metal beneath her fingertips, she looked out across the Lucadian street, observing the lighting of the nightly torches. She could almost trace the path that girl had taken with her friend in their haste, down the streets, around the bend.

"Do you think she is really A'vra's baby? *That* A'vra?" R'ta asked.

Sh'ka shrugged, tossing her silky hair over her shoulder.

"A gold medallion says she is; a truth contrary to my gold's word has never appealed to me."

She collected the last of the gilded coins from the ground. Seeing that the fire was dying out, Sh'ka pocketed the piece and began down the street. She noticed with disdain how thick the clouds were overhead.

Wet tents tonight.

Absently, she held out a hand to check for droplets.

"Are you actually going to tell those two about this?" her partner called, stopping her escape. "Alin will want a large chunk of the payoff."

Sh'ka cast her a mere glance, not bothering to turn and face her.

"It is only my duty."

She left her there.

Their caravan was arranged somewhat away from Lucadia's festival, on an abandoned street with a road of packed dirt. The buildings here were long forgotten, spiders crawling in and out of parts of cracked, stone walls, and battle-scarred birds hiding in the shadows of glassless windows. The troupe's residences looked like luxury, compared to its backdrop. The yellowed tents and buggies cut an impressive figure against

the decrepit old structures. Filthy Kala children seemed less like slaves—
which is what they were, in the end, and useful ones at that. Sh'ka stopped
a moment, admiring the sight and dwelling on the realization.

She felt a needy hand groping for her pouch.

At once, Sh'ka snatched the brown wrist and jerked it in front of
her, revealing the boy thief. He had a round face and big eyes, narrowed
though they were by frustration. The smear of mud across his cheek almost
distracted her from the ferocious desperation that scrunched his nose and
caused his sneer. He was feral, disgusting to behold, as were all the other
spawn of the camp. Yet, the strange lightness of his gaze reminded her of
another dark face, one she had beheld one too many times. Remembering it
made her taste bile.

Repulsed, she struck him.

"Keep your hands off things too good for you."

Snarling like a dog, the child scrambled behind a nearby tent.
Nearby women looked up from their fires to scowl, as if criticizing her for
not allowing the looting to take place. She couldn't bring herself to care.
She found it amusing how these women thought themselves good enough to
judge her. Perhaps they shared the same tents, or the same customers;
perhaps the same tattoo bound their right arm. But they were not the same.
She was the flower of their troupe. These women, huddled together in the
creeping cold, were nothing but rats.

She found the master's tent somewhat set apart from the rest of
them, conspicuous as always. It stood twice as large as any other, its fabric
dyed an impressive red. Akalinian markings on curtains that hung over the
entrance warned away intruders, though the two well-muscled men
standing on either side of it communicated the message without assistance.

Neither did much to deter Sh'ka. A smile granted her passage into the scarlet dwelling.

An array of stubby candles lit the area within, casting the mead-stained rugs in various yellow lights. Feather pillows were tossed here and there, a particularly large pile near the back from no-doubt recent indulgences. At the far corner of the room, covered only by a veil, lay a thick book bound by beaten leather. She could see the outline of the lock through the thin cloth—big and old, like the secrets it kept.

A bottle, still reeking of old liquor, rolled by her feet as she progressed further into the domain. It was then she found her master slumped over his short table, his gaunt face in a pile of coins. The currency did little to muffle his snores. She could see his gold vest was as stained as his rugs, and his hair – what little remained of it – was a stringy mess upon his head.

Filth.

Her thoughts mattered little. Alin owned her and every other girl in her troupe; a man of such wealth could be excused for some tasteless personal habits. Still, her situation left her with the task of waking him, one she didn't much appreciate. To deal with this efficiently, she took the half-empty bottle of mead from beside his dozing form and poured it over his balding head.

"Rise and shine, dear Master."

The man sputtered into consciousness, cursing in their native tongue. He snatched at the air for her hand, a look of murder about him. She easily evaded his drunken grip.

"You had better have a good reason for this!" he spat, wiping the liquor from his visage.

She knew words were wasted on a man with a brain soaked with mead. In response, she simply pulled a golden medallion from her heavy pouch. His eyes widened with greed; like a hungry toad, he snatched for it.

"Where'd you get that?" he demanded.

"A disgruntled child," she replied, flicking it out of his reach. "Heather, daughter of that brutish Duke. Or do you somehow not remember the man who paid your way here?"

"And why'd she give you *that*?"

Sh'ka smiled, taking a seat atop his short table.

"She wanted me to 'fix things' for a much prettier girl," she remarked. "A girl that looks very much like the little brat A'vra managed to hide."

The man was shocked, but an intrusion momentarily prevented any manifestation of his bewilderment. Akbar, the bodyguard Alin had raised by hand, appeared in the entryway. Although Sh'ka was at first annoyed by the interruption, she found herself delighting in the way the candlelight danced over the bare, bulging muscles of his torso. The woman would never deny he was a handsome man, tall and dark as he was.

"The horses are tied for the night," he reported, giving a stiff bow. "I would like to request permission to rest early."

His head was freshly shaved, she noticed, though the woman who was usually charged with doing so had recently fallen ill. He could only have done it himself.

"Forget it," Alin sneered. "This dancing whore says she's found A'vra's brat!"

Akbar, usually so calm, stood upright too abruptly. There was a strange emotion in his face, one Sh'ka had never seen on him before.

"The woman who looked in the Book, Master?"

Those were the words he said, but they were not the words in his expression. It annoyed her, somehow, but she did not complain. She interrupted Alin's response, whatever it might have been, and ignored his subsequent scowl.

"She looks only a lanky girl of sixteen, now," she said. "She's no dancer, certainly, and is of no use to us otherwise. The child probably grew up in a dirty Larascan orphanage and learned the skills of a good milkmaid."

Sh'ka observed her medallion with a detached expression, swinging it tauntingly so near her Master.

"Besides, she will be lucky if they let her be even that, after tonight."

It seemed Alin had not heard her. After another futile snatch at her prize, he gave a vulture's shriek.

"You had better give me some share of this 'reward' if you ever want to leave this camp—"

He was cut off by the clatter of a coarse stone onto his tabletop, still warm from its place in the dancer's pouch.

"There," she said, calmly slipping the medallion's chain around her neck. "It is one of only four the blacksmith makes for this ridiculous festival. Sell it, hoard it; I care not."

Alin's snarl was sated with his greed. He snatched up the aclara, bony fingers working over its every crevice before he looked up again.

"If A'vra's brat is alive, then she's my property."

Sh'ka had already stood to leave.

"Poor man," she said, unmoved.

The man stood sharply, moved by both annoyance and desperation.

"You can have anything you want if you snatch her!"

For a moment, she paused her exit. She looked back to him, now standing half between Alin and his servant. But though she first looked to him in intrigue, the sight of his frustration transformed her curiosity into a coy smile.

"I already have what I want."

She moved past Akbar to the curtain that blocked the entryway. However, it was Akbar's voice that this time stopped her departure.

"Will your performance for the Duke be…the usual?" he asked.

Though she seemed to smile at his words, it was not from mere pleasure; distant and curious memories stirred her heart, bringing about the serpentine smirk.

"Of course. It is my most inspired work."

When the curtain swung down behind her, Alin was left in his aggravated state. Still, with the object of his frustration now gone from his presence, the man had no choice but to focus it on his surrogate son.

"Do you have any idea how much it cost me when A'vra escaped?" he snapped, illustrating his point by reaching into his pile of gold and allowing coins to slip through his fingers.

Akbar only stared towards him, vacant, lost in far-off thoughts. Alin scowled, throwing the Lucadian rock at his skull. His annoyance only grew when it instead collided with Akbar's waiting palm.

"Get the girl for me and I'll make her yours."

This finally reached him, for troupe women were rarely promised to a single man. Akbar's visage betrayed his shock.

"Truly, Master?"

"You wanted her no-good mother," Alin said. "Her whelp could only be an improvement."

Akbar's stupor did not last long. Before long, the man leaned into another deep bow, his faint smile concealed. Though a man of few words, he spoke them with purpose.

"As you wish."

By the time the sun had fully set, one of the city Protectors had found Rina and Alastor, who had gotten lost among the festivities. Usually, the young woman was more wary around such men, for they were the keepers of the Duke's law, and formidable figures even without their customary armor. That day, however, she was relieved. It wasn't exactly pleasant, being lost with Alastor.

The Protector escorted Rina to the preparation tent, a space given to each of the four maidens to prime themselves for their festival duties. The boys who would serve as the Defenders were led to one as well, though some distance from their counterparts'. Rina had arrived to find the appropriate clothing already laid out for her, and a long mirror for her to ensure it was correctly worn. Beside it was a perfectly-formed glass bowl, filled with freshly heated water, and a soft cloth. She had to clean her body before wearing the gown—wash herself of any taint, the Protector had said. She didn't question it.

She found a Pillar's long, white dress almost flattering, far less stifling than her usual corset. Around her waist was a yellow ribbon tied in a plain bow, its lace ends still flowing with the dress' hem when they brushed over the floor. It was a simple outfit, yet elegant, far more elegant than Rina felt a tavern wench deserved. Even so, she found herself shyly admiring it in the mirror.

When Alastor's voice came through the tent's flap, she gave a start.

"Hey," he said. "I just saw Gwen go into the theater."

Her eyes widened; at once, she looked towards the flap, as if she would see her friend through it.

"Gwen is really here?"

She heard Alastor's laugh.

"Yeah. Our old lady is really gonna see you drop a rock in a fire."

Rina smiled, unable to help herself. She looked back into the mirror, seeing her long locks – now properly brushed – shimmer in the candlelight. For a moment, she almost thought herself attractive.

"I still don't understand why he picked me," she said, mostly to herself.

"Neither do I," Alastor replied, having heard her despite this. "Maybe you served him a bad drink."

She groaned.

"You're really no help for my nerves…"

By his laugh, he didn't care.

"Come on out, Ri. Let me see you in your costume."

Although reluctant, she knew denying him now would only postpone the inevitable. She stopped only to take her aclara from the table. Once it was securely in her hand, she finally left to see her friend.

Alastor stepped away from the tent at once when he saw her, a look of surprise coming over him. There was a strange, possessive look about him; it gave her some discomfort. But no sooner had she turned her sheepish gaze to the ground than he touched her cheek.

"Wow…you've really grown up."

When she looked at him, she saw his smile. It made her blush, and she looked away by instinct.

A nearby Protector, the Duke's jagged crest draped in cloth over his heavy armor, caught their attention with a low cough.

"The ceremony will begin soon. I have been told to escort you to your place."

Rina quickly nodded, forced to forget her embarrassment. Alastor took her arm, and she soon was walking the narrower cobblestone path to the stone theater.

She stopped when she came to its edge. Baldric's theater was built deep into the ground, many levels of stone seats rimming the area to the bottom, where a wooden platform served as the performers' stage. Around it, four giant, stone bowls held strong fires. However, it was not the sight of these fires that froze her—it was the sheer height of the ground she stood on from the ground below.

Don't push me…

She remembered Alastor's small hands on her back, and the height of the hill just outside Lucadia. She remembered her small shriek, the rolling, the incredible agony that came when a bone in her arm burst partway through her skin.

Please don't…

Her every muscle tightened when she felt Alastor's hand on her shoulder.

"Still scared, Ri?" he asked.

Rina gave no reply, too lost in the pain of her own memory; yet even if she were in her right mind, she could not have predicted his next move. Too suddenly, he had spun her towards him and pressed his lips to hers.

It was not a romantic sort of kiss, if that was what he meant it as. Rather, it seemed a shoving of his face against hers, and if his apparent eagerness to bite her lip was passion, Rina felt she could do without it. She kissed him back, in a way, and when he was satisfied, he pulled away with a smile.

"Let's go meet our adoring fans."

With her own faint smile, she took his arm again – aclara still clutched tight – and descended the stone steps, following the old Protector's lead. On the way down, she tried to glimpse the audience members that sat in the rows she passed. Near the top she saw the soldiers, all seated with an air of composure, perfectly still even without their usual armor. Next to them were the young Stags in their long tunics, chuckling and bickering in what were almost hushed voices. She looked for the dark-haired foreigner and his dog among their ranks. He was nowhere to be seen.

The girl recognized no one else for a while, save for a few men who frequented the tavern. The recognition wasn't returned, of course. She grew accustomed to blank glances until the middle steps, where she saw a line of children squabbling and whining on their cold seats, unable to sit still. Their heavy caretaker shouted curses at them from the end of the row, despite the much slighter Richard caught in the crossfire between their whines and his sister's bellowing. Although Gwen had been a feared figure in Rina's childhood, seeing her there now gave her a sense of comfort. When she passed, she offered the woman a smile. For once, a faint grin accompanied the grunt of response.

The Protector led them to their seats, located behind one of the four great fires, near enough to see cracks on the stage. When they seemed comfortable beside each other, the armored man left as silently as he had appeared—and although Rina remained perturbed by their kiss, she did not deny Alastor closeness. It wasn't her nature to shy from things that brought others happiness.

No sooner had they sat than the Duke, a cape of wolf fur draped down his back, rose up from the great throne beside the stage. Though he was seated below the large audience, so grand was his presence that he seemed to tower over its every member.

"Citizens of Lucadia, this year's festival will finish differently than in years previous," he announced, his booming voice echoing through the hollow space. "Before the Pillars perform the Blessing, there will be another presentation, to remind us that there is more to this world than what is within this city."

Even as Baldric spoke, Rina could see the unusually solemn look set on his handsome face. In past years, he had commanded the theater with an overwhelming presence, even more so than now. This time, he seemed far away. Though he seemed to see everything, from the peasants in the top rows to the royally-dressed members of his court in the bottom, his blue eyes reflected nothing back.

"Though most of you know the word Kala to describe people of dark skin, the true Kala are the troupes of Akalinian men and women who travel their country and our own to share their talents."

He made a gesture to two approaching Protectors, who escorted a tall, dark-skinned woman onto the stage. Rina grew pale, for she knew this woman's smirk.

"I present Sh'ka, a Kala of one of Akalin's oldest troupes," Baldric announced. "It is she who will perform for us."

The Protectors escorted out two Kala men as well, both bearing their wooden drums. Yet, no one saw. All sat entranced by the sight of the foreign woman, who was adorned so well by her golden skirt and the small, coined top that covered her breast. Sh'ka did not shy from this attention. She seemed to thrive in its presence, nurtured by the people's silent praise.

A drum's slow pounding began even before the Duke returned to his seat. At once, Sh'ka began her graceful dance. Her hips moved with every beat, upsetting the chains of coins that hung from a belt around her waist. At first she only smiled, hollering in response to the drummer's cries of encouragement. Then, she began her song.

"It is a strange thing, to love a beast."

Another swish of her skirt, another strange holler.

"My beast-love moved like a panther, grasped like a hawk. His black mane fell in shrouds. Human lips concealed wolfish fangs, drawing blood in the name of his lust. He believed himself invulnerable. His eyes were weak—eyes like amethyst, eyes like veins."

The drums' rhythm changed. Their beating seemed lower, echoing throughout the entire drum with purpose, each strike becoming more urgent. Before long, it became a loud, steady command.

"He loved like a dragon, hoarding what he thought his; trusting me as though I were property, as though I were prey. I could not be trusted. I was not prey. He was trapped."

Another great spin accompanied her triumphant cry, her skirt flaring out beneath her to mirror of the motion of her hand.

"My love showed me his fire. My love showed only me those flames, only me. I needed only share sparks with the rest of his world, and he flared them high."

The four flames that lit the stage gave a sudden, strange flicker. Rina jumped, her breath caught in her throat. However, Sh'ka's dance was not done. The chain of coins shimmered as they danced and jingled in the light, creating a pelt of fire for her finale.

"The furious beast destroyed all that touched him. Trust died in his eyes, fell away like cinders. His howl pierced the sky. He was lost, he was lost; he disappeared."

At last, her body settled, the golden skirt falling back against her long legs. She gave the audience a calm, chilling smile.

"The beast was best alone."

At last, the drums' pounding ceased. Sh'ka bowed instead to the music of her audience's clamor, the people of Lucadia still enchanted by the foreign dance. But Rina did not share the others' excitement. The woman's words brought pain to her heart, something she couldn't understand. She spoke softly to Alastor, hoping he might share the feeling.

"Don't you feel sorry for her lover?"

Any hope of empathy vanished when Alastor gave her a bewildered look, the same he would have given had she grown fangs.

"What kind of gibberish do you speak?" he asked.

She was as stunned as he was, terrified by the implications of this remark. Was it possible that Alastor had not understood the Kala's song?

Was she the only one that had?

When she next looked at the stage, the woman was gone, escorted back into the shadows. Before Rina could think further, the Duke had stood from his chair. Once more, his powerful voice filled the theater.

"Pillars, stand by your pyre."

Rina saw the other three maidens stand, moving gracefully behind their fire. After a moment, she realized she should do the same. Although a bit clumsier, cheeks already hot, she stood behind her own.

"Defenders, stand behind your Pillar."

Three young men took a solemn stance behind the maidens, as she heard Alastor move behind her. Though she could not see him, she sensed his smile. Holding the aclara tighter, she watched as the Duke ascended to the stage, proceeding to its center.

"This will be the fifteenth ceremony since Lucadia, formerly the capital of West Larasca, was united with the mainland—the fifteenth anniversary of our return to the Xaviers' Kingdom. However, this is more than the celebration of a date."

He extended his long arm, slowly gesturing to each of the maidens.

"This is the day we celebrate women's power, as the four chosen maidens conduct a ritual to protect the peace of our city."

Normally, Rina would have felt uncomfortable with the intensity of the crowd's attention. Yet, the sound of the Duke's voice somehow soothed her anxiety. As long as she watched him, she could forget herself.

He continued.

"With the burning of the four aclaras, the vengeful spirits from the forest beyond are forced to remain far from our streets."

With this, Baldric extended his hand towards the first maiden: a beautiful girl with brunette curls, a ribbon of blue around her white dress.

"Pillar of Truth, lend your power."

The girl's eyes fell as she dropped the coarse stone into the fire. With a great crackle, the flames shot higher, the orange turning the color of the daylight sky.

"Pillar of Justice, lend your power."

The next maiden, a scarlet ribbon around her waist, yielded the rock. This time, the orange flames became a deep red.

"Pillar of Faith, lend your power."

A young woman, her hair braided down her back, sacrificed her aclara. This time, the fire became a brilliant green, to match her ribbon.

At last, the Duke turned his blue gaze on Rina. He watched her for a long time, longer than she felt comfortable. Rina felt the blood rushing to her face, but didn't know if she was allowed to break his stare. It felt now like he was searching her, testing her, until the moment he finally spoke.

"Pillar of Hope, lend your power."

Rina gave one last look to her coarse aclara, feeling a twinge of grief at having to part with it. She had fought too hard to keep it all that while. Even so, she knew her duty. The young woman surrendered it to the flames, and waited for them to dance yellow.

There was a sudden, piercing shriek from the fire. Rina cried out, covering her ears to forego the pain it brought. The flames shot higher and higher, becoming not yellow, but black as night.

What?

The flames died as rapidly as they appeared, the shriek ending with them. When Rina could finally peel her hands away from her ears, she stumbled towards the stone bowl, staring into the ashes. She could feel the terror of Lucadia's people around her as she reached into it, pulling out all that remained—a flat, black diamond.

Raindrops pattered onto the stage. Rina could feel them sliding down her tresses, beginning to sodden her white dress. They cleansed the cinders from the diamond, leaving its surface a mirror for her shock. The rain carried away her tears.

"Hey…"

Amid the stunned silence, she felt Alastor's hand on her shoulder, its grip gentle.

"It's not your fault."

Rina managed to look back at him, through her tears. However, she tensed again when she heard a soldier's booming voice echo off the sloping walls.

"Keep her there!"

Suddenly, her arms were in the grip of two strong soldiers, jerking her away from her only friend. She cried out in shock, barely managing to hold onto the diamond when they pulled her away.

"What have we here?"

The bald general from before leered down at her, as though she were a piece of meat. Before she could say a word in protest, he snatched the gem from her trembling grasp.

"A thief, trying to destroy evidence?"

The back of his hand met her cheek, scraping her with the mere coarseness of his hand. Her tears came again; her throat was too dry to contain them.

Somewhere behind her, she heard the Duke's shout.

"LET HER GO!"

By now, the falling rain had all but smoldered the pyres. She could only see the shadow of the tall man as he rushed to the edge of the stage.

"You cur! She's done nothing wrong!"

"That was the Queen-Mother's diamond in her hand, Baldric," the General warned. "This is out of your jurisdiction. You have a problem with it, go cry to Morana."

She had already given up hope. It was only by chance that she glimpsed a Stag pointing to Alastor, accusation shaking his being.

"That's him! That's the one Kaish told us about!"

All blood left Alastor's face. He shot towards the stairs, stumbling when his foot caught the first step. That stumble was enough. A shorter, more agile Stag caught up to him, dagger drawn. With a clear slice to Alastor's pouch, gold coins spilled onto the stone steps.

"You son of a bitch!" one cried, forcing his unruly hair away from his eyes before drawing his own dagger.

The Stags wrestled him to the ground. Moving despite herself, Rina tried to worm from the soldiers' grip to get to him. She shrieked for his sake.

"Alastor!"

There was a sudden, sharp strike to the back of her head. Rina fell to her knees, the shadows in front of her beginning to blur. She barely heard Baldric's roar.

"I'll have your hide for this, Lance!"

The world went dark.

Chapter II

The rain pattered steadily outside John Keeper's inn, cleaning the windows without his efforts. Though it always seemed to be raining in the fishing town of Alore, John was beginning to appreciate its constant downpour. Something about the muggy warmth it brought distracted from the pain in his old bones, and it kept away unwanted critters and their fleas. He thanked the rain now for the quiet in the old inn – though he cursed it for his lack of patrons – and indulged in it as he swept.

A heavy knocking disrupted his peace. John looked up towards the weathered door with a start, dropping the broom to the wood floor in a clatter. On a night like this, he wasn't usually so keen to open the door. Yet, there was something about the presence beyond that struck a chord of recognition, even without a face to go with it. Perhaps it was something about the impatience of the knock, demanding entry.

"I'm coming, I'm coming," he muttered.

After propping the broom near the stone hearth, he opened the door.

At first, he wasn't sure it was a man who stared down at him, almost a full head above his own slight stature. The great thing, its bronze skin half dyed by soot, panted under the weight of a torn and sodden shirt. His shaggy mane was black, blackened further by the pouring rain. Yet, his strangest features were his narrow eyes, which seemed almost young, and glowed a color far different than John's Larascan green. John knew that this was not the first he had stared into those amethyst orbs.

"Silas?"

The young man coughed at the ground, not quite in recognition. However, when he raised his eyes again, they finally seemed to know him.

"It's getting worse. The…curse," he croaked, as if forced to recall how to speak. "Just…just let me in."

John brought the youth in from the rain, barely remembering to close the door in his hurry. He toweled him with an old quilt, sopping off the water and much of the mysterious soot. Before long, the young man looked almost comfortable by the hearth, still wrapped in the soiled quilt. He stared into the fire—distant, silent.

The innkeeper took a nearby chair.

"Silas, it's been three years. Where have you been?"

The young man didn't look at him. He shuddered beneath his blanket, like a pup having a bad dream.

"That long?"

"It was 651 when you ran off," John said, trying to see the face beneath the shadow of his dark locks. "It's 654 now. Unless I've lost all reason, that's three years you've been roaming forsaken country. My bones! You're practically eighteen!"

If the innkeeper's words reached his ears, Silas took no notice. His violet eyes were set on his right hand, the glimmer of his gold ring made bright by the fire. For the first time, John noticed the blood caked beneath his jagged nails.

"…the Protectors are after me again," Silas murmured.

At once, John gave a cry of frustration.

"Silas–!"

He stopped himself. Just that syllable of raised voice had tensed the youth's every muscle, even bristling the hair on his neck. The innkeeper forced himself to calm; in response, so did the boy.

"Why are they after you again, Silas?" he asked, his voice much gentler.

The young man in question did not raise his sights. He just kept staring at his hand, as if much more stained it than soot and blood.

"A little girl…caught me eating her father's pig."

His eyes fell even lower, long nails curling deep into his hand

"Then I burned their barn down."

John grew very pale. In Alore – or perhaps in all of Larasca – livestock was the livelihood of its people. The killing of another's livestock, be it chicken, cow, or pig, was practically murder. Burning down a barn on top of it was a death warrant.

"What were you thinking?!" John cried, this time unable to suppress his shock. "What could have possessed you to make you do something that terrible? And burn down the barn?! BURN DOWN THE—"

A terrifying sight stopped his tirade. Moved by rage, its target had shot to his full height, wolfish teeth bared in defense. No sooner had the quilt fallen to the hearth than John felt the youth's grip around his arm, growing hotter and hotter with some inhuman power.

"I was bloody hungry!!"

Though John grew paler, the burning grip only tightened.

"Can you imagine what it's like going weeks without food? Your stomach screaming at every passing squirrel and finch until you hear their screeching in your head? Do you?! **DO YOU?!**"

His roar shook the building and its keeper, almost knocking the broom from its precarious position. Petrified, John could feel the hand beginning to scorch through the thin leather of his sleeve. Then, all at once, sense returned to Silas' peculiar gaze. The man was released as abruptly as he was seized, and his visitor slumped back against the stone wall.

"I'm…sorry," he said, quietly. "My…my temper is getting out of my control. I just…snap…"

He grasped his head as he sunk to his knees, his sodden hair still dripping into his face. For some reason, his whole body shook.

"I'm losing my mind, John."

John saw Silas' jaw clench tight, though his hands concealed most of his expression.

"I didn't mean to set the barn on fire. But…the girl saw me with my prey. She started screaming 'forest freak forest freak' and I panicked…then I got angry…then…"

He reached for a piece of firewood, now stacked inside and out of the rain; he clenched it so tightly in his hand that it began to crack. Though still shaken, John could only watch in awe as Silas' palms grew red. Suddenly, the log burst into flames, burning as brightly in his hand as its twins in the fireplace.

Silent, Silas tossed the burning wood onto the hearth, leaving the stupefied John to collect himself long enough to prod it into the other fire.

"Once the fire starts, I have no more control over it than the next man. I got the little girl away from it, but not without teeth marks."

With a bitter smile, Silas pushed some tattered material away from his shoulder, revealing the fresh bite.

"I should have let her burn."

The innkeeper stood in shock, still stunned by this youth's feat. Try as he may, he could say nothing—the fire leaping from Silas' hand had lamed his tongue.

Silas raised his dull gaze towards him again, as if understanding.

"That's not my biggest problem. I have some control over that curse, now. It's this ring…"

Slowly, Silas raised his right hand towards him, and he gestured for the man to come closer. Although hesitant, John obeyed. He took Silas' rough hand, examining it. Scars mapped the darkened skin; his long nails were yellowed and cracked, all but ignored. However, what caught John's attention was the elegant ring, choking a finger marked with terrific scars. Two red petals glistened upon its surface.

"You've shown me this before." He paused, looking back to the youth's shadowed face. "Weren't there more petals, then?"

At once, Silas jerked his hand away.

"There were twelve."

He stared down at the ring himself, nearly trembling.

"Last year, they started disappearing, one by one. Every time it happened…there was this incredible pain. Then it would get worse…and worse…"

His nails curled into his palm. Briefly, his jaw clenched, haunted by anguish.

"I've done everything to get it off. I've soaked my hand so long it turned blue…I tore at it, gnawed it, tried to fawking melt it off. Nothing works…nothing bloody works…"

Silas took a pause, forcing down breath. His claws tangled in his black hair.

"It'll kill me, I know it. It'll kill me. It'll kill me…"

The older man watched as Silas' eyes glazed over, his weight falling limp against the wall. It seemed the last of him had finally been used, drained by the effort of speech. Inside, a part of John ached for the child he had once known, lost within this strange youth's torn and weary body.

Again, he wrapped the quilt around the boy's shoulders.

"Come," he said. "Let's get you upstairs."

Silas was impassive, moving with John's every gesture. Soon, the young man was seated on a cot in an upstairs room, a dry quilt around his shoulders. John busied himself by pulling things out of drawers, blowing dust off what he could.

"The room is just like you left it; I haven't had another guest in here in years. The mirror's a little dingy, but it should do you fine. There're a few new books on the shelves, I put them there before you…" He paused, catching his words. Still, he continued with the same buoyancy. "The water in the basin is fresh, and there are a few extra towels in the drawer. There's even a dusty set of clothes in the closet, though they'll be small on you now…"

John smiled, wiping the grime off an old razor.

"I'll bet you need one of these now, right? I always kept one here for when you would."

The innkeeper looked at his guest with a grin. However, the cold response he received quickly wiped it from existence. He noticed with some surprise that though this boy was all but grown – unusually tall, with muscle to spare – there was still not a shadow of hair upon his face.

"You still don't shave?"

Sharply, Silas looked away. The sight of sharp fangs betrayed his feelings: he didn't want to talk about it.

John sighed, allowing him to keep his silence. Having known the boy for many years, the innkeeper knew this was probably another of his abnormalities, none of which could be helped.

Since Silas had first arrived in Alore – a strangely tan child of no more than eight – he had always demonstrated a peculiar pattern of development. He was very small those first years, almost a full head behind many children his own age. Yet just as they had decided he would always be that way, Silas had begun an alarming stage of growth, springing up many inches in a matter of weeks. By the time he was fourteen, many of his old friends could not put their nose to his shoulder. He put on muscle whether he wanted to or not, and his hair grew too fast for him to dream of keeping it trim.

With that came other oddities. One such were his narrow eyes, which were once a glacial blue. Over the span of a few months, those pale orbs had first warmed to red, then to violet, a color that had only grown more vibrant since.

Silas was no natural youth.

When John had lit the small fireplace in the corner of the room, his guest stared into its depths, perhaps entranced by the flames. Something about him seemed worn beyond his years, like a dog stilled by weakened bones. He did not move from beneath his quilt, holding it around himself too tightly. However, just as John was about to leave him in silence, the youth spoke.

"How is Maddy?"

John paused, surprised Silas asked about the innkeeper's adopted daughter. Though he had often seen Silas and Madeleine together as children, close as siblings, Silas had never been the type to ask after someone without reason. Yet the young man interrupted him before he could reply.

"She still working for Queen Bitch?"

The words were rude enough, but with the sneer on Silas' face, it was a curse. John could only sigh, pulling up a seat near the fire.

"What happened between you and Lady Abaca is a thing of the past. Really, it's a waste of your time to hold a grudge against her. You know she is an...inconstant girl." He offered a smile, in hopes to comfort him. "She's probably forgotten all about you. Please, try to do the same."

Silas gave a sharp growl, turning his face away. John noticed then how truly feral the sound was, vibrating in the youth's chest and throat to create its low tremor. It seemed to come so naturally to him, as though his father had been some breed of wolf.

This time, the innkeeper was somewhat uncomfortable in the silence. Though it may not have been in his best interest, he continued.

"Heh, well, there's not even any proof it was her father who paid off the Kala..."

He trailed off only because he saw the look in Silas' eyes. They were narrowed to slits, hard as ice, hard as the fangs he clenched together. John was silenced.

Slowly, the young man calmed. He gazed back into the fire.

"I saw her with Edmund," said Silas, no fondness in his tone. "Are they a couple?"

John nodded.

"Yes. At least, that's what Maddy tells him."

A flicker of a smile from the boy, and then it was gone. His gaze was elsewhere – in a dream or a memory. The flames were reflected in its depths.

"What are your beliefs, John?" he asked.

The question struck the innkeeper as odd. Since its founding, Larasca had had no gods, nor any set of beliefs that resembled them. Still, John answered with a smile.

"I believe...no person is perfect," he replied, "but every one of us is capable of good deeds."

Silas seemed not to hear. He just stared, stared into the flickering flames before he finally replied.

"I believe that misery is inevitable," he said. "I believe that the all the world needs a scapegoat, and as soon as the first is too broken to be whipped, the world will move on to the next one."

He clenched his teeth, his eyes changing, seeming to take on the red from the fire they reflected.

"The world needs to see something broken for it to thrive. It wants something to laugh at; it wants to laugh at its scapegoat's breaking bones, at its blood, at its cries. It drinks all of it like a parasite, until there's nothing left..."

His grip on the quilt grew tighter, nearly trembling.

"Until there's nothing left of me..."

John had never seen him this way. He seemed to carry the weight of a kingdom on his back, a dagger in his heart. Although John didn't understand his pain, he felt he should try to help him. But when he placed his hand upon the boy's shoulder, he was met with such a violent snarl that he would have sooner tended to a beast.

"Don't **TOUCH** me!!"

Silas' eyes were savage, teeth flashing as he wrenched away. Yet, even this intense rage soon melted into shame. The violet gaze fell, and he pulled the quilt ever-tighter around his shoulders. He would speak no more.

John gave a piteous sigh, surveying him once more. All at once, he was struck by a memory. The memory led him to one of the vanity's dusty drawers.

"Here, Silas."

Soon, the innkeeper placed a small, worn leather book on the bed beside him. The young man glanced at it; his glance soon turned to a scowl.

"What would I want with that old thing?"

"You documented your early life, didn't you?" asked John, again taking his seat by the fire. "Perhaps reading it again will remind you of your...humanity."

Silas gave the man a long, hard stare, surveying his very meat. Though he tried to ignore it, John couldn't help the discomfort it brought. However, the youth soon gave in. He picked up the journal, placing it in the old pouch that had always hung from his belt.

"Doubt it."

The small flames burned for only a few hours more. By the time they had consumed the last of their wood, Silas had passed out on the mattress. John remained in his own chair, chin on his folded hands as he thought.

He's changed.

That much was too clear. John found himself saddened, because of it. He had always looked upon the boy as a son, and John played the paternal part far better than Silas' self-proclaimed parent, Giovanni Wolfslayer. Though Giovanni was a decorated man, known throughout the land as Commander-partner to Baldric Alexander and as responsible for the reunification of East and West Larasca, he could not have been a worse father to the orphan he had brought home. John's inn had been Silas' only respite from the once-Commander's bizarre methods of neglect.

John knew the boy better than any other had—every quirk, every tendency, John understood. He knew Silas had never been levelheaded. Even when he was small and surrounded by friends, the wrong phrase would send him into a frenzy that could only be soothed by restraint. But these tantrums were minor, and sometimes Madeleine, as little as he, could even coax a laugh out of him when they were finished.

Something drastic had changed in Silas, since those days. In just that evening John could see that Silas had lost all control over his volatile temper; slave to it, he was dangerously hostile towards anyone who dared come too close.

What changed?

What, he knew not. *When,* however, was something he did not have to guess. John could see that Silas, even as he now slept, had creases upon his brow left by that fateful day. As for John, it was burned into his very dreams—that day, not three years before, when the world had first seen flames leap from Silas' very body.

A mournful cry and Silas had disappeared into the forest, blistered Protectors hot in pursuit even as they licked their wounds.

John, Edmund, and Madeleine had stood by and watched—friends too stunned to follow him.

John saw sparks dancing in the hearth's ashes, and meant to snuff them out. But his body was heavy, and his eyelids were drugged by partial-sleep. He decided to stay there for a moment more. For a moment more.

Pounding on the door.

"Open up!! By order of Chief Alfric, you must open this door!"

The innkeeper sat up with a start, practically flinging himself to his feet. After a moment of light-blinded confusion, he swiftly pieced together the circumstances.

Protectors tracked Silas.

He moved to shake the boy awake but found him already alert. Silas was standing rigid, hair on end as he stared furiously at the closed door. The pounding came again, still downstairs.

"Hand over the fugitive!'

Suddenly, John realized the voice drifted up through an open window.

"We are armed, Keeper!"

Although panicked, the man tried to move as quickly as he could. He grabbed Silas' arm despite the danger, ushering him towards the window.

"You should fit through," he rushed. "Please, quickly!"

Yet Silas was not so swift to move. He stood stiff, held immobile by some new source of rage. His voice came like a low rasp.

"Giovanni told them."

Another pound, pound, pound.

"OPEN UP!"

John pushed him towards the window, though his fingers twitched with urgency.

"Please, Silas!"

But the youth was again stopped, staring out the window. His whole body shook, fury gripping his very core.

"I'll kill him…"

His veins throbbed, teeth clenched.

"I'm going to bloody KILL him!"

The innkeeper heard the downstairs door open with a mighty crack, coerced by blunt force. However, as soon as he heard metal boots upon his staircase, the object of their pursuit was gone. John could only stare at the fluttering curtains, feeling left behind.

12th Month, 644 I.R.

He says my name is Silas. S-I-L-A-S. He says I'm 8 today. I should know if that's true. But I don't. I don't remember yesterday either. I don't know why I'm in this wagon. I don't know if Silas is my name or not.

He tells me to call him Father. He doesn't feel like a Father. When I think Father, I feel happy. Giovanni doesn't make me happy.

He gave me this to write in. He told me to write in it every day I'm with him. But I don't want to go with him. But I don't want to be alone. I'm afraid to be alone.

I go with him, but I don't call him Father. I call him Vaan.

Vaan says I'll get my memory when I meet Mother. He says Mother gave me my ring. He says she'll take it off then, cause it'll hurt. I told him it doesn't hurt. He laughed at me.

The road is bumpy. Vaan says it'll be bumpy the whole way. He laughs at me when the bumpy makes me sick. I don't like his laughing. I don't like him, but I don't want to be alone. I woke up alone, and I couldn't remember.

I don't want to be alone again.

The Alize River still lapped at the sands behind that old, brick house, no more tame than it had been when Edmund had come there as a child. What brought him there now was something of a mystery to him. He still had on his Protector's armor - Duke Bayard's cloth insignia somewhat dingy from rare washing and Maddy's new lipstick still smeared on the collar. Though the young recruit had wanted to go home to change, something had instead drawn him straight to the home of Giovanni Wolfslayer.

His beautiful mare snorted at him as he tried to leave her, shaking her dark mane as if in warning. Even so, he tied her reins to a nearby oak branch.

"Don't worry, Ella," he said, gently. "I won't be long."

His companion whinnied, but stepped away. She was resigned.

An intimidating oak door stood at the end of Edmund's path, guarding entry to that dismal home. A red-flowered vine had grown around it, making a frame of beauty that feigned hospitality beyond. For some reason, Edmund found himself anything but comforted. Something told him these flowers had poison.

The door had no knocker. The young man was forced to pound on the wood.

"Hello!" he called. "Anyone home?!"

A time passed in silence. Then the door creaked open, as though pulled by some invisible force.

"Come in, come in, old boy," came a voice.

Edmund knew that voice at once: the way it seemed to chuckle behind every word, either mocking or amused at everything in life. He entered despite himself, closing the door behind him. Within, he found the front room the same as it had always been: books filling shelves that climbed to the ceiling, chess pieces and gambling chips littering the fine Akalinian rugs, and the only desk in the room so stacked with papers it was impossible to tell the wood it was made from. Used swords of strange makes, some still rusty with blood, were mounted upon the walls. It was dangerous to travel the space, unless you already knew your way.

At the end of the room was a wide window, its glass masterfully tinted so a person could only gaze out, not in. It was there he saw the ex-Commander, staring out at the vast river that supported their lives. His brown hair, once long and braided, was neatly cut below his ears, and when he turned to his guest, Edmund saw his face was nearly divided by a neat, well-groomed mustache. It lifted with his clever smile.

"Edmund, my boy," he laughed. "It's been some time, hasn't it?"

The young man chanced a hesitant grin, though he shifted uncomfortably beneath his emerald stare—it knew too much.

"I came to ask you a few questions, Wolfslayer," he replied.

He tried to put on a Protector's authority. He found it didn't fit him. Giovanni could see this too, and as his smile grew, laughter bubbled up from his gut. Soon, he was shaking the room with it.

"And here I thought you were too old to play Protect and Defend!"

The man's amused gaze fell to the sword at Edmund's hip, his eyes scrutinizing its impressive size, its bronze-inlaid hilt glinting in the morning light.

"And look: your father even let you dress with his pretty sword!"

Edmund's hand quickly pushed back the once-Chief's sword, but the man continued to laugh. He laughed until Edmund writhed under the sound, forced to retreat some. He had never liked the eerie feeling in that house, or that man. Still, he tried to stand tall.

"Do you know where your son is, Wolfslayer!?" he demanded, as if he could not hear unless he shouted.

Suddenly, Giovanni grew quiet. Though his smile did not diminish, it seemed more curious now. He turned his back to him, instead watching the window.

"I'm guessing by the smoke I saw last night that he's back in town. If he's in town, that means he's with that huggable John Keeper. You're a little late on location, though; I've already told your friends. Poor Silas is probably long gone."

Once more, his green eyes flickered back to the Protector.

"So that begs the question: why are *you* here?"

Edmund was strangely baffled by the question, though he took it upright.

"I told you, Sir," he replied. "I'm just here to ask you a few questions."

He glimpsed Giovanni's smirk before he turned back around. The young man took a step towards him, but no more.

"Ah, of course. Just like Chief Edward, always with your questions."

Another chuckle.

"I suppose I'll lend an ear."

The Protector managed to collect himself, standing tall, though out of Giovanni's view. After taking another survey of the room, he decided to chance his interrogation.

"Why haven't you taken Silas back in? Taken him to another city, where no one knows him?" He cringed, knowing already that his words fell on deaf ears. Still, he tried. "We're not going to catch him. He's too fast, and most of the Protectors are plain scared of him. All of this running and hiding…it's pointless."

As expected, Edmund's questions were met with another dismissive chuckle.

"What would he learn from that?" he asked.

Edmund coughed, startled.

"Learn from…what, Sir?"

Giovanni continued to stare out the window, silent for a time more. Looking past him, Edmund finally saw what he did: a fishing boat docked further down the shore, burly men heaving great boxes down to land.

"You see, Eddie," he said, like he had been talking all that while, "a comfortable life leads to a comfortable job, in the same comfortable situation you grew up in. If I had treated Silas like any other boy, he'd probably be one of those longshoremen, mindlessly hauling fish." The man looked back at him, his smile intact. "Just like you became a nice, neat Protector, just like your Daddy."

The youth tried to remain unmoved.

"But he's your son," he protested, "Don't you know how he's living now? How can you let him go on like this?"

The ex-Commander replied with a slow shake of his head.

"Sadly, the boy isn't of my seed."

He spoke it as though it were an excuse. Even so, Edmund tried to remain impartial. For once, Giovanni was allowing him to ask questions. He planned to make the most of this.

"So is he foreign?"

Even now, no one knew. Silas was as nearly dark as the Akalinians that visited their town, yet had a jaw like any Larascan.

Giovanni responded with another round of laughter.

"He's certainly no Kala, if that's what you're thinking. Certainly doesn't have the nose for it…"

The man grinned at his own thoughts, crossing strong arms over his tunic.

"Yes…my Silas has a purpose far beyond these waters. My job, like any parent, has always been to ensure he is ready to serve that purpose."

A smirk.

"He's not quite there yet."

The man's words struck Edmund as eerie, though he couldn't place reason to the feeling. However, he would have no chance to respond, for a great shatter soon pierced their thoughts.

A blur of muscled flesh crashed through that wide window, only a cloak shielding him from the shards. He was tall, very tall, when he leapt to his feet, and his jagged claws flashed as he pounced. Edmund could barely form a thought when he realized what had happened.

Silas.

The youth's hands had locked around Giovanni's throat. His eyes were big and red, a vein throbbing in his neck as he tightened his fatal hold.

"You bastard! You bastard YOU BASTARD **YOU BASTARD!**"

Once, Silas had been Edmund's friend. They had played the same games, eaten the same food, and knew the same people. And yet, Edmund found himself as terrified of him as he would have been of any wolf. He could not look from that horrifying youth, whose canine teeth came to points as sharp as the nails that dug into Giovanni's neck. Though it was his duty to defend the ex-Commander, Edmund found his hand frozen upon his sword. In all his life, he had never been so still.

"You couldn't let me have one day of peace?!" Silas bellowed, hands squeezing ever tighter. "One fawking **DAY?!**"

However, Edmund's fear wasn't reflected in the man being attacked. Giovanni was as calm as he had ever been, that same smirk on his face. His words came smooth as butter.

"You're getting emotional again."

A splash of blood.

A shout and Silas was on the ground, clutching at a ringed hand now half-slashed open. Above him, Giovanni stood with a reddened dagger in his hands, an object previously concealed somewhere on his body.

"I saw that Kala troupe dock down the river there, the other day," Giovanni said casually, wiping the blood on his trousers. "Did you go see that girl? Shika? Shaka? Oh, what was her name…"

Silas gave a wounded growl, the blood spilling thick down his arm. Edmund, pale as a sheet, was all but invisible to him.

"Well, I suppose it doesn't matter. I hear you're too busy stealing bread from children to deal in any more romantic matters. How's that working out for you, by the way? Kill anyone yet? Scorch the butcher? Fry the Duke?"

The beast was red with fury. But when Silas began to speak, he found the dagger's point at his throat.

"Take my advice, Violet: dig yourself a nice place to hide."

Giovanni's words were met with the most monstrous snarl. Yet the moment the dagger was lifted, Silas was gone—a trail of blood leading to the broken window.

In his absence, the room suddenly seemed very cold. Edmund stared at the crimson path that had been left behind, in denial of all that had just occurred. When he felt Giovanni's cool gaze move to him, he grew very stiff.

"He was right there, Protector. Why didn't you tie him up?"

Edmund could say nothing. All his words were drowned in that pool of blood.

"Ah." The man began to chuckle. "I'm beginning to understand."

His green eyes looked Edmund up and down, seeing something the youth would never be able to comprehend.

"What's more important to you, Edmund? Is it your simple life? Or your friend's?" The ex-Commander grinned. "You can't decide, can you?"

At last, the man again turned his back on him. He gave a long, aching sigh, for the first time showing a trace of human pain.

"My bones," he swore. "Glass all over my new rugs."

Words of dismissal.

.

Chapter III

*J*ust as the rain began to fall, Kaish took a seat on an old, rotten stump. He could see Lucadia's dimming lights in the distance as the steady rainfall snuffed its torches. By now, the Talonian was used to Larasca's constant rainfall. He was used to being wet, used to eating sodden bread. The loneliness, however, he would never be accustomed to.

His wooden flute felt familiar in his hands; he used the feeling to ward off his paranoia. The forest around him held too many shadows. Even Rajj, the moody beast that he was, paced warily in their presence, his rusty chain clinking against itself and the tree it was tied to. Not too long ago, Kaish would have been more cautious of the canine when he was in this state. Now, he was used to it.

Kaish allowed himself to be absorbed in the texture of his instrument – his fingers explored its every crevice, each hole, feeling the difference between wood the rain had darkened and patches saved by overhead leaves. He longed to hear its sound, but didn't want to annoy his feral charge, who lingered much too close. The creature's teeth were too impressive to summon.

The foreigner and the dog exchanged a cordial glance, before the black fiend settled into a damp pile of leaves. With a great yawn, fangs flashing, it lay its head down to rest. Kaish rolled his eyes, despite his relief. Rajj had a habit of sleeping just before they had to leave, and it only served to make him irritable when he awoke.

"Sleep, you pest," he said.

Even in rest, the creature growled.

The Stag returned to his flute, continuing his absent-minded scrutiny of its body. However, a horse's whinny soon pierced his thoughts. Kaish shot to his feet, shoving his flute back into his pouch. His hand was already on his dagger when a fellow foreigner and his familiar white stallion emerged from the forest.

"I've scoped out a trail," said Saito, already beginning a dismount. "If we hurry, the ground should still be hard enough for us to get the cart through to the Lesser Forest before dawn."

Kaish relaxed as he would for no other man. Saito had an air about him far different than the other soldiers of Rank 12. Kaish knew now that the man's elegant manner was reminiscent of his birthplace: the land beyond the Great River, Storm. Although Saito was not of impressive height, as he was forced to gaze up at Kaish when he usually regarded him, his understated features gave him a look of regality. Gentleness shined through the Storma's narrow gaze, complementing a more feminine face, and his short, dark locks remained perfect even in the rainfall. Since the day Queen Morana had sent him with their Rank, the man had never appeared less than immaculate.

"The General still has you pet-sitting?" Saito asked, a good-natured expression on his gentle face.

The Stag made a face resembling a smile.

"If you can call that creature a pet."

He gave a wary glance towards Rajj, who this time remained undisturbed. Breathing a sigh of relief, he again returned his attention to

Saito, who had begun to secure his horse's reins to a low branch.

"Maybe I should lend you Satoru for the night's trek," he said, lightly patting his stallion's snow-white mane. "After all your hard work, the last thing you should have is another night dragging your feet through the mud."

Kaish shook his head, giving a quiet laugh.

"That horse would miss you too much. I couldn't take him from you."

Satoru gave a huff, as if in agreement. The Talonian nearly grinned.

"I swear the two of you are one entity."

Saito smiled, lifting a burlap pack off Satoru's back and onto his own. After obtaining Kaish's nonverbal permission, the older man took a seat beside him. There was plenty of room on the large stump.

"In Storm, it is an honor to be compared to your steed. If you can be one with the animal, you and he will move like water, maneuvering any path and overtaking any enemy." A smile. "There must be a similar belief in your own country, Kairos."

At once, Kaish's pleasant look dimmed.

"I'd rather you not call me that," he said.

The Storma cringed, though he didn't yet retract his words.

"I apologize; I know you've corrected me before. Is there a reason you no longer respond to your proper name?"

Kaish gave only a dull smile.

"I'd rather not talk about it."

Saito seemed to accept this. For a time, the man watched the sleeping dog, silent in thought. Kaish took the time to examine the Storma's extraordinary armor, which seemed so different from the other soldiers'. Instead of heavy chainmail, Saito wore only thick shoulder plates, which shined like pure silver, attached to a vest that looked as if it had been laced with steel. His legs had no protection that Kaish could see, but his boots were thick enough to trek through swampland. He once thought it a strange design, but since the Rank's journey to Storm, he had seen stranger things. There, Saito's armor had appeared quite ordinary.

"Why do you stay here, Kaish?"

The question took the Stag off guard; he soon realized Saito's dark eyes were set on him.

"Why do I stay…with the Rank?" he asked.

"Your Talonian accent is nearly gone," said the man, shaking some rainwater from his own smooth locks, "and I can guarantee any Larascan city will treat you better than Lance has. I could even pull a few strings and get you a home in the Merchant Square of Joanissia."

Kaish could not help his laughter.

"There would be no point; I've been here too long. Other than gutting a boar, I have no skills."

Though amusement lit his eyes, Saito maintained his serious expression.

"You've been here far too long, Kaish. You're years older than your fellow Stags, the same age as most of the soldiers. Lance is never going to advance you; you realize that."

The Stag nodded, though he had no response. It was the truth: he should have left long ago. But he saw no point in leaving. His mother was dead, and their home long reduced to rubble. He had no skills and no master to teach them. For now, this life was the best he could hope for.

Saito sighed, again observing his comrade.

"You could be a woodsman," he said.

Kaish laughed aloud; yet, Saito's look remained quite serious.

"Honestly," he continued. "In fact, I recommend you set your sights on that sort of simple, satisfactory existence. Run away—take a wife and settle on the countryside, far away from Lance and his ludicrous beliefs. Any prey you catch won't have to be shared, and you'll always have a real bed to sleep in at night. How about it?"

He wasn't sure what to say. Although it was his instinct to refuse such a possibility – for he was too proud to desert – the idea did have some appeal.

"I'll have to give it some thought," he replied.

Saito smiled, standing to wipe the water from his fine armor. However, their calm was soon shattered by the sound of creaking wagon wheels and snapping branches. The Rank had returned.

The youngest of the soldiers, Brock and Chad, were the first to enter the clearing. The two of them were leading their horses on foot without much regard, still wildly swinging their daggers to clear the dense landscape, both cursing or laughing; it was hard to tell which. Drake trailed close behind, gritting his crooked teeth as he freed their covered wagon from the soil, the soldier's horse dragging the load as best it could.

As always, the ominous Xavier banner waved from the wagon's roof, its red cloth darkened by the rainfall. Though Kaish tried never to look too closely at it, good sense telling him not to, he could not help his glance. That night, he saw that orange dragon etched into its center, curled like a crescent, had tilted its body towards the full moon. The faint, violet veins curved differently now, extending from the figure of the beast to the edge of the crimson cloth. He swore that image changed every night, with every moon, every glance. No one believed him.

Soon came the whinny of the other stallions, followed by the appearance of the men who rode them: Thomas, Valten, Yaz, and Wolf.

Although the burly men seemed no different than before, Kaish sensed there was something changed from the time he had been told to leave them. They all seemed tense, restless. By the look on Saito's face, he saw this too.

Lance's appearance ended all suspense. The moment the soldiers parted to make way for his splotched stallion, Kaish saw the reason for the others' unrest. Sitting behind the General, her delicate wrist bound by Lance's grip, was the dark-haired girl he had met that evening.

All at once, Rajj's growl shattered his thoughts. Kaish barely managed to grab his chain before the beast shot past, testing its limits. The tree he was bound to shook with its master's strength, as the creature snarled and attacked thin air. It was all the Talonian could do to keep him restrained.

"Settle *down*!"

But the dog would not listen to him. To hear Lance's shouts, Kaish had to ignore Rajj's snarls. He could only watch as the General threw the young woman down from the horse, leaping down after her with a round of cruel laughter.

"Too scared to scream, wench?!"

He grabbed her hair in his calloused hands, jerking her off the ground to face him. Yet, this action forced only a weak cry. She was all but silent, just staring at her tormentor. Silent tears trickled down her soft cheeks. For the first time, Kaish noticed the intense blue of her eyes, so like the eyes of the Kyrons he had met on his travels. Whoever she was, she was not Larascan. He found it strange he hadn't noticed before.

"She makes a beautiful prisoner," said Saito.

Kaish managed a half nod, still trying to keep his hold on the frenzied dog. His attention was again diverted by new arrivals; his fellow stags began emerging from the forest. Colin emerged first, always gratingly eager to impress the General. As the other soldiers formed a line beside Saito and Kaish, Colin took his place beside him, his crooked nose turned up and his big head held erect. Young Craft followed him, ushered forward by his levelheaded elder, Sander. Finally, Luther and Forwin emerged from the brush, dragging a blond thief by his scrawny arms.

"Let me go, porkers!" he shrieked, thrashing against their grip, "That was *my* gold!"

A million things were happening at once, and Kaish's thoughts couldn't keep up. When his best friend Fritz took his place beside him, that strange smell wafting from his thick and soggy hair – his curls always on the fritz, the reason for his name – he didn't even notice.

"You were right about the thief," said Fritz, keeping his voice low.

These words caught the Talonian's attention.

"What?"

"I saw that guy trying to escape after we arrested the diamond-snatcher," he went on, a broad smile on his youthful face. "I remembered your description of him. Craft got his purse, and all of the coins just poured out. We managed to tackle him down before he could get two feet off. He and his girlfriend must have been in cahoots."

"Ah…"

Although he was glad for the thief's capture, his tongue was lamed by a whirl of thought. Something in his gut told him that the blond's beautiful comrade was innocent. And the longer he looked at her, seeing the perfect gentleness in her unscarred features, the more certain of that he became.

Her blue eyes were now set on the thief, such pleading in their depths. They knew each other well, he had gathered that much from their first meeting. Yet, the blond now offered no assistance to her. When

Lance's grip again locked in her hair, her friend didn't make a sound in her defense.

At last, she cried out.

"Do you have any idea what you almost did to us, little bitch?!" the General bellowed, pulling even harder on her dark locks. "Huh?!"

She didn't look right at him long. Her gaze soon fell to the soil beneath her, the rain washing away her tears.

"I...I haven't d-done anything. H-honest—"

Her words were silenced by the back of Lance's hand. A shout escaped her as she hit the ground, her cheek already reddening from the strike. Before she could regain breath, Lance had her locks again. This time, his dagger was drawn.

Kaish knew what was coming next. He had seen it many times before; it was done to all female prisoners. Yet, seeing it now was no less painful.

The bald General gathered all of her hair in one hand, unable to empathize with the pain his hold would bring. With one slice of his dagger, her beautiful locks fell to the ground. The pride of womanhood was severed from her. What was left fell across her cheeks as her head dropped, shrouding her face, her tears.

"How does that feel, bitch?" Lance sneered.

She was ever silent. Kaish waited to hear her scream, sob, to show the same torment the others' had. She did not. She was stone upon the land, frozen in her pain. It made him ache for her the more.

This did not satisfy the General. His cruel pride slowly melted into rage. Suddenly, he grabbed her arm, dragging her from her place of rest.

"That not enough for you?" he snarled. "How about the man's treatment?"

Kaish didn't believe he would do it. Although Lance was cruel to him, he had always believed it somewhat justified. He was a foreigner, after all, and foreigners were not to be easily trusted. But a slave's mark, for this innocent girl?

He watched in horror as Lance ripped the sleeve of her white gown, exposing her skin to the Rank. When he raised his dagger this time, cruelty had hardened his visage. Soon blood soiled her white dress, dripping from the X Lance had engraved into her very skin. The rain could not dilute the crimson flow.

At last, she screamed. She could only hold her arm when Lance released it, clutching at the torn flesh.

"I did NOTHING!" she shrieked.

Another strike, and she was silenced. But this wasn't enough for the General. He had to force her face into the mud, sneering down at her like a vulture. He jerked her head to the side, to shake his folded whip in her sight.

"Another sound, and I'll introduce you to this old friend of mine."

Rajj had gone rabid. The moment the girl's blood was spilled, the beast had begun to fight harder against his bind, his snarls enough to make the tallest soldiers pull back. Kaish fought to hold on, ignoring his own fury. How he longed to sic Lance with his own dog. He stole a glance at the other members of his Rank, Stags and soldiers alike. But they were frozen, expressionless as could be. Only the youngest Stags showed any sign of discontent; however, they were not brave enough to express it in more than a cringe.

At last, Lance had had enough of his toy. He looked towards his men, rising back to his full height.

"And what of *that* one?" he snapped, pointing his bloodied dagger to Forwin and Luther's captive.

The two of them threw the blond to the ground, ignoring his shout.

"The Lucadian gold-thief," said Luther, direct as always.

"Kaish gave us the description and everything," added Forwin, stealing a glance back at the Talonian.

Although he was pleased by the credit, Kaish tried not to acknowledge it. He knew better than that. Instead, he focused on restraining the beast.

As the thief sat up, obsessively wiping the mud from his face and clothes, Lance looked him up and down. There was no anger in his beady eyes. There was something else, bringing relief to the captive and unease to the Talonian. Silently, Kaish began to curse the Stag that had mentioned his name.

"State your name," was Lance's order.

The pretty youth – for he really was pretty, and that was no compliment to a man – tried to make himself look tall, drawing his head up as he sat and stubbornly crossing his spindly arms.

"Alastor," he said. "And I—"

"Shut your trap."

The boy's jaw snapped shut. The General looked him over again, walking closer. He looked to the strongest of the soldiers.

"Wolf, get him up."

The burly man took no effort to do so. With the strength of two soldiers, he easily lifted Alastor to his feet, no doubt leaving behind a good bruise as he did so. By his foul smirk, he took pride in the mark.

One hand on his sword, Lance circled the specimen. Kaish knew he was examining the boy's weakness from every angle—his scrawny legs, his shifting eyes, his smooth jaw. Kaish knew he saw all of this. Yet, the

General looked as though these things brought him pride.

"You have two options, Thief. You can become our prisoner," He gestured towards the beaten girl, smiling at the sight of her still-spilling blood, "or you can become a Stag."

Kaish could feel the blood leaving his face.

A Stag?

The scrawny cur had stolen from them, and he was being *recruited?*

Alastor's pallor had increased tenfold. His craven gaze shifted from his friend to the General, debating only how best to preserve his own life. Terrified words passed trembling lips:

"What's a S-Stag?"

A muscle twitched in Lance's face, anger leaked by the boy's ignorance. But yet, though Kaish waited for the usual explosive fury, it never came. The General's anger left with his sigh.

"The Stags are the training units of the Larascan military, part of our force since 250 I.R., the rule of Tristan Xavier III. They're named for his son, Shane, known as the Great Stag during his military triumphs in Tallk country. Get to know your history, boy."

Kaish felt his stomach lurch upon hearing that word.

Tallk.

He had heard it more in the last five years than he had in all his life. The word didn't even make sense; yet, no Larascan could decide on a more derogatory term for the black-haired people of Talon. Whether it made sense or not, it was spoken with such malice the intent never failed to come across. Even now, Kaish felt sick looking upon the man – and he knew that was the reason for Lance's grin.

"So they're not soldiers?" asked the thief.

The General grit his teeth.

"No. Travel is their training. When *I* find them worthy, they put on soldier's armor."

Despite his dumb look, it was clear Alastor was beginning to understand his options. He could end up with blood down his arm, as pale as the girl he would not defend, or he could put on a thin white shirt with a wolf etched into its breast and call it fair.

Kaish knew the boy's decision before he gave his nod.

"All right. I'll be a…a Stag."

And that was that. The coward became his comrade.

No one had a choice.

Lance's hand shot out, grabbing the boy by the wrist. With the same cold gaze, the General forced him to expose his white palm.

"What are you doing?" came the thief's shriek.

The rain had only just cleaned the dagger when the General raised it again. With a practiced hand, Lance slashed a curved, crooked cross into the pale flesh. Blood leaked from the ancient Xavier insignia.

Alastor howled like a babe. He fell to his knees, cradling his injured hand and crying like no other Stag had ever done. Kaish felt his own mark burn with revulsion, fingernails digging deep into the crooked scar. Even the feral dog seemed to loathe this unworthy new recruit.

"What?!" cried Fritz beside him, as much as he tried to keep it a whisper. "Him?! We're taking him?!"

The others were equally incensed, though all were trained to keep their objections unvoiced. Lance did not notice, or care. His beady gaze passed over his irate soldiers until they finally rest on the last person who wanted it—Kaish.

"You were told to guard the gold, Tallk," he growled.

Despite his every effort to remain vacant, Kaish sneered.

"Your dog does not wait for meat, *Sir*."

Lance's scowl only deepened.

"You have failed your Rank by letting an unremarkable, *unskilled* thief complete access to our reserves, Tallk. For your inadequacy, you will be punished."

No words could describe Kaish's rage. His jaw was taunt, his knuckles white around Rajj's rattling chain. He no longer heard the beast's racket. Even the air grew thin, burned by the intensity with which he stared at his General.

"The thief is caught and in your possession, identified by myself; you have decided to...*recruit* him," he said, words strained, "yet, you punish me?"

But no logic could have prevented Lance from sheathing his dagger and withdrawing that abused leather strap. He straightened the folded bundle in his hands three times – fwip, fwip, fwip.

"Fritz, take the dog."

It was no use hoping that Fritz would stand up for him, this time. The frizzy-haired boy jumped at the General's command, taking the chain as well as he could. Rajj almost jerked him off-balance, no doubt grateful for a weaker restraint. Though Kaish saw shame in his friend's face, he had already forgiven him. Everyone knew by now how pointless it was to defend a Tallk.

Kaish shed the Stags' marked shirt on his way to the center of the clearing, flinging it into a puddle of mud. As he stared defiantly into Lance's eyes, he felt two more gazes fall upon him, separate from the soldiers and Stags that watched from behind. The first was the thief's, who sought the sight of his pain only to salvage his own trampled dignity. The second belonged to the blue-eyed convict, who clutched her bleeding arm in the shadow of a dying tree. It was from her that he felt remorse.

The mud seeped into his pants and under his nails, marking him with its scent. It was this he focused on when the first strike came.

fawk

And the second.

fawk

And the third.

fawk

fawk

fawk

He told himself he didn't feel it. He told himself there was no stretch of skin Lance had not already broken, that had not already been calloused to the strike. But that was a lie. Each whip cut. He could feel the blood leaking, soiling other wounds. He was in pain.

His nails dug deeper into the ground. The pain didn't end. It would never end.

No sound escaped him.

A point came when Lance's frustration could no longer be sated by the sound of the cracking flesh. The striking stopped. Kaish collapsed into the mud, to join his dignity. He choked on it.

The General's bellow was hard on his ears.

"Move out!"

He heard the creaking of wagon wheels, the whinny of horses. He could barely hold himself off the ground when the men started to pass him. None could look at him. Even the thief, who seemed so pleased to have escaped the Talonian's fate, looked instead at his own bloody hand when a soldier prodded him past.

Rajj's low snarl reminded him of another face. As he stumbled to his feet, he managed to again catch a glimpse of their captive as a younger soldier led her, leashed, around the beast's restraints. Her arms were roped behind her, the bind already soaked by rain and blood. Her wounds were as deep as his own. Yet, in spite of all this, it was she who met his gaze. Her eyes looked up into his, unflinching. He could see the salty trails that streaked her face, the dirt smeared below her jaw—and her compassion. It had been so long since he had seen such an emotion that he almost failed to recognize it.

She was gone, in moments. Nearby, Fritz still struggled with Rajj's chain, waiting for Kaish to relieve him. But his mind wandered, lamed by pain. He thought of her, and Saito's words.

He imagined a world without pain, with her.

The world was still black, when Rina again stirred into consciousness. She could barely remember where she was, or how she had come to be there. A part of her hoped that she had fallen asleep in Richard's bar, or even that Alastor had somehow brought her back to his small home after a long night. He would come in at any moment, and she could tell him about her terrifying dream…

Her hopes shattered with an agonizing pain. Her arm was on fire. She groped it in shock, but it was too late—her memory had begun to return.

She had been dragged forward with a band of soldiers after their leader had marked her; she was forced to walk until the ground had grown too soft for travel, and then trudged alongside their horses, not worthy to ride with them. When she had grown weary, she tried to rest. She tried to ask for a break. The long-haired soldier who dragged her refused to listen to her pleas. And so, she had fallen into the mud, unconscious.

The floor beneath her was wood. Above her was a canvas, painted by passing shadows of the trees and moonlight. At her feet was a pile of wooden crates, and unwashed armor cradled her head. Slowly, she realized she had been tossed into the soldiers' wagon, to take her place among the cargo.

She could feel blood still leaking down her arm. She knew she had to bind it, but she didn't know how. Mud from her tight grip aggravated the wound, bringing her more pain.

She cried.

What had she done to anger the cruel spirits of the forest? She had never ventured into the woods. She wasn't cruel, and she did nothing to others that was unjust. And yet, she was trapped among them now, taken in by their rage.

People of Lucadia didn't venture into the forest. The Duke said that vengeful spirits lived there, and terrible, terrible beasts. It was a place of misfortune and death. All that came from it caused pain—its wolves attacked Lucadian pigs, its insects poisoned their people, and its weeds choked their crops. In the dark of night, the trees transformed the wooded horizon into a black mountain. No one went in; no one came out.

Now, she was trapped in that black forest.

Rina trembled at a wolf's howl, curling her body tighter, crushing herself against a large crate. Home was too far, her quilt leagues away; the wolf was too close.

There were walls all around her, but she wasn't safe. There was pain. The pain wouldn't stop. Her tears wouldn't stop it, though they flowed like a river. But she bit her tongue, and wouldn't make a sound. Not a sound, or she would be found again.

Why wasn't Alastor with her?

She remembered his eyes when the bald General had grabbed her. They were terrified, and empty. Entirely empty. Did he care nothing for her, after all their years together? Did her pain deserve no pity?

She would be drowned here. Drowned in either the darkness or her misery. Or fear.

"Are you crying?"

Her sobs stopped, robbed by shock. Someone was outside, speaking to her. She tried to be silent, pulling her knees to her chest to make herself small. The presence was not deterred. A snapping twig announced its approach.

"Calm down. I'm not here to hurt you."

Moonlight streamed past the wagon's leather flaps when he entered, illuminating his pale skin. He was bare-chested, his Stag shirt – soaked through – held loosely at his side. His trousers were stained by blood. She was afraid, at first, drawing further back into the wagon. Then, she recognized his dark, dark curls.

"You're the foreigner," she said.

The man gave her the faintest smile.

"You're the Lucadian."

At once, the air seemed somehow lighter.

He knelt beside her, tearing a strip from his sopping shirt.

"Hold still."

He began to bind her wound. She was stunned, only able to watch as the bloody gash was expertly wrapped, the cloth tied only minutes after. When he was done, she looked at it in awe, shocked silent.

"My name is Kaish," he said.

A strange name, a likeable one. She managed a smile.

"Mine is…Rina."

"Rina?"

She nodded, noticing how calm he looked. Though she had seen him tortured not hours before, there was no sign of pain in his eyes. There was distance in their pale depths, but nothing more. Yet, when he smiled, it didn't quite reach them.

"A royal name," he said.

Kaish stood, holding his hand down to her.

"Come. I'll help you clean the wound. You don't want it to become infected, do you?"

She shook her head, able to do little else. Although there was a moment's hesitation, she took his hand.

"…thank you…"

He nodded.

The man led her away from camp, deeper into the forest. Deeper into the shadows, the looming branches. Fear of what lurked there threatened to choke her; the darkness had already stifled her spirit. She was silent, her voice caught somewhere in her throat until they emerged from the dense forestry.

A long river glistened in the darkness, colored by the moon and the stars. It moved smoothly, flowing, the waters gently lapping at the shore. Along it were small clusters of milkweeds—flowery weeds, their modest beauty made impressive by the waves that touched them. Fireflies danced over the water's surface, shimmering like starlight.

Rina had never seen anything like it. She stood still, feeling the urge to fling herself into it, to become part of the waves, overwhelm her.

A hand grasped her shoulder, giving her a start.

"Kneel down by the water, please."

She moved by his will, her legs sinking into the sodden ground. He unwrapped the binding he had given her, rinsing the now-bloody cloth in the water.

"How do you know that blond youth?" he asked. "Our new…recruit?"

The mention of Alastor was another dagger in her heart. Even in her mind's eye, she couldn't bear to see his empty expression while her blood spilled before him.

"…he was my best friend," she said, her gaze set on an insect in the mud. "Everyone expected us to…marry."

"What do you think of that?"

She gave a weak smile, saying no more.

Kaish began to wring the cloth onto her arm, allowing the cool water to rinse the jagged cross engraved in her flesh. He worked in silence for a time, dressing her wound. Yet, she could see the depth of his thought in the lines on his brow, the wary flicker of his pale green eyes. When he did speak, however, there was no hesitancy.

"This river leads to a much larger one, the Alize. There is always a thick fog on the other side, which the Rank will cross into by way of an old rope bridge. It's common for soldiers to get lost in the fog. It's the easiest place for us to desert."

She paused, looking at him abruptly.

"Us?"

The foreigner pulled something from the pouch at his hip, then picked a fair milkweed from the water's edge. He knelt in front of her, meeting her blue gaze with his green. After a moment's pause, he displayed a golden bracelet and the white blossom.

"I want you to marry me, Rina."

She was shocked. She stared at the bracelet, completely speechless.

He wants me to…

He was not swayed by her silence.

"This bracelet was my mother's," he said, his voice of a gentler timbre. "I know we don't know each other, right now. But I need something to look forward to, and you need a way to escape. The two of us can help each other."

Gently, he slipped the bracelet on her wrist. The metal was strangely cool against her skin, unlike anything else she had felt. She almost felt royal.

"I promise, I'll give you nothing to regret. I'll keep you safe."

He pressed the flower into her palm.

"You'll never be hurt like this again."

Perhaps a few days before, when she was still Richard's timid tavern girl, she could have told him no. Torture had robbed her of that option.

A handsome stranger was offering a convict a life of freedom. As much as she tried to remember the girl she was, to try and remember she did have another option, she could not. She just stared at the fine gold bracelet, and spoke to seal her fate.

"Then…I'll be your wife."

At last, she saw joy reach his eyes. With the poise of a prince, he delicately kissed her hand. But although she felt a degree of warmth herself, she could not shake the paranoia that overcame her. Something was watching. She saw a pair of red eyes staring at her from the dark forest, observing. Waiting.

A beast's snarl, and the eyes vanished.

Chapter IV

$\mathscr{I}$n her Lady's absence, Madeleine Keeper sat at the royal vanity, trying on the Lady's new jewels, admiring her own beauty in the fine mirror. It certainly wasn't a proper thing to do – quite naughty, really – but she fancied herself worthy of the finery. Gold jewels suited her better than Duke Bayard's sallow daughter. The inlaid emeralds brought out the green in her round eyes, complimenting sun-kissed skin. The exotic hoops for her ears enhanced a gleam in her dusky curls, a redness in her cheeks. Certainly, if not for her questionable ancestry, she would have made a much finer Lady than Abaca. In beauty alone, she was far superior.

Alas, life was not so fair.

A strident knock sprung her from the oak seat. She scrambled to remove the jewels and cram them back into Abaca's gold box.

"Just a moment!" she cried, attempting to make her voice pleasant.

She ran first to the grand double-doors, but paused, noticing the knock came instead from the side door, which led out to a separate, minor hallway. Certainly no one of importance would come through *there*. Still, the urgent knock kept coming.

"Calm yourself! My bones..."

When she opened the door, she was stunned to see the face that stared back. There, panting, large awkward hands clutching his knees, was her lover.

"Edmund, what in the Xaviers' name are you doing here!?"

His Larascan-green eyes glanced to her through his disheveled locks. It was a moment more before he regained his breath.

"Silas is in the forest," he sputtered.

She just stared at him, dumb.

"What...?"

It had been years since either of them had spoken of him, a boy she had called "Brother." A feeling of loss at first overcame her, weighted by regret. But it was soon overwhelmed by fear.

"So?" she snapped. "He ran off. He's no business of mine."

The brown-haired youth coughed as he righted himself, despite the heavy armor that continued to fight his balance.

"I saw him, Maddy," he said, pain in his simple expression. "He's really hurting. He looked sick to begin with, but...I watched Giovanni slice his hand open. He's still bleeding, somewhere in the forest..."

"Giovanni hurt him?"

Silas' father had done many things, few of them particularly loving, but she had never imagined he would assault his own child. Yet, Edmund's weak nod confirmed otherwise.

"I couldn't believe it."

She was stunned speechless. All those years, she had heard Silas make horrific accusations about his father, never imagining they could be truth.

With a clumsy grip, Edmund grasped her delicate hands; his gaze was steady.

"Please, come find him with me. We owe this to him. We just can't abandon him to—"

A powerful voice came from the other doorway.

"Lady Abaca is retiring for the night."

Madeleine panicked. She shoved Edmund out, slamming the door shut before he could speak. She turned, calm, smiling at the armored guard.

"I'm ready for my Lady."

She didn't much appreciate the slow roll of his eyes.

Lady Abaca's arrival was an ostentatious display. Her golden dress dragged over the floor, light glaring from its ornamentation and the sheen of her applied face. Her lips were painted red today, to hide their cracks. Maddy noticed with disdain that the extravagant gown hung looser on her, for thin was the fashion, and Abaca wanted the excuse to flaunt her utter lack of a figure.

"You may address me now, Madeleine," she said, gazing elsewhere entirely.

Maddy's disgust was masked by her smile. She knelt down to kiss Abaca's outstretched hand, although Abaca's questionable birth should have allowed for Madeleine to bow from the waist to do so. The Lady just preferred her subjects low.

Abaca withdrew her hand.

"I wish to try my new Akalinian jewels. Madeleine, you will assist me."

She sat at her gold-plated vanity, and with a wave, dismissed the tall guard. Maddy stood behind her, seeming subservient. However, she tensed when Abaca lifted a golden chain from the table, eying it with more than her usual, dull curiosity.

"My sights say these jewels have been moved, once," Larascan-green eyes flashed to her Maddy, "Twice."

Her servant's smile was carefully composed.

"I was told to check for imperfections, my Lady."

Maddy's false smile was returned, a blank stare showing how quickly the exchange had been forgotten. Abaca looked back into the mirror to admire her painted face.

"Proceed, then."

With a practiced hand, she pulled back Abaca's thin locks, which were a color neither rich nor fair. Then, she began to fasten the heavy Akalinian necklace, so thick it seemed to collar and overwhelm the girl's spindly neck. Her small frame couldn't handle such gaudy adornment. But Abaca smiled, posing her head this way and that, like a pigeon caught sight of its face in a puddle.

"If only that Silas could see me now," the Lady pined, the sound accompanied by a sigh of such weight the servant feared she might swoon. "Then he would realize what a fool he was to reject my affections..."

Another long sigh.

"But alas, he is gone...far away."

The Lady lifted a misplaced bauble from her vanity, when it caught her eye—a black king from an old chess set. Compared to the other pieces Madeleine had seen, the king appeared newer, freshly painted to a handsome sheen. But already, she could see sharp cracks on its surface: the consequence of mistreatment.

"Has your father been teaching you chess again?" Madeleine asked, forgetting formality.

Abaca gave an aching groan.

"How horribly dull that game is, dear Maddy. It's nothing but mindless strategy, not a lick of romance in it. The king doesn't even have any power...he's nothing but a fancy pawn..."

Madeleine knew little about the game, so she was left in rare silence. Still, she had no real interest in it. "Chess" was a game for bored noblemen and lanky merchants. It did not pertain to her.

But Silas had enjoyed that game. She remembered it now: his long rants about Giovanni's unbeatable strategies, the nature and history of each piece, key moves and the taste of victory. She had ignored most of it. What she remembered most clearly was the passion that illuminated his violet gaze, an emotion never replicated for reason other than that game. Until that Kala came.

"What an odd look, Maddy," Abaca said, glancing back to her servant. "Care to divulge a peasant's thoughts?"

Madeleine ignored her condescension.

"I was thinking of my late brother," she replied.

A strange look came over Abaca. It was a sort of smirk, only more irritating. She touched the golden collar that choked her neck as the Lady turned her head towards her.

"Do you have news of him, then?"

"Of Silas?"

A part of her sensed just how terrible the consequences of replying would be. However, her thoughts were so clouded that she couldn't see to care.

"Edmund said he's in the forest, and he's quite injured. It's just a hand wound though, so I don't know why Edmund looked so concerned. He'll pull through, of course. He's some rare breed of cockroach, that's what I've always said..."

She felt fine after saying it, for a short time. But regret crept up on her, catching her unaware. As Abaca's coy smile grew, so did Madeleine's shame.

"Guard!" called the Lady, voice ringing like little bells. It was forced.

Soon, the burly man appeared, bowing low.

"Summon a carriage," she demanded. "I want to be taken into the Great Forest."

The man seemed concerned, a feeling shared by Madeleine herself. The Great Forest was no place to be for any reason. However, training prevented that emotion from tainting the guard's features too deeply. He only bowed lower.

"Yes, my Lady."

Abaca smiled, waving him off. She settled back into her oak seat, not noticing the man's look as he left, or Maddy's.

"Oh, how exciting, dear Madeleine! It's been many seasons since I last met him. Do you think he's grown again?"

Madeleine managed a smile.

"Like any beast, I suppose."

Her Lady smiled, lifting her alabaster brush to tame her tawny locks.

"How very quaint..." she replied, entirely absorbed in her reflection.

It wasn't quaint. It was terrifying. *Silas* was terrifying, now—arms like tree trunks, teeth like knives. But he was hurting, and it wasn't fair to loose Abaca on him in that state.

Her gut was tight, making it hard for her to claim detachment. She was again reminded of that day long ago, when that tragedy had occurred. Before Sh'ka's dance, she had had this feeling. It was an omen, looming over her, smothering her.

Silas...I'm sorry.

6th Month, 648 I.R.

I can never tell anyone what happened today. It's inhuman. I wasn't human. I don't understand what I've done, but I've done it...

A wolf attacked Edmund. We were playing in the forest, and this huge wolf just jumps on him. He was going to die: I had to stop it! He was bloody and screaming, and the wolf wouldn't let him go. So I jumped on him. I put my hands around its neck and I choked it as hard as I could, until I could feel its throat close in. I grabbed it. I tore its fur!

I don't remember most of it...but something happened, then. Edmund saw it. I know he saw it. I thought the wolf was still scaring him, but it wasn't the wolf. The wolf was making weird sounds, like crying. Wolves don't cry.

Under my hands, its fur was all burnt. It wasn't like that before.

I burned it? Burned...burned how?

I told Edmund not to tell anyone. Not until I figure this out. But he looked so scared...

I saved his life! He can't be scared of me! Me?!

But I'm scared too. I'm scared of this. My face felt hot and I couldn't think. I hurt that wolf, a lot. I don't want it to happen again. Humans shouldn't be able to hurt wolves like that. They can't...

What am I?

The blood kept coming. No matter how Silas attempted to stop the flow, blood kept draining from that gash. His hand was red, his arm was red, the ground was red – stained by a sticky, brilliant red that more resembled berries than blood. It just kept *coming,* flowing redder and redder as his body grew hotter and hotter until his rage gushed just like it.

"**FAWK!!**"

Black birds fled the treetops, cursing him in song.

His energy spent, Silas collapsed to his knees by the murky pond. He tore off his shirt, ripping a disheveled strip from that to bind his hand. But he couldn't. No matter how he wrapped it, seething, snarling, he couldn't function with one hand.

"Damn it all..."

He bore his teeth at nothing.

"Damn it...all."

He dunked his bleeding hand in the water, watching the vibrant red seep into the pool. It stung, the pond scum that brushed the wound. The sting was no worse than the injury. He ignored it.

As the blood began to separate from his hand, he could again see the gleam of a gold ring on his finger. It stared at him defiantly, unmoved by his pain or spite. The two petals etched into its surface seemed to now glow redder than his blood, as if to taunt him. His hair bristled, a growl bubbling in his throat. Someday, he would rip that ring to pieces. If not, he would rip off his own finger, watch the blood pour out thick, thicker than now.

A squirrel scampered towards him, its tail bushy and brown. It sniffed around him, sniffing, sniffing. Silas tensed, irritation rising in him like steam. He snarled.

"Scat."

The nuisance would not be deterred. It just kept scuttling and scurrying, sniffing and sniffing. Sniffing like he knew Silas' vulnerability. Like he knew he was weak. The tormenting twitch of his tail as he came closer, closer. Sniffing, snickering. Snickering at his blood.

His bloody hand shot out, cloth falling as it clamped around the small creature's throat. He squeezed slowly, feeling each suppressed muscle grow tighter. He wanted to savor that frantic shrieking.

"Not so funny now, is it?"

But as its squirming slowed, the red haze began to clear. He could see his own foolishness with increasing clarity.

What are you doing?

..

…

He set down the defenseless creature. It staggered; it scurried away. Its belly stained crimson, it painted a red path to its whereabouts. Ashamed, Silas tried not to see it.

The world fell heavy on his shoulders.

Silas took up the bandage again, head hung low as he tried to wrap it. Once, twice more he tried. He slammed the bandage down in frustration. He was incapable.

He hung his head over the water, his fingertips buried in the soil. He stared into his reflection – royal amethyst staring back, seeing shame, seeing failure – and felt nothing.

The air around him began to change. It thickened, growing damper. A fog began to settle around him. And yet, he noticed nothing until he heard a child's voice.

"Why won't you help?"

It wasn't his language. He knew that immediately. The flow, the sound, was different. Its bounce was strangely familiar. He had heard it around the docks, from the Kala, from Sh'ka – the Akalinian language. Yet, he understood it.

"Won't you?"

There was a girl floating in the water. A child whose brown locks fanned around her in the pool, her eyes set on him: blue. He had never seen blue eyes before. Her white dress looked too fine to be soaked as it was – even the lace of its sleeves was a product of careful craftsmanship. She was no ordinary girl.

"Why won't you save me?" she asked again, that strange language so sweet on her lips.

A part of him knew this was an illusion, some sort of apparition. But he was too drawn by those eyes, somehow convinced to respond.

"...why would I save you?" he asked.

A mysterious smile graced her lips.

"Because I'm drowning."

All at once, the pond swallowed her.

Instinct took over. He jumped in, icy water engulfing him. He just managed to grab her white wrist before it vanished into the darkness.

They emerged. Gasping, he dragged her to shore, having more trouble than he usually did. By the time he reached land, he realized that he was changed. He had a boy's hands, a child's strength. He realized that he was now as small as she.

She opened her eyes, and their gentleness soothed his bewilderment. He wished he could be forever held in that gaze. Her smile alone almost broke him. She drew herself up by her own strength, removing a golden bracelet from her slender wrist. As he watched, she knelt before him, slipping it over his small hand.

"Now we are bound."

Her words unnerved him, somehow. And yet, they filled him with peace. A glance to her, and then to the bracelet. It was well-made, engraved with curving lines he had often seen adorning jewelry of Talonian make, traded by sailors to the townswomen. He moved to touch it, to confirm its existence.

It vanished.

The world around him snapped into focus. The fog was gone; the girl was gone. He was grown again, still gripping his bleeding palm.

His head throbbed. He rubbed his eye, as if to rub the pain away. He smeared blood into it.

Fawk!

He grit his teeth, a red tear running down as he cursed, clutching at his hair. When the unfortunate Lady Abaca arrived, he was as angry as he could get.

The girl's arrival was announced by the snapping of twigs beneath her clumsy step. She took a heavy breath to begin a speech; Silas cut her short.

"What do you want?" he snarled.

Her reply was accompanied by a grating little gasp, her voice strident on his sensitive ears.

"However did you know? You cast me not a glance!"

His lip curled back, sneering, snarling.

"I can smell your reeking perfume three leagues off."

His inhuman growl deterred her, for a moment. All too soon he felt her approach, seeing that sickly sweet smile even in his mind's eye.

"I came to apologize for what transpired three years ago," came her grating voice, "I even dismissed my guards so we could be alone."

Like a creature struck by lightening, he turned to her. At once he saw the plain girl he remembered, her face painted to seem pretty. He was repulsed.

"What are you talking about?"

"I was just so...infatuated with you," she said, daring to come closer. "I never thought Daddy would do something as awful as paying a Kala to...oh, you remember..."

First, there was the silence of shock.

He...did...

Then, came the slow building, building up of rage.

"You...you *did* pay her off..."

She was blind to the fire in his eyes, the danger of his snarl. She had the audacity to sit beside him—*touch* him. He stared at the insolent hand upon his arm, as if it were a spider waiting to be crushed.

"Such unusual eyes..." she purred, infuriating in her naivety. "Such incredible heat from your body..."

His claws dug so deep into the mud they struck clay. But she kept moving closer, that hand *daring* to touch his powerful chest.

"I just could not help my doomed attraction...we were just children. Of course you turned me away, then..."

She leaned too close.

"I can still ignore a freakish behavior or two..."

Her lips dared too close. As though she dared to *kiss* him.

He exploded.

"You **BITCH**!!"

Silas struck her hard, hard enough to knock her over. She shrieked. Her skin sizzled like coal, black. Turning black. He stood to spit his words.

"Don't you *touch* me! **Viper!**"

She was unconscious, cold.

He began to be aware of the heat of his body, the throbbing in his fingertips. He began to recognize the stench that scorched his nostrils, rising from her cheek.

The world slowed with his breathing, settling, falling heavy around him.

Slowly, slowly he saw the scorched meat that had been Abaca's visage. Slowly, his skin turned cold.

Again. You did it again.

A rustle in the bushes. He turned, poised, snarling. Not a rabbit sound—human, boot-wearer. Protector.

"Henry, this way! I heard him!"

Not a thought. No time.

He fled.

Silas stumbled into a clearing, breathing hard, short breaths. He felt the ground moving beneath him, threatening to pull him down. His head ached too much to remember this place—its low branches to climb, the stars gazing through a palace of leaves. Yet, he was conscious of its familiar air. He was consoled enough by it to allow himself to fall, knees buckling to sink into the damp mud.

Coward.

His fist made a crater in the earth. Blood spurt from his fingers; he howled.

Freak.

The image of Abaca's disfigurement had burnt itself into his mind, searing him as she had been seared.

Monster.

He held his bleeding hand in defeat, his violet eyes glazed, dull. Their full color didn't return until he saw a yellowed envelope fluttering in the breeze, pinned to the ground by a heavy stone. It was black and smooth, polished to a shine. A paperweight—he had seen it a hundred times on Vaan's writing desk. Vaan had planted that envelope.

Why do you care?

But he was already opening that envelope, smearing it with bloody fingers. He had to know its contents. No matter what it was, he had to know.

My dear Reja,

I apologize greatly for my decision to leave you, but I know that I must. I wish I could stay by your side, for I love you dearly. Circumstances prevent this...and I am sorry...

If you still remember nothing when you wake, which I fear will come to pass, have faith in the man I have entrusted you with. Although he is young yet, he is brilliant. I know he will make a fine man of you—and when the time comes, he will lead you home to Joanissia, just as he led the Larascan people to peace and unity many years ago.

Know that you will be loved and missed. Your father cherishes you so dearly that I fear what may become of him when he finds you gone. I imagine he will do nothing but stare into the frosted windows, while the rooms grow colder with each passing day. Without you, his world will fall to pieces. As will mine...

Grow strong, Reja. Come home and set this right.

With love,

The signature was blotted out with Giovanni's pen. Though Silas felt no connection with the name the letter was addressed to, he couldn't help but feel it was meant for him. He read that letter once, twice, three times more. Soon, he felt a dull ache pain his chest.

Someone wants you...home.

A thunderclap: down poured Larasca's heavy rain. The thunder rolled, bellowing, *mocking* his joy. Denied peace, he bellowed curses at the insolent sky.

"STOP!"

He shoved the parchment into his pouch before leaping to a nearby tree. He climbed to its canopy, seating himself on a great, ancient bough. The leaves above sheltered him as the sky came down.

Disjointed feelings floated through his mind. The pain of his wound remained uncomfortably apparent; with that came the heavy resentment toward his adoptive father, the so-called "brilliant" man he had been entrusted to. From that sprang anger for this mysterious woman, the fool who had thought to abandon him to this life of abuse, neglect. But then came the hopeful image of his real father...a man who had deeply mourned his absence.

Someone wants you home.

"who? who?"

An owl floated down beside him, ruffling its jagged feathers as it settled into the great bough. Its horned head rolled, eventually twisting to rest its gray eyes on him.

Silas stared back at it, his jaw grown taut. The creature was a trespasser. He snarled, using no words to explain his disdain.

...Who? Who wants you home?

Its arched brows raised, intense eyes staring, seeing into his bloody past.

"who? who?"

Who could want you *home? A man conquered by fire?*

He snarled louder, demanding that it turn its eyes away. Clawed fingers curled into a bloody fist.

"That's not my fault..."

But the owl stared, stared deeper.

"That's not...my **FAULT!**"

His dagger impaled the beast to the mighty tree—he watched fresh blood drain, dripping, feeling pleasure. It dripped down, down, soaking and staining the bark with his malice. But as his breathing began to slow, awareness returning to him, he grew still. He saw the blood. It was no victory. This was a symptom of his damaged, irreparable soul.

If he had once been Reja, his father had mourned him well. That boy was dead now.

You can't go home.

Chapter V

The soldiers had come to accept Rina. And as they did, hope returned to her life. One by one they revealed themselves to her, humanizing the cold-hearted killers she had first thought them to be. Though all were Larascan-born, the eight men seemed to come from entirely different worlds.

Wolf was the first to accept her. He was nearly forty, but still had all the vibrancy of youth. He was loud, with a resonant, hearty laugh that shook his powerful shoulders. His brown hair was as wild as his nature; yet, his crooked smile calmed the girl. The others said he came from Argot, a lawless city on the route to Joanissia that they planned to avoid.

Yaz was the oldest of them. Five years Wolf's senior, he came from the town of Raine, a small farming town on the way to the capital. He was quiet, never one to speak when he wasn't spoken to. But there was something strange in his sunken gaze—malice beneath the surface. He seemed indifferent towards her.

Brock and Chad were the youngest, only twenty and twenty-one, and their bright dispositions were a perfect distraction from Yaz's unsettling silence. They were brothers from the town of Siette, the only grasslands in all of Larasca. They said their sprightly natures came from chasing fawns through the plains. But though their smiles brought her joy, they only irritated Drake, the only soldier close to their own age. Drake was very lean, with a generally annoyed, scholarly temperament. He said he could tolerate Rina's company above the others' because of her semblance to the bookkeepers of Pandore.

Valten was a decade older than Drake. His disposition was by far the strangest. Although he interacted freely with the soldiers, he seemed to harbor a general distaste for each and every one of them. Moreover, Rina had never seen a man with more pronounced Larascan features: his green eyes were the brightest, with a strong jaw and hair of a very uniform brown. He said all the people of Malldon shared this look, and if she were not so shamefully ill-bred, she would have it too.

Twenty-three-year-old Thomas came from the fishing town of Alore. He said it was a town of fascinating culture that sprung from the constant trade between them and the Kala troupes, who traveled there by boat up the Alize River. He himself had an Akalinian bracelet, given to him by a Kala lover before he had enlisted. Rina enjoyed his vibrant laughter almost daily, and she smiled at his foolish dances around the nightly fire.

Saito was foreign. In fact, he was the most foreign man she had ever seen. His skin was white as the first snowfall, and his smooth hair was very black, giving off a sheen she had never before seen the likes of. His eyes, above all, were strange to her: very narrow, as if he had grabbed the corners and pulled for too long. Yet, there was something lovely about his face, an elegance to his tapered chin and soft lips. He told her that he was very plain for a Storma, and that their women were much more lovely. Rina couldn't imagine this.

Unlike the others, she knew of General Lance only through his soldiers. They said he was raised in Oyban, a town he represented well. It was a place isolated by mountainous terrain, much like their capital,

Joanissia. However, the isolation did not nurture finery and creation, as it did in the capital. Oyban's mountains created a climate of rigid conformity. Its people were soldier-breeders, who trained every boy to be harsh. Knowing this, Rina felt more content with Lance's distaste for her. If it was his nature to be cruel, she could do no better than to keep the company of his gentler men, and avoid his piercing eyes.

Days with the Rank passed in a routine fashion. On the first day of the week, Lance would take half of the men out hunting, and they would return with enough meat for the following seven days. After the meat was smoked, they would travel until the sun went down, then set up camp. The next day was spent traveling, and the day after that. The fourth day of the week, the soldiers were allowed to take the morning to rest while Lance trained the Stags. Once the trainees were ready to drop, Lance gathered the rest of them and they moved again. The fifth day was travel, and then the sixth, and the evening of the seventh day was reserved for bathing in the river. The next day, the cycle started all over again.

It was morning, training day for the Stags. The sunlight was still too harsh on Rina's tired eyes when Wolf came to her place beside the wagon. He unbound her with a practiced hand, tossing her the ropes when he was finished.

"Rise and shine, girly."

She blinked once, twice. The world was still hazy, sunlight streaming down from the dense leaves above.

"Ah..."

She stood with Wolf's help, stumbling to keep her balance. He chuckled with amusement.

"Hup-two, girly. I'm gonna teach you a thing or two this fine morning."

He prodded her out to the main camp, guiding her to sit by the fire's ashes before she could fully wake. The others were already awake, sharpening their weapons with rocks, sparring in the distance, Yaz tending to the horses who were tied to low branches.

Drake dropped a piece of dried meat into Rina's lap as he passed, startling her.

"T-thank you," she managed.

He shrugged.

"I'm only being kind to Kaish's woman."

This unsettled her, somehow. Although she and her betrothed did spend time together, it was a very private affair, and she didn't expect anyone else to know about it. However, it wasn't in her best interest to question where or why food came to her. She quickly began to tear into the meat, grateful for its bland taste.

Wolf cleared his throat, taking back her attention.

"Now, a lesson. I plan to teach you a thing or two about etiquette."

"Etiquette...?"

Even the word held no meaning for the tavern girl. She just looked up at him from her meal, jagged nails still deep in the dry meat. He shook his head, his chuckle resonating deep in his chest.

"A prisoner should know good etiquette when going to meet the King."

He looked about him, observing the various activities of the soldiers. He called to Brock, who sat striking his sword on a smooth stone.

"Boy! I need you for a demonstration!"

Brock sheathed his weapon, bounding up with a smile. Wolf took his shoulders, positioning him before the girl.

"Say this is King Attlas."

Brock squared up his shoulders, crossing his arms and staring dreamily off into the distance. Wolf reprimanded him with a sharp whack on the back.

"As long as the King is sitting, your eyes remain averted to him. However, the moment the King stands, everyone else must bow and stay bowed, like so, or lower."

Wolf bowed from the waist, head down and arms wrapped about himself.

"Now, this rule goes for most members of the Xavier family, but since Attlas is the only Xavier left, he gets special treatment."

Rina looked very curiously at Wolf, not understanding.

"Xavier...?"

Wolf stood straight, a brow cocked. Even Brock looked startled.

"You don't know the name of the royal family?" asked the young soldier.

The girl felt blood rush to her cheeks. Her ignorance wasn't her fault, she hoped – they hadn't taught her anything past sweeping floors in the orphanage. Unable to reply, she looked down at her food, chewing on her own lip.

"Well, now you know," said Wolf.

He repositioned the younger soldier, again clearing his throat.

"Now, say he's Queen Azalea."

Brock raised a brow.

"Isn't it Queen Morana?" he asked.

"Morana's Queen-Mother, since Cedric passed," Wolf said, giving him a patient glance. "Although I doubt her sister much challenges her authority."

It was all too much for Rina; she struggled to understand what was being said. Wolf read it on her face. He sighed.

"All right. Say he's any Queen."

Brock took on an impatient look, pouting in a most feminine way. This earned him another whack.

"When addressing a non-Xavier Queen, married into the family or not, you must bow initially. If she extends her hand, you must kneel to kiss it, like so."

He demonstrated with Brock's hand, and the soldier gave a feminine giggle. Wolf pretended to ignore it.

"You can stand after this, but your eyes remain averted. Only the King, Commanders, Captain of the Guard, and members of the King's Royal Council can keep eye contact with the Queen. The same rule applies to any Duke, Duchess, Baron, Baroness, Lord, or Lady you might meet, although you never have to kneel to a Lord or Lady. Now then…"

"W-wait…"

Rina's mind was spinning.

"What's a Commander? A Baron?"

Wolf sighed, a slow shake of his head showing his disapproval.

"You especially should know what a Commander is. Your Duke, Baldric, is one of the most celebrated Commanders in all of Larascan history. He and Commander Giovanni conquered the part of Larasca west of the Alize River that had separated and called itself its own nation. Baldric himself unseated their King, Alasdair Talbot, crowning himself Duke of its capital: your home, Lucadia."

Her blank look made him sigh. He sat before her, bringing himself down to her level.

"A Commander is in charge of many Generals, who are in charge of many Ranks. A Rank is comprised of eight soldiers and up to eight Stags. A

Commander gives orders to the Generals, who give orders to their soldiers. A Baron – you asked about a Baron, right? – is a nobleman without any power. Either he or an ancestor was given that title by a ruling Xavier, and they are allowed to go to court and attend royal events. Any child a Baron has is born with the title of Lord or Lady, as is the child of a Duke. However, a Lady with a Baron for a father is more likely to marry into the royal family, since they tend to live in the Royal Square of Joanissia. Cuts down travel time, you see, and the Barons can more easily parade their daughters before a Prince while living in such close proximity."

"So…Queen Azalea was a Lady?"

This gave him pause. As if instinctively, he looked towards Saito, who sat on a rock by the edge of camp. The Storma paid them no mind. He looked off into the distance, looking for something. Suddenly, there was a hawk's cry—a great black hawk descended from the heavens, settling on Saito's outstretched arm.

A screech stopped short of Rina's throat.

"W-what is that, Saito?" she managed.

Saito gave her a patient smile, untying what looked like a scrap of paper from around the bird's leg.

"It is no matter."

Wolf shook his head.

"That bird gives me the creeps, Sai."

Saito laughed softly, but made no more comment.

The older soldier gathered her attention with another cough; she had to force herself to look away from the Storma.

"Since we're talking about chain of command, I should educate you about the Rank you're with. Good, useful knowledge…"

Brock had sat down with his weapon, again striking the stone against it to finish what he had started. It made an interesting sound, so close to her – *fwit, fwit. Fwit. Fwit.*

"Now, there's probably about fifty ranks, give or take a few," Wolf continued. "Lance heads up Rank 12. It used to be General Victor some years back – I was still with the Rank back then – but he had an unfortunate accident, and we got Lance."

She heard bitterness in his tone, though it wasn't shown in any part of his face.

"There've always been eight soldiers in Rank 12, but we didn't have Stags until some-odd years ago. We used to have training camps for Stags, but Attlas disbanded them after King Cedric died. Said it would cut costs, or something like that. I never heard of any costs for feeding kids scrap meat and screaming at them all day, but what do I know? So the Stags travel with us now, 'bout eight to a Rank. When the General decides they're skilled enough to be called a soldier, they're 'advanced.' Promoted. They're given their own sword and a horse upon advancement, courtesy of the King. Since our Rank is already full men-wise, the advanced Stags just travel with us until we can dump them with some other Rank that needs more manpower. Doesn't take long to get advanced, usually. Except in the case of your lover-boy, but…that's another story…"

He sighed, shaking his head. However, he continued soon enough. Kneeling in front of her again, he displayed his right palm to her. There, she saw the same crooked cross she had seen carved into Alastor's hand the night of her capture.

"What is that?" she asked, very quietly.

"It's the mark of the Xaviers," he explained. "By becoming a Stag, you swear lifelong servitude to the royal family. We bear this mark for the rest of our lives, to remind us of that choice. Art, the Captain of the Guard –

leader of all the soldiers – has the same mark tattooed over his heart."

He took her arm then, tracing the X now engraved in her skin.

"What you have is another mark of the Xaviers, a mark of slavehood. Now that you're branded with it, the King owns you. We usually give it to men who've committed treason, but I guess Lance was just having a bad day."

She grew very pale. She jerked away her arm, hand pressed over the wound. She saw sympathy in Wolf's eyes, and grew calm.

"What was I accused of, really...?"

The normally joyous Wolf grew solemn, an ancient darkness passing his face. He turned his eyes from her.

"The Queen-Mother, Morana, gave us the task of retrieving two black diamonds from the palace in Storm, her home country. She claims they're only keepsakes, but...they reek of witchcraft, if you ask me. But we got the diamonds, and we were heading back to Joanissia when we decided to stop in Lucadia for that festival. Next thing we know, a diamond's gone, and it turns up in your pyre."

Suddenly, Rina felt very cold. She looked down to her dry meat, which by now had grown soft in her hands. Her body felt stiff, her stomach balled up tight.

"He thinks I stole from the Queen?"

Wolf gave a grave nod.

"Yes. We're taking you to the capital to hand you over to Morana herself. She'll have to decide whether you're innocent or not."

She grew quiet. Her eyes remained steady on her food, too much weight on her body for it to be moved by will. Her fingers grew numb, squeezed too tight into that meat.

I didn't steal. I didn't steal anything...

The soldier must have believed her, for he gave her a familiar pat on the shoulder, shaking her from her stupor.

"Where was I?"

She managed a weak smile, shaking her head.

"I don't know. It's all just…too complicated…"

A hawk's cry shattered her thoughts. She looked suddenly to Saito, who stood tall as the creature ascended into the sky. She glimpsed a new parchment tied to its leg, a different color than the one that had been there before. Saito looked to her then, a patient smile on his lovely face. The bird was almost forgotten.

"Most of the complexities can be traced to King Raphael," said the Storma.

Wolf's brow creased in astonishment.

"You heard all that?"

Saito laughed gently, taking a seat on another large stone near Rina.

"Your voice is quite loud, Wolf. It's hard to hear oneself think."

The soldier smirked, giving a lazy salute to the foreigner. Even Brock smiled, though only momentarily distracted from his task.

"True, true," chuckled Wolf.

The Storma shook his head with light disapproval before turning his attention to Rina. The girl, entranced by his foreign gaze, had no choice but to listen.

"Raphael Xavier took power during a tumultuous time. King Draco and Queen Carmen Alexander, distant cousins of the Xaviers, had been unseated from their Kyron throne by a religious uprising. Raphael's parents, Tristan and Selena, went to Kyro thinking they were going to settle some minor dispute. They were murdered there, and their twenty-year-old son took his throne with a vengeful disposition. The day of his coronation began the forty-year Kyron War, ended only twenty years ago with the building of the Kyron Wall—Wolf, I believe you took part in that war?"

The soldier nodded, his look again turned solemn.

"Aye. As did Yaz and Valten, I believe."

Valten, who sat nearby, turned his emerald gaze towards them. There was a hint of resentment in his cool features, summoned by only the mention of that war. Soon enough though, his usual disgust returned, and he looked very pointedly from his fellow soldiers. Saito continued.

"Although there were military forces before this, it was over the course of that war that the Rank-system was officially established, and the Stags began getting the marks of loyalty carved into their skin, by Raphael's order."

Rina cringed, again feeling the pain of the dagger in her arm.

"He wasn't a very nice King, was he?"

Saito gave a soft laugh.

"No, most would agree he was not. The western part of Larasca seceded partway into that war, in hopes to escape his tyranny. And although this is mostly rumor, it is said that he never smiled at either of his twin sons."

"Twins?" she asked with a start.

"Yes, identical. Cedric and Caden. Their young mother died in childbirth, as most Queens seem to."

"But Cedric had a twin?"

As little as she knew about the royal family, she thought she had known something about King Cedric. He was their most celebrated ruler, a benevolent man who encouraged peace among Larascans. If he had had a twin, why didn't she know his name?

Saito looked ready to answer when they heard a familiar bellowing in the distance—they heard Lance's sword slicing at the brush. All at once, Wolf crammed her food in his own mouth while Brock, aided by the Storma, scrambled to rebind her hands. By the time the General had stormed into camp, they had shoved her back with the cargo.

"Men!" Lance barked. "Let's move it!"

Without another word, the soldiers packed up camp, piling their few belongings and tents into that covered wagon. When they were ready to move, it was Saito who collared Rina with rope, leading her gently forward with the rest of them. His horse, Satoru, trot along beside them, huffing with displeasure at their slow pace.

They stopped at a clearing, where the Stags were completing their training for the day. It seemed they had broken off into pairs to spar, and by now, only one battle still raged. Kaish and Alastor were one-on-one, without weapons—and Kaish was winning.

Every move Alastor made was bested by his opponent. The moment Alastor raised a hand to block his face Kaish knocked it away, implanting his fist in his throat. Alastor stepped away; Kaish tripped him. The Talonian smirked as he pushed the Lucadian down, fist deep in his gut again, again. Alastor could barely cough before another fist met his jaw.

"P-porker!" Alastor choked.

The soldiers were cheering. Kaish stood, no doubt feeling confident enough in his victory to accept the applause. His eyes met with Rina's. Her heart warmed, his soldiers' smirk softening to a smile.

And then, Alastor's knee met Kaish's groin.

Kaish toppled over, spitting colorful curses in a language Rina didn't understand. Alastor was laughing, breathing hard as he spat out blood. Rina was struck dumb.

Why?

Alastor didn't have a lot of admirable qualities, but she had never questioned his integrity. Yet, what she had seen made her question whether he had ever had any at all.

I trusted you...

Shocked, the soldiers were silenced. Only Lance's steady clapping remained.

"Looks like our new recruit just took the match," laughed the General.

Lance went to the pair, stepping over Kaish to give Alastor a strong pat on the back.

"Perhaps there's an early advancement in store for this one."

Rina couldn't stand to see Kaish curled up on the ground, cursing while Alastor smiled. When Lance spoke again, his words were salt in their wounds.

"Let's move on. If the Tallk can't pick himself up, we'll consider him dead weight."

With that, Lance led the soldiers forward. But Rina stood still. As soon as the General was far enough away, Saito released his hold on her rope collar, unbinding her with more subtlety. At once, she rushed to her betrothed.

"Kaish!"

He groaned, managing to look up towards her. His gentle smile helped calm her frenzy.

"I'll wear some armor down there, next time."

She laughed, despite herself. As she leaned over him, holding his cheek, she glimpsed Alastor lingering nearby. His mouth opened when their eyes met, words resting on his lips, wanting to be spoken.

A Stag with an obnoxious air – Colin, she thought – took his shoulder, baiting him away with praises. The words died.

"Help me up," the Talonian said, already propping himself up with an elbow.

She slipped his arm around her shoulder, allowing him to lean some of his weight on her as they stood. It was clear now that he was nursing a few other injuries; the most recent one had only pushed him over the edge.

"Your leg is bleeding," she said, seeing a trail of red seeping down his trousers. However, he showed no concern.

"I'm fine," he replied, smiling even then. "Just hold me up."

Rina helped him move forward, though the others had already left them in the dust. As she watched the last horse disappear into the forest, her hopes began to fail her. All she could do was help him along, clinging to the hope that they would make it together.

Satoru's whinny was a welcome, beautiful sound. The white stallion trot up beside them, its master looking down from the saddle with sincere remorse.

"Do you mind some company on your trek?" asked Saito.

Both Rina and Kaish shook their heads, relieved.

The three of them traveled in silence, the prisoner patiently helping the Talonian walk through his pain. However, when the air again seemed peaceful, Rina's curiosity returned. She glanced towards the Storma, who seemed far removed atop his glorious steed.

"You said that King Cedric had a twin?" she asked, watching him.

Saito nodded, clearly appreciating a break from the silence.

"Yes. When they both came of age, Raphael sent them to fight in his war. I'm sure he realized in the end how foolish that was, sending off both his heirs to be killed, but did always seem a tad…out of touch. Regardless, the story of Caden's bravery in that war has become something of a legend.

You see, when the heir apparent, Cedric, was summoned home to be married, he had already been captured by Kyron forces. Caden, next in line for the crown, could have easily gone home in his place, married the foreign princess, and become the new Crown Prince. He had a five-year-old son by this time as well, Attlas, who would have been glad to welcome him home.

"However, Caden chose a route no one expected. Rather than going home to a bride and his child, Caden orchestrated a massive rescue for the brother who shared his face, and ended up taking his place as a prisoner of war. The Kyron leaders executed him, thinking he was the heir apparent: and so, he died a hero."

Somehow, this story saddened her.

"So...did Cedric raise his brother's son? Attlas?"

Saito nodded.

"The boy took to him very well. He knew no other father, since he had been conceived during one of Caden's brief visits to the castle and the man had been gone to war since Attlas was an infant; if people hadn't told him all his life that Cedric wasn't his sire, he probably wouldn't have known the difference. Attlas and Asyrias got along very well because of it."

"Asyrias?"

The man nodded once more, though it seemed harder for him to do. He was silent for a moment, his tongue weighted by some forlorn memory.

"Cedric's only son. He passed when he was only a child."

"Oh..."

This memory seemed very close to Saito, and she felt ashamed for prying into it. However, the discomfort of silence seemed the more unbearable alternative.

"You seem to know a lot about the Xaviers. Have you...known any of them?"

Once more, Saito nodded.

"I accompanied the Princesses Miyuki and the child Princess Arisa from Storm, when they were first summoned to the castle. Raphael had a…dispute with their father, Emperor Ryuu Shioya, and the two of them were sent as tokens of peace. You know them best as Morana and Azalea, for they were told to change their names upon arrival to something more befitting Larascan royalty."

Rina's eyes grew wide, startled.

"You came with the Queen?"

He smiled gently.

"I was a favorite of the Emperor. When he discovered I could speak Larascan, he trusted me to accompany his daughters to the capital and remain with them as their tutors. It was he who gave me this fine horse."

Satoru gave an approving snort, as if pleased with the compliment. Saito smiled, patting his silvery mane.

"The Princesses knew enough Larascan to get by without me around the time of our departure, but I decided to accompany them regardless. Little Arisa was only five, and I couldn't bear to send her off alone, not with a half-sister who barely liked her. I can barely leave her alone now…"

His eyes took on a distant look, one she had never quite seen in him before. He seemed too logical a man to wear such a look. She watched him, blinking, thinking she had imagined it. It remained.

"Do you still care about her?" she asked, gently.

At once, he shook away his wistful expression. Recomposed, he got a tighter hold of his reins.

"Attlas has married her. I cannot."

The response was too strange. Unfortunately, a soldier's call silenced her quiet inquiry. Saito, still looking somewhat shaken, was quick to start his horse into a gallop.

"Duty calls! Follow my tracks and stay safe!"

A wave of his hand.

"Best of luck – Rina! Kairos!"

This confused Rina most of all.

"Kairos?"

She heard a sigh from her betrothed, who now seemed to be walking more on his own two feet.

"Saito memorized a list of all the soldiers and Stags in this Rank before he was sent to travel with us. When he's distracted, he forgets nicknames." When he saw her confusion, he adjusted his answer. "Or he screws up my name completely."

She reflected on this answer for a time, watching Saito and his white stallion disappear into the forestry. Without them, the forest seemed quieter, only the nightingales still singing in the distance.

"Then…he must love her."

Kaish nodded, standing even more on his own two feet.

"I believe he does. But he's common, and she's the Queen. An Xavier Queen."

He held his neck, rolling his head to work out knots. He stood on his own now, looking about for some other path, as though the one they were on would somehow lead them astray.

"It might sound awful, but there are two rules I've decided one must follow when dealing with Xaviers, whether an Xavier by marriage or by birth," he continued, still looking. "The first: don't befriend one. The second: never love one."

Chapter VI

When night fell, the soldiers and Stags retreated to the nearby river to bathe. After days of trudging through forest muck, everyone agreed that a bath was best, even if the river wasn't much cleaner. The soldiers rubbed themselves with stones to help rid themselves of the grime; the Stags slapped mud across each others' faces.

Two souls remained at camp. The first was Kaish, who tended to the Stags' fire, tossing chunks of hard meat to the dog chained to a nearby tree. They were his own rations. Unfortunately, by the end of the week it was Lance who decided who received what cuts of the remaining meat. The soldiers generally got the nicer cuts, with a bit of herb to flavor it, and the Stags got most of the jerky. Kaish was handed whatever was deemed too hard to chew.

The second soul was Saito, who had bathed quickly and privately in a nearby pond. Kaish could feel the Storma's eyes on him from across the way, not needing to look to know their pity. He continued chucking meat into the beast's waiting jaws.

"Why do you do that?" came Saito's inquisitive voice.

Kaish smiled, though he was unable to help the cynicism that tainted it.

"I've started to hope that Lance will come by and yell at me for doing it, so I have an excuse to make rude gestures when he turns his back."

This brought Saito's patient smile.

"Fortunately, he's too preoccupied for you right now," he said, taking a seat much nearer to the Stag, "When I passed them, Lance had started his rant about our useless Pacifist King and how he's going to decree some law requiring all men to mate with Kyrons, – or something of the like – all while Lance himself was standing naked in the middle of the river, waving a rock."

Despite Kaish's sour mood, laughter took him all the same. Something about Saito's nature calmed him, even in the worst of times.

"Maybe it's best he won't let me bathe with the others."

Saito chuckled, nodding gently.

"It's a safe assumption."

Kaish's smile remained.

"I take it he doesn't like his new leader?" he asked.

"Loathe is a more correct word," Saito replied, gently prodding a log in the fire. "It's not surprising though. His rants about Cedric are surprisingly similar. The only Xavier he seems to like is that tyrant of a King, Raphael, and his gore-filled policies for the treatment of outsiders."

Kaish's laugh was filled with resentment. He grew silent, dropping most of his rations into the rag they had been given in. What was left, he slipped into his pouch. Saito, likely sensing the dangerous change of mood, spoke to alter it.

"It's odd. That girl reminds me very much of Baldric Alexander."

This caught the Stag's attention.

"The Commander?"

Saito nodded.

"His hair had a nice wave to it, when it began to grow out. More than anything though, it's her eyes—surely, you must have noticed their gleam. I've never seen another with such sharply blue orbs."

This was relatively surprising, but Kaish didn't think much of it. Though the notion was intriguing, he knew the chances of Rina being related to the legendary Commander were slim.

"Did you know Commander Baldric?"

Once again, Saito gave a nod.

"Briefly. Baldric and young Giovanni were a part of Prince Cedric's Rank when he served in Kyro, and they accompanied him back to the castle when the Prince was summoned home. I had only been there a few days myself when they arrived. Baldric brought with him a boy named Antonio, who saved him from capture some time during Baldric's service. Antonio now serves on the King's Council as an expert on Kyron affairs, and an overseer of the Kyron Wall. Giovanni brought with him a young girl named Twyla, whom he saved from torture at the hands of a pair of Kyro's corrupt priests. Because her arrival coincided with the Princesses', Morana saw her as an ally, for they were both foreigners in the King's household. Twyla has been Morana's right-hand ever since. Both Kyrons have become friends of mine, so…I am grateful to the men who saved them."

Kaish smiled at the man, who gazed so distantly into the night.

"You're a walking anecdote."

Saito laughed, the sound warming the air more efficiently than the fire they tended.

"I'll introduce you when we arrive. They would like you very much."

Rajj's sudden snarl chilled the atmosphere. Kaish looked to him with initial annoyance, but was soon grateful for the creature's warning. Too soon, his fellow Stags emerged from the bushes, whooping and hollering as they smacked each other with damp shirts. Saito stood then, politely bowing his head to his friend.

"I should return to the soldiers' fire. It's not far."

Kaish forgave his haste.

"Good night, Saito."

The man disappeared into the forest.

At once, Fritz plopped down beside the Talonian. His frizzy curls were weighed by water, lying nearly flat against his head even as he shook them. He laughed, looking up at Kaish with his boyish grin, oblivious to the worlds' troubles. Fritz was the youngest of the Stags, just turned fourteen years, and always he looked it.

"Can you play your flute again? Pleaaase?"

Taken off guard, it took Kaish a moment to understand his request.

"My flute?"

"Yeah, the one you keep in your pouch? You used to play it all the time..."

Forwin sat down on his other side, his pale face flushed from laughing. His green eyes had a trickster's gleam, though his smile made him the picture of innocence.

"I wanna hear it too, Kaish!"

Craft jumped on Forwin's back, covering the boy's eyes with his muddy hands.

"Me too!"

The boy's sandy-brown locks were a sopping mess upon his head, and his water dripped from his clothes onto his victim's still-bare back. Craft was only months older than Fritz, though he acted years younger.

Kaish gave him a stern glare, and Craft blushed. He released Forwin, rolling out of his reach when the fellow Stag tried to smack him.

"If you two behave, maybe I will," said Kaish.

They both gave good-natured smiles, agreeing with guiltless looks. The Talonian found himself smiling, unable to help it.

"All right. Just don't kill each other while I'm not looking."

He retrieved his wooden flute from the pouch at his waist, taking a moment to look it over. There were no new cracks, not even an unusual scratch. It gave him some comfort, knowing that his mother's instrument remained pristine, even now. With another glance to his small audience, he began to play.

A slow, haunting melody rose from his instrument, coaxed by his soft breath. It seemed to twist and bend around the Stags until it enveloped them, calming them from their childish mood to a restful one. Luther and Sander, already the more solemn of the trainees, were lured closer by it, until they finally seated themselves near to the fire. The last to give in was Colin, whose unpleasant disposition would not let him move from his superior perch upon a moss-covered boulder. He only turned towards them, acknowledging the music with a bitter huff.

Kaish lowered the flute from his lips, observing the spectators. Dark-eyed Luther, whose pale face never displayed motion, had hidden his gaze from him. His hand gripped his knee, knuckles white, as if to contain something. Sander looked upon Kaish with a haughty sort of approval, seeming incapable of any other sort. When the Talonian looked to Fritz, he paused—tears had welled in the boy's eyes.

"What's wrong?" he asked, worried by the rare sight.

Fritz rubbed his green eyes, smiling as he shook his head.

"N-nothing," he said, voice wavering. "It just...makes me miss Argot. There were Tallks that would play for money on the street...Mum would take me to listen to them..."

The word made him cringe, but Kaish dismissed it. The boy knew no better. He placed his flute in his pouch before looking back to his friend, very calm.

"How long has it been since you've seen Argot?"

"I dunno…" Fritz scrunched up his face, thinking. "A year…?"

Colin's mocking laugh came from that boulder, tightening Kaish's jaw.

"I last went to Oyban four months ago," the boy said, smirking, "While you losers got dragged to Storm and back, Lance gave me leave to do what I wanted. I went home to see my parents *and* got a new dagger from Pandore."

This made Sander roll his eyes.

"Why a Pandore blacksmith would make anything for a sniveling brat like you, I'll never understand. Personally, I find Pandore has had nothing to offer me after I graduated from their Academy."

Fritz' eyes grew very wide.

"What's an Academy, Sander?"

A long sigh was his only response.

"I miss the deer, in Siette…" said Craft, drawing circles in the soft soil beneath him. "It's mating season for them now. I liked to watch the bucks fighting…"

Kaish looked to Luther, somehow sensing that he wanted to say something. But he hadn't moved since he last saw him: still looking at the ground, still clutching his knee. He wondered if everyone from Raine was of that disposition; Yaz had a similar attitude around others. In truth, the two of them were deeply unsettling.

"Well, I don't miss Alore," said Forwin, shaking out his tangled brown locks. "Things were getting weird, there."

Craft sat up straight, curiosity in his round eyes.

"What do you mean?"

Forwin shook his head

"Before I enlisted, some weird stuff happened. A Kala girl publicly accused a guy named Silas of witchcraft, and the Protectors tried to arrest him for it. Then he went crazy, and…I swear, I saw flames jump out of his skin!"

Even Kaish looked at him, startled.

"Maybe you were seeing things," the foreigner suggested.

The boy shook his head with conviction, staring hard at the flames that danced before him.

"The Protectors all got burned. Chief Alfric's hands haven't been the same since…all red and raw…"

He shuddered, visibly chewing his lip.

"I'm glad I left."

Suddenly, the new recruit wandered into camp. Alastor was half dressed, shirt held at his waist, – as if his bruised chest was anything to look at – his blonde hair still messy and damp. The youth flashed his suave smile, pretending to be elegant.

"What'd I miss?" he asked.

As much as Kaish tried not to hate him, he did.

The others accepted Alastor into their circle, talking with him as if he were any other Stag. Kaish tried to shake his bitterness towards him, for he was sure it wasn't his bitterness: it was Rina's. Yet, the longer he sat there staring down the youth who had all but abandoned the girl Kaish would marry, the less sure he was of his own feelings. The bitterness only seemed to grow, coursing through him like his own blood.

Fritz' voice cut through the resentful fog.

"You should go see her, Kaish," he said, nudging him with his elbow

"Who?" Kaish asked, startled.

"You know," laughed Craft, "Your *girl*."

Forwin looked up with a smirk.

"You know, if you steal her away now, you could probably take her *bathing*…"

Their immaturity was trying, though they had a point. Rina hadn't been given time to properly wash since she had arrived there, and it was best if she could at least rinse off. If he could sneak into the soldiers' camp as they were starting to fall asleep, he could probably take her to the river without notice.

It's for her own benefit.

The younger Stags, sensing that they had made headway, at once began to pester him until he could barely stand it.

"C'monnn, Kaish!" they goaded. "Don't be a baby!"

He was just about to shut them up when another voice came to him, somewhat deeper, yet more tiresome.

"Leave him alone," said Alastor, challenge in his eyes, "I don't see any reason why he should be helping Rina…*bathe*."

Somehow, this convinced him more than anything else.

"Actually, I believe I should."

Kaish stood, watching as Alastor's fists tightened.

"Maybe *I* should," the boy snapped, "She's *my* friend, after all."

Sander scoffed.

"I don't see your name on her. She doesn't seem to like you much anyway."

Although easy to summon, Alastor's envy brought Kaish pride. He was smiling as he turned to leave camp, his comrade's cheers at his back. However, Rajj began to snarl. As he passed, that snarl turned into a growl, and then a loud, raucous barking. It was as though Rajj knew where he was going, and planned to stop it.

"Shut it," he whispered.

Kaish crammed the rest of his rations from his pocket into the dog's mouth. The creature was silent, seething, chewing. The Talonian left his sight.

He managed to unbind Rina when the soldiers fell asleep, taking her out of their camp without difficulty. The moon shone bright that night, making their walk to the river a simple one. Yet, despite the light, Rina remained skittish. He held her hand, which comforted her some. Even so, she was afraid.

"I'm sorry," she whispered to him, squeezing his hand tight. "I was always told never to go into the forest, especially at night. I'm afraid of the creatures that live here, and spirits…"

Kaish gave her a patient look.

"Spirits?"

She nodded weakly, though she laughed.

"Silly, right? Alastor always said there aren't any, but…I believe. B-but I have all sorts of irrational fears…like my fear of heights…"

He sighed, offering her a comforting smile.

"Why are you afraid of heights?"

"Alastor pushed me down a hill, when I was small…"

Although this upset him, he wasn't quite surprised. He just squeezed her hand, and she seemed soothed.

"Oh...I've been talking a lot about Alastor, haven't I?" she said, her cheeks taking on their usual blush.

He only smiled.

"It's fine."

The small river was lit by fireflies, that night. They cast a golden glow across the surface as they danced, illuminating the darkness with light more beautiful than the sun. The sight must have calmed Rina, for her grip grew lax. Kaish saw the water's surface reflected in her eyes, though they were much bluer than the water they beheld. He was charmed.

Soon, she had slipped into the river, her clothes in a neat pile on shore. Kaish had had the courtesy not to watch while she stripped, and didn't look back to her until she was submerged up to her shoulders. She turned back to shore then, the ends of her short locks barely touching the cool water.

"Aren't you coming in...?" she asked, her soft voice full of hope.

It almost hurt him to shake his head.

"I'm not allowed to bathe, this time," he explained. "If Lance sees I'm wet at all, it'll be a lashing."

Normally, he would take that chance. However, his back was still too raw this time to survive another round. Rina looked down, disappointment clear in her gentle eyes. However, she expressed it only in silence. She disappeared under the waves for a moment, reappearing with a smooth stone from beneath. She turned from him to begin scrubbing her body.

"Saito mentioned a Prince, before..." she said, after a time. "Asyrias, I think. For some reason...well, the story made me so sad, I couldn't stop thinking about it. Everyone says Cedric was such a kind King, and then…his only son dies…"

Kaish watched her back, somewhat entranced by that glimpse of her naked skin. She was very pale, the moonlight giving her the faintest glow. He couldn't look away.

"I'm not sure he's dead," he replied.

She glanced over her shoulder, her eye sparkling with intrigue.

"What makes you say that?"

"Saito's told me enough about the castle. I sense foul play. Cedric's wife, Morana, isn't the innocent foreign Queen everyone took her to be, that much is certain. And Cedric, wonderful as he might have been to his people, couldn't have been an angel in every aspect of his life." He leaned back on his hands, more relaxed as he watched her. "There's a Talon belief my mother had, that a child born into deep adversity has a destiny to overcome it. She said it about me, of course…but I believe it applies better to a Larascan Prince, no? It makes for a more romantic tale."

Rina laughed gently.

"That doesn't have anything to do with him being dead or not."

Kaish smiled in return.

"Someone with a destiny is terribly hard to kill."

This seemed to confuse her, though she asked no more about it. Even so, she moved a little closer to shore, her gaze meeting his.

"Can you tell me something about Talon…?" she asked.

How he wished he could satisfy those inquisitive eyes. Unable to stop himself, he reached out to her, his calloused hand upon her smooth cheek.

"I was very small when I lived there," he said, his voice quiet, just for her, "My earliest memories are of Levanche, the Larascan town where my mother raised me."

She seemed saddened.

"Do you miss her?"

He nodded, holding back his emotions. She didn't need to see them.

"Yes. But she died, a long time ago."

Again, there was beautiful compassion in her eyes. He was lost in it, so grateful to finally meet another person capable of that sincere emotion. Rina placed her hand over his, holding his palm against her cheek. She still wore his bracelet – water fell from it, rejoining the river.

"I'm so sorry, Kaish."

His thoughts weren't with his mother, though. They were with the young woman who stood before him, whose brown tresses were lit by fireflies, soft skin shimmering in moonlight. He saw her virgin lips tremble, a gentle breath passing them.

"May I kiss my future bride?" he asked.

She blushed, at first, eyes averted. And then, she gave one slow nod.

"I-if you wish."

At once, he leaned down and kissed her. He found her lips supple, her taste as sweet as her nature. His hand slipped into her hair, pulling her closer to him. Their lips would not part. He had to savor this, for as long as he could.

My bride.

Alastor had slipped out of camp moments after Kaish, too proud to let the foreigner have Rina without a fight. But when Rina began to shed her clothing, he had decided to allow them peace, in order to observe.

Alastor had settled among the dark foliage, watching the two interact from behind low branches. He realized too late that he had lost his chance. Suddenly, they were kissing.

They were *kissing*.

The kiss never seemed to end. It just stretched on and on, Kaish sucking her face like some kind of animal. Worse, she seemed to be *enjoying* it, her arms wrapping around his neck, as if she needed him.

He grew cold, his heart beating faster and faster with fury.

Rina was his. Didn't anyone realize that? Since the day they had first shared a room in Gwen's orphanage, she had always been his. Always.

Something changed within him. Something took hold of him, squeezing his heart in its clawed grip, laughing in his ear. His whole body lurched. His face grew hot, stomach turning on its side. He was going to be sick. And still, they were *kissing*. Kissing like dogs, like rodents.

He heard Kaish laugh when it was done, that smug smile on his face.

"Tomorrow, we'll disappear into the fog," Kaish said.

Not if he could help it.

He stumbled back into the forest, his legs seeming independent of his body, carrying him. He still felt hot, still sick, sick until he let it out into the roots of a tree. And then he was panting, his body growing heavier, his forehead against his arm against that tree. Slowly, slowly, the world fell into focus around him.

I'll see him dead.

At some point, he ended up back in camp. He still didn't feel right, still felt hot. He held the back of his neck, feeling sweat slick his hand.

"Hey, are you ok?"

Colin – the Stag with a prominently crooked nose – jumped down from his boulder to meet him, since the others had drifted to sleep around the fire. The boy was startled by his appearance, for some reason. He saw it in his eyes.

"You're…different, Alastor—"

"No shit," he snapped, fists tensed like claws. "I'm pissed and I don't know what to do to stop being so bloody pissed!"

The boy drew back, clearly a little overwhelmed.

"Wait wait, pissed about what?"

"*Them*!" he snarled. "Rina and that TALLK!"

Though the volume made Colin cringe, the words brought out his smile. He crossed his arms, sighing and shaking his head.

"I've really got no problem with your blue-eyed little girlfriend, but I'm up for knocking Kaish off his high horse. If he cares about her, I say use that—really find a way to make him squirm."

This cooled his temper, somewhat. He was intrigued.

"And how do we do that?"

Colin shrugged, rubbing the tweak above his nostrils.

"We have to cross an old rickety rope bridge to get across the Alize. We could always make her go first."

All at once, Alastor remembered Rina's terrible fear. If she got anywhere near that rope bridge, she was likely to faint. As her friend, he wouldn't have considered such an option. And yet, the idea now gave him vindictive pleasure. He wanted nothing more than to force her across that bridge, if only to watch her lover writhe.

It's all in good fun.

He had discovered just how easy it was to lie to himself.

The sky was thundering that morning, as the rain poured down. Kaish didn't understand why they had to travel in such conditions, but he had learned not to protest. All he could do was try to restrain Rajj, who was only moodier in the poor weather. He went where he pleased, threatening Kaish with his great teeth when the Talonian tried to veer him any direction he did not find to his liking.

The entire Rank moved sluggishly through the rain, everyone unhappy being woken so early by thunder. It seemed to be an eternity before they came to the Alize. However, it was soon on the horizon. Kaish saw the rickety old bridge swaying in the wind; beyond it was the rolling fog, shrouding the east. His new life lay somewhere beyond that fog, waiting for him.

He glimpsed Rina at the back of the Rank, collared like an animal. Though it saddened him, he forced himself to look away.

General Lance advanced first towards the rope bridge, watching it sway with a wary eye. As tough as he seemed, he clearly couldn't bring himself to cross. Despite being soaked and bitter, Kaish found it easy enough to smirk. It lasted until Colin's shrill voice came through the downpour.

"Why not have the prisoner go first, General?!" was his shout.

The Rank grew quiet, the sounds of thunder echoing louder. Kaish could see that cold smirk spreading across Lance's face.

"Bring her forward!"

Kaish could feel the blood fall from his face. His tongue went numb as Rina was brought forward, led by Colin himself.

"Her? Lance, don't be ridiculous!" Wolf bellowed.

"She's only a child!" Saito cried, stepping forward from the Rank. "Let one of your soldiers cross first—that bridge doesn't look stable!"

"All the more reason why a prisoner should test it!" Lance snarled, stepping aside. He gestured Colin forward, who now nearly dragged the girl by her rope. She was digging her feet into the ground, her body visibly trembling. At once, Kaish realized her fear.

"Lance!"

His own voice came forth without him calling it, his grip on Rajj's chain growing tighter every moment.

"Lance! Let me go instead!"

Kaish had stepped forward from the rest—alone. He stood face to face with Lance, realizing he was now as tall as the man he so loathed.

"I'm not afraid, General," he said, strength behind each word. "Let me cross."

Rajj snarled, beginning to fight against the Talonian's hold. Kaish tried not to let it distract him, just holding his firm stare. The General stared back, his Larascan eyes filled with contempt. And then...he smiled. At once, General Lance pushed the prisoner onto the rope bridge.

"Move, girl!"

Rina stood, white like ice, like Kaish.

Shit.

"MOVE!" Lance barked.

She took small steps across, her trembling hand gripping the rope rail. The wind wailed, slapping the bridge she clung to.

"**GO!**"

Suddenly, Rajj was feral. He was snarling, snapping his jaws, fighting Kaish's grip with strength that shouldn't have belonged to him.

"Stop this," Kaish whispered, trying to keep his hold.

The chain was slick, slippery in the rain. And the more Rajj fought, the less control Kaish managed. It was like some ancient beast had possessed the dog, taking advantage of the elements to win this battle.

Rajj broke free. Kaish grabbed for the chain, but the creature was already bounding towards Rina, already on the bridge. The ropes began to creak, strained. Rina turned in time to see the dog as it leapt for her, jaws wide.

The bridge snapped.

Kaish saw her eyes widen as she went down, down into the raging river beneath.

"Rina!"

He had almost dived into the river before someone held him back – Fritz on his left, Saito on his right. They were shouting at him, Saito's well-kept fingers dug deep into his muscle in hopes of shocking sense into him. But his sense was gone. She was gone. Just like that, she was gone.

He was screaming in Talonian, screaming into the rain.

My hope is dead.

Silas stared out over the Alize River, watching the waters rush past, slapping up against smooth rocks. The water was deep here, the surface rippling with the drizzling rain. He could almost see his reflection in it as he towered above—his shaggy hair tangled with leaves, lips stained with some animal's blood. He could still taste raw flesh, veins caught between his teeth.

Why are you here?

Some force had beckoned him here. He remembered wandering for days through that forest, hearing the rushing river so near. Perhaps he had come to rest his eyes on something other than the never-ending trees that had become his refuge. Perhaps he had come to see himself in the water, to know he was more than just a creature who could rip rabbits to pieces, feast on their bones.

Would your father mourn this creature?

The youth heard a bitter chuckle echoing, echoing in his mind. He realized that it was rolling out of him, filling the air around him with half-sane laughter. He reached into his pouch, retrieving that yellowed parchment from its place: the letter to his past self. It was smooth against his bandaged, throbbing hand, like royal silk. He stared down at it, seeing the red stains from where his tainted fingers had traveled. Bruises, they seemed.

He opened his hand, letting the breeze carry the letter into the water. It swelled as it was swept away, shuddering beneath the surface. It sank.

"Disappear."

A growl, behind him. He spun about, dagger drawn, snarling. There was nothing.

Baffled, Silas lowered his weapon. He knew there was an animal near; its scent was heavy on his senses. But he saw nothing.

The bushes rustled, something big disturbing them. He hurled the knife into the leaves, hollering to deter the beast. The world was silent again.

"…Bastard…"

Irked, he went to retrieve his dagger. He parted the dense bushes, searching. The weapon was nowhere to be found. He continued searching, frustrated, until he finally came through to the other side. There, in a small clearing, was his pest: a great mutt with fur of matted gray, bat-like ears held up playfully, a twinkle in his startlingly black eyes. The dagger was in his mouth.

Silas bore his teeth, kneeling low to meet his black gaze.

"Give it," he snarled, hand thrust out towards it.

The dog showed understanding, large ears twitching as he cocked his head. His mouth stretched wider, as if to grin. And then, he bolted to the river.

"FAWK!"

Silas pursued, as fast as he could manage, cursing the dog as he ran, panting, running. The beast seemed intent on leading him all the way to Kyro. He ran, faster and faster, but could never gain on the creature he chased.

And then, the dog stopped. It stood in front of a body, half washed onto the shoreline, face down. There was dark hair upon its head, short and tangled; yet, there was a white dress clinging to its form, tattered. This was a female.

Silas stood still, frozen. All at once, the creature looked up at him, black eyes meeting violet with playful curiosity. Slowly, it set the weapon down in the damp soil, by the girl's head. It stopped to look at its reflection in the water, tilting its head this way and that, intrigued. Then, without another sound, the beast bounded back into the forest.

The man remained still, uncertain what to do. He thought for sure this woman was dead, for no one could survive being swept away by the Alize River. However, something led him to kneel beside her, roll her over to examine her body. He found a beautiful face smeared by dirt. Her jaw was shaped finely, her lips soft and plump. She was thin, her pale skin abused by the waves. She was scratched everywhere, bleeding into the white gown. Upon her right arm, he found the mark of slavehood: the Xavier 'X'. However, on her left, he found a Talonian bracelet.

...her.

This was the girl from his vision. Battered by the river, barely breathing, was the young girl he was supposed to save.

Why? Why should you save her?

It was too dangerous for him to go back to town, even to get her treatment. Every man, woman, and child knew by now what he had done to Lady Abaca. He couldn't set foot in Alore, not unless he wanted a hanging.

He stood, sliding his dagger in his belt. However, the girl's soft groan prevented him from leaving. He looked back to her, finding she had begun to stir.

"...who...are you...?"

Her eyes partially opened, revealing their color. He stared into those blue orbs, azure as the sky. He wondered if the world regarded her eyes as they did his—an abomination, a shameful difference.

"I am no one," he said.

She seemed to smile, choking when she meant to laugh.

"…you look like…someone, to me…"

Her eyes fell closed, her breath slowing again. And yet, he continued to watch her. Was he intrigued? Entranced?

Slowly, he knelt by her body, eyes still set on her closed lids. He slipped his powerful arms beneath her, lifting her from the shore. Water cascaded from her ruined garment, dripping like the rain.

Fool.

He found his way through the forest, home.

Chapter VII

Rina's world was hazy after the water's rushing had ended. She barely remembered being lifted from the river, supported in someone's strong hold. Once, she had opened her eyes to see her savior. She saw a strange man through the haze, whose skin looked darkened by summer heat, his eyes a hue of sunset. A dangerous air seemed to emanate from him. And yet, she thought him beautiful.

She drifted back into darkness until she felt a cot beneath her, a quilt against her battered skin. She heard the voices of two men: one old and fatherly, the other deep, haughty.

"You shouldn't be here…"

"I'll go where I please."

"You have to leave, for your own sake!"

Her eyes half-open, she saw the shadowy figure of her savior jump onto the window's ledge.

"Take care of her."

He vanished out the window, out of her view.

Slowly, she drifted back into darkness.

Edmund always felt very tense when standing among fellow Protectors. He could always feel their eyes boring into his skull, always hear those nagging whispers.

"He doesn't look like his father."

"Bet I could take 'im."

"Why would the old Chief give him his sword?"

"Bet he falls over when he pulls it out."

He tried not to hear them. He just focused on Chief Alfric, who paced back and forth before the Protectors' straight lines. The Chief's dark hair was thinning as he aged, his green eyes grown sunken and tired. Familiar leather gloves, worn thin by use, concealed his scarred palms: Silas' gift to five senior Protectors. Yet Alfric's preaching was as passionate as it always had been.

"This time, that abomination has gone too far!" he exclaimed, still pacing. "Time and time again that sorcerer has violated the peace of this town, and he mocks us by avoiding capture! Cedric's Code must be enforced!"

Edmund knew most of the soldiers had already stopped listening. Though Cedric had died nearly six years before, all Alfric could talk about was the late King's Code: that a disturber of the people's peace must be removed, tamed, and corrected. If the disturber refuses correction, they must be removed more permanently. Cedric himself had set the precedent with the public burning of Dayu, the foreign sorcerer, in the Noble Square of Joanissia.

"How do you expect us to capture him?" snapped Henry, an arrogant youth who had been a Protector for only a few months longer than Edmund. "Even if he wasn't a walking furnace, he's got teeth like knives, and I hear he's not afraid to use them anymore. It's like trying to apprehend a bear!"

"There is always a way," was Alfric's retort. "Throw a net on him for all I care!"

Suddenly, Edmund heard tapping on the window beside him. He tried not to seem bothered by it, attempting to stay still at the end of the line, but the tapping came with more persistence. When he finally looked, he was mortified to see his lover gesturing him outside.

Oh no...

He shook his head, trying to plead with his eyes. He told himself that Madeleine just didn't realize how highly important it was that he stay and listen to his Chief, that is was a sign of great disrespect if he did not. However, the more she stared him down through that glass, the more he realized that she really just didn't care.

But...but...

He couldn't stand her insistent look. As much as he knew he would regret it, Edmund waited until Alfric had paced to the other side of the room, and he slipped quietly out the side door.

Outside, the rain had finally dried up. The overcast sky seemed a little brighter, a lighter gray than even the cobblestone road. Both Madeleine and John Keeper awaited him, Maddy regarding him with her usual scowl. But there was a third presence that he didn't recognize, wrapped and hooded in a black cloak.

"Who's this?" he asked.

John pulled back the hood, revealing the lovely face of a girl no more than sixteen. However, her beauty did not lessen his caution when he saw the crop of her dark locks.

"She's been marked for a criminal," the Protector said, looking at the innkeeper in shock. "Who is she? What are you doing *here* with her?"

"She says her name is Rina," Maddy replied, sighing heavily. "Silas dumped her in Father's inn a few nights back."

"But why in the Xaviers' name—?!"

He paused, lowering his voice.

"Why in the Xaviers' name would you bring a marked criminal to the Protectors' headquarters?!" he whispered.

John spoke this time, his calm look hushing Madeleine.

"She said her only goal is to reach Joanissia, to catch up to someone. It just so happens that your most wanted felon has his origins in the same city."

This gave Edmund pause.

"Silas came from the capital?"

The innkeeper nodded, placing his hand on Rina's shoulder.

"Giovanni has always refused to disclose much about the boy; however, that's one fact he has remained consistent on."

The girl never once met Edmund's gaze, her blue eyes steadily rest on the cobblestones at his feet. There was such a heartbreaking look about her that the Protector couldn't bring himself to judge her past.

"All right, even if that's true, what do I have to do with this?" the youth asked, somewhat bewildered.

Once more, John was quick to respond.

"Find a way to get the Protectors' off Silas' tail, so that he and Rina can flee to the capital."

Edmund could feel his blood run cold. He stared blankly at John, and then to Madeleine. Only John seemed to have any sympathy for him.

Maddy's arms were crossed with impatience, her foot tapping determinedly until such time that he bow to her wishes.

"You're asking me to go against my Chief, my vows," he said, mouth so dry he could hardly speak. "If I help a criminal with a death sentence—"

"Edmund, who helped you with your reading when your father gave up hope?" John snapped.

At once, the Protector's protests began to run dry.

"…Silas did…"

"Who saved your life three times in the Great Forest?"

The youth looked down, scratching his head in nervous agitation.

"Silas did…"

"And who did you turn your back on the one time he needed help?"

The heavy hand of regret came down upon Edmund as he remembered that day, when the three of them had watched Silas disappear into the forest. The sour taste in his mouth returned, and as much as he tried to rationalize his continued dissent, he knew he had been cornered.

"Even…even if I did decide to help, how are we going to get her out of town?"

The cloaked girl further averted her gaze, no doubt uncomfortable being referred to at all in speech. He sighed, feeling remorse.

"I'm risking serious consequences by not apprehending such a deliberately marked criminal on sight. Even if she leaves Alore intact, she'll be seized as soon as they stop for shelter."

John pulled up her hood then, which she seemed grateful for. Yet, the innkeeper didn't seem as worried as the Protector thought he should be. With a look to Madeleine, the man soon stated his case.

"We've decided it would be best to dress her as a man, until her hair lengthens."

Edmund gawked.

"W-what?"

"We know it's illegal, unheard of, dishonorable, blah blah blah," said Maddy, tactful as always, "but I certainly can't figure out how to make a short-haired girl look feminine. It's simply unnatural."

"But…" he croaked.

"How about it, Edmund?" John asked, his gaze never faltering. "Will you help your old friend out of the hole he's fallen into?"

It was too hard to respond. His reason had been pitted against his feelings, and his reason had never been strong. He was a Protector, Chief Edward's only son—but above that, he had been Silas' closest friend.

He looked once more at Madeleine, whose haughty look beseeched his reply, and then to the hooded girl, Rina. Her strange blue eyes regarded him with true sincerity, such hope glistening in their depths. He could only say one thing.

"Of course I'll help."

Madeleine smiled, kissing him then and there. Though his thoughts were spinning, he tried to enjoy it.

The Alore sky began to drizzle.

Late that night, when the moon was high and Madeleine had grown used to the creaking of the castle walls, she was disturbed by an unusual sound. Though Duke Bayard ordered that all windows were to be secured after sunset, she thought she heard the sound of her own swinging open, hinges creaking with a cool autumn breeze. When she sat up, she saw a figure silhouetted on the stone ledge—a bare-chested youth with powerful shoulders and narrow, piercing eyes.

"Silas?!"

Her initial fear was forgotten. She leapt out of bed, rushing to the window before her passion died down.

"Where the fawk have you been, Silas?! Three years and you've never even dropped me a letter! I thought you were dead!"

His eyes grew narrower, a twitch of his brow betraying silent irritation. She was not deterred.

"And then you come back into town after burning half our Lady's face off?! Granted, she probably provoked it, but that doesn't make it any less—"

"Shut up."

He said it with such forceful intensity that words died on her lips.

In utter silence, Silas reached into the weathered pouch he had always kept on his belt, pulling out a sizeable scrap of paper, folded in two. This, he handed to her.

"Take this to Abaca."

She looked it over, baffled, tongue-tied. But when she looked back to the window, Silas had disappeared. Maddy looked over the edge to see him descending the stone wall, climbing with beastlike agility. It was astonishing how effortless it seemed to him now.

The servant closed the window, this time taking a moment to secure it. As much as she wanted to wait until morning to deliver the letter, something told her it was best to complete the task quickly. Before the sky grew any darker, she found herself wandering the familiar halls of the small castle to find her Lady's room.

The double doors were already open, which was unusual at that hour. Madeleine entered to find her Lady sitting on the bench-sized ledge of the glass window, staring out into the massive courtyard. Since that fateful accident in the forest some days before, Abaca had taken to wearing well-crafted masks to hide her disfigurement. Yet, tonight her face was bare to the world: raw, pink skin blistered and oozing, sickening to behold.

Madeleine approached, trying not to see her face.

"I have a letter for you, my Lady."

Abaca ignored her. Maddy went closer, wanting to see what had so entranced her. What she saw left her cold. There, in the courtyard, she saw a great force of armored Protectors surrounding one man. Their swords were drawn, points making a lethal star around their victim, who tried to run despite them. He was forced to the ground, his mournful howl shaking the window the women watched from.

"They've been waiting for him for days," said her Lady, forgetting all attempts at formal speech, "I've been waiting to watch him suffer."

A vengeful smile twisted her grotesque features, leaving her servant repulsed, trembling with disbelief. Madeleine was furious.

"He didn't come to do any harm!" Again she thrust out that letter, ready to scream. "*He's* the one that wrote you this!"

Abaca smacked it from her hand, spitting at it as it fell.

"Your brother got what he deserved, peasant."

She turned back to the window, without attempt to mask her vindictive pleasure. Madeleine was dismissed with an inattentive wave.

"Go, or make yourself small."

Maddy's nails dug deep into her palms as she watched a Protector knock Silas over the head with the hilt of his weapon, rendering him unconscious. The felon left limp, he was bound and dragged through the mud, into the night.

***

Abaca,

　I know what I've done to you is inexcusable. As much as you might have deserved my anger, it wasn't right to raise my hand against you. I am sorry.

　Maybe I misjudged you. Beneath that selfish façade, perhaps there's a heart capable of forgiveness I could not muster. That would make you far stronger than I.

~Silas

Chapter VIII

*R*ina looked sadly upon the four well-made corsets still hanging in Madeleine's closet, barely faded by a light coating of dust. "Made from the finest whales of the Griffon Sea," the innkeeper had said. "At least, that's what my daughter would have you believe." They seemed now to represent a world Rina had lost, one of feminine wiles and a quest for beauty. With only a glimpse in the mirror, she was grounded in reality.

"You make a fine lad," said John, clasping her shoulders in a kind, fatherly way.

Indeed, in the long mirror was a figure even she didn't recognize. Her cropped locks were pulled back at the nape of her neck with a simple strip of leather, a tightly wrapped cloth concealing her sizeable bosom beneath a shapeless tunic and vest. Long sleeves hid the slaves' mark scarred into her arm. She wore workers' trousers barely tapered at the ankle to allow room for stiff boots, both of which had an unusually musty scent about them. She had never been proud of what she saw in the mirror, but what she felt now was close to shame.

"This is illegal, isn't it?" came her own meek voice.

Though remorsefully, the innkeeper nodded.

"Yes, but only if you're caught."

She tried to swallow her uneasiness, without luck. John's look of sympathy could only ease her so much. Still, she allowed him to move her away from the mirror, turning her towards him in a stern sort of way.

"Now, you should understand a few things about men before you pretend to be one. It'll help you make the most of your experiences."

"But aren't they just like girls…?"

This was met with a soft chuckle.

"Except for some minor extremities, I think you're right. But Larascan law doesn't see it that way. For example, there are three laws that apply to women that don't apply to men: the law against gambling, buying horses, and owning weapons. I'll bet you've never even held a sword, have you?"

The girl shook her head, realizing she had not. John didn't seem surprised.

"You might also want to learn how to read while you're disguised. It's a rather handy skill, and I find it a shame peasant women are prohibited from knowing it."

He continued on, telling her the best way to stand, ways to speak, as much as he could to help her play her role. But her mind began to wander. She touched the bracelet hidden by her long sleeves, remembering the dark-haired Talonian who had given it to her. Rina missed his gentle touch, his elusive smile. This façade would be for him, so she could meet him in Joanissia. Maybe then, she could save him from the General's unjust treatment. Maybe then they could be together.

"Why are you helping me?" she asked, always hesitant.

The man looked at her in some surprise, realizing she hadn't been paying attention. His look was forgiving, however.

"I don't believe it's a coincidence that you and Silas both have ties to Joanissia. This town has become poison to him, and he needs to move on to the next part of his life, there. I don't know how the two of you crossed paths, but I plan to make the most of this twist of fate."

Rina smiled weakly, managing a nod. Generally, fate meant very little to her. She knew only what goals she could see before her, and thought little of anything past them. She didn't yet realize that she shared this belief with most of her countrymen.

"Are you looking forward to traveling with him?" John asked.

The question shook her from her daze.

"With who?" she asked.

"Silas, of course."

She cringed, her anxiety written on her face. The thought of going back into that forest with anyone was frightening enough, but to do it with a complete stranger was terrifying.

"Well…what's he like?" she asked, quietly.

He thought quite intently on this, arms crossing as he stared towards the cracked window. It was as if he hoped Silas would appear there any moment.

"Silas is special," he replied. "As much as he pretends he's otherwise, he has always been kind-hearted and courageous, with blunt honesty that never fails. I'll admit his temper can sometimes get the better of him, but there's something within him that drives him to succeed despite it. He was peerless at endurance sports, in his youth. He's also incredibly gifted in logic, when he chooses to use it. Lately though…I feel he's forgotten himself."

He looked to her a moment, his smile returning.

"Perhaps you're meant to soften him, again."

Rina smiled gently, liking this description very much. If this was her savior, she was certain to be in very capable hands.

"Do you know him well?"

The innkeeper nodded, taking a seat on the small cot. He gestured that she sit beside him, to which she complied.

"Silas' guardian, Giovanni Wolfslayer, had this disturbing habit of locking Silas out of the house for weeks at a time as a form of punishment—punishment for what, I'm not sure. The boy was little more than nine when he started doing it, and when Giovanni locked him out during snowy months, Silas started coming into my inn to escape the weather. After watching this boy show up fairly consistently at my inn, I offered to let him have a room upstairs for his own. He began living with Giovanni the months he would allow him to, and the rest of the time he spent with my adoptive daughter and me. He and Madeleine got along well, though they bickered like a married couple."

He chuckled, amused at some memory.

"Before long, he was dear as a son to me. He's the only brother Maddy's ever known, and he protected her like a younger sister. We were happy enough, until…"

He trailed off, his gaze somewhere far away. Strangely, she found herself recalling the intense air about her rescuer, the icy look of his strange eyes. Something must have changed him from the kind boy who had been Madeleine's brother. But before she could ask, the door swung open. Madeleine rushed in, her hair escaping her normally neat bun when she stopped, breathless.

"Silas is going to be hanged!"

John grew rigid, face pale white.

"They caught him, Maddy?"

She nodded, as pale as he.

"I was planning on going into the forest to tell him our plan, but..." She had to stop, choking on the words she would have said. Finally, she continued. "You'll have to go down to the prison without me. I can't take it. Edmund's outside waiting to escort you, since you can't get in without a Protector."

The innkeeper helped Rina to her feet, trying to hasten her out the door.

"Please, we have to hurry!" he urged.

Outside, Edmund sat atop his dark horse, clearly as anxious as his lover had been. But they proceeded quickly despite this, maneuvering the narrow streets of Alore by the Protector's lead. John was near silent, brow creased by deep thought. However, though she sensed the gravity of the situation, Rina was most aware of the Protector's steed. It was a magnificent mare, with a long mane and a coat as black as Satoru's had been white. The young man must have noticed her admiration, for his gentle voice soon broke the tension.

"This is Ella," he said, patting her mane. "She was given to me when I first became a Protector."

"She's beautiful," said Rina.

Edmund smiled with sincerity.

"I feel she's a part of me, at times."

The creature gave a snort.

Soon, they came upon the small prison. Its four walls were made entirely of stone, the double-doors barred with a massive steel beam. On each side of the door was a Protector, both broad and menacing. And yet, the innkeeper's attention was focused on another man who lingered near the entry. He was of a modest build, with short, dark hair and a mustache that divided his features. There was something unsettling about the way his smile deepened John's rare scowl.

"You!" the innkeeper cried, "What do you think you're doing here?!"

The man chuckled, welcoming the confrontation.

"Am I not allowed to ask about my poor son's health?"

"You have no right to call him your son, you bastard! Haven't you done enough to him?!"

Rina was startled by the intense anger coming from a man who had seemed so docile. But his fury was very real: it was written in his eyes, his brow, his fists. And yet, it rolled off its target like feeble rain. The man only smiled, his clever gaze set on Rina. She paled, shrinking away when he approached. Her tongue ceased to function.

"You're a new face," he said.

Like a curious jackal he began to circle her, judging her hair, her clothes, her face.

"How very strange," he said, that smile ever set upon his visage. "I've never seen a lad with such long lashes."

"Leave him alone, Giovanni. He's none of your concern."

The innkeeper stepped in front of her, using his own body to distance her and this man. At last, he took the hint. Giovanni gave a regal bow, smirk never faltering.

"For now, perhaps. Something tells me our paths will cross soon enough."

He moved past them, gracefully as a ghost.

"Until we meet again, my lady."

Rina was white as a sheet. But the man was already gone.

"Forget about him," John said, squeezing her shoulder. "He's a callous ass, but he won't tell another soul about this meeting. He's already given up all the friends he might have had."

Edmund dismounted, handing Ella's reins to the innkeeper.

"There's a stable around back, Sir Keeper, if you would be kind enough to take her there."

John nodded, looking once more to the girl.

"Stay here until I get back."

He left, leading Ella around the stone wall while Edmund – somewhat timidly – approached the guards. Rina was left to stand as still as she could, trying not to seem out of place.

A gray dog wandered out of a nearby ally, sniffing the cobblestones with purpose. Sniffing, sniffing, he approached her, bat-ears pressed tight against his head. Rina's body grew stiff; she stared at the creature, throat closing, mouth dry. All she could remember now was Rajj's snarl, and the bridge snapping beneath her feat.

Please, go away...

The beast came closer, sniffing her boots, her hands. He was oblivious to her fear. He seemed to smile as his large ears perked up, black eyes alight with a curious gleam. His tongue slicked her hand before she could dodge it. Her every muscle locked, and for a moment, tears clouded her vision. Yet, the world went on. The dog finished licking her palm and – finding the taste was not to his liking – sneezed, and bounded away. She remained, stupefied, until she heard the prison doors creak open.

"Come on," Edmund hollered, "Sir Keeper will meet us inside."

It was a moment before she could hurry to his call. Try as she might, she could not shake the foreboding feeling that curious creature had given her, or the anxiety caused by Giovanni's smile. She felt she never would.

This is too much.

1ˢᵗ Month, 650 I.R.

I hate our cellar. I don't like the stone walls, or the way it keeps in cold or how it creaks at night. I wouldn't care a lick about Vaan's drinking habit if he didn't keep sending me down there to bring him bottles. I know he only sends me down there to piss me off! He knows I can't take the shadows...

They haunt me, now. The shadows. They remind me of something I've seen before, but I can't remember it. And when I try to remember, the voices come. I hear them down there, in the cellar. They whisper to me— some woman, or some girl. It makes me sick to hear them, or maybe I hear them because I'm sick.

Vaan tells me that everything has a logical explanation. But how can that be true when my hands burn with flames and I hear imaginary voices echo off stone? How much longer can I keep these things from everyone? I'll be stoned, or worse.

Sometimes, when the woman speaks to me in the cellar, she'll sing a song. It's always the same, but the words are blurred.

Oh my pretty little son,
Close your eyes in gentle sleep
Feel my hand ...
Pressing ... sigh...
My lovely little boy
My cursed ... little ...

It frightens me. I feel that I should know her voice, and I don't. I just don't know anything anymore. I can't go through life not knowing anything.

Everyone expects me to be honest, but how can I be when I don't even know my real name?

I feel this will tear me apart, soon. The fire that controls me burns brighter every day, and I lose more of myself. I have to stop it, somehow. I have to regain control.

The prison wall was ice against Silas' bare back, adding frustration to his misery. Above him, his hands were cuffed with iron, and his ankles were bound below by heavy chains attached to metal boulders. Although he could feel his broken body healing, it felt heavy, detached from him. He was filled to the brim by rage, deep and potent.

They've done this to you.

He gnashed his teeth, snarling into the dark and empty air.

All those people you trusted. They led you here.

His jagged nails dug deep into his skin, agitating the deep wound his so-called father had inflicted upon him. Fresh blood trickled down his arm.

This is how they kill the Abomination.

He howled at the ceiling, to hear it echo off the walls. Something, anything to drown out his thoughts. It was futile. Alone, he had only himself to fight. And so, he grew limp. The dense air surrounded him, choking him with thoughts of what he had been: skilled, revered, envied. He was reduced to nothing.

His vision began to flicker. He thought he saw a young woman resting against the cell bars, staring out into the long, torch-lit hall. Her chestnut locks fell in tangled waves to the floor beneath her, very dark against her white complexion. The dress she wore was thin and tattered, exposing much of her slender body. She was a prisoner, as he was, but imprisoned for something very different.

"Come here," came her gentle voice, echoing from the cool walls.

He wanted to call her a fool; clearly, he could do no such thing. Yet suddenly, he was unbound. His arms fell, knees buckling under the sudden weight of his upper body. At first, he was thrilled. But he was suddenly overwhelmed by pain, spreading from his core to the most insignificant bone. It was as if nails moved through his veins, ripping through them until his heart had no more reason to beat. He couldn't manage the breath to speak.

She looked back at him, the faintest concern softening her blue eyes.

"Is that why you won't come?"

He choked, barely able to lift his head to see her. He collapsed to the ground, breathing slowly, heavily, as the agony began to overcome him. And then, she was there. She lifted his bleeding hand in her own tender hold, her finger tracing the ring that had never left his skin. He saw now the black veins that extended from it, grotesquely pulsing, pulsing.

"Let go..."

She slipped the gold band from his finger as if it were cloth. At once, the black veins disappeared, settling back into his flesh. Slowly, the pain ended.

"Now you'll remember."

Silas managed to sit up, rubbing his finger in astonishment. He had never felt the skin beneath that band. He was so relieved, he tried to speak again, wanting to thank her. She pressed a finger to his lips.

"Tick tock...tick tock..."

She leaned closer, that finger tracing his smooth jaw as she closed her eyes. Unaware of all else, he relaxed. He closed his eyes as well, going to touch her, kiss her.

A chain went taut, movement stopped. His eyes snapped open, realizing he was bound once again. And yet, he saw that young woman, this time through his prison bars. Her hair was short, tied back, and she wore a man's clothes. But her eyes could not be so concealed.

Her. Her, again.

Silas didn't notice John Keeper's presence until he spoke, stepping very close to the iron bars.

"We have a plan, Silas," he said. "We're going to set you free."

He just…blinked, staring. His thoughts were slow to process, after such a long isolation.

"When?"

"Tonight," he replied, "Edmund will cut you loose before the drop."

Another slow blink, eyes adjusting to the light. He felt incapable of understanding any of this, though the words were so clear. He looked from John, his old friend, to the cross-dressing girl, and then to the Protector he had glimpsed in the shadows—Edmund, he realized. Neither youth wanted to look too long at the other.

"Why?" he managed.

"Because you need to go to Joanissia," said John, clasping the girl's shoulders. "And so does she."

The capital. The letter in the forest had wanted him to return there—*Reja* to return there. There were answers there, tucked within those frozen mountains. A part of him knew that was where his future lay. However, those were not the words that spilled from his mouth.

"I can't."

John tensed, clear frustration leading him to grip the cell's bars.

"Please, Silas, you have no other choice. Alore isn't a home for you anymore; the capital is the only hope you have left."

His grip tightened, such care in his face.

"Please, trust us."

They were the wrong words. Anger bubbled from his gut, clenching his teeth and clenching his fists. The chains rattled as he snarled his retort.

"What reason do I have to trust *any* of you?"

The innkeeper grew solemn, slowly stepping away from the bars. Seeing his grief, Silas regretted his anger. And yet, he was silent.

"You can find faith in your friends, or you can die alone. The choice is yours. Just agree to take Rina with you when you flee the city, and you'll have our undying loyalty."

This disturbed him. His rage was the only thing that was certain now, and he clung to it. But he knew he could not keep to it long. His body was weakened, strength compromised by chains. Now, his past friends had returned to right their wrongs. What right did he have to rob them of that chance?

His gaze fell to the floor, feeling the strain his weight put on his suspended arms. He carefully composed his reply.

"Leave the girl on the western outskirts of town. Take care that no one *sees* her. If Edmund does his part, I'll be out of this shithole faster than you can blink."

Sudden light blinded him. Silas howled, closing his eyes tight as the guard shouted down at them from the open entry.

"Visiting time is over!"

Edmund gestured them quickly forward, never willing to be caught out of line. In any other situation, Silas might have been amused. The innkeeper smiled at the youth before he left, though it had a somber nature.

"Stay strong," he said.

The girl turned to leave as well. However, his low grunt caught her attention. His gaze met hers, wanting her to know his power. He could smell her fear.

"Listen well, girl."

He narrowed his eyes, watching as her foot shifted back ever so slightly.

"I am not your savior, guardian, or anything of that nature. Lean on me again and expect to fall."

She barely breathed as she nodded, meekly crossing her arms. She looked ridiculous, pretending she was a man. No clothing could hide her fragility, give power to her helpless, mindless nod. Only a fool would ever fear a sheep in wolf's clothing.

The girl vanished into the hall, her shadow disappearing with the light. There was no more mystery about her. She was only the girl who would be his ward, the reason for his imprisonment and the key to his escape. Yet, her gaze lingered in his thoughts, the same blue eyes that had haunted his visions. He tried once more to feel nothing.

Silas was woken by a smirking group of self-righteous Protectors, who freed his wrists from the wall first to snicker when he collapsed to the ground. Their laughter incited his rage: he leapt to his feet, snarling as he grasped futilely for his confiscated dagger. But they overpowered him, six men to one. It took four to pin him down, while the last two shackled his arms and feet. The last chain became his collar.

He was paraded through Alore like a dog, ridiculed by the townsfolk who felt confident of his restraints. They spit on him, throwing rotten meat, jeering.

"Freak!"

"Thief!"

"Murderer!"

In those moments, he didn't know if their accusations were true. Yet by the time he stood in the gallows, staring out over the sneering crowd, he began to feel that they were.

They're winning.

They all congregated there, his faceless enemies. Vanity mocked him, rocks in hand. Lust, the sweet poison that had led him there, smirked on the sidelines. Wrath was there, front and center—but he would never be satisfied.

Chief Alfric unrolled the record of Silas' misdeeds with his scorched hands.

"Silas Wolfslayer: guilty of thievery, arson, the premeditated slaughter of livestock, the attempted murder of our Lady Abaca, and sorcery. He is a man who shows neither remorse for his repeated crimes, nor any attempt to reform his ways. By Cedric's Code, the consequence of this is death."

Edmund himself placed the noose around his neck, eyes solemn. At once Silas grew tense, knowing something was terribly wrong.

Isn't he supposed to save you?

Suddenly, the scene solidified. The laughter, the chanting, his fear became real.

You're going to die.

All he knew now was regret. It choked him, tighter than the noose that groped his neck.

"For the good of Larasca!" The Chief bellowed.

Silas closed his eyes tight.

A fate you deserve.

The floor dropped.

He rolled onto the ground beneath. Loose rope slapped his back as a sword and sheath hit the ground beside him. It was an impressive weapon with a blade shined to gleam, a hilt inlaid with bronze—Edmund's sword. Silas looked up to the platform above, seeing his old friend smiling, shaking with adrenaline. The youth's mouth formed silent words.

"Use it well."

That moment seemed suspended in time. Silas felt something had been returned to him, lost long ago. His lips stretched in a forgotten way, to smile.

Time began. He grabbed the bronze hilt and began to run. The crowd parted for him, screaming, shrieking, as Protectors bellowed orders in their midst. Silas looked behind him once, glimpsing Edmund's arrest. John restrained Madeleine near the platform, preventing her from reaching the condemned man. Silas knew he would never see them again.

They've paid their debt.

He left the gallows far behind, running as fast as he could though the alleys to the Western side of Alore. He had almost outrun the Protectors that pursued him when his path was blocked. Two horses prevented his passing, one light, with a yellow, feathery mane, the other dark brown—atop it, a mustached man with an infuriating smile.

"No...no fawking way..."

Silas gripped the hilt of his sword so tightly it threatened to crack, teeth clamped together to prevent his fury from becoming a roar. But Giovanni *smiled.*

"Having a bad day, my boy?"

Vaan tugged the reins of the blonde horse at his side, chuckling when she tried to step away.

"This is Charlotte, Silas. Charlotte, remember?" He chuckled. "She's reliable enough. She'll be your trusty steed on this long journey."

The youth snarled, forgetting his sword to threaten with his teeth.

"You're *not* coming."

"Really?"

His adoptive father smirked, retrieving one yellowed scroll from his stallion's leather pack.

"And how do you plan to find the capital without a horse? A…map, perhaps?" His cool laughter was an infuriating sound, more so than the gleam in his eyes. "Come now, you must have realized with all that 'forest living' that you have no sense of direction."

Silas knew he had been cornered. Though he did not lower his weapon, his stance deflated. He snarled in reply, his last defense.

"I *hate* you."

Vann only laughed.

"I've found 'hate' is a rather temporary thing. Open your heart, dear boy, and you'll notice you have no choice."

The man looked up suddenly, smirking.

"Ah! I see the Protectors have caught your scent. I do suggest you quicken your decision-making."

Indeed, Silas heard the clanking of armor approaching, hollers as some men tripped over themselves to catch up. He looked over the mare, seeing her sturdy form and well-made reins. He saw the map.

"Don't say a word to me."

He swung himself atop the blonde mare, gripping her reins and securing his sword in his belt. Then, they were off. The horses' whinnies drowned out the Protector's shouts as Alore passed them by, building by building, street by street. The lapping of the Alize River was far behind them.

The blue-eyed girl was waiting at the western edge of town, as specified. She looked up at them with delicate, joyous relief that didn't match her disguise. But despite his annoyance, he had every intention of taking her on his own horse. However, it was Giovanni who offered his hand down to her.

"Hurry up, my dear," he said, "Silas has caused quite a stir in town."

She nodded in obedience, allowing the man to help her up without a thought of her own.

"Thank you," she whispered.

Irritation was overshadowed by urgency. Silas looked back to his hometown, seeing the orange shadows of torchlight across the walls. A mob was forming, demanding blood.

Without a word, he sent his mare into a gallop. Vaan whooped as he followed suit. Soon, the three of them disappeared into the Great Forest.

Part II:
Journey

Chapter IX

24th day of 11th Month, 654 I.R.

To the Queen-Mother:

There was an unfortunate accident at the Alize River. The bridge snapped before any member of the Rank could cross. I regret to say the female criminal accused of stealing your jewel was lost in the water below. Fortunately, a new bridge was located and travel has continued on schedule. Both diamonds remain safe and should arrive before winter falls too harshly. I will continue to keep contact.

Also, I ask you to remind Tahn to better tend to Tobias. The hawk is beginning to look sickly; one eye has turned an unfortunate yellow, and I worry how quickly my messages will come to you if he is to go blind and lose his way.

I remain your faithful servant.

Saito Niigata

にいがた 紗人

Lesser Advisor, King's Council

Though the world outside Joanissia castle was already white, the Autumn Ball was alive with color. The Ladies and their Baroness mothers wore extravagant gowns of crimson and saffron, while their husbands flaunted their lace-fringed sleeves and gold leggings. The ballroom was a whirl of ostentatious beauty, its marble floors the stage for the young nobles' vanity. Yet, Morana's usual revulsion was lessened by her wandering thoughts. Though her gaze was set upon the dancers as she sat upon her sister's throne, her mind was with the letter she had read that morning.

Winter comes soon.

While the loss of the criminal was a shame, it did not change anything. So long as the Rank arrived with Dayu's diamonds intact, there was no reason to concern herself with the girl who had almost stolen them.

Soon...

Her hand brushed the yoke of her silver dress, feeling the black diamond still tucked beneath. It never left her person.

The man on the throne beside her sighed in his usual way, touching a jewel in his golden crown.

"I'm too tired for this," Attlas said. "I didn't sleep...and my shoulders are killing me..."

He yawned, tugging on the low ribbon that bound his blonde locks.

"There should be a law against hosting the Autumn Ball past midnight," he said.

Morana had never attempted to hide her disdain for her nephew-brother. Even the day of his marriage to Azalea she had scowled in the front row, trying to whittle away at his slight form with her penetrating stare. She was baffled now as to how he remained so at ease while she sat beside him, taking up space while her flighty sister danced with the lesser nobles.

"Is the crown too heavy for you, My Liege?" she asked; glancing sideways, her sneer consciously restrained.

"Perhaps," he said, resting his cheek casually upon his closed fist, "but though I'm sorry to disappoint you, I'm not quite ready to hand it over—I believe you would find it far less flattering than you anticipate."

Her scorn manifested itself in the twitch of her brow, which she concealed from him.

"And here I thought the brat-Prince would outgrow his insolence."

"Insolence?"

He laughed aloud, pressing himself back against the golden chair for its support.

"I am King, Morana. If anyone is being insolent, it's you."

He feigned such confidence in his power. It infuriated her to see the slender and doe-eyed youth order her about like a commoner. Life had given no color to his skin; he was as pale as Cedric had been, and his terrible grandfather Raphael before that. A sickly, lean, arrogant Prince: that's all Attlas would ever be.

"I apologize, Morana, but I never could admire your barefaced lust for power. Your sister is Queen now; I wish you would respect that."

He set his emerald gaze upon her, such a gratingly weary look about it.

"Please, stop trying to make my life difficult. Until Azalea has a child, I alone must bear the weight of the Xavier bloodline. It is more oppressive than you seem to think. All of your efforts to undermine me, like that stunt you pulled with your silent prisoner, have to stop. Please, for once, will you obey my wishes?"

Morana defied his gaze, looking instead over the ballroom. She saw her sister switching partners, the girl laughing like a fool. She looked out of place in that sea of chestnut curls. The Queen was as pale as her husband, face even whiter against her teased black locks and painted, red lips. Her dark eyes were not as narrow as Morana's; on the contrary, they seemed rather round, wide and glistening with naïve joy. Their father had given her the necklace she wore: three strings of blue crystal that sparkled against her elegant white gown. Morana had been given oats for the horse.

"I've made no attempt to 'make your life difficult'," she said to the King, choosing not to see his reaction. "I merely take care of issues of importance that you're still too young to handle, which is most of them."

She didn't have to see him to know his scowl.

"I'm twenty-three years old, just two years younger than Cedric was when you married him. I don't know what age you consider 'grown' in your country, but in Larasca I am many years a man. Yet you fire workers at your leisure, imprison any man who displeases you, and even dispatch a Rank to another *country* to retrieve some old jewelry you used to fancy?! I will not tolerate you side-stepping me for any more decisions! Your husband is dead: you *have* no more power!"

As passionate as his speech might have been, it was hushed. He wasn't one to cause a stir among his subjects, and treated his emotions as a private affair. When she finally did turn to him, she saw his jaw taut, his eyes like ice. It was a look Cedric had given her many times, once he realized she would not love him.

"Let me rule, Morana," he said, his timbre somehow changed. "The world might crumble if you don't."

She might have said something, if only in spite; however, the King's Grand Advisor chose then to approach the Royal Platform.

"My King," said Raoul, bowing in his refined way. "How do you fare this fine evening?"

Raoul's fair hair was also pulled back with a golden ribbon, which matched well with his fine shirt and elegant stockings. The apparel flattered him, and pleased Morana.

"Well enough," the King replied, "although I grow tired of sitting. Whoever came up with the ridiculous custom that 'no one can stand when King Xavier is standing' deserves a sharp kick in his rear end."

The grey-eyed advisor chuckled, bowing a little lower.

"I come to ask permission of a dance with the Queen-Mother."

The title itself was grating to her ears. Six years since Cedric's death and Morana had yet to adjust to that clumsy word: *Queen-Mother.*

Attlas nodded, making no secret of his relief.

"Do attempt to enjoy yourself."

Raoul extended his hand to her, a smile adding to the faint lines on his face. She accepted him, graciously leaving her King's presence to mingle with the noblemen.

She was not usually one for dancing. The Larascan way of twirling across the dance floor, stepping when the flute and drum demanded it, was foreign to her. Yet she danced, allowing Raoul to spin her, hold her. It was tolerable, with him. She was used to his bony hands upon her body, guiding her in some ancient ritual. However, lacking the darkness that usually accompanied their closeness, she was forced to maintain an affectionate look.

"You look lovely, my dear," he said.

Morana almost smiled, her dress billowing in another guided spin.

"I thank you," she said.

"Almost as lovely as your sister, I believe."

No element of impudence prevailed in his tone, though it irritated the former Queen. There was, however, a sense of knowing in his gaze that did not sit well with her.

"I know not what *you* see," she replied. "She looks pale and sickly to my eye."

"Sickly, perhaps, but she has already begun to glow."

Raoul had a tiring way of dancing around issues. He had always been a philosopher at heart; it was the reason Cedric had first employed him. The late King had a theory that Princes should be taught by scholars, not warriors.

"She looks much the same to me," Morana remarked, twirled again by his pale hand.

"Give it some time." He smiled, glimpsing the young Queen as she again switched partners. "A baby can only be hidden for so long."

For a moment, everything stood still. Morana stared at the man in shock, mind raped of all reply.

"…ah…"

Oblivious to her stupor, the dance carried on. Raoul must have taken her blank look as delayed excitement, continuing as if nothing had changed.

"I expect she's waiting for the right time to tell the King," he continued, mostly musing to himself. "A pregnancy is a delicate situation. Perhaps she does not want to cause unnecessary worry…"

The Queen-Mother did not hear him. Her mind was a whirl of dangerous thoughts that would not cease, spinning and spinning, colored by fury.

An heir…

The Boy-King was no threat to her will without an heir. With one, his reign was assured. Even if he were to suffer an accident, the Xaviers would live on through Morana's own bloodline.

"Morana, are you well?" Raoul asked, concern on his face.

She reassembled her mask of grace, finding a smile as she did so.

"Of course. I'm merely a little nostalgic," she replied. "It would have been my own son's birthday in a month's time."

He nodded, made weaker by sympathy.

"I had almost forgotten. My condolences, Your Majesty."

She didn't need his pity. Already, she had forgotten it, letting her thoughts sweep her up again. As she became more aware of herself, she began to realize the depth of her discontent. It vexed her like a burr buried in her very gut, churning and churning with her every breath. She was sick from it. The churning had to end.

Something must be done.

It was a treacherous, beautiful thought.

A young guard fetched Azalea to her husband's study shortly after the Autumn Ball's late conclusion. She was still flushed with laughter, her face warm, despite chattering teeth. It seemed only to grow colder the deeper she went into the castle. Mosaic dragons were cooled by frost, though their icy eyes followed their Queen despite it. She shuddered, trying not to see them.

The guard opened the door for her, but would not enter. He was impassive to her smile; he slammed the door when she stepped inside.

Attlas' study was cozy, in an oppressive way. A fire danced in the fireplace, casting an orange glow upon Raphael's buck-heads still mounted from some hunt, and the large desk resting upon a gray wolf skin—another of the late King's conquests. His grandson sat reclined at the old desk, his feet atop a stack of papers on the desk that he never meant to read. Despite his informal posture, he seemed tense. He had let down his blonde locks: a sign of anxiety. Even when he met her gaze, he was distant.

"Sorry about the cold. Even with the fire, it's not as warm as it is outside."

She shook her head, quickly taking a place by the flickering flames.

"No no, it's fine. I'm used to it," she said, shivering.

Her lie made him smile, though it didn't reach his eyes. He had a look of Cedric about him, trying to mask solemnity with pleasantness.

"Antonio's been breathing down my neck with talk of some new uprising in Kyro," he said, staring up at the stone ceiling, "but I have no patience for it. I have no patience for…much of anything, anymore."

She pitied him for his somber look.

"You must have some patience, since you summoned me."

He smiled briefly, bowing his head in a single nod.

"Of course. For you, I have endless patience."

This gave her some peace. She watched as he swung his legs down from the writing table to rest an arm upon it, and his head upon that. He was weary—it was written in the shadow beneath his eyes.

"Did you sleep, Your Majesty?" she asked, concerned.

He shook his head.

"Not long. I had an unsettling dream early in the night, and after I awoke, I feared it so greatly that I could not sleep again."

Attlas glanced towards her, his faint smile still present.

"Do you think I'm…silly?"

Such a casual word did not come easily to him anymore. He said it now for her benefit, to relax her. But while it did calm her some, the foreboding air quickly undid his work.

"That depends on the dream," she said, trying to be gentle.

He looked from her again, emerald gaze set on Cedric's black quill.

"Do you remember that hooded man who came to the Autumn Ball ten years ago? Who told that prophecy about Asyrias?"

"The month before he died?"

She could remember that man's words at any moment. The sight of his gnarled beard, the rotten smell wafting from his black robes, had forever engrained itself in her memory. The words he had spoken spilled past her lips before she could stop them.

"Do not be deceived by your Prince's slow growth, for the runt will grow tall, harboring strength unmatched by any man. However, that strength will bring him grief. By that man, two women will fall: the one who bore him, and the one who succumbed to his whim."

Attlas pushed back his loose locks, reaching for Cedric's quill. He held the feather between his fingers and watched it tremble.

"I dreamt of that hooded figure, last night," he said. "He looked right at me with his snake-eyes and said, 'the Bastard King will have a shortened reign.'"

At first, Azalea felt only shock. She tried to pretend that his fear had no merit; however, seeing his utter stillness, she knew that was not true. Although she did not usually act upon affection, she went to him, bravely touching his shoulder.

"It was only a dream," she soothed, "even if it wasn't, he was wrong about Asyrias. The boy never grew up, and he didn't foretell that. If he was wrong about Azzy, he could be just as wrong about you."

The King shook his head, silently placing his hand over his Queen's. The brief contact made her heart swell, remembering her love for him. She wished their meetings weren't so rare. She thought briefly of telling him of her news—that there was a child within her that would continue his legacy, even if he were to pass. But even now, she was not brave enough to form those words.

Attlas reached into a desk drawer, withdrawing a sheathed dagger with an elegantly carved, black hilt. When he slipped it from its leather binds, he revealed a weapon of stunning craftsmanship that reflected every flicker of the firelight. She could see her own surprise reflected in its blade.

"This was Caden's dagger," he said, his voice sodden with old feelings. "It's the only thing of my father's that Cedric ever gave me."

He looked towards her for a long moment, his gaze searching her. And then, he sheathed the dagger, pressing the elegant hilt into her palm.

"I want you to have it."

Her mouth was open, speechless.

"Me?"

The man smiled, squeezing her hand over the hilt.

"I want you to have something of mine, when I'm gone. And…this is the only object that matters to me."

Her eyes were glossy, though she wasn't one to cry. Their marriage had always been one of formalities and brief nightly meetings; they were never together long enough to nurture deep love. Yet he now offered her a gift of the most intimate nature, without bitterness, despite even his own country's customs—for it was illegal for anyone to know he had given a woman a weapon. For the first time since their union, Azalea felt right in her affection for him.

Quickly, she brushed away the tears that threatened to fall.

"Thank you, Attlas."

He stood, allowing her to hold the dagger fully on her own. After a moment of hesitation, he slipped his arms around her body. For the first time in days, the King kissed his Queen.

Twyla, Morana's faithful handmaid, usually made it her habit not to interfere with her mistress' affairs. Morana was good to her, and it was unwise to try a good woman's trust. Yet, she couldn't convince herself not to see the once-Queen's mysterious prisoner. His presence had disturbed the castle's delicate atmosphere, somehow darkening the world. She had to know why.

Flickering torches cast shadows on the walls when a guard escorted her to the dungeon's foreboding entry. The heavy doors loomed high above her, their hanging chains curving to make them scowl.

"The Queen-Mother has ordered very limited interaction with the prisoner," the guard explained. "You may be called up at a moment's notice."

She nodded, shivering beneath her fur shawl. She tightly gripped the small bag she carried.

"I understand. I won't be long."

The response was accepted. The guard loosed the chains, heaving aside the heavy plank to open the doors. Beyond, steep stairs disappeared into darkness.

He handed her his torch.

"Ariel's cell is down the center passage, to the right."

She smiled.

"Thank you."

The handmaid found the passage with the torch's light, wandering past cell after cell. Their rusty bars had turned the color of the dirt below, gaps providing passage to scuttling creatures. It smelled of death. Every cell was disquietingly empty until the very end of the row. There, curled up in a dark corner, was the battered young man she had come to see.

"Are you Ariel?" she asked.

He lifted his head from his knees, revealing narrow, sapphire eyes—Morana's eyes. His silence was confirmation enough.

Despite her shock, she smiled at him. She knelt down in her heavy skirt, digging a plump, red apple from her bag. She slipped her hand between the bars, offering the ripe fruit to him.

"I know it's not much, but it's all I could take from the kitchen. I hope this is all right?"

Though his eyes were vacant, there was hesitation in his stillness. It was a time before he dragged himself forward, taking the apple from her hand. He ate no more hungrily than any rich man, taking one disinterested bite after another. His Storma eyes remained set on her.

Suddenly, he spoke.

"Morana will soon turn the tables on the Xavier family."

She was caught unaware, looking to him in confusion.

"What?"

The man stared back at her, inexpressive.

"Go to the royal graveyard tomorrow, during the late hours of daylight. Lift King Raphael's gravestone, and you'll find symbols engraved in a stone beneath. Copy the symbols and show them to me. With them, I may prove her foul intentions."

The concept was ludicrous; she had never heard a more fantastical request. It was all but sacrilegious to disturb a late-King's resting place, a fool's errand. And yet, the longer she stared into Ariel's vacant eyes, the more she doubted her own hesitancy.

"Why should I do as you say?"

She thought she glimpsed a smile on his face.

"You need not," he said.

A rat scurried by, squeaking as it passed. She paid it no mind, never one to be squeamish. As she considered a reply, she watched him eat, one slow bite at a time.

Finally, light streamed down from the dungeon entry. The guard hollered down.

"Come, Twyla!"

She stood at once, brushing the dust from her skirt.

"Be well, Sir Ariel," she said, always pleasant.

He said nothing, just staring after her, the red apple still against his lips. She saw something, then. His eyes were Morana's, perhaps, but they were not the only reason the sight of him inspired familiarity. His shaggy black locks, the curve of his jaw, his intense stare, had all belonged to a child she had hoped to forget.

Pale, she knelt before him once more.

"Asyrias?" she whispered.

Slowly, a true smile stretched across the man's impassive face.

"Not I."

Chapter X

By the following night, the men had taken Rina far from Alore. They stopped in a clearing in the dense forest where her companions began to set up camp, paying her no mind. Rina stood awkwardly by a tree, left to observe them.

Her savior turned out to be a sullen figure indeed, saying little and glaring whenever he did. She thought it strange that the cool air didn't chill him, though his torso was bare—it was nicely toned, however, and it made her blush when she looked at it too long. At times, she thought she saw the glimmer of goodness in him the innkeeper had spoken of. However, the bestial snarl he somehow made in his throat would quickly extinguish that light.

His adoptive father wasn't at all what she had expected. The cruel, conniving man she had anticipated had proven himself instead to be a clever, lively spirit. He was never without a smile. She didn't understand why Silas was so cold towards him, even if their past had been bitter. It seemed unfair.

Silas did his part that night by tying up the horses, which put a great deal of distance between him and his father, who worked diligently to start a fire. Giovanni sang quietly to himself as he worked.

"Our Lady of the Light, faceless, shimmering, white, hath named the sacred objects three…that one day, lovely Justice will bestow to me…"

She had never heard the song before. It unsettled her, though she didn't know why. She occupied herself by attempting to stay in the fire's light, still avoiding the darkness of the forest around her. Even now, she thought she heard some forsaken entity rustling in the bushes. They rustled, rustled, as her muscles tightened to stone.

It's all in my mind…all in my mind…

But the forest kept rustling behind her, mocking her trembling body. It grew louder and louder, her body growing tighter, until something finally leapt from the trees—a mass of gray fur.

She screamed, pressing her hands over her face.

Help—!

Giovanni was laughing. Realizing she wasn't dead, she peeled her fingers from her eyes in time to see a mangy dog sniffing the leaves beneath her feet. She remained stiff, her terror only lessened; however, Giovanni came to pet the creature.

"I could have sworn I've seen this beast around town…" He chuckled, scratching one of its large ears. The creature shuddered with delight, bushy tail wagging back and forth.

"I guess he's come along for the ride," he said.

Rina almost smiled, though her look showed more fear than joy.

"M-maybe…"

Strangely, she did recognize the dog. He was the same shade of gray as the beast that had approached her outside the prison, with the same ears and the same eyes, black as night. How had that creature followed her there? Why?

Giovanni continued to scratch his ears.

"Ride, hm? You like that?" he asked.

The dog barked, stretching back on his hind legs like a self-absorbed cat. The creature seemed to grin, and the man laughed.

"That'll be your name then. Our curious mongrel, Ride."

The man then turned his gaze to Rina, who stood very still. For some reason, the sight made him chuckle.

"My, my, you're stiff as a board," he said. "Why don't you sit down and pet him? Takes all your worries away, so long as he doesn't bite."

She didn't find the remark as amusing as he did. Even so, it seemed he knew best. Despite the scar Rajj had left on her courage, she knelt down in front of the animal and forced her shaking hand near its fur. Slowly, she began to stroke a very small patch.

Ride's lips stretched back to show all his teeth, practically smiling. He licked her hand before she could move, and before long, she found herself enjoying it. Her muscles loosened, calm washing over her. She began to smile back.

"You know what you need, Rina?" said Giovanni, standing before her. "Rina – that's your name, right?"

She nodded, though unsure which question he wanted her to answer.

"You need to exercise your new rights as a man," he said, "really find a way to relish this unique opportunity."

Once more, she nodded, if only because the pause seemed to call for it. He began to pace back and forth, stroking his mustache as he thought. She took the opportunity to settle against a tree, letting Ride lay his head in her lap. His friendliness was startling, but she convinced herself that as long as she didn't make any sudden moves, he was unlikely to attack.

"Ah! I've got it!"

Giovanni's exclamation caught her off-guard: she jumped, causing Ride to whine in her lap.

"G-got what?" she asked.

"I'm going to teach you how to identify and judge people who are different than you. Bigotry: a man's real power."

Already, she didn't like the direction of the conversation. However, she expressed her caution in silence, hoping he would interpret it as disinterest. He paid it no mind.

"The Kala are easiest to pick out of a crowd," he began, sitting comfortably in the leaves before her. "The men are the big, dark ones with vacant stares. The girls are cheap though, if you know what I mean."

She didn't know what he meant.

"You won't see them much outside Alore and Levanche though, since the Alize is the only way for them to travel up into Larasca. However, they still aren't as rare as those romantic, dark-haired Kyrons, always making googly eyes at each other, hollering words of love across city streets. Passionate bunch, fine lovers. It's a shame Raphael had us wall them out."

He shook his head, tsking in disapproval at the long-dead King.

"Then again, they were a little different after the Catsavions rose to power."

A difference in his tone caught her attention, rousing her from her silence.

"What are Catsavions?" she asked, having learned to be direct with questions.

The man sighed, solemnly shaking his head.

"A rather depressing group of religious nuts that drove the Alexanders from power in Kyro. Alexanders were the distant cousins of the Xaviers, you see, and that really didn't sit well with our breed of royalty. I don't know the details of the religion they claim to follow, but it seems to be a rather exclusive one: exclusive in this case being 'all those unfit to be one of us will be promptly cut up and burned at the stake'."

She shuddered, wishing she had not asked.

"We seem to have gotten off topic," the man said, chuckling to himself. "Talonians, that's where I was. Tallks are the only foreigners left without some sort of wall or mountain or river to prevent them from scrambling over the border. They're pretty easy to spot: hook noses, black hair growing all over. They breed like rabbits, smell like cheese, and they're always doing something with their hands. I had a conversation with one once, and he had me so distracted by his flailing hands I completely forgot he was saying words."

Giovanni laughed, no doubt expecting her to do the same. Yet, she could not. Talk of Talonians made her heart ache. His words baffled her, for Kaish hadn't talked with his hands, or smelled of cheese. The Talonian had been gentle, with a dry sense of humor and a soft smile.

"Are all Talonians like that?" she asked, feebly.

He shrugged.

"That's not the point. The point is to easily dismiss people who are different than you, so you can continue thinking you're the superior one. *Comprendéis?*"

In all her life, she had never felt such confusion. Of course, this did nothing to stop his lesson.

"Storma are a serious bunch; I've certainly never heard one laugh. Black hair straight as sticks, and they've got such narrow eyes it's like they're always staring you down. They're almost as pale as Rionans, but they're not quite as bitter. Those northern folk are certainly a sour lot, that's for sure. Too much ice, I say. They're almost as easy to spot as a Storma, though – their hair is almost as white as their faces. It would be a shame to call it yellow, it's so fair…"

Rina managed a smile when he looked at her, but could think of nothing to respond with. She was relieved when Silas returned begrudgingly to the fire. The flickering light illuminated his sour expression, lighting his sneer when he thrust his hand down to his father.

"Hand over the map," he demanded.

"The map?"

The man laughed, looking up at his hot-tempered ward.

"You don't need it, I'm afraid. I've already decided our course," Giovanni said, standing and brushing off his trousers. "We'll go from here to Argot, then Raine, and perhaps take a *very* brief stop in Malldon before braving that snowy mountain-pass to the capital."

"Let me *see* it," Silas snarled.

Giovanni shook his head, tsking as he stood, brushing the leaves from his tawny garments.

"I'm afraid you haven't yet earned that right, my boy."

"Just hand it **OVER!**" the youth barked, hand upon his sword. "I refuse to play one of your bloody games! **GIVE IT!**"

Although Silas' hostility frightened her, Giovanni was all but unresponsive. He steadily held Silas' heated gaze, though the youth stood nearly a full head taller than him.

"No games, then," said the man, chuckling to himself. "Just good, old-fashioned combat."

With that, Giovanni whipped his sword from its leather sheath. Silas, seemingly unfazed, drew his.

"If you can disarm me," said his father, "then I'll hand over the map and leave your company. I assure you, you will never see me again."

"Good riddance," Silas growled.

Rina shot to her feet when their weapons clashed, pressing herself back against the tree. Even Ride howled, scampering into a nearby bush to escape the noise. The men entered into a terrifying dance of skill – each strike was parried, every move mirrored, dodged, countered. Neither the fire nor their audience was of any consequence to them. Twice, Rina had to duck out of the way of someone's blade.

Finally, it appeared Silas had gotten the upper hand. By brute strength, he had backed Giovanni up against a tree, blade nearly overpowering his father's. He was a horrific figure, violet eyes aflame with such rage, hair wild about him. Yet, Giovanni began to smirk.

Suddenly, Silas fell.

"FAWK!"

His sword clattered to the ground at Rina's feet as he collapsed to his knees, gripping at his hand. Giovanni stood above him, a cool smile the mark of his triumph.

"You might learn to switch hands, dear son, when you've suffered such an unfortunate injury so recently. A sword is only as strong as the hand that wields it."

Silas continued to grip his hand, snarling, spitting that word again and again.

"You…fawking *pig*…"

Giovanni slipped his weapon back into its sheath, returning to the fire without another glance towards the defeated youth.

"It's a good thing you're no longer living under my roof," said the man, settling before the flames. "A loss like that would have earned you at least three weeks on the streets."

Ride crept back out from the bushes, sensing the world had settled. He rubbed his snout against Rina's leg, though she only tensed further. Her eyes were set on Silas' sword, which seemed eerily still on the ground before her. She jumped again when Silas snatched it up, fury written in his every feature. Again, he snarled that word.

"Fawk…"

Although she was he frightened her, her curiosity overwhelmed her fear. Words spilled past her lips.

"What does that mean?" she asked.

At once, he turned his intense stare on her.

"*What* mean?"

Rina swallowed air, as if hoping to swallow her newfound bravery with it.

"That word…'fawk'."

The silence stretched for a long, long time. Silas stared her down long enough to see her own eyes reflected in their depths—trembling, weak.

Suddenly, he flicked his sword up, swinging it over his head and across his body, swinging it towards her. It made a purposeful sound as it sliced the air, stopping short of her throat: *fawwk.*

"That's what it means," Silas said, holding that blade against her neck.

The blood drained from her face, leaving her cold. She could say nothing. In that moment, she saw just how terrifying her savior truly was.

For some reason, she noticed then how loudly Ride was panting. His long tongue hung out of his mouth as he stared up at the armed man, maintaining the most unconcerned look Rina had ever seen. Drool dripped with each pant. Silas, disgusted, withdrew his weapon.

"Mind your mutt," he ordered.

The young man disappeared back into the forest, in the direction of the horses' whinnies. Rina slid down the tree, deflating with her lungs. She held her head, hoping that would stop the world from spinning.

"Relax," came Giovanni's voice, as he turned to her from the fire. "He's mostly harmless."

She took a deep breath, staring at the ground.

"That doesn't seem harmless," she whispered.

"Just you wait," the man chuckled. "You'll warm right up to him."

She focused on calming her trembling fingers, trying to breathe steadily until her heart stopped pounding. This time, when Ride placed his head in her lap, she did calm. He was no threat when compared to the towering youth who had once saved her life.

Giovanni approached her, paying no attention to the way she flinched from him.

"Let's see if he nicked you."

The girl sat very still while he examined her neck, trying not to look at him. However, when the job was finished and he moved away, she noticed something. On his hand, she glimpsed the scar of a crooked cross: the same mark that Kaish bore, and Alastor had been given.

"Were you a soldier?" she asked, suddenly.

He paused, though he seemed more startled by the sound of her voice than the words she spoke. Slowly, his smile returned.

"As a matter of fact, I was a Commander. Joined the Stags in 633, when they promptly sent me off to Kyro to help with that little military effort. I was such an asset that they advanced me in 634 and put me with Rank 1, the Princes' Rank. A few clever deeds here and there and Prince Cedric called me Commander."

His words left her speechless.

Commander...Giovanni?

She remembered the brief tale Wolf had told her of Baldric and Giovanni, and how they were responsible for the reunification of the eastern and western halves of Larasca. Yet, this man seemed too young to have been the partner to her Duke, who looked many years his senior. Even the dog seemed confused, rising just out of her lap to cock his head.

"Was there another Commander Giovanni?" she asked.

He chuckled.

"No. I am exactly who you think I am."

Giovanni stood tall, slicking back his earthy hair with his hand before he gave a regal bow.

"Commander Giovanni Wolfslayer, partner to Commander Baldric Alexander and unifier of the great Kingdom of Larasca, at your service."

She stared up at him, eyes wide with shock.

"But you're so young..."

"So he would say," he laughed, staring off into some memory. "Perhaps he was right. I was only fourteen when I advanced. But what is age when one has skill?"

The man knelt before her again, elegantly lifting her chin with his finger. She was forced to stare into his eyes, forced to see the flash of cunning within them. They were indecipherable, in a terrible way.

"Was your father a soldier?" he asked, abruptly.

"N-no," she answered, the word startled out of her. "I-I mean...I don't know. I'm...an orphan, so..."

She tried to look away, but his grip held her there, forcing her to keep his gaze.

"You have a soldier's eyes," he said. "They flash about without your knowing, observing all of your environment at once – that's what gives them such intensity. The men with those eyes survive the longest in harsh circumstances."

She didn't know what to say. Yet, by his look, he expected such. He almost moved from her again, but something more caught his attention. He took her hand, lifting it to see the golden band around her wrist.

"What a lovely bracelet," he said, curious. "Distinctly Talonian craftsmanship; definitely not a mimic's work."

Rina withdrew her arm, overcome by inexplicable paranoia. Unfortunately, this reaction only further provoked his curiosity. He took her hand again, more firmly.

"Would you mind telling me where you got such a fine artifact, dear Rina? An old friend? A lover, perhaps?"

It would have been simple enough to answer him, to say that a Talonian man had given her the bracelet to represent their engagement, and that she was traveling with them in hopes to see her betrothed again. But her wary trust in him had been tried, and his forwardness had overwhelmed it. For the first time in her life, she told a lie.

"My boss gave it to me, when I used to work in a tavern. It was a birthday gift."

The man seemed surprised, almost intrigued.

"A tavern girl, hm?" He chuckled, releasing her hand. "You seem too fragile for that line of work."

He stood tall, cracking his knuckles before stretching.

"Get a good night's rest, dear girl. Argot is no place for the sleepy-eyed. Brutal place, really. We'll be there by mid-afternoon or so, if the rain allows…"

Rina wasn't listening to him. She stared at the gray dog, who still rested happily in her lap. She stroked his head with a trembling hand, trying not to think. Never before had she told a lie. And yet, one had slipped off her tongue more effortlessly than anything she had said in months.

What's wrong with me?

The world around her was changing too fast. Perhaps it was safest to change along with it.

By mid-day, the stench of Argot was upon them. Men tossed knives at each other for sport while their sons wrestled in the streets amongst mud and waste. The stone buildings rose high around them, their former glory tarnished by the soiled garments hanging out their windows. Once, after dismounting, Giovanni jerked her out from under the contents flung from a top-story chamber pot. Silas scowled when he saw her feminine disgust and told her to smother it—she would get them all killed.

Giovanni abandoned them partway into town, though he assured them he was only going to buy supplies, and a shirt for Silas.

"Try not to talk to anyone, Princess," he said to her as he climbed back onto his steed, "We'll improve your disguise for the next town. Until then, Silas' quick wit should be able to explain away your pretty little smile."

And then, Giovanni left her alone with his son.

For the first time, she was grateful Ride remained so strangely near to her. She could reach down and touch his mangy fur to distract herself, trying not to feel that youth's cold eyes upon her. It seemed an eternity before he spoke.

"Follow. Say nothing."

She did as she was told, staying a good distance behind him and his horse. He led the mare by her reins with surprising control, very comfortable beside the great beast. Curious, she forgot his orders.

"Are you around horses a lot?" she asked.

He stopped, turning his icy sneer on her. She was frightened into silence; they continued on.

Before long, they came to a stop in front of a rundown building, boards on the windows and cracks in the walls. The swinging sign above the door pictured an open book.

Silas held the mare's reins out to her.

"Take Charlotte around side," he ordered. "Stay by the window. Don't move until I get you."

Rina looked to the mare, Charlotte, who snorted in annoyance. Although it left the girl flustered, Silas had already disappeared into the shop. She had no choice but to bring the ill-tempered mare around the building, praying she wouldn't be bitten along the way.

She found the window he referred to, or what had been a window. What was left of the glass protruded from the frame in jagged shards, sharp as knives. Standing near it made her nervous, afraid a piece would fall and slice her foot. Yet, the dog that followed her was unaffected by her mood, bravely padding around the broken pieces in the alley. He stopped to examine a larger piece, raising his ears up and down, as if observing their reflection. His amusement made her smile.

Suddenly, he looked up from the glass, eyes perked to catch some far-off sound. Before she could stop him, he bounded into the street.

"Wait!" she cried.

But he was gone, swallowed by the boisterous town. Though she hadn't known him long, she couldn't help but feel abandoned. Rina sighed, busying herself by tying Charlotte's reins to a sturdy part of the exposed frame. Yet when she looked up, Ride had returned, head erect as he stood at the mouth of the alley. A twinkle in his eyes beckoned her to come to him.

"Is that it?" she asked the dog. "Do you want me to come with you?"

Excited, he barked, bushy tail wagging behind him. It was answer enough.

"Well…"

She remembered Silas' command, and was almost frightened enough by the memory to obey it. Yet she was tempted by the prospect of adventure, for she had never truly gone anywhere on her own.

It'll only be a short while…

Rina tested the frame the mare was tied to, convincing herself of the horse's safety. Charlotte's expression only implored her to leave. Feeling more certain in her precarious decision, she left the mare, this time following the dog when he bounded into the streets.

She followed Ride down a long road until they came to a massive gathering of people – mostly men with heavy beards. Because of her slight stature, she managed to weave her way through the crowd in pursuit of the black-eyed mongrel, until she came to the front lines. Before them was an older man, streaks of gray through his thinning locks, and a girl standing atop a wooden crate. She was slender and tall, no older than Rina, with chestnut locks that fell down her back in waves. She had such a strained smile.

"Twenty silver!" a man cried.

"Thirty silver!" came another.

More men bellowed, the amount increasing until Rina realized what she was witnessing.

"An auction?' she whispered.

A bearded man beside her cast her a scowl.

"You an out-of-towner, boy?"

At once, she remembered her terror. She was dressed as a man, even though she was not a man, *far* from a man. Although petrified, she nodded, trying to silently maintain what she could of the illusion.

"Don't you think yourself too proud for our ways," he said, sneering down at her, "It may not be *your* custom for a father to auction off his daughter, but even in Joanissia, a girl goes to the highest bidder."

Silence was deepened by shock. She looked back at the girl, seeing her chestnut curls, her honest features. She was not cattle, not a pig. Yet, they bid on her like a common animal.

"Two gold pieces!"

"Four!"

Rina grew dizzy, sick with contempt. In Lucadia, women had been honored – the Blessing called them bringers of truth, faith, light, and hope. They were the caretakers, the wives and mothers of farmers and soldiers. Naïve, Rina had thought all places treated them the same.

"Six gold pieces!"

She left, as fast as she could. Men's faces blurred as she passed, their features uniformly revolting. Without thought, she took Ride by a scruff of his fur, breaking his gaze from a puddle in the street. Her world was tilting, tainted.

Disgusting...

The world was disgusting.

Though she released her hold on the dog, he continued to follow her, oblivious to her changed mood. She thought of nothing, determined only not to look behind her.

A loud whinny told her something was amiss. She quickened her pace, Ride following, barking. When she came to the alley, her blood ran cold.

Shit.

A shadowy man was there, untying Charlotte's reins. Grime stained his skin, his hair long and greasy, lips cracked. A bloody dagger slapped his side, sharp enough to threaten her very courage.

"HEY!"

She cried the word in sheer horror, realizing too late that she had no defense. Too soon, his eyes flashed towards her. A long tongue wet his cracked lips, a hungry look distorting his features. Forgetting the panicked horse, he wrapped his fingers around his dagger, advancing towards her.

"You're no lad," he hissed. "You're…just a girl. Just a pretty little girl…"

Before she could run, he had her by her locks, scaly fingers tangled within them. He smirked, as if knowing she was already too terrified to scream.

His rough lips scratched her ear, his words breathed with sour air.

"Let's have a little fun."

Silas was glad the library had been abandoned. He wasn't yet patient enough to deal with bookkeepers, who were finicky by nature. If they didn't harass him about his "partial-nudity," they would have kicked him out for having "big, page-ripping hands." Still, a part of him was pained by the layers of dust that coated the shelves, the tell-tale sign of a city that had forsaken intellect.

He remembered being here once, ten years before. During that foggy first year of Silas' memory, Giovanni had taken him many places before finally settling in Alore, Argot included. It had been a prosperous city then, its libraries the envy of even Pandore's. Its Duke at that time had been a scholarly man, who greatly encouraged the upkeep of such places. He died young, however, and his son, Duke Brown, had proven just how little he cared for his father's pursuits.

Silas ran his fingers down a row of leather spines, seeing familiar titles etched on their surfaces. *The Xavier Kingdom* – he had read it a hundred times. Then came *A History of Man, Storma Emperors, Hierarchy and Society, The Complete History of Riona,* works he had studied cover to cover under Giovanni's astute eye. Only nostalgia for his childhood gave him any fondness for these books, for the act of studying them had been torture. To remember Giovanni's worktable now, remember every day he spent at that man's beck and call, made him sick with hatred.

You'll be rid of him soon.

He came upon what he had been searching for. The youth pulled it from the shelf, carefully blowing a cloud of dust from its cover. *Larascan Maps* was etched into its surface in pristine, golden letters. To have found it so easily was disconcerting. Silas glanced warily towards the broken window, seeing his mare tied sloppily to a part of the broken frame. Though irritating, the sight was nothing to be concerned about.

He began to flip through the old book, cautious of the fragile pages. There were detailed maps of every area of the nation, from the mountains that hid Joanissia to the plains of Siette. However, there was only one map of the country as a whole. At first, it seemed no different than any other map he had seen – yet, he noticed one minor difference. At the base of the northern mountains that cradled the capital, he saw a marking for a city he didn't recognize: "Citris."

Citris?

The marking itself seemed to be an error, for it had been placed within the mountains, not below or above them. After raking his brain for some knowledge of the city – as he was certain he knew them all – he decided that the map was outdated. Even so, it was the best he had. He carefully tore out the page, returning the book to its place.

A loud whinny pierced his calm. He snapped to attention, no time even to put the map in his pouch. By the time Silas saw the repulsive thief, the man already had Rina in his grasp. He hissed something in her ear, raising his bloody dagger.

Silas leapt through the window with a roar.

"Let her **GO!**"

His fist cracked the thief's skull, sending him down. Rina gasped, stumbling away from the body as quickly as she could. She held her head where she had been grabbed, eyes wide, dumb. Slowly, his thoughts began to catch up with his actions.

Why did you protect her?

He clutched the map in his trembling fist, staring at the man he had felled. Blood leaked from the thief's forehead, staining the cobblestones.

"I-I'm sorry," Rina said, barely able to choke out the words. "I'm s-sorry, I only left for a minute…"

Silas' gaze snapped to her, cold. Fury began to well within him.

"You *left?*" he growled.

She shrunk away from him, her terror growing with his rage.

"I-I came back before he could get Charlotte, I—"

She cried out when he grabbed her wrist, jerking her back towards him.

"You **IDIOT!**" he bellowed. "You LEFT?! You FAWKING LEFT?! I can't leave you alone three **MINUTES** with my bloody horse?!"

He could feel his skin growing hotter and hotter, though his anger did not cease.

"You **STUPID girl! USELESS** thing!"

Too late, he realized the heat of his hand. By the time he released her, his grip had left a bright red mark upon her, steaming. He dropped the map, but found it was too late—the parchment had been burnt to a cinder.

Great.

His last thought before he was overwhelmed by pain. His blood was boiling, scalding his insides. He doubled over, seeing black veins traveling into his hand, into his immoveable ring. They pulsed, pulsed grotesquely, as a single petal disappeared from the gold band. One remained.

He couldn't think, couldn't breathe. He barely looked up to see Rina coming closer, still holding her injured wrist. He barely heard her voice.

"Silas...what's going on...?'

The dog was barking; the horse whinnied. The world was turning, turning on its side, turning black.

"Silas!"

He passed out.

Chapter XI

Since before her husband's passing, Morana Xavier had seen Grand Advisor Raoul Markovich on a nightly basis. Their activities varied with her mood, as they made no effort to conceal their meetings. Often, however, they met only to play the game of nobility: chess.

As always, Morana's opponent championed the black pieces. She preferred the white, for they were polished from the finest crystal and reminded her of the diamonds in her forfeited crown. Black was a poor man's color, dyed with common charcoal. Since she was a child, she had been taught that finery prevailed over commonness.

Raoul was usually very talented at defending all of his pieces; however, this night, Morana took his knight very early in the game.

"A careless move," she said, neatly placing the piece on her own side of the stone table. "You must be distracted."

He nodded, though his gray eyes did not leave the board. His slender fingers already hovered over the pieces, calculating the best counter.

"Forgive me. A hawk arrived at the aviary early this morning with a rather interesting letter from Duke Baldric of Lucadia. I was deciphering it in my mind, for it seemed like rubbish when I first read it. I did not take Baldric Alexander as a man to lose his wits with age."

Although mildly surprised, she was not foolish enough to avert her attention from the game.

"What business would Cedric's Favorite have with Joanissia Castle?" she scoffed. "He has not set foot in the capital for seventeen years."

"He claims that something of his has been abducted by our forces, and that he will take drastic measures if it is not returned to him."

Raoul advanced his king—a strange move for the circumstances. Unable to understand his strategy, she bought time by moving a pawn.

"It sounds like the ravings of an aging man," she said. "I would pay the letter no mind."

"Perhaps," Raoul replied.

For a time, the game progressed in silence, only disrupted by the sound of sliding pieces over the marble board. Even when her queen was taken from her side, she was unshaken—the event had been planned.

"You have the Xavier glow about you, Morana," her opponent said, suddenly.

The words irritated her, though she did not understand them.

"I'd prefer you not waste your rubbish philosophies on me, Advisor."

"It is no philosophy," he said, moving a black pawn past her defenses. "You merely have the pale glow that Raphael had in the end of his reign. He would not leave this cold castle to mingle with anyone, and grew agitated with the slightest interrogation. They say he was even dabbling in the dark arts."

She alone knew the irony of his words, though she chose not to dwell on it. The Queen-Mother was more threatened by the black bishop that had crossed into her back rank and remained there, sitting idly by. However, she was soon reassured after Queening one of her own expendable pawns.

"Raphael looked that way because he was sickly," she said, capturing another of the pawns he had organized so carefully. "He was a very old man, Raoul. I doubt he had the energy to dabble in 'dark arts'."

"I suppose you are right," he agreed, yet again.

His king began to retreat. Soon, with the sacrifice of her own knight, she had captured his remaining knight and his queen. It seemed the odds had begun to tilt in her favor. Yet as soon as she had grown confident in her victory, he Queened one of his own pawns. One by one, her pieces fell to it, as he expertly defied her every strategy.

When she grew more certain of defeat, her thoughts began to wander. The sight of the Xavier insignia on the wall – the curved, orange dragon set upon a background red as blood – inspired her contempt, as it always had. Yet, it was intensified now by the knowledge that her own blood would soon continue the legacy it stood for. The cold-blooded creatures who had torched her homeland, ordered her away from home, would live on through her own sister.

In desperation, she attacked the black king with her last remaining pawn. Raoul humored her, allowing the piece to advance until it could move no further. By now, both she and her opponent knew what the outcome would be. Left without option, she tipped over her king.

"I resign."

Raoul nodded, a good sport until the end. He returned her pieces to her and began to reorganize his side of the board. However, her attention remained on that red insignia.

"There is always such relief to see the king removed, don't you agree?" Morana rolled her pale king in her palm, feeling its fragility. "The game ends."

The Grand Advisor chuckled, placing his own black king on the board.

"I don't believe so, Your Highness," he replied. "It only means a new game must begin."

Despite Twyla's hesitation, something drove her to carry out the prisoner's mysterious instructions. She went to the graveyard behind the palace during daylight, brushing snow off the grave of Raphael Fabiyus Xavier. The handmaid reached beneath the stone, expecting it to be very heavy; instead, it was weighted only by the snow.

Beneath was another stone, with a tilted, six-point figure carved into it. At each point, and in the center of the figure, was a rounded depression with a foreign symbol carved within it – and in four of these seven depressions, there were black diamonds placed in the stone. Encircling the six-pointed figure was strange text, different than even the symbols within the carved craters.

Witchcraft.

It reeked of it; she grew dizzy just to see it. She couldn't understand how her mistress could be responsible for something of this nature, something so dark and wicked. Remembering the prisoner's words, she pulled out the blank journal she had brought with her and began to copy the foreign symbols.

When night fell, she returned to the damp prison. The sound of scurrying rats greeted her as she descended the steps, feeling the guard's wary eyes following her into the depths. It took little time to find the blue-eyed prisoner. Ariel remained against the wall in his far cell, eyes half opened to stare into the darkness. Before she could say a word, he spoke.

"You copied what you saw?"

Though surprised by his quick understanding, she nodded.

"What are they?" she asked, kneeling before the cell, the journal held close. "They have an evil look about them, and…I do not believe my mistress could be responsible for their existence. But I must know what they are."

Slowly, he rose from the damp ground, taking his place very close to the iron bars. He set his eyes on the journal she held.

"Show me each symbol. I will tell you its meaning."

Twyla sensed she was starting down a shadowy path, away from the certainty she had known for nearly ten years. Yet his strange eyes beckoned her down that path with only a single, cool look. She did as she was told, opening her journal to each sketch.

高慢

He knew it in a moment.

"It is a Storma symbol. *Kouman* – Pride."

貪欲

"Storma as well. *Donyoku* – Greed."

嫉妬

"It is *Shitto* – Envy."

暴食

"*Bousyoku* – Gluttony."

肉欲

"The symbol *Nikuyoku* – Lust."

激怒

"*Gekido* – Wrath."

怠惰

"*Taida,* they say – Sloth."

Her drawing of the text that had encircled the diagram took him longer to decipher, though he seemed to already know its meaning.

Фавориты зла, я ваш хозяин.

"Minions of Evil, I am your master."

His whispered words sent shivers down her spine. Unsettled, she quickly closed the journal.

"Why would these things be on King Raphael's grave?" she asked. "What do they have to do with my mistress?"

His bones seemed to creak as he raised his head to see her, that stare eternally vacant.

"The Storma symbols represent the creatures that control the Xavier family," he said. "The gems you no doubt found in the stone will someday provide the power to control those creatures."

Her body trembled, shaken by inexplicable fear. Her rational mind blamed the frigid air.

"Even if I believe you, there were only gems on four of the symbols. Where are the other three?"

A chilling smile graced his lips, for the briefest of moments.

"At this time, Lust, Wrath, and Sloth are missing," he said.

It wasn't a question, though she had not divulged that information.

"Dayu Mazaki, the sorcerer who first carved the stone, possessed all seven Avdotian diamonds to complete the spell. However, he found it impossible to bring all seven into the country at a single time. Instead, he began to bring them in sets—one, perhaps two at a time. By the time King Cedric caught him, he had brought five into Larasca. Rank 12 brings the last of them."

"But *three* are missing," she cried, attempting to cling to disbelief.

The prisoner gave one slow nod.

"Lust's gem never leaves her person. Since Dayu burned, she has learned to use its power to make more puppets like herself."

Her terrible uneasiness had begun to shift her soul. Twyla realized she was gripping an iron bar, fingers shaking.

"She?"

He would not answer.

The guard's voice came down too soon, calling her away. She was forced to leave his presence, his words casting shadows on her once-loyal heart.

Chapter XII

*R*ina tried not to be awake late at night, a part of her still afraid of unseen forest spirits. But she had traveled in the forest for some time now, and had seen no sign of them. Slowly, her superstition was giving way to reason. She was no longer afraid to be alone at the shallow stream near camp, submersing her wrist to cool the bright mark Silas' grip had left behind.

The girl watched the icy water gurgle as it rushed over her skin, numbing her fingers and soothing the burn. The memory of its origin now seemed a dream – it wasn't possible for a mere man to burn her flesh so brightly. Yet, proof of otherwise was red upon her skin.

She was right to fear him, now more than ever. And yet, she now feared him less than before. After seeing him fall unconscious before her, limp, and helping Giovanni lift him onto the blonde mare, she had begun to feel pity for him. Something was very wrong with him, a curse or otherwise, and he had no control over it. The innkeeper had seen goodness in him; she wanted to see it too.

Ride settled beside her as she tried to soothe her smarting flesh, the creature raising its ears up and down as he tried to catch a glimpse of himself in the waters. However, they moved much too quickly for any hope of such. He sighed heavily before laying his head upon his paws, disappointed. With her uninjured hand, she rubbed his ears to console him.

"Silly thing," she whispered.

A rustle in the trees behind her frightened her to her feet, sending Ride scampering to a nearby bush. Her breath caught when she saw Silas there – wearing the long shirt Giovanni had purchased – watching her. The usual ire in his countenance had lessened, replaced by annoyance. For a moment, she glimpsed remorse in his narrow eyes. Then, it was gone.

In silence, he unsheathed his sword and tossed it at her feet.

"Take it," he said.

The power of his voice alone compelled her to do so, without question. In the same puzzling silence, he reached up and cracked a sturdy bough from a tree, quickly stripping it of its smaller branches. At last, he addressed her.

"Come at me."

She watched him, blank-faced. Visibly irritated, he clutched the bough tighter.

"*Attack* me," he snapped.

"A-attack you?"

Despite her confusion, hesitation, Silas stared her down with impatience. He expected that his will would be done. If he knew that what he asked of her was illegal, he did not care. So she gripped the weapon with a trembling hand, swinging it towards him. Faster than light, the bough knocked the sword from her unsteady grasp.

"Again," he said. "Firmer grip, this time."

Although startled, she gripped the sword again, tighter. As soon as she swung at him, the weapon was once more knocked away.

"You're dully predictable. If you must dress like a man, fight like one."

His cool words startled her more than he realized. He held her gaze firmly, intimidating and strong. She began to realize that he was trying to help her—training her to be more like him.

"Aim. Don't just swing at me," he said.

Rina retrieved the weapon, tightening her hold on it. It felt strange enough to hold a sword, let alone use it. But she tried to do as she was told, grateful for even his strained patience. She aimed for his shoulder, and though she had no intention of hurting him, focused only there as she swung. This time, he had to step away to block – his lips twitched, a smile suppressed.

"Better."

He trained her for hours, instructing her on when it was best to run, how to block an attack, and the necessity of knowing potential weapons in your environment, if she were caught without one. Most of all, he taught her to focus on her goal, for that was what would bring victory.

At the end of the night, he asked for her burnt wrist. In solemn silence, he wrapped a damp, green herb around the damaged skin. The pain began to lessen—but by the time she looked up to thank him, Silas had disappeared back into the forest. She couldn't find him at camp, or anywhere nearby. He didn't appear again until the next morning, when Giovanni brought her up onto his horse and they went on their way, following the stream northwest.

Silas told her to meet him by the stream each night. Because he had no spare weapon, he trained her by moonlight to handle his own sword, never using more than a branch against her. When his time with her was finished, he would disappear back into the forest, not to be seen again until dawn.

One night, her curiosity got the better of her. Bravery born of Silas' teachings led her to leave Ride in camp and search the area around it, trying to find the place her instructor spent his nights. Instead, she found Giovanni standing by a still pond.

"Are you looking for someone, my dear?" he asked, watching the rustle of colorful leaves that had yet to fall.

She stiffened, more uncomfortable around him in recent days. Something about him was unnerving—his constant smile, or the way his eyes searched her.

"No," she replied. "I just couldn't sleep."

Another lie, to avoid his inquisitive gaze.

The dark-haired man nodded, not even glancing to her.

"Come here, Rina," he said.

Though not without hesitation, she did as commanded. She stood beside him, staring at the full moon reflected in the pristine waters. Soon, he began to walk around her, observing. She felt him scrutinizing her as a hawk would his next meal. Then, he gripped her shoulders, correcting her posture so drastically she felt joints crack.

"Stand like a boy," he said, ignoring her startled choke. "Keep your chin up. Everyone expects you to be indestructible."

Rina stared at him, shocked by his chilling tone. His smile was gone, replaced by the General Lance's commanding stare.

"It's about time you stop chasing boys, Rina. Let go. In only a matter of days, your lover will forget about you entirely."

Her shock left her numb.

"What are you talking about?"

"That's why you're traveling with us, aren't you?" he asked, disregarding her question. "You long to see him again. You're convinced that someday you'll just happen upon him in your travels, and he'll whisk you away to the life you've always dreamed: a fairytale ending, where luck fixes a hard life, and longing is rewarded with a home and a lover's embrace."

He gripped her wrist, calloused hands over her golden bracelet as he jerked her to face him.

"That's why your disguise fails you," he said, cool eyes set on hers. "The world can see that foolish hope in your every look. Feminine naivety shines through, no matter what trousers you might wear, or how you tie those short curls. You fail to realize that your dream is a fantasy that will never come true."

Lance's whip had never dug so deep. All of her trials faded to obscurity, for none destroyed her as completely as Giovanni did with those few words. She did not feel her tears as they trailed, her face and body numb to her. She knew only the tightness of his grip.

"Please, stop," she whispered.

He tightened his hold on her.

"What is it you expect from your hopes?" he asked, a sinister gleam to his gaze. "No man is truly loyal. Even as he kissed you, you can be certain he was comparing you to every girl that came before. He'll find another, just as he found you. Perhaps that one won't bore him so with her silence."

"Stop it," she pleaded, desperation shaking her core.

"What were you to him, anyway? A toy? A warm body? Did he say he would marry you?" He laughed aloud, the sound all but daggers in her soul. "You're nothing more than an orphan, far from home. A man couldn't ask for a more expendable woman."

At last, Rina broke.

"SHUT UP!"

She didn't realize she had struck him. Rina saw the mark upon his face before she felt her hand begin to throb. Stunned by her own conduct, she stepped away, holding her smarting hand to her chest. Yet she felt no remorse, not a speck of sympathy. He deserved that print upon his cheek.

Slowly, the ex-Commander reached up to touch his face. He was baffled a moment, tapping the red skin. And then, he began to smile.

"It seems you can think for yourself," he said.

It so disgusted her to look upon his face that she could say nothing more. And still he smiled at her, so content to bask in her hatred.

"Consider this my lesson to you, Princess: learn to speak for yourself, or people will walk all over you."

She looked sharply away from him, staring instead into the deep waters.

"No wonder he hates you," she whispered.

He laughed even at this. With no regard to her disposition, he took her chin in his hand, forcing her again to meet his gaze.

"You have a beautiful face, even streaked by tears. Most people do not see past such a face. But I see your potential, Rina. You were born with vast, untapped abilities that are only starting to manifest. You are like a fine coal: with only pressure and time, you will become the world's finest gem."

A cold gust disturbed the trees, shaking leaves from their branches. Soon, one crimson leaf drifted onto the still water, sending ripples across its untouched surface.

Silas stood in a forest clearing, the sky above black as pitch. The trees loomed around him, casting shadows without light's aid. He knew he was alone here. Yet, his senses told him he was not.

Something crawled beneath his skin. Things slithered in his veins, slowly, writhing like smooth, slimy snakes. He could see them crawling under his skin, pulsing forward with each beat of his heart.

Who are you?

The sound of his own thoughts seemed foreign to him, in this black dream. It was as if they belonged to someone else.

Who do you think you are?

He turned to see himself, standing amongst the trees. It was only a shadow of him, with the same black hair and his own clothes. But his nails were like claws, long and dripping with blood.

"What have you done?" Silas asked, staring at the shadowy creature.

"You have done this," it said.

It raised one hand, one long, gnarled finger pointing to his doppelganger. Puppetted by his own reflection, Silas did the same. He found his own nails long and bloody, caked with the flesh of some unknown foe.

You will become as I am.

His voice, and not his. His thoughts, and not his own.

Silas began to change. Red scales erupted from his veins, bringing with them fiery pain, fiery rage. Wings ripped from his spine, and he grew – teeth slicing his lips as they became fangs in long, bestial jaws. With a predator's sight, he saw his twin became something else: a man of an old world, with fair hair and eyes like blood.

You are what your father made us.

He didn't understand why this inspired such rage. Yet wrath grew within him, shaking his great body until he roared to the heavens. The fire that billowed forth lighted the black sky.

Silas awoke to a dark night, heaving, his brow drenched in sweat. It took time for his senses to settle. He glimpsed camp in the distance by the light of Giovanni's fire, and heard the faint gurgle of the stream nearby. The youth stumbled in that direction, dropping to his knees once beside the water and splashing his face with it.

His head hurt, his hands still shaking from thoughts of his dream. Though the cool water helped ground him in reality, he could not entirely banish the memories. Something about it was too real. It haunted him in every shadow, every sound in the forest. It was as if that creature lived within him, now wishing to make its presence known.

He stared into the bubbling stream, seeing nothing in the darkness. He did not move again until something growled in the forest before him. The youth looked up to see a wolf emerge from the trees, head bent low to the ground as he snarled at his opponent. Even in the darkness, Silas saw the red gleam to his eyes.

The youth stood tall, snarling back as he drew Edmund's sword. In silence, man and beast stood their ground, one gaze never wavering from the other. Not once did the wolf's tail twitch.

As silently as he had come, the creature vanished back into the trees.

Alone again, Silas sheathed his sword. He didn't further attempt to find peace, knowing it wouldn't come. Vaguely, he remembered his nightly appointment with Rina. Each night she would meet him somewhere along the stream, her blue eyes bright with zeal. She was so ready to learn from him, never less than attentive. Although he would never admit it to her, he enjoyed seeing how quickly she progressed. Her company, as well, was…tolerable.

He buried his turbulent thoughts to follow the stream to their meeting place. However, it was Giovanni, not Rina, who stood where they had promised. He had brought the horses with him, Vaan's dark stallion and the blonde mare drinking from the stream. The ex-Commander smiled at him when he arrived, impervious to Silas' irritation.

"Where is she?" Silas growled, gripping the hilt of his weapon.

"So sorry, little Rina had to search the forest for 'feminine necessities'," Giovanni replied, that infuriating smile set upon his face. "I'm afraid we won't be able to travel for at least a few days."

"What?!"

He tried to control his outrage, so not to spook the horses. Still, his displeasure manifested in a deep snarl.

"I don't care what her problem is," he snapped. "We can't afford to delay for any reason. If the snow falls, we're as good as dead!"

Giovanni only smiled, stroking his horse's mane.

"Let the girl rest, Silas. She's in no condition to travel right now."

Though angry, he turned away. Now more than ever, he was in no mood to deal with Giovanni's presence. He tried to leave.

"You're changing," Vaan said, suddenly.

Silas stopped in his tracks, though he would not turn back.

"I'm not," he snarled.

"You are," his adoptive father laughed. "You are, and so is she. You've stopped roaring at me, and she's begun to glare. You're changing each other, little by little."

The youth would not respond to this. He tried once more to leave, only to be stopped by one of Vaan's grating inquiries.

"Why sleep so far from camp, my boy?"

He answered this, if only to rob Giovanni of any reason to pursue him.

"Because there's someone following us. I won't be caught off-guard by him."

As quickly as he could, he left him there. He returned to the place he had chosen for rest: a tall tree only near enough to camp to allow him view of that flickering firelight. It had become his custom to climb trees and rest in the sturdy boughs above, to put himself out of the way of predators and give him a wide view of the forest around him. It was the safest place. And yet, he could not bring himself to climb the tree that night. He tried, but could not.

Perhaps the dream had made him hate isolation, instilling the fear that solitude would allow those images to return. Perhaps he was only tired of being alone. For whatever reason, he returned to camp that night. He saw Rina sitting by a tree, knees pulled to her chest and her head resting upon them, while Ride laid with his body curled around her. Both were fast asleep.

Despite hesitation, he laid down by the fire, watching them. Before long, he too had drifted to sleep.

5th Month, 651 I.R.

I have paid little attention to the Akalinians for most of my life. Although I often hear their drums pounding by the Alize, any fascination I might have had with their culture was overshadowed by resentment, for I myself have been called "Kala" too many times. I have made it a point to the morons that surround me that though my skin may resemble theirs, I do not know those foreign ways. However, an accidental encounter has drawn me into their world.

It was a fortnight ago when I met Sh'ka. She is a few years older than I, but below my eye level. Although she is beautiful, I would have passed her by were she not in the situation I found her in. It was dark, and a couple of rugged-looking longshoremen had stolen her bag and decided to play keep-a-way, tossing it just over her head as she screamed Akalinian curses. Vaan always tells me not to involve myself in a stranger's business, but it made me furious to see her treated as such. I knocked them unconscious and returned the bag to her. In thanks, she kissed me.

Something about that kiss drew me back to her. To continue seeing her, I began to linger by the docks where the Kala's tents were. Whenever they set up their nightly fire, I was there, observing them from the shadows. Lately, Sh'ka has begun to include me in their rituals – simple dances, mostly, for it seems they too have no god. Yet even before I mingled among them, I could see the dynamic between the women and the men. The women do nothing without some sort of nod from a man, and say very little around any male counterpart. The men are all but silent, and each of them is armed with a brutal, curved dagger. However, man or woman, they share the same tattooed chain around their right arm.

The closer I grow to Sh'ka, the more I want to take her from that world. That kind of unfeeling society is a breeding ground for oppression and duplicity. Were it not for her, I would have no part in it.

As soon as they could travel again, they were off, faster than before. They covered many leagues in a single day, stopping only when the horses refused to move. If Silas had had his way, they wouldn't have stopped at all. He had once been caught out in the forest when snow began to fall—he had no intention of repeating the incident.

Fate had other plans for them. On the second day of their travels, before the sun had set, Giovanni brought their progress to a halt.

"We stop there," he said, gesturing to a shadowy place over the next hill.

"There? There's nothing *there*!" Silas growled, impatiently gripping his reins. "We have hours left of daylight: we keep going."

Giovanni didn't listen. He smiled, making sure Rina was still secure behind him before he started off again, towards the place he had specified. The girl's mongrel loyally pursued them, barking all the while. Furious and without a map, Silas was forced to follow suit.

Soon, crumbling pillars rose up around them. Vaan led them to the heart of a ruined temple, its marbles walls crumbling under the weight of parasitic vines, thick roots splitting the stone once laid so neatly upon the ground. Something about this place unsettled Silas. He felt he had seen these ruined walls, these broken statues—the familiarity of their eyes haunted his thoughts.

"You can tie up Charlotte on one of those pillars, my boy," Giovanni said, already dismounting his stallion, "her reins should fit around it quite snugly."

Silas pretended not to hear him, though he did dismount. As he fastened Charlotte's reins, he could hear Vaan helping Rina off the stallion, being sickeningly sweet to her as he did so. He glanced to them, all but relieved to see she was ignoring him. Rina ruffled her dog's mangy fur, smiling only at him.

"You want to go explore, Ride?" she asked the creature.

Ride barked, licking at her nose. With no regard to Giovanni's chuckle, she went further into the overgrown ruins without her comrades, the loyal beast at her side. Oddly, Silas found the sight amusing.

The young man pat Charlotte's mane before leaving her there, wanting to survey his surroundings. He happened upon a pile of colorful glass, each shard glinting brightly in the sunlight. He lifted one to the sky, seeing its lilac gleam.

"That's real Asyrian violet," Vaan said, appearing behind him like a specter.

Though startled, Silas stiffened to stone.

"You made up that word."

"I might as well have, it seems," the man said, calmly observing the ancient surroundings. "The vast Empire of Asyrias isn't documented in any written work, though it stretched from the far reaches of Riona to the sands of the Akalinian desert. Larasca was the peace-loving state of Larasha, then, its people the sole worshippers of the almighty Neschume: the faceless Lady of the Light."

Silas tried to keep himself from being swept up in one of Giovanni's fantastical tales. Yet, he could not help but watch the man's pacing in attentive silence.

"They say there were five temples in her honor on now-Larascan soil, each built to house a sacred object Neschume herself had blessed. One sacred object in each, one Priestess to protect it—except in the Grand Temple of Avdotia, which housed three objects and three Priestesses. Profoundly beautiful, these women, so the legend goes..."

"If that's true, where are the temples now?" Silas asked, unable to curb his intrigue.

"Destroyed, reduced to little more than what you see around you," Vaan replied. "All but the Temple of Avdotia, which disappeared into thin air. No remains, not a single stone left behind."

Silas' gaze returned to the pile of shards, carefully using the piece he held to shift them about. Vibrant colors gleamed from under the dust, from the darkest green to the most brilliant yellow. They were an unsolvable puzzle now, a colorful remnant of the masterpiece they had once been.

"This is one of Neschume's temples?" asked the youth.

"Right you are. You kneel in the glorious Temple of Silas."

Giovanni laughed at the youth's shock.

"Don't you recognize your namesake, my child? The place you first awoke in my company?"

Slowly, Silas realized that he did. He remembered lying on the cracked floor of these ruins, hearing the birds singing high in the treetops. Sunlight streamed through the leaves when he opened his eyes and first saw the man who loomed over him now.

"Rise and shine, Silas," he had said. *"Your new life awaits."*

Silas rose to his feet, clutching the violet shard.

"I'm not your child," he snarled.

"Ah, yes, I had almost forgotten…"

Suddenly, Giovanni snatched his hand, examining the bewitched ring. He only chuckled when Silas promptly jerked from his grasp.

"Yes, I suppose you will be a man, before the month is out," he continued, oblivious to the youth's threatening scowl. "Perhaps I should start treating you like one."

"Freak," Silas spat.

All at once, a scream echoed through the forest. Their eyes snapped to an overgrown entry they had overlooked, where their comrade and her dog had vanished long before.

Rina.

Wielding the jagged shard, he rushed through the entryway and into the black hall. He didn't know what he expected to find there; however, any expectations he had could not have been further from reality.

Rina was standing over the body of a strong Akalinian man, whose blood now dyed a massive shard of glass that jutted from his side, and dripped from the girl's hands.

Shocked, Rina stared at her handiwork. Silas stared at her.

"He snuck up on me," she whispered, her red hands trembling.

Giovanni came up behind them—smirking, and most unwelcome.

"Would you look at that, boy?" he laughed. "It seems you've created a monster."

Despite Silas' objections, they laid the injured man atop the broken altar until he regained consciousness. Rina herself pulled the glass from the wound. Giovanni left briefly, returning to announce that he had discovered the man's stallion tied at a nearby location. Once they confiscated his dagger, they had nothing more to do but wait.

Not long passed before the sun went down. To keep them from being cast into darkness, Silas discreetly used his abilities to light a torch still perched upon the wall. If his comrades noticed, they were kind enough to make no remark of it. It seemed that the three of them would stay here this night, whether they liked it or not.

To pass the time, Silas explored the small space. The large shard of glass Rina had grabbed had come from a pile behind the altar, knocked from what had once been a great window. Large branches reached in through the open arch that had been left behind, rustling in the breeze. He found three other torches along the walls, which he lit as the sky grew darker. For the most part, however, the place was empty. The only statue within that space was a small one: a man with feathery wings arched from his back, a white candle grasped his right hand, a black one in his left. They had no wicks, however; Silas left them alone.

The moment the Kala groaned, Silas' sword was at his throat. It was Rina's soft voice that stopped him from doing anything worse.

"Leave him be," she said. "He's injured and unarmed."

"She's right," Giovanni said, observing them from his seat upon a broken pedestal. "But if he assaults us, I give you full permission to burn his face off. Fair?"

The youth refused to react to the remark. Stifling his growl, he sheathed his weapon, allowing Rina to approach the altar. The injured Kala, barely conscious, rolled his head to see her. He was silent, still lacking the awareness to speak.

"Do we have any needles?" she asked, looking towards Giovanni.

With his usual smirk, he pulled a fine needle from his pouch.

"Doe-bone," he replied, handing it to her. "Picked them up in Argot. Figured we would need a couple, with Silas' luck."

She nodded, as unamused as the target of the comment.

"Do we have water?" she asked.

Giovanni produced the water pouch, this time without any sly remarks. He only watched her, apparently pleased by her new apathy towards him.

In silence, Rina pushed up the man's thin shirt, revealing the bloody gash. She poured water over it, allowing it to drip from the altar with a reddish tint. When she was finished, she corked the pouch and returned it to Giovanni, then proceeded to pull a long thread from the hem of her own tunic. She thread the needle with a careful hand, ignoring the gray mongrel as he lay by her feet.

The Kala grunted – his first sound – when the needle pierced his flesh. Yet, he didn't fight back. He gazed at the girl with the same wonder as her comrades, stunned by her steady work. It was Giovanni who spoke.

"Where did you learn such a handy skill, Princess?"

"I'm accident-prone," she replied. "And please, stop calling me that."

Vaan chuckled, eternally amused.

Silence returned to the room, only the man's occasional grunt any sound of life. Silas found himself watching Rina's every move, more fascinated by her now than he had ever been before. To stitch another man's wound was no small task. And yet, she did it so well, so calmly. It wasn't a skill that belonged to an unlucky tavern girl. He was beginning to feel that somewhere along the way, he had misjudged her.

"I'm sorry for what I've done to you," she said to the Kala, finishing her work. "You startled me, and I've stopped thinking before I act. Traveling with my companions would probably do that to anyone."

There was a sudden thunderclap in the dark sky, and water came down hard upon the weathered roof. Rina stood, looking strangely disoriented as she returned the bloody needle to Giovanni.

"You look pale, Rina," he said, unusually understanding.

She shrugged her shoulders, holding her head. With remarkable gentleness, he took her towards the entryway. Ride followed close on her heels, whining in an almost comforting way.

"Let's go check on the horses, shall we?" Giovanni soothed. "Enjoy the refreshing drizzle."

The youth's gaze followed her until she left, feeling…pity. He had not felt pity in a very long time.

Once they were gone, his senses returned to him. At once, he whipped his sword from its sheath, pointing it again at the Kala's neck.

"Drop the act," he barked. "If a needle in your skin doesn't wake you up, you're a corpse. Who are you? Why were you following us?"

The man looked to him from the altar, his reflexes much quicker now that Rina was away. His black eyes were penetrating, as sure a sign of strength as his powerful shoulders. Although he did not challenge him, he did not seem intimidated by the blade at his throat. Instead, his piercing eyes were searching Silas, as if recalling something.

"I have seen you," he said. "You were Sh'ka's toy."

Rage coursed through his body. He gripped the bronze hilt tighter, using every ounce of his control to stop himself from decapitating him.

"*Answer*," Silas snarled.

Even then, he seemed hesitant to obey. However, after another wary glance to the weapon, he spoke.

"I am Akbar, of Alin's troupe. I have been promised A'vra's daughter as my own, should I successfully return with her."

"A'vra's daughter?" Silas asked, a faint growl to his words.

"R'na," the man replied. "The woman you've dressed as a man."

This revelation shocked him, so much so that he lowered his weapon. He just stared at him, temporarily left without emotion.

"She's not a Kala. She can't be. She doesn't look like any of you."

"My race is not as homogenous as you seem to believe," Akbar replied. "A'vra herself was fathered by a Larascan. It did not surprise us that R'na was born as pale as she was."

"But she doesn't bear the troupe's mark," Silas snapped, grasping at reason. "Even if what you say is true, your world has no claim over her. She isn't yours to take."

Slowly, Akbar closed his eyes. His breath was uneven for a moment, no doubt brought on by the pain of the wound. Even so, he was soon calm again.

"Sh'ka always said you claimed to know our ways, thought yourself too righteous for our 'primitive traditions.' It amused her."

A bestial growl rumbled in Silas' chest, though Akbar ignored it.

"Whether or not she has been formally marked is of no consequence. At her birth, she was given a name from the Book, the same as every other woman of Alin's troupe or any other. The name they go by is not the name they are given. It is an arrangement of sounds that results from their given name. So long as they do not know their true given name, they are Alin's property. This law is enforced by the mark they are given: if they run from us and are caught by another troupe master, and they cannot produce both their spoken name and their given one, they are returned to the troupe whose mark they bear. It prevents escape and teaches submission to our law. That is how our troupes have survived hundreds of years."

Silas did try to understand Akbar. In so few words, he had explained the submissive nature of the Kala women and their undying loyalty to the oppressive world they had been born into—something that Sh'ka had utterly refused to admit to him. And yet, the concepts were so foreign they eluded him even now.

"Why don't they just run on Larascan soil?" he asked. "Or just look in the bloody Book while the master isn't looking?"

"Larascan Generals have learned that returning a woman to a Kala troupe brings a sizeable reward. They are as big a threat as other Akalinian troupe masters. As for looking…only one woman ever tried."

"And what became of her?"

For the briefest moment, Akbar's indifference turned to pain.

"A'vra was beat to death."

Even Silas grew cold, hearing this.

"And so, you want her daughter."

"A'vra's death was expected," the man said, apathy returning as he again closed his eyes. "Although she was the most talented dancer of our troupe, she was always of the rebellious sort, and grew restless after R'na's birth. She kept R'na from getting her mark at the proper age, and caused all sorts of trouble for Master Alin. That woman even ran away with the girl; by the time a General had returned her to us, she had already hidden R'na somewhere, and she refused to give her location. Soon after, she looked in the Book, and that was the end of her. Since then, however, other women have started to attempt similar things. It has caused Master Alin much unnecessary pain—he feels that the return of A'vra's daughter to the troupe will correct her wrong, and prove that resistance bears no fruit."

Silas sneered, again clutching his sword.

"How do you know R'na—*Rina* wouldn't share her mother's fate? You claim to want her as your own, but if she shares her mother's rebellious spirit, she'll slip through your fingers."

The youth narrowed his eyes to slits, finally raising the blade back to the man's dark neck.

"That's what happened to A'vra, isn't it?" he said. "You wanted her, and she got away. That's why you've come all this way for her replacement."

This time, the man gave no response. He only lay there, still as a monument.

Silas lifted his chin with the tip of his blade.

"Listen well, Akbar. I don't plan to stand by and let you take an innocent girl into captivity. So do as I say: leave tomorrow, and say nothing to her of your motives. Not a word, or I'll carve you like a pig. Do you understand me?"

The youth saw agreement in his black gaze. Only when he was certain did he sheath his weapon, going to reignite the dimming torch. However, Akbar's low voice stopped him once again.

"Sh'ka still sings of your eyes," he said. "Those eyes: like veins, she says."

With only the mention of that serpentine name, anger threatened to take hold of him. But Silas held his ground, diluting his snarls with deep breaths.

"I want you gone by sunrise," he growled.

Rina and Giovanni returned then, dripping from the rain. Vaan draped his wet coat around her shoulders, leading her to sit by a warm torch. Again, the temple was overcome by a silent night.

Rina awoke to the sound of a horse's whinny, as the sun began to light the horizon. She looked about to find only the sleeping Ride as her company – even the injured man had left the altar.

I've been abandoned.

She choked with fear of it, trying to perish the thought. But the horse's whinny came again, jolting to her feet. She quickly rushed from the temple, terrified of being left behind. However, it was neither Giovanni nor Silas she happened upon. It was the Akalinian man who mounted his black steed, still wearing his bloodstained shirt.

"You're leaving?" she asked, startled. "But your wound was deep, Sir, and you can't possibly have healed enough for travel…"

He shook his head, his silent gaze searching her.

"Your black-haired companion returned my dagger to me this morning. It is all I need for travel."

She found it strange that Silas trusted him with his weapon; he had threatened the man with his own only the night before. Still, the man had demonstrated no ill will towards them, even after the wound she had caused. Perhaps that was reason enough.

"Then…swear to me you'll be careful," she said, offering a smile. "Try not to take anyone else off-guard."

Her words must have been strange to him, for he seemed bewildered. However, his calm demeanor returned with his nod.

"I swear it, Nasaria."

She smiled, thinking that in fatigue, he had confused her name for another's. Yet he seemed very serious, entirely unaware of his error. He observed her a moment longer, absorbed by some deep thought. And then, he left: his horse's gallop faded into the sounds of the forest, leaving the marble ruins far behind.

By the silence of his departure, he had forgiven her for his wound. Even so, it left her without closure. He had robbed her of the opportunity to do anything more.

I'm sorry, Good Sir.

She turned, and was startled to see Silas standing by the shaded entry. There was a contemplative look about him she had never seen before: violet gaze staring far into the distance, his normally taut features relaxed, gentle. However, the look vanished when his eyes met hers, replaced by his usual impatience.

"Get your dog, girl," he said. "Vaan is waiting for you."

She nodded, and he abandoned her there. Yet even as he left, she couldn't wipe that image of him from her mind—that cool, thoughtful visage he had never shown before. For a moment, the wrathful being had resembled something human.

Chapter XIII

$\mathcal{K}$ing Attlas usually stayed far away from the Hall of Portraits. The isolated hall was deep within the castle, its very air made damp by memories of Kings and their miserable lives. Cedric had brought Attlas there for only one lesson during his lifetime, for he himself had thought it a haunted place. Yet the young King found himself drawn to it that dark night. He found himself aimlessly observing the grand portraits mounted upon the weathered stone, the dim moonlight casting shadows over ghosts of the past.

The pale faces of Tristan and Selena, his great-grandparents, were foreign to him. Though they were pictured in the peak of youth – Selena's chestnut locks in perfect ringlets, her husband's shadowed face free of lines – there was no joy about them. Even in the picture, they were distant from one another: Selena standing a pace away from Tristan's throne, both of them staring listlessly at their painter. Attlas had felt that gaze often from his heartless grandfather, who had never spoken more than two words to his son's only child.

"Bastard Prince."

Raphael, more than anyone, had made it known that Attlas was not a welcome heir. It had made the young Prince so cold towards his own mother that he had not cried when she abandoned him, run away with the former Captain of the Guard. Attlas wondered now if it had even been Rishiel's fault that Caden had not married her, for he had been away to war again only weeks after they had met.

King Raphael had only one portrait with his Queen – Diamond Ayres, child sister to the still-living Envoy of the People, King's Councilman Gabriel Ayres. Many years younger than her husband, Queen Diamond had gentle eyes, their hue very different from Raphael's pale green. It was she who sat in their portrait, while her gray-haired husband stood behind her modest chair. He displayed the smallest smile, so foreign on his visage that it altered it. Attlas wished he had known that smiling man, for even a day. However, Queen Diamond was gone in the following portrait—and with her, Raphael's smile.

The adjacent image showed the stone-faced King seated in his throne, his adolescent sons on either side of him. Cedric stood on his right, his short locks brushed neatly from his brow, his eyes of his mother's gentle gleam. Caden stood to his left, his dark locks somewhat longer, smirking when he was supposed to be smiling. He was rumored to have been a mischievous Prince, far more unruly than his docile brother. Yet in all other ways, the brothers were identical: they were of the same height, the same build, the same handsome face. In too pronounced a way, they had resembled the mother whose life they had compromised; for this, Raphael had hated them equally.

Attlas had studied this portrait many times, for it remained the only image of his sire. He knew every detail of Caden's face, from the curve of his smirk to the most insignificant line about his eyes. It was all he knew of Caden, the man who had given his life for his brother. And yet, the King did not care to know anything more. It was Cedric who had come home from the war and taken the little boy into his arms. It was the Crown Prince who had first called him son.

The image beside this portrayed a part of Attlas' own life. When his own blood-son was old enough to sit still, King Cedric had commissioned a family portrait. Although all the country knew that yellow-haired Attlas was not his child, the ruler had insisted that he be a part of it. They made an interesting image, the blonde boy standing at Cedric's side, the King behind his seated wife, who had been forced to keep their young offspring on her lap. The Storma Queen had never tried to conceal her disgust for her son; even in the portrait, the artist had been forced to lessen her scowl to a more vacant look. It was no mistake that she had named the child for a fallen empire—Asyrias.

There had always been an interesting look about the Prince. As far as anyone knew, he was the first child of both Larascan and Storma blood. Asyrias had inherited the narrow shape of his mother's eyes and her black locks, which were never allowed to grow past his ears. From his father, he had inherited the shape of his jaw and the wave of his hair, as well as the pale glow of his skin, which was shared by all Xaviers. He had been of sour temperament, no doubt brought on by his mother's constant cruelty; however, it was kindness that had most animated his features. Attlas remembered the ring the child had always worn, the only gift his mother had ever given him. Yet, the artist hadn't bothered to paint it.

The child's existence had not changed Attlas' relationship with Cedric, though he knew it should have. Despite Cedric's overwhelming love for his true son, he had continued to have Attlas trained for succession.

"Asyrias is a sickly boy," the King had explained. *"It's best that you are prepared to take my place."*

Indeed, everyone had called Asyrias sickly, though Attlas himself had never seen evidence of any illness. His paleness was no doubt the result of isolation, for he was kept inside for all his life, and Raoul would only tutor him in the somber darkness of his own chambers. The boy had been small for his age, but never ill. Still, it was likely the others had known something Attlas did not—the child had caught a fever and died before his eighth birthday.

Although Azalea's engagement to Attlas had been planned the day of her arrival in Larasca, when the two of them were only five years of age, it was not formally announced until the year after Asyrias' death. The day after the announcement, Cedric took the fourteen-year-old boy into the Hall of Portraits for the first time.

"Do you see the hollow look to our forefathers?" the King had asked him.

He could see it now, in all the portraits: the dead eyes, the pale complexion.

"It's because someone surrendered our souls," he said. *"Our ancestor struck a deal with Evil to have our land. He wanted power, wealth, and superiority. He was given that, at the cost of our afterlife."*

"How do you know that?" Attlas had asked. *"No one knows what happens after you die."*

Cedric had smiled, though it lacked its usual comfort.

"Some of us are born with...abilities. Your father and I were born with the ability to know things others cannot."

"Abilities?"

He had not answered him. The late King had only placed his gloved hand upon the bewildered youth's shoulder, his grip keeping Attlas firmly in reality.

"What makes us different from others is not that we're rulers, or that we're any brighter than anyone else. What divides us from them what's called a Grace Period. While others will pass into a peaceful world in their death, we are given only a week to remain in our conscious bodies, sleeping when we should have died. That is our Grace Period: a week to come to terms with our flaws, our regrets, our lost dreams, until our soul disappears into nothingness. That is all we have to look forward to."

The words were destructive to a young boy's spirit. Though Attlas had had nearly a decade to ponder them, each thought of them pained him anew. At first, he hadn't believed the tale, as Prince Asyrias had died in a very natural way, buried the day after he had stopped breathing. However, Cedric's death had proved his words.

On a cold morning in the 12th Month of 648 I.R., a guard had opened the King's Chamber to find a knife wound in Cedric's chest, the knife in his mistress' stomach. She lay sprawled across him, cold as ice. Yet the King, who bled from his heart, continued to breathe. He slept and slept, never waking, even as his body grew pale and cold. A week later, serenity smoothing his tired features, he finally took his last breath.

"We must be grateful for that time."

Someone was behind him.

Attlas tensed, forced to turn from the portrait of his lost family. A young man stood behind him, with hair dark as midnight, vacant eyes narrow, sapphire. Cast in moonlight was the image of their lost Prince, the aged ghost that would not rest.

"Asyrias?" the King whispered, fear draining the color from his face.

The man gave one, slow shake of his head.

"I apologize, my King. This is not my will."

The pale man advanced, whispering foreign words as he revealed the black diamond in his hand. Attlas, too stunned to move, stared into the man's eyes as the gem was pressed against his throat.

Tangled lights danced before him, clouding his vision. Misery came over him like a disease, infecting his every joint, weighing down his very heart. Control was lost.

He felt the cool hilt of a dagger pressed into his hand, the man's lips very close to his ear.

"Your reign ends."

His vision distorted, hazy, he glimpsed a woman's silhouette in the hall. Attlas could feel her eyes upon him, feel her smile.

The man's hand guided his own, raising the weapon. He closed his eyes, allowing the spell of misery to lead his hand.

This is what's meant to be.

Blood seeped into the King's tunic. His knees buckled, and he collapsed to the ground. The woman beckoned the man away, leaving the last Xavier to fall.

The guards found Attlas Elijah Xavier's body in the early morning, when he didn't come to the weekly Council meeting. By the entry of the dagger in his gut, they concluded that it could only have been suicide. To escape the chaos of grieving scullery maids and frantic pages, Morana had slipped into the aviary, awaiting a message from Lesser Advisor Saito.

Since the beginning of the Larascan Kingdom, the Xaviers had communicated with their Generals, Commanders, and Councilmen by way of birds. They had hundreds of hawks, falcons, and other birds of prey at their disposal, all trained as if by magic to convey messages to those important people. Their aviary was the entirety of the second eastern tower, where the birds were able to fly as high as the ceiling would allow. There were perches all along the stone walls, and maids cleaned the floor daily. Each bird responded to its name, and would promptly cease its circular flight pattern up and down the tower to come and receive its obligation. The errand boy Tahn was usually in charge of receiving and writing the birds' messages. Today, however, the Queen-Mother was alone in the tower.

Though the birds' shrieks were grating on her ears, she was distracted from her original ambitions with the sight of one of Cedric's grand mosaics. There was only one in the aviary, yet it held her gaze better than any other. She had newly been his wife at the time of its construction, when she was pregnant and still pretending to care. He once showed her the charcoal sketch that had become the masterpiece, drawn by his own hand.

"It came to me in a dream," he said, in his animated way. *"The creature was so overwhelmed by grief that he called out to me, as if he knew I would understand."*

Morning light now lit the mosaic, illuminating the image he had seen. A great crimson dragon arched back, wings unfurled as black lightning pierced his breast. Flames billowed from his mouth, their orange glow now summoned by sunlight.

"He breathes fire, roaring because he cannot cry."

"That makes no sense," she had said.

"The Dragons are not like us," he said, never discouraged. *"There are some feelings they simply cannot express."*

The Queen-Mother brushed these memories away, trying not to dwell on the mosaic's haunting glow. She raised her arm high, her gaze on the circling birds above.

"Tobias," she called, her voice echoing in the tower. "Come to me, if you have arrived."

Soon, a hawk's cry pierced the air. A great black bird swooped down to her, his talons digging into the white sleeve of her gown. He ruffled his feathers, eying her diamond necklace with his discolored, yellowed eye. The Queen-Mother offered him a scrap of meat, which he choked down greedily.

"Let's see what you have…"

She untied the scrap from his leg, attempting to unroll it with one hand. However, the bird soon disrupted her task, uncouthly snapping at her necklace. She swatted him away, scowling as he took flight.

"Ill-mannered pest!"

Tobias vanished back into the sea of birds, camouflaged by others of his kind. Though unsettled, the Queen-Mother unrolled the parchment she had taken from him. Upon it was the message she had anticipated, written in a familiar hand.

1ˢᵗ day of 12ᵗʰ Month, 654 I.R.
To the Queen-Mother:

Winter fast approaches, and game is becoming scarce. The soldiers kill what they can and share amongst themselves, but a rabbit or an owl can only go so far. The Stags are often left without any meat at all, which worries me. A few of the younger recruits have already begun to waste away.

General Lance continues to move us on schedule. Despite my pity for the young Stags, I will try to eat enough to survive. He says we should arrive within a week, perhaps two. I can only hope we move fast enough.

Your loyal servant,

Saito Niigata

にいがた 紗人

Lesser Advisor, King's Council

She smiled, unable to help it. The Xavier King was dead, and the last of the sorcerer's gems would soon be in her possession. One by one, the pieces were falling into place. Soon, Dayu would breathe again.

A light patter of footsteps announced the errand boy's arrival, before he had even opened the aviary doors. The pale boy heaved and heaved, still unable to catch his breath before he bowed to Morana.

"Y-your Highness," Tahn stammered. "Terrible, terrible news…"

"Spit it out then," she said.

"Y-your sister," he managed. "Your sister has lost her child, in her grief…"

Morana feigned sorrow to the best of her ability. But her façade was cracked, joy leaking through her twitching lips.

"How…regrettable."

"She wants to see you, Your Highness." He bowed deeper, unable to see her countenance. "She's waiting in your chambers."

"Then I will go to her."

She moved past him before he could stand, her slender hands gripping the handles of the aviary doors. However, she paused.

"Write a letter to Saito," she said to him, not bothering to turn. "Inform him of the tragedies that have occurred in the palace."

"Right away, Your Majesty."

She swung open the doors, feeling the cool castle air wash over her.

"And do tame that bird," she snapped.

He stammered some apology, which fell on deaf ears. The great doors slammed behind her, leaving the errand boy to his petty duties.

Azalea paced by her sister's window, pacing and pacing in the dim light, trying somehow to bury her misery in her step. Her voice was lodged in her throat, somewhere beneath her moans, her sobs. When Morana entered the room, it all broke free.

"They're both dead, Ana!" she sobbed. "Husband…child…gone…"

Morana was impassive to her pain. Without a glance to her, she seated herself at her vanity, coolly reaching for her alabaster brush.

"It's for the best," she said. "The Xaviers were a blight upon the land, a curse to all they touched."

The Queen's eyes grew wide, body cold with distress.

"How can you say that? Your husband…my husband…"

"Both descendents of the man who ordered the burning of our land. We were a prize to them, nothing more."

Morana only stared into her mirror, brushing her locks with a steady hand. Her sister's pain could not shake her—it didn't even draw her glance.

"Cedric was not Raphael," Azalea whispered, "nor was Attlas. They were gentle, kind spirits."

"You did not love your spouse, nor did I love mine. Don't let your mind be clouded by grief."

Salty tears stung the Queen's raw eyes, shock silencing her sobs.

"How…dare you…"

Anger rose within her, tears growing hot.

"You only hated Cedric because he killed Dayu, that sorcerer—"

"An innocent man, our *only* ally!"

Morana's shriek took her aback, though it was not strong enough to stop her thoughts from turning, transforming. Azalea's misery was overshadowed by her growing suspicion.

"Cedric would never have killed an innocent man without proof. Not as angry as he was. Not unless…"

The pieces fell into place: Cedric's fury as he threw the dark-haired man to the guards; his Queen, heavy with child, shrieking as the flames licked the man's foreign garb. Cedric's face had never been so changed by wrath, never so resembled the cruel King that had passed only months before.

"You were sleeping with that sorcerer, weren't you?" the young Queen asked, numb.

Morana never looked from her vanity.

"I paid for it in full."

Azalea stared at her sister, feeling all her rage beginning to grow. Her hands began to shake so terribly that she was forced to grip the window's frame.

"You're sick!" she screamed. "You were having Cedric's child! He *loved* you! How could you be so heartless?!"

"My heart beats well, Sister."

"Then you're a living corpse!"

Then, Morana began to laugh. The sound was so chilling it stopped all thoughts, leaving Azalea to stare vacantly at the woman she thought she had known.

"You're becoming hysterical," said the Queen-Mother, once more drawing her alabaster brush through her locks. "If you become too excited, I will have to have you escorted out."

She said it with such absolute detachment, feeling nothing for her sister, for Attlas, or for the husband she herself had lost.

And then, all the pieces came together.

"You killed them both, didn't you?"

Morana said nothing. Her cold smile was reflected back at her as her brush slid through her hair again, again.

Azalea began to feel ill, so overcome by rage that she retched with it, shaking.

"Saito…I'll tell Saito!" she cried. "He'll report this to Father; you'll pay for your treason!"

The woman began to laugh again, the sound cold as a knife's edge.

"Saito will not bow so easily to your whims. His concern for your well-being has always offset his concern for this crumbling kingdom."

The Queen stared at her, thoughts thrown.

"What are you talking about?"

"He was not blind to your admiration, Azalea. I am only surprised how blind you were to his."

Azalea's heart had been weakened enough by tragedy. Hearing this, its muted beating began to slow to a feeble thud, until her body began to quake.

"You're lying…"

"Do you honestly think it was coincidence that he left with Rank 12 the day of your marriage?"

As the Queen stood there, distant, bewildered, her sister reached for the silver bell hanging by her vanity.

"Don't bother trying to tell anyone about this meeting," she said, setting her brush on the polished wood. "If you do, I'm afraid you may never be allowed to retrieve Caden's dagger from your dear husband's corpse. Now, be a good girl and let the guards escort you back to your chambers."

The silver bell chimed, ushering in the three heavily armed guards. With only a gesture from the Queen-Mother, they took Azalea by her arms and tried to guide her to the doorway.

"You shouldn't be up and about, Your Majesty," one chided, though softly.

She did not hear him, still trying to understand how that dagger, safe in her possession, had ended up in her husband's fateful grip. How had her most prized artifact become the instrument of her destruction?

As the guards led her out, the Queen caught a glimpse of Morana standing by her vanity, her sapphire eyes observing the departure.

"Oh, Azalea," she called, voice deceptively gentle. "I hope you enjoyed the wine I sent to your room last night."

All at once, she remembered the putrid taste of her sister's gift, the horrible pain that had kept her tossing through the night. She remembered the blood upon her sheets, the tiny life gone from her body—gone.

She began to shriek.

"I'll **KILL** YOU! I'LL RIP YOUR THROAT OUT!"

The guards tightened their hold on her as she screamed and shrieked, spitting at her sister's feet.

"**MURDERER!**"

Queen Azalea was forced from her sister's chambers, the sight of Morana's smile forever burned into her mind.

Joanissia's Town Crier was alerted of the tragedy before mid-day. By evening, the citizens of the capital's Noble Square had gathered beneath the castle's northern balcony, weighing the air with their mourning. As silently as they could, they listened to Gabriel Ayres' powerful voice fill the courtyard.

"Citizens of Joanissia, it is true that the last Xavier King has taken his own life."

A chorus of voices rose from the grieving crowd.

"Why?!"

"How could he do this?!"

"What will become of us?!"

The eldest Councilman silenced them with a single wave of his weathered hand.

"The Council has discussed the matter in depth. We do not know why young Attlas ended his life, but we know that with no heir, there is only one possible manner of succession."

Gabriel turned, setting his emerald gaze on Morana, who had waited on the balcony with such solemn patience.

"Morana, Azalea, please come forward."

The woman had not noticed her younger sister's presence, so absorbed by her own joy. It threatened to overwhelm her mask of grief, exposing her to all. However, she suppressed it enough to step forward. She glimpsed her sister standing further down the marble rail, her face veiled, wearing a gown of charcoal black. The only color about her was her golden crown, its diamonds still glistening in the snowy light. She was a blight upon the scenery, so dark against the icy world. In one night, she had lost her place within it.

"Cedric's Queen has proven herself a capable leader many a time," said Gabriel, taking his place between them. "In these dark hours, she is the only one suited to guide our people."

The gray-haired man lifted the crown from Azalea's head, inspiring no reaction from the Storma. The woman only stared forward, all expression concealed behind her dark veil. Unshaken, Gabriel carried the prize to her elder sister.

Beyond the castle's open doors, Morana could feel the eyes of every Councilman upon her, as hesitant as the nobles who watched below.

The crown was set perfectly upon her head, as familiar as the power it bestowed.

"Long live the Queen!" Gabriel cried.

The crowd echoed him, in a crowd's way.

Snow began to fall, though it did not cool Joanissia's strange warmth. It could not dampen Morana's concealed joy. Yet, Azalea did not demonstrate the emotions her Queen expected of her. The young woman only smiled, bowing formally to her new ruler. She said only one thing before disappearing into the palace.

"May you reap all you have sown."

Chapter XIV

*R*ank 12 had fallen on hard times. They had managed without a hunting dog well enough, until it grew harder to find game to hunt – and the closer they came to the northern mountains, the less game there was. The less game there was, the less the soldiers ate. The less the soldiers ate, the fewer scraps there were for the Stags, until there was nothing left for them at all.

Although all the Stags were now starved and thin, the youngest, Fritz was in the worst condition. He had fallen ill, and with no food to help his body fight it, he was only getting worse. He would pass out on long treks, forcing Brock or Chad to take him onto his horse; at night, the other Stags would give him what clothes they could to stop him from shivering. But despite all of this, Kaish was forced to watch his best friend waste away.

It had been hard enough for Kaish to lose the woman he was going to marry; to see Fritz in such a state threatened to destroy him. To ease some of his friend's pain, the Talonian began to play his flute at the boy's request. Fritz's eyes would light up when he did, happy for those moments. However, when the sound ceased, the boy would grow quiet again and succumb to pain and shakes. After almost a week of this, Kaish made up his mind to do something about it.

After much persuasion, the General had decided to take a break from travel. As always, the Stags and the soldiers set up separate camps. However, that day, the soldiers' cart was wheeled a little further from the soldiers' resting place, parked between the two camps. Any jerky made from the remains of the hunt would be stored within it. Kaish knew that the position of the cart, the distracted gaze of the soldiers, and the unusual warmth of the day had created a one-time opportunity—he had to steal food for Fritz.

Kaish tread carefully over the fallen leaves around the cart, trying to avoid any dry crunch. The soldiers' camp was very near, concealed by only a few trees. If he were caught, he would get far more than the usual lashing. He got very close, able to pull aside the curtain to see its contents; however, a hawk's cry startled him from his task. He looked up in time to see the familiar black bird fly overhead, towards the soldiers' sleeping place.

Wolf's voice cut through the silence.

"What's it this time, Saito?'

A long time passed as Kaish stood very still, not wanting to draw their attention his direction. Soon, Saito spoke.

"King Attlas has committed suicide."

Silence again fell over camp. Kaish could feel his own throat tighten, dried by shock. Attlas had been their King for only six years, the last Xavier. And now, there was no one left to rule

"You don't look well, Sai," said Wolf, the first one able to break the silence.

"I'm not," came the response. "Morana has taken over. She may be capable, but...she's no Xavier. If I've learned anything since coming to Larasca, it's that an Xavier must have the throne."

"Why's that?" Wolf asked, his gruff voice strained by uncertainty.

"This whole country revolves around them. There is no record of the northern or southern mountains existing before Fabian Xavier, the first King, took control; Storma history tells of a time when patches of the 'Great River' were once dry enough to cross on foot. Somehow, the Xaviers' existence created Larasca and all that divides it from the rest of the world."

Kaish stood very still, as if bewitched by the words.

"Those are some crazy ideas, Saito…"

"I have seen proof of their connection to this country," said the Storma. "These birds, for example – do you honestly believe they are trained to seek out each and every General? Each Councilman? Do you believe they are born knowing their own name?"

Silence.

"Yet, these birds allow the Xaviers contact with their underlings, obeying them and their servants more loyally than the Grand Advisor. And if these birds were not enough, I have seen with my own eyes proof that the very land is subject to their well-being."

"But that's impossible," came Brock's youthful voice.

"Impossible were the things that happened when Cedric Xavier tried to refuse his throne. Random fires started throughout the Great Forest; the Balle River overflowed, ruining crops; wolves broke from their packs to attack humans, unprovoked. Disasters continued, unrelenting, until Cedric finally knelt to be crowned."

Troubling stillness settled over the soldiers as these words were absorbed. To Kaish, they seemed an omen of dark times to come.

"Pigshit," said Wolf.

"Believe it or not, it's true."

"True or not, that's not why you've got that look on your face," the soldier snapped. "What else does that paper say?"

"Only that Attlas' widow has...miscarried..."

Suddenly, a leaf crunched behind Kaish. He whipped around to see his nemesis standing by the cart, still pale and green with hunger—Alastor.

"What are you doing here?" Kaish snapped, taken off guard.

Before he could stop him, Alastor had snatched a box from the cart, stumbling back.

"Trying to get to the food before you take it all for yourself, bastard!"

Kaish growled a Talonian curse, trying to usurp the box from the boy's bony hands. However, driven by hunger, Alastor was a willful opponent. The two of them tried to wrestle the box from the others' grip, each growing more furious as the others' clutches grew taut.

"No wonder you couldn't catch Rina," Alastor taunted, attempting to twist it from Kaish's hold. "You've got such girly hands!"

"Don't you dare bring her into this!"

"If you had just let her stick with me, maybe Lance never would have made her cross that bloody bridge!"

Alastor's gut caved under Kaish's foot, almost sending him back. Even then, the Lucadian refused to let go of the container.

"Like she ever wanted to look at your sniveling little face," Kaish growled, teeth clenched even as Alastor coughed. "Now get your selfish hands off this—"

Alastor slammed Kaish's wrist into a tree—something cracked. Kaish choked on his tongue as he finally dropped the object, sending Alastor tumbling back with his own force. The Talonian gripped his scratched and broken wrist, watching the box fly out of the boy's hands and crash against a large boulder. One black diamond rolled out; the other cascaded down in shards.

Kaish stared, stared into nothing.

I'm dead.

His rival barely managed to clamber to his feet before the soldiers rushed to the scene, swords drawn. Lance pushed through them, grabbing Kaish by the back of his yellowed tunic.

"What's the meaning of this?!" he barked.

Alastor, still covered in autumn leaves, was quick to point to the shattered gem, pieces of it glittering upon the rock.

"Kaish busted it," he said. "He emptied that box out on the rock thinking it was scraps of meat he could steal. I tried to stop him, I really did…"

The Talonian had never seen Lance so terrified. The General stared at the gem in horror, as if already feeling their Queen's wrath upon him. Kaish, too, felt fear far greater than his rage. As much as he wanted to tear Alastor to pieces, he already knew the futility of the action. He had only one hope now.

"Saito, you can't believe him," Kaish said, seeing the Storma standing so near. "Please, I didn't do this!"

But his friend was useless. Even now, Saito clutched that letter in his hands, staring forward as though he were dead.

All was lost.

"Bind him, Yaz!" Lance bellowed, the spell broken. "I'll have him hanged!"

All at once, the sallow-cheeked man was upon him, tying back his arms with the same rope that had once bound Rina's. Kaish screamed curses no one would understand, clenching his teeth as he fought back hot tears. He would not let them fall.

Useless…

Lance tore the leather pouch from Kaish's waist, emptying its contents on the ground. Everything Kaish cared for was spilled for all to see: a gold coin, three smooth rocks, and his wooden flute.

"Break the Queen's diamond, will you?!" Lance growled. "I'll break your skull!"

The flute cracked beneath the General's foot, pieces buried beneath the autumn leaves—lost. Destroyed.

Chapter XV

12th Month, 648 I.R.

Why am I so sad?

I started bawling in the middle of one of Vaan's history lessons. I couldn't help it. I couldn't stop. I made a mess of my books, and he locked me out again, said he would let me back in when I got control of my emotions.

I ran to the edge of town, but I couldn't stop crying. I was practically in the forest when I finally collapsed into the mud. Maddy must have seen me running. When it got darker, she came out and brought me a blanket and a loaf of bread. She asked me what was wrong, and I couldn't tell her. All I knew was that it felt like my heart was dying, that the world was different.

When I was crying less, she told me the Town Crier had come with news that morning, that the King was dead. I'm still too miserable to care.

*D*ead leaves concealed the cobblestones of Raine's central street, crunching beneath the hooves of Giovanni and Silas' steeds. Their pace slowed, Rina was able to release her hold on the ex-Commander, observing the town with weary eyes. There was an eerie silence about it.

Dusk cast shapeless shadows over buildings of withered brick, the sun's light already fleeing countless allies. People on the streets would not look towards the travelers, their listless gazes reserved only for one another. Whenever the horses did catch someone's sight, the stranger would stare after them with alarming intensity until they could look no more.

"Cheery, isn't it?" said Giovanni.

"Like a funeral," she murmured.

The man chuckled, directing the stallion that carried them down another darkening path, Ride panting close behind.

"Raine just hasn't been the same since Duke James gambled away its Protectors. Living in isolation has its expense, I suppose, and it is only rational that he chose to maintain his own standard of living over his peasants'."

He gestured to a castle atop a solitary hill, its weathered stones eclipsing what remained of the sun.

"He gambled away all the Protectors?" Rina asked, stunned. "Is that possible?"

"You're free to gamble with anything you possess, Princess, so long as you have boy-parts. As Duke, he possesses every component of the city, from his courtly entertainers to the most insignificant spider. He gambled his Protectors to the city of Alia quite legally. Of course, the act caused such problems that King Cedric himself traveled here in attempts to remedy them. He was in the process of naming a new Force – brand new Chief, new Protectors – when he had to abandon the job. His son was dying, they say, and he loved that boy far more than the apathetic Duke. After Asyrias passed, Cedric never left the castle again."

They fell back into silence. Rina glanced behind them, seeing Silas directing his horse with a vacant, unusual look. She wondered what was disturbing him.

Around another bend, there was a boy standing on a corner, wearing a bright yellow cap; the insignia of a Duke's court was etched upon his coat. He cupped his mouth as he hollered, the sound filling the square.

"King Attlas is dead! Long live Queen Morana!"

Rina was filled with inexpressible horror. She grew sickly white, staring at that boy until the stallion had carried them to the next street. Yet, Giovanni's amusement was only fueled by this tragedy, deepening his smirk.

"Well, we're going that way," he chuckled. "We'll have to give them our condolences."

The girl looked back to Silas, longing for a reasonable companion in her distress. His look had only grown more vacant, as if he had been forced to retreat very deeply into his own mind. He remained that way.

Giovanni purchased two rooms that night from a sallow-looking girl who ran the town's only inn. Despite her better judgment, Rina had agreed to a room with the once-Commander, while Silas stayed in a room down the hall. The news of King Attlas' death was overshadowed by the promise of a warm bed. She was relieved to know she would have a blanket that night, after spending so many with a pillow of leaves. She took advantage of the cold bath the inn provided, grateful afterwards to feel her skin without the dirt caked upon it.

When she returned from her bath, Giovanni stood before the dingy vanity mirror, regarding his rugged reflection before prepping his face for a shave. She paid him no more mind. She went to her bed, the smaller of the two, and pulled the ribbon from her hair in preparation for the night. She had pulled off her shirt, about to remove her chest's bind when she heard Ride's bark rise through the cracked window.

Curious, Rina pulled her tunic back over her head and went to see the view. The sun still lingered on the horizon, barely lighting the world below. From the second story, she could glimpse Silas quieting the roped dog with a pat before he disappeared into an alley across the street, towards the forest just beyond.

"He's escaping, hmm?" came Giovanni's voice.

She turned to him in surprise; however, surprise soon turned to horror. Before her eyes, he was unsheathing a curved Akalinian dagger and coating it in froth, to shave.

"That's the Kala's dagger," she said, words cracking.

Giovanni only grinned.

"Indeed."

All at once, unfamiliar rage overwhelmed her. She was frozen by it, sputtering words.

"You stole it *back* from him?! That was his only protection! He'll die in the forest thanks to you, you unfeeling bastard!"

But the man laughed and laughed, immune to her fury. He finished shaving his cheeks, wiping the residue with his clean hands. Humming to himself, he rinsed the blade in the shallow water basin and held it towards his comrade.

"Take it," he said, smiling his whiskered smile. "Go chase my boy."

He held the sheath to her as well, his gaze never wavering. It seemed he knew what he asked of her was forbidden—yet, he did not care.

Unable to tolerate him a moment longer, Rina took the weapon and its sheath.

"You're a despicable human being," she spat.

He only smiled, his eyes following her until she left the room.

Rina untied Ride from the post by the entrance, wrapping his rope back around her own waist to hold her dagger's sheath. He barked and whined, licking at her hands.

"Did you see where Silas went?" she asked him, somehow feeling he would understand her words.

Ride whined, turning his head towards the alley across the way. On the other side of it, spindly trees rustled each other's branches, loosening brown leaves to fall. With a bark, he bounded into the alley, past the trees and into the forest. Rina pursued.

She followed him deep into the forest, where the tree's bare branches locked in tangled patterns above her head, forcing the moonlight to cast webs on the ground below. Owls called out from the branches like lost souls, eyeing the living who passed them by. Rina tried not to think of them, blindly following the gray dog as he padded his way through the dying wood. Her fear of the forest had been dwindled to suspicion, faint enough to be suppressed by will alone.

They stopped in front of a small structure, with stone walls and a battered door that hung strangely off its hinges, abused and neglected. It was here she heard Silas' roar—a sound of anguish. It shook that structure by its foundation, frightening owls from their perch. Even Ride backed away, whining.

She put a hand on Ride's head, stopping his departure. More curious than afraid, she pressed a hand to the old door, pushing it open enough to see what was inside.

Inside, the walls were lined by old wood planks, most rotted and brittle from long winters. On the right, she glimpsed rusty shackles hung from the ceiling; to the left, she saw a chain-link wall filled with the Protectors' abandoned tools of interrogation, all browned, unusable. Amongst these rotting things, was Silas. He stood in the center of the hut, where a large branch had fallen through the roof and made a home for itself upon the stone floor. Moonlight streamed down from the hole above, barely illuminating his dark hair, his cracked nails. He was hunched over the log, powerful arms wrapped around his powerful body, as his shoulders shook with some suppressed force.

He roared again, throwing his head back to be sure the sky heard him. It was inhuman in its strength—human in its pain. Suddenly, he threw his fist into the wall behind him, shaking the building once again.

"**WHY?!**" he bellowed.

He pounded again, again, until the wood began to crack.

"**WHY DO I FEEL THIS?!**"

With his last blow, flames burst from his hand. They burned through the plank in a flash, forcing his knuckles to meet the rock wall concealed behind. He wrenched his fist away, leaving scorched wood to frame the blood upon stone.

Silas cursed, though not as loudly. He stumbled back, holding his fist, staring dully at his handiwork. His fire was fading.

The sight of his blood held Rina bewitched. Not even her own blood was so vibrantly red, like the berries of summer months. She had never seen anything like it.

She pushed open the door, at first not realizing she had done so.

"Are you all right?" she asked.

At once, his vigor returned. His body jerked towards her, fury intensifying his damp gaze.

"*Leave,*" he snarled.

But she couldn't. Even if Ride had not wriggled past the old door, giving her strength with his presence, she would be held still by the sight of the youth's narrow eyes, glistening with the beginnings of tears.

"You're hurting," she said, gently. "Please, tell me what's wrong."

Her words must have threatened him; suddenly, he drew his sword from its sheath, raising its point towards her.

"Get out, you **moron,** you **dolt**," he growled, bloody hand tight upon the bronze hilt. "I told you to **LEAVE!**"

But it was he who had sharpened her instincts. His own teachings had taught her not to stand there and allow fear to hold her captive.

Her dagger's blade struck his sword.

"You're no better than Giovanni," Rina spat, her dagger shaking as the adrenaline coursed through her. "Both of you constantly telling me what to do and what to say, how to do things and when, how to bury my feelings when neither one of you has the guts to show a single real emotion towards anything at all!"

Her own tears began to well—one weakness she had yet to control.

"I could help you, Silas, but you've made it very clear that you won't let that happen. So don't expect me to be there when you can't hold yourself up anymore."

Rina lowered her weapon, her hand still shaking. She couldn't look at him, blinded by frustration.

"Come, Ride."

The dog bounded out ahead, whimpering very softly. Without a glance behind her, Rina left the hut, slamming the ancient door shut.

Silas had never seen Rina with her hair down. It has grown quickly to an almost feminine length, whipping about her so wildly, tangled and free. He had focused on it when shock forced him to break from her gaze—too soft, too hurt.

The door slammed; he was alone.

No longer masked by anger, his inexplicable misery returned. It forced him to his knees, making him dizzy, sick. Yet through that fog of emotion, regret crept in.

Why won't you pursue her?

He couldn't. Not in this state. The sadness that had smoldered within him since that morning had rendered him useless: his body ached, water like steam in his eyes. He could only try to grow numb to it.

Worthless.

Silas pushed back against the planked wall, staring at the mossy branch that lay in the center of the room. He gripped his bloody fist, feeling its sting.

Weak.

He watched a black spider creeping down a tiny branch raised from a larger one to return to his silvery web, carefully constructed between the two. The arachnid was still when he reached it, content upon threads of support. The youth envied the creature that could be so easily contented.

Silas thought of the girl who traveled with him. He thought of her soft eyes and fair skin, so like the girl who haunted his waking dreams. It distracted him from his misery, if only for a moment. Although he had made little attempt to know her, through actions alone she had proven herself a kind spirit, braver than her delicate features could portray. She stood still in the face of danger, no matter how she trembled – and though he had never been anything but cruel to her, she had given him words of compassion without provocation.

That you threw back in her face.

Rina didn't deserve to leave in the state she had. He had apologized to Abaca, who deserved far less. Despite his own state of mind, he knew his obligation. His heart wasn't as frozen as she believed it to be.

The forest was eerily still as he walked the trodden path, his injured hand buried in his pocket. He focused on the pain of the rough cloth grating against it, agitating torn skin. When he finally heard the rustling in the bushes around him, it was too late.

"Take a look at that sword," came a raspy voice. "I'd say it's worth at least fifty gold pieces."

"Sixty, if we pass that hilt for solid bronze."

Silas whipped out his weapon, muscles taut as nine men emerged from the shadows around him. They were burly and menacing, built like boars. The youth stood still, scowl set on the largest of them.

"Leave," he snarled. "You'll regret this fight."

"You must think you're pretty tough," the man said, accenting his words with cracking knuckles. "You're a pretty big guy—biggest guy in your town, I bet."

Silas was silent, trying to quell his welling rage.

"This one's not a talker," laughed another, who had a scar down his right cheek. "Let's just take the sword and go back to the tavern."

They circled him like vultures, cackling through their snaggled teeth. Silas' hair bristled, his own nails digging into the palm of his injured hand.

A waste of time.

He wouldn't dull his blade on them. As they threw their fists, he threw his, ducking and dodging their haphazard blows. Most of them were half intoxicated, hitting their comrades in their eagerness. Silas, body still throbbing with anguish and ire, enjoyed having their throats to cushion his blows. His own blood stained each impact.

He imaged Vaan smirking at him from behind.

"Enjoying yourself?"

That thought, and the men ceased to be people. Overcome by rage, Silas fought with lethal intent, not satisfied by even the sound of cracking bones. He wanted to hear them howl for mercy he would not give.

Flames leapt from his fists. Two of the men began to shriek: *fire,* then *witch.*

Silas drew back, horrified to have again lost control.

Monster.

The men who weren't burned tried to restrain him, before he could gather his wits. He didn't resist.

"We'll see how *you* like being torched!"

Suddenly, a loud sound shook the trees; all the men looked up at once. Silas saw a man of fiery hair standing on the path to town, holding a weapon the youth had never seen before. It was like a hollowed rod with a shaped handle, attached beneath and four times as thick as the shaft. Smoke billowed from the hollow end.

"Scram!" the stranger barked. "Get back to your tavern!"

They rushed away like frightened cats, still nursing their injuries. Silas was left alone, staring into the hollow shaft of the man's weapon.

"What is that?" he asked, forgetting to be grateful.

"One of my brother's crackpot inventions," the man replied, slinging the weapon onto his back. He took one determined step forward, thrusting out his slender hand.

"Creed Temlar, at your service."

The man was of no impressive height, with a face wrinkled by his knowing smile. His fiery locks were almost curly—and yet, he had the green eyes of any Larascan. He stood like a fortress upon the landscape, powerful in his own right, and intimidated by no one.

Although hesitant, Silas shook his hand in silence.

"Firm grip you've got," Creed said. "A bit hot from that court-trick you pulled. I don't know how you got that fire going in such a pinch, but the execution was flawless. You must be a fine entertainer for some Duke, or you'll be one someday."

Even if Creed had given him the time, Silas could have said nothing.

"Now go," the man said, giving him a push towards the town. "You might have burned and broken their limbs, but you've damaged their pride most of all—and thieves know best how to start a riot."

Silas hesitated, not wanting to be forced anywhere. However, Creed pushed him forward again.

"*Go,*" he warned.

At last, Silas ran. By the time he reached Raine, the streets already echoed with angry shouts, torches lighting the windows. The youth passed Ride, tied at the inn's entry, as he rushed inside. He had to kick down Rina and Giovanni's door. When the girl didn't stir from her slumber, he grabbed her arm, jerking her to sit.

"We have to leave," he said, his hold firm.

Her eyes shot open, half-hidden by her tangled locks. She gasped for breath.

"W-what?"

He heard Giovanni stirring, yawning in the next bed. He didn't care.

"Don't ask questions. Come to the stables."

Silas left her in disarray, moving swiftly to the stables behind the inn. The horses greeted him with raucous sounds, spooked by the slamming doors. He went quickly to his mare, stroking her mane as he soothed her.

"Hush, Charlotte…"

He could hear the shouting growing louder and louder outside, the mob beginning to take shape. His heart was pounding in his ears, though he managed to feign composure for the sake of his steed. As soon as he could, he fastened her reins and mounted the creature.

"We'll sleep elsewhere, tonight," he told her.

In his rush, he looked about the stables, seeing no sign of Rina. He was growing agitated, too impatient to wait. However, just as he was about to leave, he heard Ride's incessant bark. The girl came into the stables with him – her hair a tousled mess, her breasts very round and prominent beneath her tunic. The sight took him off guard; he realized her usual bind was held in her hand.

"We're leaving, then?" she asked, still shaken.

He nodded. Before he realized his own actions, he had held his hand down to her.

"Get on."

Rina stared at his extended hand, as startled as he. She had never once ridden on his horse, no doubt having become used to Giovanni's grating laugh and his habit of jerking his stallion to a stop. Silas offered her a change.

Giovanni appeared before she could make a decision, yawning and scratching his neck. He ruffled Ride's fur as he passed him.

"Good night for a midnight ride, isn't it? Those murderous chants really get the blood pumping."

At last, Rina made her choice. Her soft white hand clasped his dark palm, allowing him to help her onto the mare. For the first time, her arms wrapped around his waist, her body against his back. Her breath was warm.

The ex-Commander mounted his stallion, riding up beside them.

"Let's depart, shall we?"

Silas didn't need his permission. He whipped Charlotte's reins, sending her off. They rode out onto the streets, past buildings lit by fiery torches. The townsfolk's vicious cries bid them farewell.

Chapter XVI

They rode deep into the forest, far from Raine. Although it was very dark, Silas seemed to guide his horse without difficulty, never hesitating at the reins. Not once did he look back at Rina, as much as she wanted him to. She regretted her harsh words and longed to see forgiveness in his eyes. For now, she could only content herself with his closeness.

His body was unusually warm, she found. She had only felt such heat from sick children in Gwen's orphanage, when fever colored their cheeks. His heartbeat, too, was strange. It beat much slower than her own, yet each pound was forceful: *thu-THUD, thu-THUD.* She concentrated on it as they rode, her ear against his warm back.

thu-THUD.

The forest was thinner where they stopped, trees scattered amidst large clearings. Silas dismounted beside a great boulder, taking a moment to calm Charlotte before he held his hand towards the girl. Unnerved as much by his action as by his silence, she accepted his help, flinching only when he took her waist to guide her down. His grip was strong, hot.

Still guilty after their confrontation, she caught the youth's attention as he took Charlotte's reins.

"I can bandage your hand, if you like," she said.

He shook his head.

"That won't be necessary."

Before she could ask why, he showed her the injured hand. His red blood was dried upon his knuckles, barely darkened; however, the wounds that had spilled it had closed. Shocked, she took his hand, thinking she had made some error. Even up close, she could find no split skin, not a crack around even his golden ring.

He allowed her to turn his hand, to be certain. Yet while she found no sign of his recent injury, she saw a long, grotesque scar down his palm, ready to bleed again with the slightest agitation.

"What's this?" she asked, startled.

At once, he jerked his hand away.

"None of your concern."

Giovanni soon dismounted beside them, clapping her shoulder the moment he passed by.

"Feel free to rebind yourself behind that rock," he said, smirking his usual smirk. "Don't want those bouncing bubbies to distract my boy from his fire-duties."

Though mortified by his words, she did disappear behind the rock, taking his advice.

Before long, a fire blazed in the clearing. Silas had set it up in his habitual way, with rocks around the flames to discourage their spread. Although disappointed that she would not wake in a warm bed, Rina resigned herself to fluffing her pillow of leaves. She tied back her hair to lie upon it, hoping to lessen how much of the foliage tangled in her locks. Ride, who had lingered behind with Giovanni's stallion, lay down beside her as she closed her eyes.

She heard Giovanni stand, nearby.

"I'd better take the horses to drink," he said.

"Leave the supplies," came Silas' snarl.

"Fine, fine. Poor boy, so afraid that I'll abandon him…"

There was a thud as the leather pack hit the ground, crunching scattered leaves beneath their weight.

Silence settled over the camp. The horses whinnied as Giovanni took their reins, luring them away from their resting place. Rina relaxed again. She was beginning to drift into slumber when she felt something cold come to rest upon her cheek.

Startled, she sat up, touching her face. It was wet, cold. When she looked up into the dark sky, she saw a flurry of white flakes beginning to drift down.

Snow?

She saw Silas looking up as well, his scarred palm towards the sky. He mouthed one single, recognizable word.

"Unnatural."

He was right. Snow had never fallen this early in Lucadia, no matter how cold the air had become.

Wolves howled in the distance, frightening Rina and pausing Giovanni's departure.

"Ah, a creature with a howl like yours," the ex-Commander said, his emerald gaze regarding Silas. "Indeed, you have much in common with those beasts, it seems—they too wither when shunned from their pack."

Rina heard that familiar growl rumble in Silas' chest, warning of the danger in his tight fists.

"Hmm? You disagree?" his father asked.

"*Go,*" Silas warned.

Ride licked snowflakes from Rina's hand, reminding her of his presence. She ruffled his fur, not seeing Giovanni's last smirk.

"Pleasant dreams, my son."

He led the horses into the night.

Rina awoke to a white world. She had grown so numb to the cold that night that she had not felt the flakes piling upon her, smothering her in a blanket of ice. She sat up, shivering violently; Ride, disturbed by her sudden movement, got up and shook the snow from his coat and onto her tunic.

On the other side of the frozen fire-pit, she saw Silas asleep in a sitting position, his head resting against the sheathed sword he held upright against his body. There was no trace of snow upon him, though his clothes were soaked through. Seeing him content in sleep, she looked about for Giovanni.

There was no sign of him. He was gone, as were their horses. All the man had left was his jacket draped across the fire pit, peeking out from under a pile of snow.

Her teeth chattering behind blue lips, she snatched the icy jacket from the ashes, wrapping it about her body. Where it had lain, she saw a note fluttering in the breeze. Overwhelmed by curiosity, she lifted it from the soot, shaking the dust away before she tried to decipher what she saw as gibberish upon the page.

Silas' deep voice took her off guard.

"What are you holding?"

She found his violet gaze boring daggers into her soul. Terrified and cold, she held the note towards him.

"I found it in the ashes," she said. "I swear, I couldn't read it."

Silas snatched it away, irritable even for him. However, as his eyes scanned the text again and again, irritation turned to anger. He gripped the paper tighter and tighter, until to ripped between his shaking fists.

"He's gone. That son of a bitch is…"

He stumbled to the place Giovanni's pack had fallen the night before, finding only a depression in the fine snow.

"Gone…"

He grabbed a handful of the weightless snow, letting it slip through his fingers.

"The supplies, our horses, that map…gone…"

All composure crumbled to rage. The torn note fell into the snow as he clutched his hair, trembling with such fury that the veins in his eyes pulsed red.

"I'll SLAUGHTER him! I'll slice him in **HALF**! I'll **RIP OUT THAT BASTARD'S TONGUE!**"

The wind howled as he howled, screamed as he screamed, as if the very air bowed to his whim. Yet, all the grandeur of his rage could not hide his pain. Behind the storm, he was just as frightened, as abandoned as she.

Rina looked down, holding the wet jacket tighter around her body. The action distracted her, though it could not quell her shaking. Ride laid his head upon her lap, less concerned about her well-being than he was about her body-heat.

"So…we die here?" she asked, the question directed into the empty air.

Silas wouldn't look at her. His breath like steam, he stared at the ground, watching the snow melting beneath his boots.

"No," he said. "We find shelter. We survive."

Rina was slow to move, slow to trust him. However, as the cold began to seep into her bones, she grew less willing to remain where she was. She stood, slowly brushing away the snow caked onto her trousers, her other hand warm in Ride's fur.

With a nod, he gestured her forward. She came.

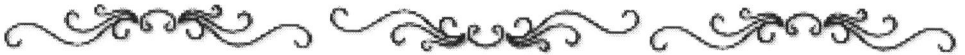

My Dear Silas,

Today is the day: 8th day of 12th Month, 654 I.R. Today is the eighteenth anniversary of your birth, the day you are considered a man. In honor of this fateful day, I have decided to give you exactly what you have always wanted: complete independence.

Continue North to Joanissia. I will await your arrival.

Do try to keep the girl alive.

Very best wishes,

Giovanni Wolfslayer

Commander, Ranks 1-5 (disc. 643 I.R.)

The unusual blizzard only worsened as they traveled, flurry of ice distorting Silas' sense of the world. Even Ride was disoriented, walking in zigzags behind Silas and the girl. Silas was protected from the worst of the conditions by his own abnormalities: his heated skin melted the snow on contact, making him wet and irritable, but not cold.

However, Rina was not so fortunate. The youth kept her very close, becoming accustomed to the sound of her trembling teeth. She was miserable, shivering violently—and then, her shaking stopped. As the wind wailed, her body was utterly still.

Unsettled, Silas gripped her shoulder.

"How do you fare?" he asked.

Silence. The girl stared forward, all but dead.

Fawk.

Silas acted on instinct. He lifted her into his arms, holding her against his warm chest. Ride began to bark, as if concerned for his companion.

"Shut up," the youth snarled.

The beast was quiet.

Silas saw a mountainous formation in the distance, almost concealed by the white storm. He rushed towards it, the dog close behind. All the while, Rina was very still. Her eyes were barely open, half seeing, half lost in some distant dream.

Luck guided him to the mouth of a dark cave. Inside, vines clung to the rocky walls, browned by the shock of a sudden winter. The cave provided shelter from the bitter wind. The air was so very still there that Silas stumbled into it, his bones still swaying with the storm's gust.

The youth laid Rina by the cold wall; Ride came to settle beside her. Even now, the girl was unresponsive. Gripped by unusual urgency, Silas ripped vines from the walls, tossing them in a pile on the cave floor. They burst into flames beneath his fingers, lighting the darkness.

"Strip down," he said to her, relieved to see her move. "Those wet clothes aren't going to help you warm."

With an obedient nod, the girl began to remove her icy garments. Silas looked away to preserve her modesty, collecting what she discarded. He laid her trousers and her tunic out by the fire, her boots, dagger, and his own sword beside them. After wringing out the tawny jacket Giovanni had left her, he dried it with the heat of his palms.

"Here."

He tossed it back to her, without a glance. However, when silence stretched too long, he finally convinced himself to look.

Rina appeared puzzled by the article of clothing, holding it on her head, then her face, trying to peer through the armholes. She was like a child trying to play dress-up. He was concerned, more so when she began to hum an Akalinian lullaby.

"Just hold still," he said.

Silas knelt before her, wrapping the jacket around her slender shoulders. He was relieved that her chest remained bound.

"I feel…tipsy," she said, smiling strangely.

"You're not," he said. "You're freezing. Your brain is shutting down."

As her Talonian bracelet began to slip off, Silas pushed it back on, then again corrected her jacket about her body.

"It's like…after a sip of mead that Richard gives me, or after a whole mug…"

Rina giggled at her own words, as if she hadn't heard him at all.

"Have you ever done that…?"

"No. I've never had liquor."

"Oh…"

Suddenly, she fell against him, forcing Ride to scamper out from between them. Silas, startled, was too tense to react.

"You're so warm," she said. "Like…sunlight…"

Despite himself, Silas began to relax. Her skin was still too cold against his, though the jacket shielded her better from the chill. If she was going to survive, he would have to keep her warmer.

With a sigh, he shed his wet shirt. He sat with her, his back against the rock wall, cautiously holding her in his lap. He tried to be still, to avoid provoking more inquiry. However, now warmed by the heat of his skin, her gaze had begun to explore him without restraint.

Suddenly, she pressed her hand against his cheek.

"It's so soft…no bristle…not a scratch…"

He pushed her hand away.

"I've never shaved. Don't ask me why."

Because he didn't know why. Though he had once looked forward to that rite of manhood, his cheeks remained perfectly bare, not a single hair upon them. He had come to accept this.

The disoriented girl then touched his lip, then past it—her finger pressed against his canine tooth.

"Like Ride's fangs," she said in awe. "Pointed…"

Mortified, he forced her hand from his lips.

"It's no sharper than yours," he snapped.

"But it is," she giggled, "They're like fangs…"

He sighed, realizing the futility of arguing with her in this state. It would be more productive to humor her mood.

"It's just the way I was born."

"Did your Mama think they were pointy?"

This question shook him. In truth, he had never pondered the absence of a mother in his life. Giovanni had brought women into the house now and again, but none of them had ever assumed a substantial role in his upbringing. Women, in general, played very little role in his existence.

"I never knew my mother," he said.

The girl's spirit fell quickly in her delusional state.

"Me neither…"

Seeing this heartbreaking look upon her face, misery dampening her soft eyes, he thought about telling her what he knew: that her mother had been a beautiful Kala, who had saved her from an oppressive life. Silas wanted to tell her that A'vra had loved her. And yet, he said nothing.

Rina slumped back against him. As if guided by another's will, his arms tightened around her.

"You're so warm," she whispered.

He hesitated, at first. However, it seemed talking was keeping her coherent.

"It's…my blood," he explained. "I can't rationalize it, but it's true. That's where the fire comes from. That's what heals my wounds."

"But…this one?"

Her light pressure to his scarred palm gave him a great deal of pain, forcing him to wrench it from her grasp.

"A wound Vaan gave me. It's unusual."

She accepted this explanation, distracted by the glint of his golden ring.

"And what's that?" she asked, touching the cool metal.

This time, he didn't pull away. Somehow, he was compelled to allow her to touch that immoveable object.

"It's just a ring," he replied. "I've had it for as long as I can remember."

Satisfied, she dropped his hand. Soon, she moved very close to him, her head upon his chest. He saw her breast rising and falling beneath the jacket, summoning the soft steam of her breath.

"Have you ever had a woman?" she asked, suddenly.

Although he was unnerved by the question, he found that she had begun to shiver in his arms. She was recovering, though slowly.

Relieved, he again decided to humor her.

"One," he admitted. "I was fourteen. The woman, Sh'ka, was a Kala."

Rina smiled brightly.

"Was it wonderful, like all those stories…?"

He paused, unable to say much of anything. Disappointed, she tried again.

"Did you love her?" she asked.

At last, he breathed a great sigh.

"It's a long story."

But the girl looked intrigued in her dream-like state, those blue eyes imploring him to speak. Something about her made it difficult to deny that heartfelt look. She was childlike now, too trusting of a dangerous man. He couldn't bring himself to again damage that naïve faith.

Staring into the flickering fire, he began.

"Since the day I moved in with Vaan, he worked me like a dog. I shined that filthy sword collection, beat his rugs, scrubbed the floors and watered his wretched flowers. Once he decided I was old enough, he added lessons to my grueling chores: I learned laws and hierarchy, logic, tactics, swordsmanship, horseback riding – if it could be learned, Vaan would teach it. I collapsed into my bed at the end of the day, all but dead. However, the slightest refusal to comply with his methods – as subtle as losing a game of chess – and 'Father' would lock me out, refusing to accept me back for weeks at a time.

"Although I occasionally found refuge in John's inn, I learned my way about the streets. I didn't see people much, locked up in Vaan's house on the edge of town. It was when he locked me out that I met others of my own age. Their games were child's play after what Vaan put me through, and my skills earned their reverence. I was Prince to my peers, unchallenged and adored. Yet, though I had many admirers, only two had my confidence: Edmund, son of former-Chief Edward, and the innkeeper's daughter, Madeleine – who admired me very little, and treated me more like a dirty brother. The two of them were always there, checking on me even when Vaan took me back in.

"Things became routine. I would put up with Vaan's torture until I slipped up, losing a duel, forgetting a law, and returned to the inn and my peers when he put me out. It was the fifth month in my fourteenth year when Vaan locked me out for the longest time: a full month. It was during that time that a series of…events occurred."

Rina seemed engrossed in his words, though it could well have been her delirium.

"What events?"

"Duke Bayard's daughter, Abaca, had fallen for me. She even hired Maddy as her servant in hopes to win my favor. Although my peers swore that she was a catch, I was not so convinced. She was the Duke's child, perhaps, but she was more daughter to the harlot that bore her. When she made the grand proclamation to me that it should be my honor to marry her, I laughed in her face. All the world's diamonds could not make me love that spoiled girl. However, arrogance made me forget her influence in

Alore. I was too foolish to know her tears would make me the Duke's most despised subject.

"It wasn't long after that that I met Sh'ka. She had everything Abaca lacked: grace, poise, mystery, beauty. Being young, I did not realize how effortlessly she seduced me. One kiss became many, and before long I had convinced myself that I…loved her."

Silas stared into the flames as they slithered along the woody vines, leaves already crumbling to ash.

"I was naïve, as most boys are with their first love. I thought that because she smiled at me, she could be trusted. I showed her what I would show no one else: the flames that leap from my hands."

"No one else had seen?" Rina asked, entranced.

"No," he said. "Not a soul, especially not Vaan. But…"

He found himself staring at his scarred palm, blind to it. Memories played over and over in his mind, each dancing like shadows across his vision. He began to feel ill.

"Silas…"

Rina touched his cheek again, concern in her eyes. Again, he shoved her hand away.

"She betrayed me," he said, forcing each word. "I found her in the town square the next day, a fresh bag of gold at her waist as she shrieked that I had assaulted her with magic. She called me a sorcerer of dark arts, the source of all misfortune in Alore. She shrieked, crying those fake tears, pointing at me as I stared.

"All the town was there, terrified as they saw me. The Protectors descended, six men to one, as if I was no longer human enough to be handled by any fewer. I saw John and Maddy there, Edmund beside them. I screamed for them to help me. They just…*stared* at me, believing her…"

He closed his eyes, as if that would erase the images that haunted his thoughts.

"My fury overwhelmed my fear. All my anger welled in this...scream, that wasn't a scream. It was a howl...a roar, that parted the crowd. The Protectors released me—my clothes singed, their hands burnt beyond recognition. Everyone saw. All my peers, all their mothers and fathers and siblings, stared at me as though I were a monster. Women fainted...children cried, and..."

Silas stared into the fire.

"I escaped into the forest, away from them."

He didn't expect to hear sobs. Yet he was shaken from his own recollection by the sound of them; he looked down to find Rina crying, dampening him with her tears.

"What did I do?" he asked, startled.

She wiped her eyes, choking on a sob.

"I-it's just so...so sad...what happened..."

Silas wasn't one to accept pity, what little there usually was for him. Still, there was something so sincere about her unrestrained weeping – she certainly wasn't pretty as she blubbered, water running from her eyes and nose. Despite himself, he began to smile.

"I'm fine," he said, kind of patting her shoulder. "It's past."

Rina almost smiled, in a delirious way. Her sobs had turned to hiccups.

"Have you...ever had a man?" the youth asked, unpracticed in the art of comfort.

The girl shook her head, hiccupping again.

"No," she murmured, still wiping her eyes. "But everyone thinks I have, just 'cause I work in a tavern..."

This amused him.

"A virgin tavern wench?"

Even she giggled, her spirits lifted.

"Silas…why did you save me from the river?" she asked.

He shrugged, as the question required far more introspection than he was presently ready to give.

"Instinct."

A smile brightened her face, even as she yawned.

"I'm glad," she whispered. "I'm glad…to have someone like you around."

"A beast?" he asked, dryly.

Rina leaned against him, curled like a child.

"A defender," she said.

The dog finally returned to them, settling between Silas and the fire to warm his own pelt. He wanted to kick the selfish pest out of the way; however, Rina had fallen asleep in his arms. To move would be to wake her.

Silas forced himself to be still, for her sake.

He returned her clothes to her when she awoke, now dried by the fire. They didn't speak as she dressed. He wondered if she remembered what occurred in her delirium, but did not ask, half-afraid that that would spark the recollection.

The youth distracted himself by tossing more vines onto the dying fire, then proceeding to shine his sword with the ragged tunic. The wind outside howled in their silence.

Suddenly, the mangy dog rushed to the mouth of the cave, barking at the wind.

"Stupid mutt," Silas grumbled.

He pulled on his tunic, re-sheathing his sword. In the corner of his eye, he saw Rina examining her curved dagger, running her fingers over crevices in the hilt. She didn't notice the dog's panic until he rushed into the snow, vanishing.

Rina shot to her feet.

"Ride!"

She was at the entry by the time Silas grabbed her arm, jerking her back.

"Don't be a fool," he growled. "That selfish creature never cared about you, don't squander your well-being trying to save him."

She did not listen. His hold was too gentle; she broke free, disappearing into the roaring winds.

Furious, Silas pursued.

He didn't feel the snow melting about him as he ran, too focused on pushing forward, keeping the girl in his sights. He grasped her wrist the moment she stopped, again jerking her backwards.

"You stupid girl!"

But she was as frozen as the world around them, staring at a gruesome sight.

Silas smelt the blood before he saw it, its stain spreading beneath a wolf's black paws. It dripped from the pelt of a mangy gray dog, whose neck was broken between the beast's mighty jaws.

"Rina, come," Silas urged, his grip growing tighter. "Wolves don't travel alone."

At last, the spell was broken. Rina turned to escape with him, clutching his hand in her panic. However, her hesitation had sealed their fate. Snarling wolves encircled them – vengeful ghosts, snarling in twilight.

Rina drew her weapon as he drew his, though he could feel her trembling beside him.

"I'm sorry," she whispered.

The creatures attacked.

Silas killed three before another gust blinded him. He swung at nothing as another beast attacked, its great teeth shredding his arm. The creature howled when Silas slit its belly, its guts slop upon the ice. The youth turned to see Rina fall, a gray wolf upon her back, its teeth sunk into her shoulder. With a slice, its jaw disengaged, its head rolling aside.

"Get up," he snapped, ire masking concern. "*Up!*"

Rina was still, her face in the snow.

Another snarl turned him from her body. The last two wolves advanced towards him, mindless bloodlust driving their step.

Snatching Rina's dagger from her hand, he hurled it into one beast's skull, watching it collapse as blood leaked down its eyes. A sweep of Edmund's sword, and the second creature bled from a half-severed neck.

Silas breathed hard, hard as he collapsed to his knees. His heart was pounding, pounding, pounding in his ears. He thought it was the heat of the battle still driving him. However, the pounding grew more and more severe, until he could feel his blood creep with every pump of his heart.

The girl.

He smelt her blood.

The youth stumbled towards her, barely able to hold himself upright. He turned her over, finding her shirt torn, her shoulder ripped and red. There was no trace of blood left in her face.

He lifted her into his arms, as his own body began to shake. All he could feel was pounding, pounding in his veins.

As he rose, he saw one lone wolf standing before him, once hidden by the swirling wind. He was very large and very old, with eyes that held no color. He made not a move, not a sound. Then, without a speck of blood upon his paw, he left in silence.

Silas could not enjoy relief, for his throbbing had become agony. It was the pain of Argot upon him again, poison creeping in his veins, black veins, to his ring.

That curse.

He slung Rina over his shoulder to collect their weapons, telling himself he felt nothing. That was a lie – the tremors in his hand were so strong he could barely sheath his sword.

Your curse.

He soon held Rina in his arms again, her dagger returned to her belt by painstaking effort. It was all he could do to stand again, to move forward.

Your demise.

The scent of her blood still filled his senses, urging him through the pounding anguish, pounding, beating.

A light in the distance, brighter than the dimming sun. Hope.

He adjusted his step for his tilting vision, step by step. Breath by breath.

A house, a cottage, in the snow. A light in the window.

Silas collapsed on the doorstep.

Chapter XVII

*H*er shoulder ached.

Rina stirred when she felt it, that terrible stinging far stronger than her peaceful dream. She awoke to a dark room, candlelight shifting shadows on the walls.

"Awake already?"

The woman's voice took her by surprise, its elderly warble unfamiliar to her ears. As Rina's eyes adjusted to the shadows, she saw an old woman hunched over her – wispy hair asunder, age etched into her face like rings in a stump. The girl stiffened, frightened.

"Calm, child," said the old woman. "I fixed you up. You're lucky you're not as bad-off as that friend of yours."

Suddenly, she realized why she felt so alone.

"Where's Silas?" she asked.

"Interesting name for a boy, Silas…"

Rina tried to get up, but was forced to hold her shoulder as pain sprung from it anew. The woman sneered with disapproval.

"Don't move so fast, girl! You'll rip those stitches right out. Wolf gnawed you down to bone, he did…"

The girl forced herself to breathe, hoping the pain would lessen with stillness.

"Who are you?" she asked, her voice weak.

"Pem," the woman replied. "I usually take care of gruff old diamond traders on their way to Citris – was expecting a few tomorrow morning, but I expect that storm has them all cold and horizontal. You're one lucky girl to have stumbled onto my doorstep."

Indeed, Rina was lucky to have survived that day; however, concern for another made her forget gratitude.

"Where is Silas?" she asked again, trying not to panic.

The old woman moved from her bedside, gesturing her forward.

"Come—*slowly*," she ordered.

Pem led her down a short, dark hallway, so dim that Rina had to keep a hand upon the wall to prevent herself from stumbling. The woman pushed open a door, which creaked on ancient hinges.

"I suggest you say your goodbyes," she said.

Rina saw Silas laid upon a dusty cot. His arm was bound, the bandages now as stained by blood as the rest of his clothing. His skin had lost its chestnut hue, now pale and sickly; his hair was slicked across his brow, dampened by sweat. It was heartbreaking for her to see that powerful youth so ill, trembling upon the sheets.

In silence, Rina knelt at his bedside. She grasped his scarred hand, finding it cold. The inviting warmth of his body was now a hazy memory.

I'm so sorry…

She felt his ring against her palm, colder than his skin. The single petal was gone from it now. It was very gold against his flesh, a stark contrast to his black veins. Its gleam mocked her now, too beautiful on this tragic day.

Slowly, she removed it from his finger. Behind it was a pale ring of flesh that was stranger to both sun and air, whiter than even her own hand.

"Come, child," Pem said, gesturing to her from the doorway. "It's time to change your dressings."

Rina nodded, feeling no joy. She stood, reluctantly releasing his hand.

Goodbye.

A dream.

It was 646 I.R., the summer light leaking in through Vaan's boarded windows. Silas sat in that stiff oak chair at the ex-Commander's desk, books open and strewn across the varnished surface. It was a familiar memory – yet, the books were not. They were bound in silk, their page-edges painted with gold.

Silas heard the pacing of his adoptive father behind him, boots falling heavy against the wood floor.

"Tell me what you know of Prince Asyrias," said the man.

The boy stared at an open page, finding the words meant nothing to him. He recited from memory.

"Prince Asyrias, son of King Cedric and the foreign Princess Miyuki Shioya, now Morana Xavier. Born 8th day of 12th Month, 636 I.R. Succumbed to a fever on the 7th day of 12th Month, 644 I.R."

"Are you so certain?" Vaan asked.

"Yes."

Suddenly, the man snatched his wrist, dragging him up so fast his chair toppled over.

"Liar."

Had Silas been his natural self, he would not have been so afraid. But he was only a child, and a small one; his neck hurt to look into the Commander's face, to see a soldier's intense gaze. Silas was afraid.

"I'm not!" he pleaded.

Giovanni began to laugh his mocking laugh.

"Lying won't get you anywhere in this life, my boy."

The man began to drag him mercilessly towards the door, his grip growing ever tighter.

"Why should I know anything else about him?!" the boy cried, trying to fight Vaan's grasp. "The porker is dead! Dead dead dead!"

A tinkling melody began to tangle with Vaan's laughter. The mechanical sound was haunting, warped, yet too familiar to the boy who listened.

*"Let me go, Vaan!" he cried, panicked. "Please, let me **go**!'*

Giovanni tossed him into the street – the child tumbled, landing in the poison flowers that blossomed between the cobblestones. The door slammed shut behind Silas, as the tinkling melody overcame his senses.

A woman's voice gave meaning to the song.

Oh my pretty little son,

Close your eyes in gentle sleep

Feel my hand upon your throat

Pressing down until you sigh

My lovely little boy

My cursed little toy

The world was dark, too bleak for the child. Helpless, alone, he curled up and began to cry.

Suddenly, there was a warm hand upon his head. Silas looked up, seeing a man standing over him. He was tall and pale, with a smooth face and warm, inviting eyes. Black was his garb: black tunic, black gloves, a black hood upon his black cloak. He seemed little more than a shadow, standing in the boy's path.

The man extended one hand towards Silas, his emerald eyes agleam.

"Come home," he said.

Everything faded.

Rina sat upon the bed she had woken in, her back against the wall. She held her bandaged shoulder as it throbbed, while she listened to the wind wail outside. All her tears were spent, dried upon her cheek and her borrowed dress. Pem had not asked about her bind, or her trousers, or the X carved into her arm. The woman had been kind enough to allow her peace.

A fire flickered in the fireplace, dimming. All the candles had been burnt to wax. She had wasted their light on wandering thoughts, and sobs.

Where were the men in her life?

Her best friend Alastor, who had shared a room with her since childhood, had turned his back on her in her time of need. It might as well have been he who carved the traitor's mark into her flesh.

Her betrothed, Kaish, had watched her fall into the Alize River. He thought she was dead. Though she wore his bracelet even now, she knew she was clinging to a fantasy. The Talonian was far away; she would never see his smile again.

Now, Silas was slipping away. Silas, twice her savior, now lay dying in a room down the hall.

Rina had to let them go. If she wanted to survive this day, she had to live without thoughts of them.

Why?

What reason was there to wait out the storm, to continue to Joanissia? There was nothing for her there. All its legendary beauty could not bury her regret.

The old hinges creaked as Pem entered the room, carrying an icy cup.

"Drink up," she said. "Try to relax. Things will get better."

Rina sipped the water, feelings its chill as it trickled down her throat. She could say nothing.

The woman sighed, dragging a rickety chair towards her bedside.

"I know a place you can start over," she said, taking the cup when it was drained. "It'll make you forget all about this day."

Rina nodded, halfheartedly intrigued. However, as she closed her eyes in exhaustion, the door creaked open. She opened her eyes to see Silas standing in the entryway, holding his bandaged arm. The color had returned to his skin; his eyes were vibrant, like the ruins' stained glass. He looked perplexed.

"Where's my ring?" he asked.

Tears streaked her face anew. Rina rushed to him, slamming against his chest as she wrapped him in her arms, squeezing him tight. She laughed as much as she cried.

"I was so scared," she whispered.

Silas stiffened at first, as she expected him to. However, soon, he accepted her into his strong arms.

"You're…all right, then?" he asked.

She had never been so happy to cry.

Part III:
Trust

2nd Month, 651 I.R.

A reflection on my tenth year:

I played my first chess game with Vaan on the 5th day of 7th Month, 647 I.R. Naïve, I had begged him to teach me the game for months; however, he always told me that my mind wasn't yet trained to handle that sort of logic. I insisted and insisted until he gave in – of course, appeasement came at a price. He would teach me only if I gathered my pieces on my own.

Everyone laughed at me when I told them my quest. The notion of gathering together "throwaway chess pieces" – if such things even existed – was absurd. Yet, I did just that. I asked court servants if the Duke had retired old sets, asked the woodsmith if I could whittle shapes from his leftover blocks, even knocked on the doors of well-to-do merchants to see if any had pity for my plight. A longshoreman gave me a knight at the docks when I asked, and when I had made two rooks and a pawn of my own, John gave me my king.

I painted them all black and brought them to Vaan. He would be impressed, I thought. He wasn't. He laughed at my mismatched pieces and told me that gathering them had taken much too long. Still, I got my wish. He beat me in the game twice that night, and as punishment, sent me to bed without dinner.

I blamed my imperfect pieces, then, for my loss. I was too young to realize that the shape of my pawns made no difference. Though they were not as refined, they served the same function as my opponent's. Once the mind that guided them had grown in intellect, my mismatched pieces were a first-rate army. I repaid Vaan for my losses a hundred times over.

Skill will triumph over beauty. That is a lesson I taught myself.

Chapter XVIII

*I*t was a week before the King could be buried. Although all agreed that his deep wounds meant his death, the man hired to prepare the body insisted that Attlas Xavier was, in fact, breathing. He was not *alive* is any natural sense, for his heart had indeed stopped; yet the servant swore for seven days that he could not bury the King in good conscience, for the sound of Attlas' breath would haunt him.

However, this claim ceased by the end of that week. Attlas' body was dressed for death, and laid in the earth beside Asyrias and his father, while the Council and his widow watched in silence. With this, the family cemetery was complete.

A Council meeting was scheduled for the day after the burial, to make up for lost time. Twyla was escorted to the Queen's chamber early that morning to aid in preparing her for the assembly: Morana would have to look her best to appear before the Council.

"No no, not that necklace," the Queen snapped, pushing yet another string of diamonds back into her handmaid's hands. "Choose another."

Twyla was accustomed to her mistress' outbursts. Unfazed, she placed the jewels in her jewelry box and returned with a necklace of rubies.

"It is a shame, the tragedies that this palace has suffered," said the servant. "To think I once thought we would now be celebrating the marriage of your Asyrias to the Rionan Princess."

"That girl was a terror," Morana spat. "Perfect little Princess Natasia, always screeching her unwanted opinions in unwilling ears."

Twyla began pinning the Queen's raven locks into a regal twist upon her neck.

"Whatever became of her?" she asked.

"We received a letter from the Czar of Riona not three years ago. He said she was assaulted by a Demon and ran away from home."

Though her servant was shocked, Morana continued to paint her lips with the juice of a crimson fruit, unaffected.

"Riona is a dangerous place," Twyla remarked. "Were there not so many stories of those blood-sucking creatures wreaking havoc in that icy land, I would not believe their existence."

Morana scoffed.

"Stories of men bleeding women dry? One doesn't need to be 'Demon' to commit such an act," said the Queen.

"But the magic that could create such creatures—"

"Magic is nothing to be feared, Twyla," the woman replied, continuing to stain her lips with red. "The majority is exaggerated superstition. Everyone who's ever claimed to have seen it has always heard the story from someone else – there's nothing more dangerous than a trail of second-hand information."

"True, Your Majesty."

But Morana didn't know what Twyla had seen in Kyro. The Catsavion Priests that controlled her homeland had made it their quest to eradicate all such 'superstition' from the world. While she had been enslaved by them, she had seen the Priests imprison fire-breathers, illusionists, and telekinetics alike. She had seen the things such people had done during imprisonment, such unimaginable things. Even after Giovanni had taken her from their temple, she had witnessed Baldric Alexander, one of Rank 1's most talented soldiers, using sorcery to create rock charms that warded off misfortune. If Twyla knew anything with certainty, it was that magic was far more than hearsay.

"That hooded man who came to the Autumn Ball those years ago spoke like a Rionan," Twyla remarked, slipping the last diamond pin into her mistress' locks. "Do you believe he was a Demon?"

At once, the Queen grew very cold and still. Her sapphire eyes hardened to ice, staring deeply into their own reflection.

"He's no Demon," she spat. "The word is too kind for a creature like him."

There was a knock on the door before the guard entered, his gaze cast respectfully to the floor.

"The Council is gathered and ready to see you, Your Highness."

Morana nodded, calmly rising to her feet.

"Then let us depart."

The Council never varied in its seating. The six Councilmen always placed themselves the same way at the curved table: the twin lawmakers Reade and Reginald, so old now that their silvery locks were beginning to fall out, seated themselves at opposite ends of the table; Lesser Advisor Antonio Carrera sat to mirror the empty seat beside Reginald, where gentle-eyed Saito would sit upon his return. Closest to the royal seats were the Grand Advisor Raoul Markovich, who sat very upright in his seat, and the

Envoy of the People Gabriel Ayres, whose wise eyes did not waver from his new Queen.

Morana took Attlas' place in the chair opposite the Council, because of the circumstances. Although a woman had never before occupied that seat, she was their monarch now, and that was her rightful place. However, the Queen's seat beside her was not empty. Her sister, now-Princess Azalea, retained her position. The woman had put no effort into her own appearance: her face was pale as death, narrow eyes as black as her gown. She looked at nothing, saw nothing; however, her gaze lingered on the empty seat across the curved table.

Twyla took her place by the entrance to the servants' hall, in order to observe. She glimpsed the Captain of the Guard positioning himself by the entryway before he grew tense again, not to move until commanded. At last, the Council could begin.

Gabriel's commanding voice stilled the room.

"We have one very clear problem, Morana," he said, his hawk's stare set on her. "An Xavier must have your seat, and the last of them has died."

"I do not see why it must be an Xavier," the woman replied. "Any boy with half a brain can be trained to be a King."

"What of the Alexanders?" Reginald piped, his screeching voice distracting from the Queen's words. "Weren't they descendents of Princess Aurora Xavier?"

His brother scowled from across the table, barely looking up from his scroll and the quill that furiously scratched upon it.

"Idiot," Reade spat. "The Alexanders were evicted from their own palace over sixty years ago. Bet they're all feeding trees by now…"

It was the young Antonio who cut in, such hope in his dark eyes.

"They were overthrown, but not killed. They've been living in hiding. Baldric said he was raised by Alexanders, though they may have been descendents of Draco and Carmen – that's where he got his name, you see. His adoptive parents had a little girl, he said: Isabella, who wasn't much younger than Baldric himself."

This caught even the Queen's interest; Twyla, however, found herself quite shaken. Antonio had known this fact all these years, yet had never said a word of it to the handmaid, who considered him a dear friend. She couldn't help but wonder what else her fellow Kyron had kept to himself.

"That is quite a revelation," said Gabriel. "Has Duke Baldric kept in contact with his adoptive family?"

Antonio's bright look fell. He sharply turned away, pushing his fingers through his short, dark locks. Twyla recognized this nervous habit.

"He said he wasn't allowed to disclose their location," he replied. "You can contact him, but I do not think he will talk."

The room lapsed back into silence, customarily talkative men quieted by grief. Reade's quill continued to scratch against the open scroll, recording each moment of the cumbersome muteness.

It was the philosopher's refined voice that jarred them from their stupor.

"Does anyone else find it peculiar that our three Kings all died in such strange ways? That Raphael choked on a bone in his meat not three months after Cedric's return from the war; that Cedric was murdered by his mistress, who showed only adoration towards him? And now Attlas, barely a man, who was never without a smile—"

"Inner turmoil is rarely expressed openly, Raoul," said the Queen. "Perhaps his secret burdens proved to be too much for him."

Twyla saw the others' reluctance written on their faces, for they were too contemplative a group to readily accept this explanation; however, it was then the entry doors swung open, distracting them from disbelief. The handmaid looked up to see Tahn, the errand boy, waving a letter over his head.

"I have a very urgent message from Duke Baldric of Lucadia, Your Highness," he announced. "This is the second one this week—"

"Ignore it," said Morana. "I'm certain it's the same rubbish as the last one. Return to your duties."

Twyla recognized the look of a servant forced to swallow his tongue. Tahn bowed low, crinkling the letter in his hands.

"Yes, Your Majesty."

He departed without a fuss, the swinging doors sweeping away his trail. No sooner had the doors closed than they were pushed open again, this time by a guard. The man said something to Art, who became more rigid in his Captain's armor. As the guard left, Art bowed to the Council.

"Someone has entered the castle through an unauthorized entry," he said. "I must investigate."

Morana gave a nod of dismissal.

"Do as you must," she said.

The Captain's departure gave Twyla an unusual feeling of foreboding, unshaken even by Gabriel's calm words.

"The problem remains: we need a male heir to prepare for the throne. If an Alexander absolutely cannot be located, we must choose the son of a Baron or a Duke."

"I do not see why we're in such a hurry to find a Prince," said Morana. "I know perfectly well how to rule alone."

"The Larascan people will not tolerate a ruling Queen for long, no matter how capable a ruler you may be," Gabriel replied. "Women are not permitted to hold weapons, let alone command Ranks. Riots will overwhelm the land."

The argument continued, Morana growing more and more tense with anger. Her handmaid tried to ignore the churning in her gut, praying that her mistress would remember how to control her disagreeable nature. However, the discourse ended as the doors creaked open once again.

"What's with all these bloody interruptions?!" Reginald cried.

The man in the entryway was too familiar, so familiar that the sight of him choked Twyla with memories. She knew that clever gleam in the man's emerald eyes, that smirk raising the tips of his dark mustache. His hair was short now, brushed with such care that it distracted from his tattered clothing. Ten years had passed since Giovanni's disappearance, when the man who had saved her from Kyro vanished without a word. Yet, his voice was entirely unchanged.

"It's always so cold inside the castle," he said, sighing lugubriously as he rubbed his arms. "If only that warm air outside could come past the gates…"

All the Councilmen stood, as shocked as Twyla herself.

"Commander Giovanni?!" Reade exclaimed.

"I thought you had been ripped apart by bears, you little pest!" his brother cried.

Indeed, each Councilmen seemed similarly unsettled by the ex-Commander's presence. Like wolves of a different pack, they regarded the newcomer with unease, trying to determine what had brought the loner into their midst. Even the Princess appeared unnerved, though she had only been a child when he had last been in the castle. Morana herself seemed more then unnerved—she was furious.

"Get out!" she warned. "Cedric's not here to tolerate you anymore! I want you OUT of my SIGHT!"

However, she was silenced by a gesture of Gabriel's hand.

"No matter what your personal feelings towards this man may be, he is an esteemed Commander with an honorable discharge," he said. "He has earned the utmost respect."

Moved by the most begrudging reluctance, all but Antonio returned to their seats. The Kyron Councilman who stood had been the only one to show no disdain towards the ex-Commander's presence; in fact, he regarded him with an elated smile.

"Have you any news of Baldric?" he asked. "Is he well? His daughters?"

Giovanni shook his heard, breathing a great sigh of what might have been disappointment.

"Baldric and I had a terrible falling out. I fear he may assault me if we ever meet again."

Disappointed, Antonio took his seat.

Twyla watched in awe as Giovanni began to circle the Council, that familiar smile curling his lips. Her heart began to pound, her tongue too lame to spare a word for his attention.

"If you ask me," he began, "I believe we should allow our competent Queen to continue her rule. However, it is advisable that she choose a pawn to crown her Prince – any half-brained boy will do, as she so eloquently put it. A questionable lineage can be changed with little more than an announcement and a stroke of a quill. In the meantime, I suggest a public execution to entertain the masses. Public executions always take the people's minds off their troubles – surely you remember the turn-out for Dayu's burning?"

He chuckled, oblivious to the Queen's mortified stare.

"Also, I suggest you hold the Winter Ball on schedule: let all things proceed naturally, as though nothing has changed. That is the key to smoothing over tragedy."

Suddenly, the Captain of the Guard burst through the entryway. He seemed at first shocked by Giovanni's presence, then threatened. Yet, the ex-Commander's prideful smirk somehow deterred any form of interrogation. Art ignored him, bowing low towards the members of the Council.

"Rank 12 has returned. Lesser Advisor Saito accompanies them."

Visible relief eased them all – especially Azalea, whose miserable gaze was lit with the sound of Saito's name.

"The meeting can be postponed," said Gabriel, rising to his feet. "Morana, see to your...pet project."

The Queen stood as well, smiling despite even Giovanni's presence.

"Certainly," she replied.

The Councilmen began to file out the main entry. Reade and Reginald argued loudly as they went, Reade shuffling his scrolls as he kicked open the door, while Gabriel and Raoul did their best to press past them. Twyla wanted desperately to confront Giovanni about his disappearance; however, the sight of the Princess fleeing to the servants' doorway stole her attention.

"Azalea, where are you going?" she asked.

The girl answered her in sobs, the door half-open.

"I can't...I just can't see him..."

She fled, the door swinging shut behind her. The handmaid's instinct was to follow, but was stopped by a calloused hand upon her wrist. Against her will she was turned, familiar lips meeting hers in a long kiss.

When they parted, Giovanni smiled down at her.

"You want answers," he assumed.

Twyla stiffened, remembering her anger.

"You didn't even say goodbye!"

"My dear, it was you who sent me off."

Bewildered, she stared challengingly into his calm visage. He remained unaffected. As she watched, he withdrew a small, weathered book from a bag slung at his side. He pressed this book into her hand.

"This is Reja's journal," he said. "It documents every day of his life since you gave him to me, until around three years ago. I can summarize the details of that recent time period in my own words, once you've read his."

Her hands shook as she stared at the journal.

"Reja is dead," she whispered.

"Quite the contrary, my dear."

He kissed her again, stealing her breath from her.

"I will explain everything, once you know his story."

Giovanni released her then, pushing open the door to the servant's hall.

"Ah, and before you hate me…"

He flashed another of his perfect smiles.

"I must say that you are as beautiful now as you were the day I stole you."

And then, he was gone.

Twyla was alone in the Council room now, all but abandoned. Her body still trembling with shock, she took Raoul's seat, opening the journal to its first page.

She recognized Reja's handwriting in a moment: perfectly formed, perfectly dotted 'i's.' Yet, that lost boy had been taught to call himself by a different name.

Silas.

In the first entry, her Reja had become Silas. And as the days went by, the handwriting grew less and less recognizable. It became coarser, refinement giving way to swiftness and frustration. Page by page, she witnessed his transformation.

Rank 12 arrived in Joanissia at sundown. The Stags had grown quiet since Fritz's passing, their laughter buried with his body. They were impassive to even the snowy splendor of the Noble Square, cold even to the unusual warmth of the capital's air. Their silence caused Saito great pain; yet, what wrung his heart most was the state that Kaish had fallen into. Saito's young friend had grown pale and thin, eyes so sunken that his very gaze was cast in shadow. The youth no longer fought Lance when the General came to bind his wrists. Kaish just stood still, staring at the crooked cross carved into his hand.

Saito could not look upon Kaish as a guard led him down the castle halls. Lance had dragged him to the front of their lines, and jerked him along as though he were cattle. The Talonian didn't resist. Although it was against Saito's nature to challenge authority, seeing this cruelty made him want to drag his General to the dungeons.

An old guard with a limp led them to the throne room, never quite turning to see the miserable troupe. No sooner had he parted the grand doors than he abandoned them with their Queen.

Morana was seated in the King's throne, the distinctive Xavier crown atop her head: seven carved dragons were its peaks, precious gems glistening in their bellies. Beside the Queen was the Captain of the Guard, a man resembling Lance in his physique. However, there was strength to his upright stature that the sour General could not imitate.

The Queen regarded Saito first, beckoning him forward with a slight nod.

"Good to see you survived," she said.

Though they were comforting words, they were more chilling than anything Saito had heard before.

He bowed to her properly.

"The journey was difficult, but we are well."

She nodded, but he knew she had not heard him.

"The jewels?" she asked.

At once, misery turned to tension. Saito himself grew uncomfortable, his instinct to step further away from the throne. The General released Kaish's rope to come forward, though not by bravery—he was urged by the others' forceful stares.

"You see, Y-your Majesty," he stammered, "there was a mishap in the forest…"

The sallow soldier Valten came forward, pressing the wooden box into Saito's hands. Immediately, Morana's impatience turned on her advisor.

"Well?" she snapped. "Open it."

Saito sensed what the consequences would be if he obeyed. He sensed the coming tragedy, and yet, he could not bring himself to ignore an order. As the others averted their eyes, he revealed the box's contents. There, laid upon a bed of silk, was one diamond, still intact—and beside it, a pile of black shards.

Morana was ominously quiet. She eased her pale hand into the box, and let the shards slip through her fingers.

"You idiots," she snarled, beginning to shake with rage. "This is glass. *Glass*, you idiots!"

She turned the General's face with a strike.

"Who's responsible for this? WHO?!"

All were silent. Lance touched his reddening cheek, struck dumb. Even Art, usually so expressionless, showed disbelief.

It was Alastor's voice that next came forward.

"The Talonian broke it," he said. "That's why he's roped now. Maybe he switched the diamond with the glass one to begin with."

Saito stared at him, as sickened as the rest of the Rank. Yet, relief eased the lines on Lance's face, his sneer stretching to a smile.

"Is this true, General?" Morana asked, her dangerous stare set upon the young man who had betrayed his comrade.

"Yes, my Queen," Lance said, bowing low. "In an attempt to steal food from our reserves, the Stag Kairos shattered the gem upon a rock. He has been bound ever since."

The Queen approached Kaish, taking one step off the raised platform and onto the crimson rug. Saito's gut tightened when he saw the youth's vacant stare, still unchanged.

He's resigned himself.

Nothing could be done.

"Art, I want this Stag imprisoned," ordered the Queen.

The Captain bowed his head.

"As you wish."

Art's guards came forward with shackles in their hands, pushing past the speechless Stags and soldiers. At last, Saito knew fear. He forgot himself and stepped forward, shaken by panic.

"The diamond was clearly false to begin with," he pleaded. "Your Majesty, he deserves a lashing, not imprisonment!"

"A criminal of any race deserves punishment," she replied, returning to her throne. "You make excuses for him because he is a fellow outsider. I will not."

Kaish was taken away, never fighting. He looked behind him only once, meeting Saito's gaze. Reflected in those pale orbs, Saito saw himself: the bystander. The traitor.

"Your Rank is dismissed, General," said Morana.

Lance bowed deeply enough to hide his grin. However, Alastor, who did not know to bow, could not conceal his deepening smirk. Saito was horrified, so repulsed by the sight that he drew back. He did not watch their departure, erasing each soldier, each Stag from his mind as they passed through those heavy doors. Saito forgot them all, all except two.

"Tell me, Saito: who was that blond youth with the Stags?" Morana asked, settling back against the throne with a pensive look.

Saito was forced to swallow his sensibility.

"Alastor of Lucadia," he said. "A selfish, brainless terror."

The Queen seemed only pleased by this revelation. Slowly, she removed the Xavier crown from her head, examining its gems.

"Indeed…"

With a wave, she again gestured the Captain forward.

"See to it that Lesser Advisor Saito is settled."

Art bowed.

"Yes, my Queen."

Saito had planned many things to say to Morana, after such a long absence. However, one glimpse of her cool gaze, her absent smile, proved to him that all his planning had been wasted.

"Tell Azalea I am sorry for her loss," he said.

The Queen did not look to him.

"No, you're not."

Morana would say no more, not to him. She examined the Xavier crown in silence as the Lesser Advisor was escorted back to his permanent chambers, far away from her.

Chapter XIX

*I*t was nighttime, the moon high outside Reja's window. He liked to stand on his bed to press his hands against the glass, feeling how the air outside had warmed it. The child didn't know what it was like to be outside, to feel that air against his pale skin—pale as the moon he watched. Sometimes, he would press his face against the glass, pretending he could push through it to the outside world.

He sat on his bed properly when the door creaked open, his father entering with a tired smile on his face. Reja envied the slight color his father had developed from the touch of sunlight from his travels. It made him more handsome.

"Will Mama see me tonight?" Reja asked, almost hopeful.

The man shook his head, slowly shedding his cloak.

"No, Reja," he said, sitting upon his bed. "But I promise, I will try to convince her to come tomorrow."

By now, the child was old enough to understand what his father really meant: not today, not ever. Yet, he did sense his mother near. He could feel her outside his doorway, pressed against the wall. She was there often, like a shadow at the doors; she had never once entered his room.

"Papa, why don't you call me what Mama calls me?" the boy asked.

The man kissed his forehead, his gentle hand guiding the boy to lie down.

"Your given name was not my choice," his father explained. "I call you Reja because it means 'good fortune,' for that is what you are to me."

This made the child smile, though it gave way to a wide yawn. His father chuckled with amusement.

"I have a gift for you," he said.

Reja watched curiously as his father pulled a round, metal box from his deep pocket. Its appeal was in its understated embellishment, with vines carved into its sides, and a rose-shaped handle atop its silver lid.

"What is it?" Reja asked.

"One of Clarke Temlar's inventions," the man replied. "He said it's been in his shop for months, but he couldn't bear to give it to anyone but you."

The boy remembered Sir Temlar's description of his shop: the strange objects littering dusty tables, contraptions with numbered faces filling the room with a mechanical tick:

'Tick tock. Tick tock.'

"What does it do?" the child asked, his heart pattering with innocent excitement.

His father smiled, amused by his enthusiasm. He opened the box in silence, revealing a bright mirror beneath the lid, and a small, carved flower upon a turning table. As the flower turned, a tinkling melody began to play, entrancing Reja with its tender sound.

"This is your music box," the man said, placing it on Reja's windowsill. "Do you like the song it plays?"

Reja nodded, beginning to smile.

"Then it is my gift to you," said his father. "Now every day that I must be away, you can open this music box and remember I am with you."

This soothed his child. Content, Reja closed his eyes, allowing the sound to envelop his senses. Before long, his father tucked him beneath warm blankets.

"Sleep well, my son."

With a kiss, his father left him. The child curled up in his blankets, peeking through half-open lids to the window. The turning blossom was a silhouette against the moon, the sight so peaceful, so beautiful to the sheltered child.

However, a shadowy figure haunted the mirror behind the flower. Reja glimpsed his mother's raven locks in the doorway, shivered at the flash of her sapphire gaze. Her soft voice sang as the flower turned.

Every time I see you hatred for you only grows

Lovely boy

I never wanted you to be

So close your eyes in sleep.

Disappear, my little spawn.

My lovely little boy.

Silas awoke suddenly, choking on the winter air. Sunlight streamed through the windows, small flecks of dust drifting in its rays. He felt displaced, as though he were stranger to his own flesh.

The youth raised his hand to the light, seeing the rays against his dark skin. He clenched a fist to see his veins rise, then fall with its release.

The hand belonged to him, yet seemed no more than an apparition. It was the pale hands of his dream that now haunted him.

A dream?

The youth had had many unusual dreams since he had awoken in Pem's home. While their healing injuries bound them to her care, strange images had begun to disturb Silas' waking world. At night, disjointed dreams troubled his sleep – a collection of images that teased his elusive memory, and made his head pound when he awoke. However, none had been so complete as the vision of that gentle man and his music box. Each moment, each sight, seemed too real to be dreamt. No dream could capture such subtle smiles, nor the warmth of human touch.

A memory.

Silas dragged himself from bed and to the oak vanity, splashing his eyes with cool water from the basin. In a cracked mirror, he glimpsed his bedraggled countenance: shadowed eyes, his long hair tangling about his shoulders. He would have to cut it soon. Still, he made no effort to prepare himself for the day. He pulled on his shirt before going out to the kitchen, expecting to see Rina already finishing her mourning gruel.

She wasn't there. Pem was alone in the kitchen, her lined face set in a knotted scowl as she pushed her spoon through a bowl of slop.

"Where's Rina?" Silas demanded.

"Don't you growl at me with that tone," the old woman sneered, "and don't you make that face at my food. I used to run a respectable inn, you know, before that bloody Kyron wall barred out all my customers."

Silas continued to scowl.

"Where *is* she?" he growled.

"If you must know, it's her feminine cycle – now sit down and eat your gruel, boy."

The youth sat begrudgingly at the table, prompting Pem to slop the lumpy mixture into a wooden bowl before him. Silas cringed with disgust.

"When will this 'cycle' be finished?"

"When it's finished, that's when. Now eat! The two of you are skin and bones."

Silas grit his teeth, forcing himself to swallow a spoonful. The consistency was questionable and the general taste was foul, though it varied depending on whether he decided to chew or slurp the concoction. Sill, brown slop was better than nothing at all.

He distracted himself by observing the room. It was homely, comfortable enough. The fire in the stove warmed the air, and sunlight leaked through the cracks in the old walls. He had learned to avoid the light, for cold gusts came with it.

The wrinkled old woman planted her willowy body in a chair by the fire, as was her habit. However, today, there was a book in her hands, bound in fine black leather. The sight took Silas by surprise.

"What is that?" he asked.

"A book, moron," she snapped. "Some old diamond trader left it, and I get bored."

"Who taught you to read?"

She was certainly no noblewoman, nor did he see how such an isolated woman could have found the resources to teach herself.

Pem scowled at him.

"What a condescending question. Who taught you, boy?"

Many others had asked that question, for Giovanni had never needed to teach him literacy. Always, the answer had been the same:

"I don't know."

But as he was about to form these words, a thought made them wither on his lips. He thought of a fair-haired man—he recalled a gray-eyed man with a dry, impatient look, standing beside his own dark-haired father.

"Do not make such faces at him, son," his father had chided. *"He is a revered scholar, a man of sound philosophy. He will make a fine tutor."*

Silas shook his had, forcing himself from this stranger's memory.

"I am not...certain," he said.

Pem grunted, opening her book once again.

"Finish your gruel. Use some snow to clean the bowl when it's gone."

The youth nodded, reluctantly beginning to eat again. For once, he was grateful that the rancid concoction overwhelmed his senses.

It was two nights before Silas found himself at Rina's door. Her absence gnawed at him during that time, until he could take it no more. He had to see her—just for a moment.

Her door seemed heavy, ominously creaking with the slightest pressure. His own hesitancy made him recoil.

What are you afraid of?

The door made him recall another, one much broader and higher. That one creaked behind many boards, and rustled their heavy chains. It had seemed wondrous to his young eyes.

"Why can't I go in there?" he once asked his father.

"One day, you will," the man replied, touching the great lock that sealed the door. *"One day, when you can understand the secrets of this tower."*

Silas placed his hand on Rina's door, trying to bury these disjointed thoughts. As gently as he could, he guided it open.

Before he could see through a crack, he heard her voice.

"Who's there?"

The youth was still, silent. Soon, he heard her soft laughter.

"I thought you might come, Silas."

Caught. He flinched back at first, but remained. He was compelled to stay as he was, in her presence, out of her sight.

After a moment's hesitation, he spoke.

"How are you?"

A pause.

"Better," she said. "But...I miss Ride. I don't like dogs much, but he was sweet to me. It's hard to be without him."

He nodded, though she could not see it. Out of his element, he tried to retreat; however, her voice gave him pause.

"I still have your ring. I promise to give it back to you, as long as you promise not to wear it. It just...gives me a bad feeling."

Her concern startled him. What reason did she have to care whether or not he wore his own ring, cursed though it was? Yet, he found himself nodding, a word of agreement falling from his lips.

"Fine."

It was silent, after this. He stood by the wall, motionless until he heard her soft breath slow. Unable to help himself, he opened the door another click. Through that crack, he glimpsed her dark hair upon her pillow, some locks strewn across her pale cheek. He thought he saw her lips, so pink against her skin.

Silas had seen another girl laid upon her bed in such a way. She had been only a child, her blonde locks spread across her pillow, her cheeks rosy with youth. He had disliked her when she woke, forced to deal with her taunts in her cruel foreign tongue. It was only when she slept in that bed across from him, so peaceful in rest, that he could appreciate her noble beauty.

His head began to throb. Silas closed his eyes tight to right his vision, only wanting to see what was presently before him. He was uneasy, his thoughts out of his control.

He let the door creak closed as he fled, wanting the isolation of his own room.

By the end of the week, Rina was well. Her wounds had healed to scars by now, and she had regained enough energy to travel. However, Pem had no trousers to spare – she said that Rina's hair had grown enough by now to do without them, so there was no point in sewing a pair. Although Rina was wary of becoming a girl again, her hostess gave her no choice.

Rina had forgotten how restrictive a corset could be. She had grown accustomed to breathing in one's absence, and gasped more than she liked as Pem tightened its springs.

"Suits you much better than that feeble boy's costume you had, I'll say…" Pem gave the strings another jerk; Rina choked. "You ready to be a girl again?"

The girl managed a strained smile.

"I'll miss my dagger," she said.

Pem rolled her eyes.

"Being a girl doesn't mean you can't have your dagger, just that no one can see it. As long as it's sheathed, you can shove it down the front of your corset and no one will give a rip."

Rina smiled some, though she didn't consider her advice. As Pem left to find her a dress, the girl stared at herself in the long mirror.

The first thing she noticed was her bosom, which had always been the last to catch her eye before. It seemed very strange on her now—burdensome, distracting. Next were her dark locks, now long enough to curl about her shoulders. They were too brown against her fair skin, overwhelming her face without their tie. Then, there were her eyes—blue. In all their travels, she had never seen another soul with blue eyes. Seeing them now, so very large, so very blue, she felt like a foreigner herself.

Vulnerability began to play with her mind. Instinctively, she covered the X upon her arm, her other hand concealing the scar upon her shoulder. She missed the anonymity of her trousers and her bind, the security of a dagger at her side. Without them, she was soft, doe-eyed: prey.

Pem returned, a leaf-green dress draped across her arms. She gestured for her to come and accept it.

"This was my daughter's, before she ran off with that smooth-talking diamond trader, foolish girl. It's yours – I'd rather not look at it again."

Reluctantly, Rina took the dress.

"Thank you."

She pulled it over her head, beginning the time-consuming task of lacing the front. Pem settled onto the nearby bed, watching for a time. When she grew tired of silence – for she was a more talkative companion than Silas – she got Rina's attention.

"Your friend has decided that you'll go to Citris," she said.

Rina was startled, confused.

"Citris?"

"An underground city with a huge diamond market. The traders usually stop at my place on their way there, since the entrance is close. It's got a passage into the capital, I expect – that's where you're going, isn't it?"

Rina nodded, flustered though she was.

"So we keep going, just like that?"

Pem nodded in return, her old bones creaking as she stood.

"The both of you are fixed up. There's no reason for you to sleep here anymore."

She shuffled over to the door, grumbling something about the state of her walls.

"Be ready quick," she said. "You'll need to get to Citris before that storm blows back."

And then, Rina was alone again.

She finished lacing the dress before glancing in the mirror again, seeing that it suited her. The sleeves covered the telling scars upon her arm and shoulder, and the fabric was thick enough to ward off the elements. The sight wasn't enough to keep her interest. Rina went to the window, staring out over the landscape. Although she was still terrified of heights, she found they weren't so terrifying when glass kept her safe.

Silas was beneath her window, scooping snow into a bucket with his bare hands. He did it hastily, as the ice melted quickly against his palms and dripped back to the ground. When Pem emerged from the door beneath Rina's window, the youth cast her a scowl. The glass distorted the sound of their argument, muffling the youth's snarls and Pem's nagging screech.

The debate ended with Pem snatching the bucket and storming back inside, slamming the door hard enough to shake the house. A mound of snow was loosened from the sloping roof, burying Silas in white ice.

Rina began to laugh. She couldn't stop herself – she laughed and laughed so hard that Silas stopped shaking slush from his hair to look into her window. He glared; yet, the act had lost its venom, and disappeared in the face of her smile.

Breathless with amusement, she pulled the curtains closed. For the first time in a very long while, she felt content in her surroundings. No longer vulnerable, she took the sheathed Akalinian dagger from her vanity and slid it down the front of her corset.

"Hurry yourself, child!" came Pem's shriek.

The young woman grabbed Silas' ring from her dresser, ready to begin again.

Silas waited on the doorstep for the women to emerge, rubbing the white band of flesh that his ring had once bound. Although he wasn't in the best of moods, his sword was at his waist again, and his arm was freed of bandages. He was ready to depart.

A little bird landed at his feet, pecking at a mound of snow. Its feathers were a gleam of yellow, at first – but with a blink, they became brown. Baffled, entranced, Silas held his hand out to the bird.

"Come," he whispered, his own greeting unfamiliar to his ears.

The bird flew away, startled by the sound. With a sigh, he withdrew his palm.

Too gentle a creature for the likes of you.

A soft voice disturbed his thoughts.

"Hey."

Suddenly, Rina was beside him, her soft fingers pressing cool metal into his hand.

"Remember, you promised not to wear it."

Startled, he clutched the ring tightly. It was by accident that he met her gaze; and yet, he could not look away.

He had never seen such a girl. Her blue eyes were so bright, her skin a warm color against the frozen landscape. Her body curved with regal elegance, more tempting than even Sh'ka's form. How had he traveled with her all this time, and never seen her? Never see through that futile disguise?

The spell was broken when Pem pushed them apart, tossing Rina a warm blanket as she adjusted her own fur jacket.

"Come along, you two. I refuse to be snowed out of my house for you."

Rina followed after her, gone too quickly. Silas did not realize how quickly he stood in pursuit.

Foolish. She is no different than before.

That was what he tried to believe. However, he could not dwell too long on his own delicate thoughts, knowing how little it took for them to deteriorate.

Chapter XX

No one would visit the Royal Graveyard. It was an eerie place: its air was too still, not a whisper to haunt the environment. There, in the vast, snowy landscape behind Joanissia castle, the flowers never died. Frost preserved the red blossoms until the sun returned to thaw them; the trees' leaves could not be coaxed to fall, not even by the capital's warm winds. The graveyard, like the rest of Joanissia, was frozen in a perpetual state of existence—never changing. Snow came, snow thawed, and the world stood still.

Although Morana was as wary of this place as her subjects, she had a duty here. As night fell, she descended the castle steps to the snow-covered cemetery. Joanissia's unusual warmth greeted her at the base, bringing her relief from the castle's frozen air. Even so, she did not shed her black cloak.

She walked along the tombstones of Xaviers' past, noticing the similarity of their gray faces. Not one of them prayed for the deceased to 'Rest in Peace.'

The Queen touched her husband's grave as she passed, drawn to it. The snow had not settled into the dragons etched into its surface, who curled like guardians around the solemn epitaph:

Here lies King Cedric Raphael Xavier

Champion of Peace, Honor, and Love

(611 I.R. – 648 I.R.)

Beside his grave was a smaller one, its gray stone faded by time, as pale as the child buried there.

Prince Asyrias Xavier

A loving and brilliant son.

May he feel heaven's warmth.

(636 I.R. – 644 I.R.)

Morana had seen Cedric himself carving this epitaph, his hand still while the rest of him shook. Kings did not usually do a servant's task, but he would not let anyone else touch his son's stone. His devotion was almost admirable.

At last, she came to Raphael's grave. It stood the tallest of the royal headstones, its stone face shadowed by the spindly branches of an old tree. The Xaviers' insignia was carved beneath his name: the dragon curled to the sky, lines curving from its body like veins. Its epitaph was simple:

King Raphael Fabiyus Xavier

Our Leader

(570 I.R. – 636 I.R.)

The Queen recalled that bitter, scowling man, who had treated her as though she were some exotic pet. His death had been Dayu's greatest gift.

She remembered her task. Smiling, she brushed the snow from the false slab laid upon the ground, already drawing her newly-obtained diamond from her breast. Beneath the slab, she found Dayu's spell, still carved into dark granite.

At once, she remembered her anger towards the arrogant General and his soldiers. Were it not for their inattentiveness, she would have the last pieces of this enchantment. However, the fools had allowed someone to replace the last gem with a counterfeit, adding years of searching to Morana's quest. Lance was fortunate that she was willing to take a Stag's head in place of his own.

Of the three bare symbols, Wrath and Sloth were all she needed. Lust was tucked within her corset; Sloth, being the center, should be placed last. Morana knew this—yet, when she tried to place the new diamond upon the mark of Wrath, a painful shock forced her away. When she tried again, her fingers burned, hissing smoke eating her nails.

With a furious shriek, she slammed the diamond upon Sloth. The gem sighed into its hole, melting, until it too became a part of the stone. She gripped her hair, trying to quell her own anger with slow, methodic breaths. The Queen was nearly calm when a rotten cackle snatched her attention.

"Having difficulty, my Queen?"

She stiffened as she saw the hooded man standing behind Raphael's headstone, his long beard soiling the snow beneath his feet, his yellowed teeth peering out from cracked lips.

"Perhaps if you made more effort to control your own wrath, you would have more chance of controlling mine."

Enraged, Morana slammed the false slab over the carving, standing to face him.

"You have no place here," she said. "Your last puppet is dead!"

The man's gnarled grin began to grow.

"Did you honestly believe I would sit idly by while you schemed to steal my Dragons from me? I could not allow the last Avdotian diamond to come into your possession so easily."

Morana sneered.

"Why don't you crawl back into the fiery chasm you came from?"

"I wanted to congratulate you on finding a mindless pawn on such short notice," he replied, cackling like a crow. "I doubt your dear Raoul has praised you much for it. Certainly, he rightfully believes that you have cheated him of both a marriage and a throne."

"My relationship with Raoul is none of your concern, Creature!"

But the man paid her no mind, the tip of his claw scratching along the headstone as he trailed around it, a smirk stretching his lips.

"It is quite a feat to reanimate a corpse," he said. "Even if you do bewitch my Dragons to your command, there is little chance that the diamonds' power can manage it without taking your blood as well. Why risk such tragedy?"

The Queen grew rigid, drawing away as the shadowed man advanced. Though she said not a word, his rotten breath billowed forth in another cackle.

"You loved him, is that it? You loved your Dayu so deeply that you would surrender yourself just to bring him life?"

She smacked his gnarled hand away from her chin, her scowl inspiring his grin.

"Do you truly love Dayu?" he asked, "or did he command you to love him?"

He pulled a long, dying insect from his beard, chuckling as it writhed. Morana was too mortified to hear the guards' heavy boots upon the stairs.

"Here comes your prisoner, brought at your request," Jaska informed her.

Repulsed by his grin, she stepped away.

"I did no such—"

"He poses a problem to your scheme," he said. "Consider it a favor from your adversary."

The hood's shadow seemed to extend further as the man faded into the shade of the spindly tree. Morana swiftly turned to see Ariel struggling in the hold of two guards – the youth's eyes bright, a scowl upon his face.

"Where is my father?!" he cried. "I know he's here! It's 654, he has to be here!"

The Queen stood in awe, as shocked as she was angry. By will alone, the youth had broken her spell.

"Guards, leave him with me," she ordered.

They seemed hesitant, but a firm glare coerced them to abandon their prisoner at her feet. His shackles rattled as he fought them, writhing in the snow.

"You're sick if you think I'll let you—"

Ariel's protest was silenced by her hand upon his mouth, her flat diamond against his throat. Once again, a web of lights crawled over his skin, charmed by the Queen's foreign whisper. His spirit fled his narrow eyes, leaving them empty once again.

"How did you break my spell?" she demanded.

He would not reply. Even so, Morana relaxed. She rose to her feet, observing the stubborn youth. There was dark hair upon his cheek now, and his once-regal locks were shaggy and knotted. A life in the dungeons had taken its toll on him.

"You have not won," he said.

Morana actually laughed.

"It seems I have."

Ariel rose to a kneel, his sapphire gaze searching the frozen graves.

"There will be an uprising soon. Two young leaders, a man and a woman, will organize a force from the depths of Citris to overwhelm you."

She stared at him, uncomprehending.

"I have never heard of this 'Citris'."

"It is a city that flourishes without your laws and decrees, thriving under your very nose."

The Queen felt new rage spring from these words, although Ariel gave her nothing to direct it towards. He was all but transpired, filtering everything through an unfeeling haze.

"Liar," she spat.

"I do not lie," he said.

His strange eyes again observed the landscape, drifting, until at last they rest upon the smallest headstone.

"You did not bury Asyrias in that grave," he said. "You believe him to be rotting in some mountainous ditch. However, you cannot be sure of that, for Twyla no longer remembers that night, nor the ditch she might have buried him in."

Morana's blood grew cold in her veins.

"What nonsense are you spouting?" she snapped.

"It is a wonder how Cedric never noticed a stranger's child beneath a royal shroud. I can only assume that after his return from Raine, he was too distraught by news of his son's death to look upon the corpse. Perhaps he knew all along that *you* were the cause of his fair child's last breath. Perhaps that it why he found comfort in a peasant girl – perhaps that is why Cedric's eyes would never again linger upon you."

Ariel hunched over – his shoulders shaking, either laughter or sobs dead in his throat.

"I suggest you remedy the situation in Citris. Otherwise, you will be troubled by the ghosts it will stir from the shadows."

"Shut up, shut **UP**!" the Queen shrieked. "It will be done!"

As he rose, she saw a smile possess his enchanted visage. A strange wind whispered in her ear, spinning her about. In the far-off shade, she saw Jaska's haunting grin; Ariel's had grown in reflection of it, as though he were puppet to that fiend.

"Begone," she commanded the creature.

Jaska faded into the night.

The coronation of Morana's chosen heir took place a fortnight after Attlas' death. Although her handmaid wanted very much to see the mysterious young man up close, her social rank forced her to stand by the entrance. Try as she may, Twyla could not glimpse the face of the blond youth as he proceeded down the crimson carpet.

With the coronation ritual already proceeding, the nobility who planned to attend were already seated. However, the door beside her opened once more, as ex-Commander Giovanni Wolfslayer entered to observe.

The moment the door shut behind him, Giovanni's cheek met a harsh strike.

"You bastard!" Twyla whispered, her shriek stifled out of respect for the ceremony. "How could you treat Reja in such a way?! Such neglect would make a monster out of anyone!"

Although the pain startled the man, he did not seem perturbed. He smiled as he touched his cheek, as if the strike had been a loving tap.

"I was only acting in his father's stead," he said.

"His father would never—"

"You believe so?"

Giovanni smirked, giving his cheek a last rub before he took a place beside her.

"His father was not the flawless man he pretended to be. I watched him take woman after woman into his personal tent in Kyro, sometimes two or three at a time. The only sign of monogamy he showed was an interest in an Akalinian girl, Reja, who had fled from a Kala troupe – I expect his interest ended shortly before he executed her, she being an expected spy and all. I believe it was he who gave Baldric the okay to massacre countless West Larascans, to murder the Talbot family and marry their daughter for the Lucadian throne. It was not by chance that he took that servant for a lover only months after his son's death. You see, without a child to protect, one quickly reverts to old habits."

Twyla stared at him, numbed by shock. She did not want to hear these words, to know this side of the man whose tragic life she had cherished.

"You're wrong," she said. "He took Genevieve as a mistress because he loved her. Anyone would deserve love after such a loss. Every could see how cold his wife had become towards him, and no one frowned upon his choice."

Giovanni bowed to kiss her palm; repulsed, she pulled from his grip.

"I am only proving that my parenting was not as abominable as you believe it to be. While his father's love might have fostered a more compassionate youth, mine has given him resilience and strength. There is no weakness left within him – except, perhaps, a genetic fondness for the female form."

"You're a monster," she hissed.

The man grinned, her words at last persuading him to put a polite distance between them.

"If nothing else, take heart in this: unashamed of my own raw nature, I raised the boy to bear only his true face to the world, unabashed, without a mask of loyalties or expectations to bind him. That is something his true father could not have done—not without disappointing his cherished son."

Twyla was silenced. Though rage pumped her heart too quickly, she forced herself to focus on the beginning ritual.

Morana and Gabriel stood upon the throne's red platform, before which the blond youth knelt. The Councilmen stood behind the throne, lining the wall beyond it like statues.

"...to witness the coronation of the chosen heir of our Queen, our Prince, Alastor Ayres."

The name took Twyla by surprise. However, her questions were answered by a whisper in her ear.

"It was clever for them to use Gabriel's name," Giovanni said. "It alludes to royal lineage, while avoiding the claim that he is something as displeasing as an illegitimate spawn of Cedric."

The coronation continued, with Gabriel stepping forward to draw the royal sword: a weapon with a hilt as gold as the finest coin, dark etchings making the veins upon the glistening surface, and a blade as white as a dragon's fang.

The noble Envoy touched the blunt side of the white blade to the youth's golden hair, reciting the many vows of Princehood. Alastor agreed to each with instructed grace, forgetting no courtly phrase. The ceremony ended with the noblest of promises:

"Do you, Alastor Ayres, swear to be loyal to the Xavier crown, and continue its legacy with honor?"

The youth replied simply.

"I do."

The nobles in attendance applauded as Morana placed a Prince's gold circlet upon his golden locks. Twyla, forgetting her anger towards Giovanni, spoke hushed words to him.

"I am glad my mistress had found our future King so quickly."

The man chuckled.

"He looks more like a quean to me."

Her elbow dented his rib, and he was quiet. Soon, their Queen had silenced the nobles' applause.

"As Prince, your first official duty will be to accompany the Commander of Ranks 1, 2, and 3 on a secret mission. Are you willing to accept this task?"

Alastor stood, then, prepared with a practiced bow.

"It would be my honor, Your Highness."

A shiver crept down Twyla's spine, seemingly unprovoked. The nobles again began to applaud as their crowned Prince turned to face them. At last, she could see the boy's handsome features, so perfectly shaped. And yet, she glimpsed an unnatural greenness to his eyes.

"What a pretty puppet," Giovanni laughed. "Indeed, it will be hard not to forgive such a lovely face."

The applause soon ended, the nobles soon departing for their homes. However, that blond youth remained, now another stitch in the tapestry of an ancient world.

The dungeons were a dark, damp place. For each day Kaish spent there, there was another rat bite, another wound infected by mildew. His bones ached; his lungs swelled with the smoke of dying torches. Sill, thin and hungry as he was, he was no longer subject to Lance's whip. For that, he was grateful.

Kaish no longer had any way to judge time. It was morning, perhaps noon that day when the doors above swung open, blinding him with intense light. He shielded himself from it with dirty hands, barely hearing the familiar voice that drifted down the stairway.

"Thanks, Sir Guard. I just want to visit him for a little while."

The guard's voice followed.

"The Stag Kaish may be visited. You will find him in the cell at the bottom of the stairway. However, you may not come in contact with the prisoner Ariel, by the Queen's decree."

"Whatever you say, Sir."

The light vanished, sending Kaish into a darkness more absolute than before. By the time he could see again, the Stag Colin stood before him. His plain, brown hair seemed greasier than before, that serpentine smirk set upon his face. However, Kaish could still see the tweak in the middle of his nose—the ever-present proof of the Talonian's greatest triumph.

Kaish didn't have the strength to humor any visitor, let alone one as unwelcome as the General's favorite. Even so, he spared a few words.

"What do you want?"

Colin was too pleased for Kaish's taste. For once, the former Stag was grateful for the many shadows.

"I just wanted to let you know that Alastor's been advanced further than anyone."

Kaish was merely annoyed, at first.

"To soldier? Before you? Shocking."

"No, *Tallk*," Colin spat, "to Prince."

The Talonian didn't believe this, at first. He knew it wasn't beyond Colin to lie, if it would make Kaish squirm. However, a lie this far-fetched required a depth of thought that Colin had never possessed.

At first, Kaish felt anger well within him. It simmered, growing, until a cool sort of bitterness doused these infant flames. Kaish fell back against the cold cell wall.

"A fitting Prince," he murmured, "for a country deserving the inferno."

The concept was too complex for Colin, who stood frustrated in the face of Kaish's apathy. He knelt outside the cell, gripping the rusty bars.

"Bet I could break your neck now," he jeered. "You're just a scrawny little twig now."

"Like you were when I broke your nose?"

Colin's scowl breathed life into Kaish's smile.

"It's a waste for you to hate me," said the Talonian. "I'll be executed soon enough. Even if you have somehow surpassed me in strength, you'll never get the chance to prove it."

"Whatever," Colin snapped. "I've got a message from the Prince."

Kaish gave no response, staring into the cracked wall on the other side of his cell.

"The Prince says you deserve the sewers," said the boy.

The Talonian still had no reaction, though he began to fondle a small, jagged rock upon the ground beside him.

"He also says he kissed Rina first," said Colin, "and that yours rubbed your filthy Tallk luck on her. That's why she died—your little kiss of death."

Something broke, deep within Kaish. Something pure, something gentle. In that moment, it shattered.

He hurled the rock through the cell bars, barely missing Colin's skull.

"Why don't you give that message to your scrawny Prince?!"

The rock broke against another set of bars, causing such a raucous noise that the Stag clambered back up the stairway. The doors opened, again blinding the prisoner with light. Then, all was black.

Chapter XXI

$\mathscr{S}$ ilas kept his attention on Pem's back during that long walk. He memorized every ridge in the brown leather jacket, every loose lock of her wispy hair, to avoid looking at the young woman who stood beside him – whose chestnut locks waved just at her shoulders, whose breasts were very prominent and white, rising and falling with each cloud of breath.

"I have a question for you," Rina said, suddenly.

He refused to look towards her, but acknowledged her words with a grunt.

"Why are you going to Joanissia?" she asked. "The innkeeper told me that you have some connection to it, but he didn't say how."

The youth shrugged.

"I don't remember my childhood. Perhaps I spent it there. Even if I didn't, it's the only hint Vaan ever gave me."

When she fell silent, he allowed himself a glance.

"You?" he asked.

She seemed hesitant to respond; Silas noticed a strange movement of her hand, towards the Talonian bracelet that never left her wrist.

"I'm looking for someone," she said.

Although his curiosity was not yet satisfied, he would say no more.

Soon after, Pem stopped in her tracks. The northern mountains now rose high in the distance, barely concealed by the white fog that dampened the world around them. The woman knelt in the snow – then, like a mad woman, rapped on the ground.

"Garrick! Open up, you old porker!"

All at once, a little old man popped up from the ground, a trapdoor making a roof of snow above his head.

"Finally bringing those bloody diamond traders?" the man sneered.

"Travelers," Pem said.

The wrinkled man scowled, coming up further to peer upon Silas and Rina.

"Ugh, that one looks foreign," he grumbled. "And the girl must be someone's bastard—she's got Kyron eyes."

Instinct summoned Silas' growl, his nails digging into his palm. However, it was Pem who whacked Garrick in the back of the head.

"Shut up. You owe me."

The man surveyed them again, his scowl only deepened. However, he gave one slow, reluctant nod.

"Fine," he mumbled. "Here's to hoping they didn't kill anyone."

He climbed up and out of that hole, gesturing that they proceed down it.

"Hurry up!" he snapped. "It's freezing out here!"

Silas hesitated longer than Rina. After a gracious 'thank you' to Pem, she was the first to descend into the darkness. Not wanting to be outshone in bravery, he quickly followed to the entry. He found a wooden ladder leading down into a dimly lit cave at the bottom of a steep, steep drop.

"You take care, boy," said Pem.

The youth nodded towards her in return.

"Thank you…for saving her," he said.

The man, Garrick, coughed loudly as he shivered.

"Move it along," he muttered, "you'll let all the cold air in."

Silas observed the withered old woman for the last time, his gaze tracing her knotted face and the wispy locks that stemmed from her pale head. Harsh as she was, she was one of the few truly kind people they had met on their journey. She had nursed them back to health without payment, and given them both shelter and a destination.

The youth was not trained in the art of gratitude. If he had been, he might have found more words for her. However, speechless with ignorance, he could only mutter a simple farewell.

"Take care."

Pem rolled her eyes.

"Quite the master of eloquence, this one."

"Just get down," Garrick grumbled.

The youth scowled, at last descending into the unknown.

Rina was gone when he reached the bottom. Though the passageway was lit well by flickering torches, Silas' companion was nowhere to be seen. Anxiety gripped him, though he tried to smother it – he moved quickly through the passage in pursuit, cursing her nature, as though it was her intention to anger him.

He found her at the end of the passageway, stopped. By the time he reached her, though she had done nothing to provoke him, he had worked himself into such a foul temper that he spun her around to snarl in her face.

"Stay close," he ordered.

Yet, she scowled at him, no longer intimidated. She pulled from his grip, pointing forward.

"Look," she said.

Despite annoyance, Silas lifted his gaze. Beyond was a world he could never have imagined: a metropolis amongst the caverns. Children climbed wooden ladders to join the women who stood atop sturdy rope bridges, which crossed in levels reaching to the rocky sky. Men sold handcrafted necessities out of carts that lined the smooth roads, the salesmen needing only to holler to grab the attention of the families passing by.

A yellow bird swooped past Silas' gaze, soaring high into the maze of rope bridges. Startled, he tried to keep it in his sights; however, the creature vanished as quickly as it came.

"We should try to find some food," said Rina, her voice catching his attention. "Maybe there's somewhere we can work for a meal."

Silas agreed with a grunt, allowing her to lead. He continued to observe the strange environment they found themselves in, trying to understand the mechanics of it: how they could keep the torches burning for so long, how the bridges were held up, how the ladders were fastened to stone. Yet, a more pressing matter compromised his attention. He began to notice the stray glances cast towards his companion, the smirks from the burlier salesmen. Silas tensed, irked. He made it his priority to stay a pace behind Rina, a hand on his weapon.

Suddenly, a small pup wandered across their path, coming to settle near Rina. His chestnut coat was very soft, his ears but flaps that hung past his cheeks. He seemed lost, and whimpered in regret of his aimless trek. Naturally, Rina cooed with delight.

"Hi there…"

She knelt to rub its soft ears, smiling sweetly. Silas was not so amused.

"Leave it alone," he said. "Any pup is old enough to carry disease."

However, its owner appeared before Rina could rise. A young boy, not yet tall enough to reach Silas' hip, rushed to the pup. The moment Rina released it, the child had his pet cradled in his arms.

"Hero," he murmured.

The child was strikingly pale, as if some creature had sucked the color from his flesh. His nails, too, were very white, and come to points as sharp as his pup's. However, there was color to his eyes, bright as emeralds, and his hair—as vibrantly red as the blood that fled his skin.

At once, Silas knew danger.

"Let's go, Rina," he demanded.

She stared at him in confusion, but he would not be swayed. He knew the boy before them from every Rionan work Giovanni had placed before him. *The Complete History of Riona* called him thus:

Demon.

    A creature of the night. Only male. Born to a human mother, fathered by a creature of his own kind, it will thrive on her milk until it dries. Once the mother can no longer provide nourishment in this way, the babe will make her his first feast of human blood, its true sustenance.

    Creatures' origin, unknown.

A woman's voice stopped their quick departure.

"Sen!"

A tall woman slid down a nearby ladder, rushing to the boy and his dog.

"Sen, I told you not to run off on your own!'

The child looked down, regret dampening his glasslike eyes. He buried his face in her skirt, murmuring his apology.

Silas stared in bewilderment at the woman, speechless. The Demon child was too old to still have a living mother – all accounts of Demon children said it was strange to even see a toddler still at his mother's skirt. Yet, she lived.

Why?

He observed her, fully, as if that would provide some explanation. The woman was of average build, not too round in any one place, though her golden hair was regally well kempt. The beauty of her face would have been inviting, were it not for her stubborn scowl, determined to repel any who might admire it. And yet, Silas almost knew her. He felt the wall of caution fall as it was overwhelmed by inexplicable familiarity—and by the gleam of her wary gaze, she felt this too.

"Do I know you?" she asked, words clipped on a sharp tongue.

Despite the alien emotions that stirred within him, he could only shake his head.

"No."

She did not seem willing to accept this, but her attentions were shifted to another man, who slid down the ladder she had come from. He was handsome and strong, with broad shoulders and a masculine jaw, which was shaded by the same russet brown as his shaggy locks. There seemed an infectious cheeriness about him, resistant to any fog.

"Is he all right?" he asked the woman, moving quickly to her side.

"He's fine," she replied. "Hasn't killed anyone either, as far as I can tell."

Silas noticed an unusual pattern to the woman's speech, as if her Larascan accent was a manufactured, practiced thing. He noticed how pale her eyes were – not Larascan green, but gray, almost brown.

A foreigner.

Rionan, if she was truly the Demon's mother. Logically, it made the most sense. Demons were not seen past Rionan mountains. This made the presence of the foreigner and the child all the more intriguing, troubling though it was.

The man looked to Silas, then, an apologetic look on his rugged face.

"Excuse my betrothed," he said. "She is not the docile type."

The woman's scowl seemed to harden she tucked her child behind her skirt.

"*Betrothed,* now, is that what you call me?" she snapped. "I don't remember ever saying yes."

Silas was impressed by the man's lack of reaction.

"You two must be new to Citris," he said, politely continuing the conversation.

At last, Rina spoke up.

"How can you tell?"

"I'm the graveskeeper," he said. "I've met everyone here, at one point or another. There aren't a lot of newcomers. Most people come to visit the graves of their grandparents, great-grandparents, great-great-grandparents, all born and buried here…"

He trailed off momentarily, lost in some thought. However, a smile appeared the moment he collected himself.

"The name's Caine," he said. "This golden-haired vision is Tasha, and her sweet child is Sen."

The woman clearly did not appreciate her description, but made no comment of it. Her child peeked at Silas from behind her skirt, observing him. Silas could feel his emerald gaze exploring his every joint and crevice, surveying his very flesh. It made him tense.

"Is there anything you need?" Caine asked. "I'm more than willing to help you out for a day or two, at least until you're settled."

Silas wasn't yet that trusting.

"Why would you do that?" he asked, wary.

Even Tasha glared with feline irritation, eyes narrow and jaw tight. Still, Caine's cheerful disposition could not be swayed.

"I know what it's like to be alone in a new place. I would have had a much easier time if someone had offered me a helping hand."

Silas looked to Rina, who blushed under Caine's gaze. Silas tensed.

"You look hungry," said the man. "I can show you where to find fresh fruit, if you like."

The girl nodded, smiling graciously.

"That would be wonderful, Sir."

Tasha could no longer bite her tongue. She tugged hard on Caine's sleeve as her harsh whisper scathed his ear.

"You can't just lead random strangers to Sanctuary!"

But Caine smiled, easily sliding from her grip.

"A stranger is only a friend you haven't met," he said, a hand already on the ladder. With a jerk of his head, he gestured them to follow. "Stay close, you two."

Despite Silas' reluctance, Rina was already climbing the ladder with him. Even Tasha, whose sour look had not lessened, soon hoisted her son and his pup onto her shoulders to follow. Silas had little choice but to follow suit.

The graveskeeper led them over rope bridges and up the many ladders, greeting anyone familiar who passed by. Silas quickly grew accustomed to maneuvering in those heights, but his companion seemed tense, paler than her natural hue. When she did stumble, once, she was righted swiftly by Silas' hand. After this, she seemed calmer.

Their destination was a long cavern closer to the surface, where a wide crack in the rocky ceiling filled the room with sunlight. Rows of trees stretched as far as the eye could see, still alive with green leaves and burdened by fruits of yellows and oranges, some as green as the leaves that sheltered them. It was a startling sight in winter – and though white flakes fell through the cracked rock above, the air was warm and inviting.

Caine's smile was even calmer here, no doubt soothed by the environment.

"Welcome to Sanctuary," he said.

The sight was surreal. The sun set the trees aglow, lighting the stray white flakes that crowned the leaves. Silas recalled a similar sight, from some dream, some other world—red roses, vibrant blossoms adorned by frost.

"What's that smell?" Rina asked, a dizzy smile on her lips.

"Citrus fruit," Caine explained. "That's where this town got its name. A bit of a rarity in these parts, but they're our sustenance – that, and the birds that fly in through that crack and lose their way."

Two nightingales flew in, then, singing to each other as they surveyed the many leafy perches. The red-haired child watched hungrily as they soared overhead, tightening his hold on his mother's shirt. Caine chuckled.

"This way, please."

Caine led them past the rows of fruitful trees with a purpose, while their heady scent permeated through the air, so strong upon Silas' sense that he began to salivate against his will. Surviving on Pem's gruel for as long as he had had left him ravenous, and though he craved something of bloodier substance, anything would do—even foreign, sour-smelling fruit.

Towards the center of the colorful orchard, they found a large pond of clear water, its surface glistening in the sun's white light. A small island rose from its center, crowned by a magnificent tree: roots so large they rose from the soil and cast shadows upon the water, leafy branches rising to the heavens, burdened by crimson fruit. Silas stared into the treetops, awestruck.

Unnatural.

"Those are Kyron fruits," he said, looking to Caine. "How did they end up here?"

The graveskeeper paused, surprised by the question.

"We're lucky here, I suppose."

A girl sat before the pond, sitting cross-legged in the snow – which had already dusted her curly mane white – with a book open in her lap. This inspired Silas' curiosity, as she seemed to understand more than just the pictures.

Caine caught her attention with a cough.

"Alice, I have visitors."

The girl looked up briefly – looking longer at Silas – before she looked back down.

"Outsiders. Interesting."

She would say no more on it, absorbed in her book. Tasha rolled her eyes, speaking in another harsh whisper to her companion.

"Her father must be gone. Don't bother her."

Caine was not so easily deterred.

"Is your father allowing anyone to pick from this tree yet?" he asked, loudly. "I doubt these young people are as used to sour fruit as we are, and I don't want them to starve."

The girl shrugged, still making no effort to look up.

"If they want to swim it," she muttered.

Caine sighed, taking Tasha's hand as he moved to leave. Silas, annoyed at the girl's apathy, meant to follow suit—however, there was a loud splash in the pond. He turned in time to see Rina swimming clumsily to the island, laughing.

"It's warm, Silas! Come in!"

The youth was certain she had lost her mind. Silas stared vacantly towards her, as annoyed as he was ashamed. Yet, Caine's laughter did not mock them.

"What a lively girl you have," he said.

Lively wasn't the word he had in mind. The moment she swam back towards shore, he thrust his hand towards her, expectant.

"Out," he ordered. "You look like a fool."

She shook her head defiantly as she bobbed at the surface.

"You should come in," she said again. "The water's fine."

Silas growled his reply.

"No."

Rina sighed, clearly disappointed. She took his hand, and he gripped her strongly to pull her up. However, he found she was suddenly very heavy—and all at once, he found himself tumbling into the pond.

Silas quickly resurfaced, coughing and sputtering. Everyone was still laughing at him; even Alice snickered behind her open book. He couldn't scowl hard enough. He turned to find Rina already climbing onto the tree's roots, her chiming laughter unrestrained. Yet, seeing that bright smile on her face, almost enough to distract from her dripping, clinging garb, made it difficult to be angry.

She dangled one pale foot in the water as he swam to her, her look too demure.

"I'm sorry," she said.

He squeezed her foot, just hard enough for it to hurt.

"You're not."

And yet, he forgave her.

Silas was the one who had to climb the tall tree to get their meal, since Rina was accident-prone and lacking in any great strength. It was simple for him to pluck the red fruit from the branches, tossing one down to his companion and keeping another for himself. From the treetop, he could see Caine and Tasha sitting in the shade of an orange-fruited tree, very close to each other, while the Demon child nuzzled with his pup in the powdery snow. It was a serene image, untouched by troubles, though troubles had surely led to it.

The youth climbed down, finding Rina happily consuming her fruit amongst the dense roots, her gaze also on the strange family across the way.

"Do you think they love each other?" she asked, suddenly.

He gave her a strange look, sitting near her.

"What does it matter? They're together."

There was a vulnerable softness to her visage that he had never seen before. It wasn't naivety, or that foolish blankness she would sometimes get. For a moment, in her distant gaze, he glimpsed the depth of her thought.

"Because love will keep them together."

She was silent after that, enjoying her fruit. Silas found he had little interest in his own, in a position to watch her without her knowing. He didn't understand why he liked to observe her. At first he had attributed it to her newly displayed femininity, but now, he wasn't so certain. He had begun watching her before that – out of frustration, he then justified. Rina had never been a good "boy." The girl was too graceful, too soft, too warm. Her lips were too pink, her eyes too blue. She was too…

Distracting.

He forced himself to look away from her, at last taking a bite of the crimson fruit. The sweet juice caressed his tongue, promising relief from long weeks of tasteless nourishment. However, the moment it touched his throat, his blood burned.

Silas began to cough violently, everything about him squeezing and burning, his heart pumping hard enough to force lead through his veins. There was too much light, too much light in his throat, in his hands. His claws scratched his skin, which burned, screamed. Another voice roared, overwhelming his mind.

StopstopstopstopSTOP

He heard the fruit roll into the pond, as another voice overcame him—Rina's.

"Silas, what's wrong? You're getting red…"

He was falling, falling deep into the roots.

"Silas…Silas, wake up!"

It was dark there. Dark like Giovanni's cellar.

Silas moved through a fog as dense as memory, alone. He was no longer sure if he was awake, if anything around him was real. Lost, he stumbled forward. Weak, he fell to his knees.

And then, a voice, too airy to exist.

"Silas?"

He turned, seeing Rina. She was dressed in golden finery, golden pins holding her chestnut locks like a crown upon her head. Yet, her welcoming smile outshone even her grandest adornment.

"Dance with me."

She took his hand in her pale grip, while her arm slipped around his neck. As though it were old habit, he slid his arm around her waist, bewitched by the sight of her.

The whisper of a Talonian flute guided each graceful step. Rina moved like a ghost, moving where he led her, each twirl making her golden dress fan out, shifting like a flickering flame. He held her like glass, afraid to break her.

Though the flute grew louder, Rina grew still. She warmed his cheek with such a soft touch, leaning him down to her. He could almost taste her, but was afraid her lips were poison.

A raven croaked a laugh as it flew overhead, distracting Silas from the young woman he held. As he watched its black feathers disappear into the night sky, he realized that his hold was slipping. He looked down to find an arrowhead had emerged from Rina's breast, blood seeping into her gown.

"Rina!"

His own voice was too far away. Too late, he saw the fissure in the earth before them and the young man beyond it—his face a blur of color, with a serpent's eyes. In his hands was a cocked bow, as red as the Xavier insignia.

Rina's body grew too heavy, sodden with blood. She slipped from his arms into the black fissure, swallowed by the sound of a rushing river.

"RINA!"

He roared her name, as all warmth left him. He howled for his love, who would never return.

Silas coughed his way into consciousness. He found himself in someone's bed, staring up at a rocky ceiling he had never seen before. Disorientated, he tried to sit up; however, a young woman's touch forced him back down.

"Don't get up so fast," Rina said, her voice trembling. "You still look sick."

Though groggy, he saw the dried tears upon her cheeks, the redness of her eyes and nose. She hadn't looked this way since the night he had first woken in Pem's home.

Despite her, he rose again, though slower.

"What happened?" he managed.

"You started seeing things after you ate that fruit," she said. "It must not have agreed with you, I think."

Understatement, but he didn't correct her. She seemed so relieved that he was breathing.

"Caine and Tasha helped me bring you here," she continued. "This is where Tasha used to live before she moved in with Caine. They said we could use it until you got better. You're wearing some of Caine's old clothes, and Tasha let me use one of her dresses."

This sparked his interest. He looked about, trying to find a trace of Tasha's Demon spawn anywhere in the small lodging. Yet, there was nothing—not even a separate bed for him to sleep on.

"I'm fine now," he said, standing. "Just…don't talk too much."

Rina complied, though he doubted she would have done otherwise even without his request. She was too quiet, lost in her own head. Still, he left her to herself.

After another survey of the room, he went to the dingy mirror mounted on the wall, old and partially cracked. Even in the weathered surface, he could see the sorry, shaggy state of his hair. It grew fast, and months had passed since he had last cut it. More than ready to remedy the situation, he grabbed his hair in his hand and drew his sword from his side.

"Stop…"

Rina's hesitant voice gave him pause, despite himself. He looked back at her expectantly, annoyed.

"Let me do it," she said. "I used to cut my friend Alastor's hair, once upon a time. He said I was good at it."

Silas was not, by nature, a trusting person—especially when it came to knives. Yet, it took only a moment for him to bend to her whim.

"Don't take too long."

He stood in front of the room's lone window, staring out it as she began. Because of Silas' unusual height, she was forced to balance on a rickety chair to work. Even so, she didn't complain. The young woman didn't have Maddy's habit of mindless chatter. Silas admired her dignified silence.

Outside, he could see the venders packing their things, while men with long torches ensured that each lantern remained lit. There was no sun to monitor time, here. Every hour of every day, there was only the orange glow of firelight. Yet, something told the youth that the moon was high above them, and a black sky stared down upon this buried city.

"Finished."

Rina sheathed her curved dagger, climbing down off the chair. Silas ran his fingers through his hair, disturbed for a moment at the feel of its cropped length. As she cleaned the hair from the floor, he went to the mirror, looking again. He found that his dark locks fell smoothly along his jawline, only some straying across his brow.

"You look regal," Rina said, standing as she finished her cleaning.

Silas saw his smile in his reflection before he realized its presence. He suppressed it at once, though he was truly delighted.

"…good work," he said.

Her smile pleased him, more than he would ever admit.

They avoided each other until it came time for bed; Rina brushed her hair at the vanity, and Silas skimmed the few books on the Larascan language he found on the shelves. None of them had a single picture, so Silas could only assume that someone had taught Tasha to read. However, as soon as he heard Rina's yawn, he put the book away and stood from the bed.

"Get ready to sleep," he said.

"I am ready," she said, setting down the brush as she stood.

He rolled his eyes.

"Then get in bed."

Rina stumbled towards the cot when he pushed her, gently though it was. Startled, though, she stood stiff before it.

"Where will you sleep?"

He was already lying on the floor beside it, unstrapping his sword from his side to hold in his arms.

"The floor?!" she exclaimed. "Silas, I can't let you sleep on the floor while I sleep here…"

"Quit talking," he snapped. "Just sleep."

There was enough finality in his voice to hush her. Silas heard the bed shift as Rina lay down, settling beneath the quilts. Soon, the candle on the nightstand went out.

"Sleep well, Silas," she said, gently.

The youth would say nothing; yet, he felt peace. Her breathing fell into rhythm, soothing him with each gentle sound. Before long, he too had fallen asleep.

Rina woke to a ruckus in the street, so loud it seemed to be pounding at their window. She sat up at once, edgy after their long travels. The torches outside were flickering strangely, casting ominous shadows in their borrowed residence. Somehow, she knew something was wrong.

Silas?

He was still asleep beside the bed, looking exhausted. She didn't want to wake him if there was nothing wrong. For now, she trusted herself enough to investigate alone.

She took her dagger and opened up the trap door, climbing down the ladder that led to a back alley in the street level. All at once, she swept away by a flurry of terrified people—women screaming, children crying.

The girl fought the wave of people to the main street, trying to find the source of the terror. What she found made her heart turn to ice. Up and down the street, soldiers carrying golden-hilted swords stormed the unsuspecting denizens, apprehending those who weren't fast enough to run.

Their bald General, the Xavier insignia branded upon his iron chest plate, roared over the commotion

"Search their homes! All insubordination must be corrected!"

She grew cold, terrified as the memory of Lance overwhelmed her. Her hands shook as she gripped her dagger, feeling dizzy.

Suddenly, a powerful grip turned her around.

"What do you think you're doing?!" Silas growled. "It's dangerous out here!"

Rina stared at him blankly, uncomprehending. In frustration, he led her back to the ladder, pushing through the crowd like a battering ram. They only stopped when they heard Tasha's strident shout.

"You two! This way!"

Next she knew, Silas' arm was around her waist as he shielded her from the commotion, pushing down another alley. The blonde woman stood in front of an open door, beyond which was perfect darkness. She beckoned them quickly.

"Don't just stand there, idiots!"

Rina turned, once, before Silas dragged her into darkness. In that moment, she glimpsed a young soldier in golden armor, with hair of the same vibrant color. In that glance, she knew his emerald gaze.

Alastor.

Tasha slammed the door behind them, shutting out turmoil.

Chapter XXII

The passage led to the darkest corners of Citris, where the townspeople buried their dead. Little light could reach it, the few torches only casting more shadows on the rows of carved, cracked headstones. The atmosphere of the place was stifling to Rina, filling her eyes with tears that did not belong to her – and though the air was still, she thought she could feel it whispering in her ears, begging her to stay.

The blonde woman led them to a sturdy shack constructed a small distance from the graves, the walls of which had taken on a damp color, absorbed from their environment over many years. With some force, she swung open the creaky door before beckoning them inside.

"It'll be cramped, but it's better than being up there."

Rina glanced to Silas out of habit, as if searching for his approval. Although he seemed wary, he did not refuse their host. They entered the hovel.

It was small, with a bed just large enough for two people and a dresser pushed as far against the opposite wall as it could go; beside it was an oppressive black chest, secured by a heavy lock. The only feminine touch to the space was a golden brush laid atop it, beside a clay water basin.

"If you need water, you'll have to get it from the spring by the outer wall," Tasha explained, drawing back the dusty curtains of the barred window. "You'll get used to the chalky taste."

Rina took a seat on the cot, noticing curiously that the red-haired boy from before was curled up on a pile of blankets in the corner, squeezing his pup to his chest like a doll. It was a sweet sight; yet her companion tensed in the presence of it, jaw tight in his usual look of disgust.

"I need air," he said.

With that, he left the shack. Rina, now abandoned, could only fiddle with her bracelet as Tasha stared out the window, silent. The bracelet's existence affected her less, now. Though very present, the memories that usually accompanied its touch had recently become muffled, warded off by some force. It was as though Kaish had only existed in her dreams, long ago.

The uncomfortable stillness ended when Caine hurried through the door, helping the old gatekeeper, Garrick, into the room. The wrinkled man was cradling his arm, bent at a strange angle, as he grumbled and cursed.

"Fawk…"

Caine helped him sit on the other edge of the bed, away from Rina. Tasha gave the two of them a sympathetic look, as though the sight were commonplace.

"Bloody mob," Garrick muttered.

Caine sighed, examining the man's arm for a moment longer before he stood.

"I'll get you a sling."

Garrick grumbled, finally looking about. At last, he noticed Rina.

"You're that part-breed, aren't you? I remember those eyes."

Rina was grateful for Tasha's quick retort.

"Caine thought it was good idea to go save the out-of-towners. You'll have to make room for her and Loverboy."

Both remarks made Rina uncomfortable, but not enough to correct them.

"I'm sorry we couldn't meet again under better circumstances," Rina said, gently.

The man shrugged.

"I was only a matter of time before this happened, I say. There's only so long you can live under the capital before the capital comes crashing in."

"What's happening up there?" Rina asked.

The graveskeeper returned with a strip of cloth, using it to secure Garrick's arm.

"The soldiers just stormed the passages, outta nowhere," Garrick grunted, allowing Caine to tie the sling around his neck. "They're spouting gibberish about some rebellion. I couldn't make much sense of it."

Rina touched the mark upon her arm, which was still hidden by the sleeve of Tasha's old nightgown. Mere talk of the soldiers made it burn now, the memories of the pain entwined with memories of the men. It was Caine's voice that brought her from her toxic thoughts.

"Are you injured?" he asked.

She shook her head.

"It's an old wound."

Tasha glanced towards her, briefly, before looking back out the window.

"I don't know why Caine decided to take pity on you, but I suppose you're allowed to stay here for the night – assuming you're used to sleeping on the floor."

Rina was grateful, and she politely thanked Caine for his hospitality. Curious, she looked out the window as well, seeing what Tasha saw: Silas, pacing back and forth behind a headstone. His brow was furrowed, and he scowled so deeply that there was no doubt of his foul temper. Though the girl's instinct was to comfort him, she still didn't know how.

Suddenly, the red-haired boy was at his mother's side, tugging her sleeve with urgency. Tasha leaned down to hear his whisper.

"He wants you to play your flute, Caine," said the woman.

Her lover smiled at the boy.

"Is that what you want?"

Sen showed his approval with a nod, before again hiding his face in his mother's skirt. The endearing sight brought a smile to the graveskeeper's face. After a moment of digging through drawers, he pulled out a wooden flute – its shape reminiscent of the one Kaish had kept in his pocket.

"Where did you get that?" Rina asked, startled.

"It was a gift," he replied.

He examined the instrument, rubbing off a speck of dust here and there. Soon, though, he began to play. Its warming melody filled the room, soothing the cloud of uncertainty that threatened to overwhelm them. Sen sat down, lifting the little dog, Hero, to cradle him. Garrick grew quiet, still holding his injured arm; Tasha watched Caine with affectionate eyes. Rina, however, felt no comfort. The sound summoned images that had been suppressed: the soldiers' camp in the Great Forest, where she had first heard Kaish's song in the distant camp. Her betrothed could breathe life into his instrument, its sound filling Rina with such warmth, such hope. She could not bear to hear its mimic.

Rina left the shack quietly, knowing she would not be missed. She thought of telling Silas she was leaving, but a glance towards the pacing youth compelled her to turn the other direction. The young woman wandered aimlessly through the graveyard, drawn from torchlight to torchlight like a lost moth. She tried to clear her head; but no matter how she tried, she couldn't stop the memories that clouded her thoughts, now stirred from the depths. She thought of Gwen, of Richard, of John and Edmund, of Alastor—of Kaish. She wished now that thoughts of him could return to dormancy.

Along a wall far from the shack, Rina found a ladder leading to a trap door in the ceiling, its latch rusted and loose. Above it, she heard a soldier's voice.

"Smack her around some more, she'll talk."

A sharp whack brought a woman's scream, followed by another. The soldier's bark came again.

"Sir Alastor, where do you think you're going?"

The world snapped into focus. Suddenly, Rina remembered the glimpse of the blond man in golden armor, rushing through the streets with his fellow soldiers.

Alastor.

It wasn't a dream. He was really there, just beyond that trap door. All at once, the ill feelings she had had for him melted away. The memory of his selfishness was overshadowed by nostalgia, a need for the world she had left behind.

Well aware of her foolishness, she climbed up the ladder. The trapdoor above was lined with small cracks, allowing her to see what was just above. The General was pacing near it, frustration on his young face.

"No one in this bloody sinkhole knows the first thing about a so-called rebellion…"

The bald man paced for a time more, the occasional step thudding loudly upon the trap door, as another soldier continued to beat some screaming, unseen girl. Rina stayed very still, swallowing her fear. Before long, the General bellowed again.

"Let's move on!"

He disappeared from view, another soldier's boot passing over her head.

"Pick up the pace, Sir Alastor! We can't have you getting lost!"

Her heart jumped as she heard her friend's familiar voice sputter an apology, his clumsy step passing overhead soon after. When Rina heard the clinking of chainmail begin to lessen, she bravely pushed the door open a crack, to glimpse the world above. For just a moment, she saw him: blond hair and golden armor fading into the distance.

No…

She would not let her past escape again.

Silently as she could, she hoisted herself out of the trap door, grabbing a loose cobblestone as she quietly pursued them. The caverns of Citris were strangely still now, every shop and ladder now abandoned. Only the soldiers remained, their cool eyes posing an ever-present danger to her quest. She kept to the shadows until she again glimpsed that golden armor.

The blond soldier was standing some distance from the General and his other men, dully picking his teeth with a wood sliver from a broken bridge. Rina was so relived to see him that she could ignore this grosser habit. Her tears welled as she realized just how much she had missed him.

My friend.

Although eager for his attention, she would not let her feeling compromise caution. Carefully, she readied the cobblestone she had taken from the alley, aiming for the broadest part of his body. With a thrust, the stone echoed off his shoulder plate.

"What?!"

He looked around, clearly confused. After a moment of frustration, however, he seemed willing to let this pass. To prevent this, she at last stepped out of the shadows, revealing herself.

His eyes widened, filled with shock and awe. Mouth agape, he turned very white, as though he were seeing an apparition.

"See someone, Sir Ayres?" his General snapped, strained disdain prevalent in his bark.

Alastor sputtered, no doubt trying to look natural.

"No, Sir!"

The General returned his attention to other troops, though not without a look of annoyance. It seemed Alastor's mere presence was grating to him, as if the man was being forced to tolerate a gnat flying about his head. Once this danger had passed, the youth forgot all formality. He pushed her into a dark alley and crushed her with his embrace.

"My bones, Ri! It's Rina! Fawk, I thought you were fish food, but you're here!"

Her breathless laughter was stifled by his chokehold.

"I missed you," she whispered.

"How did you get here?!" he stammered. "We all saw you fall and now you're...*here*!"

She managed a smile.

"It's a long story."

Alastor finally released her, observing her with such bright eyes. She didn't think she had ever seen him so happy.

"Is the rest of the Rank here?" she asked.

The question dampened his look considerably, though he gave a prompt reply.

"In Joanissia."

She thought of asking him about Kaish, but intuition subdued her curiosity.

"Maybe this is fate," she said.

"What?"

Rina's smile widened as hope filled her once more, forgotten dreams resurfacing to become tangible things.

"I've been traveling with a friend who really needs to go to Joanissia," she said, "and I've been trying to find the Rank since we were separated."

Rina grasped her friend's soft hands, asking the world of him with her gaze.

"I know things weren't great between us back in the forest, but I want you to help me now. I *need* you to help me now."

She squeezed his hold.

"Please?"

Her forwardness must have taken him by surprise, for he said nothing for a long while. However, his old smile began to resurface, almost out of place on a new, more hardened countenance. He brushed her hair behind her ear, the sensation intimate enough to chill her.

"It's dangerous for me to do that, Rina. Still…if you introduce me to this friend of yours, I'll see what I can do."

Overwhelmed by her good fortune, she led him like a leashed animal through the caverns, to the trap door where she had first heard his name. A part of her was made anxious by the thought of Silas' usual hostility towards strangers, but she buried these thoughts with a feeling of accomplishment; somehow, she felt she was walking fate's path.

As she held her hand up to Alastor from the bottom of the ladder, he asked her only one question.

"What kind of friend is this person, Ri?"

She smiled, deciding she would be clever.

"A boy-friend."

His eyes gleamed strangely, too green for a moment. He did not seem pleased, but said no more.

It was a long time before Silas realized the girl was gone. When he first found Rina missing from the shack, he asked no one of it, convincing himself that she had gone to explore the graveyard. However, further investigation of the stone field yielded no sign of her. He began to feel annoyance, then ire, but continued to search. By the time he returned to the hovel, he had worked himself into such a fury that he nearly tore the door from its hinges.

"Where *is* she?!" he roared.

The hovel's inhabitants looked towards him in bewilderment, Tasha glaring him down in irritation.

"Your pet left a long time ago," she snapped. "I didn't know she had to get your permission before leaving."

He snarled, in no mood to humor her. It was the graveskeeper who came to him, bravely squeezing his shoulder in a gesture of peace.

"Calm yourself, friend," said Caine. "Have more faith. If she's not back by the end of the day, we'll search for her."

Although Silas still didn't understand how to know *when* the day was ending, Caine's words provided a degree of comfort. His rage defeated, he sat where he had last seen Rina, a short distance from the injured old gatekeeper whose presence he did not question. Silas allowed his gaze to wander the room, observing the mundane artifacts Caine surrounded himself with. He was most intrigued by the large black chest, burdened by a lock made from fine metal. He wondered what treasures a common graveskeeper would want to secure.

As his eyes wandered again, Silas made the mistake of looking at the Demon child in the corner of the room, sitting atop a nest of blankets. There was a furry thing in his clutches that might have once been an animal, but was now mostly lifeless and soaked in its own blood, the red liquid also smeared and dripping from the boy's mouth. Silas grew nauseous, watching with disgust as the inhuman child buried his face in its fur, sucking the rest of the life from that twitching, wriggling mass.

"Nasty, ain't it?" the gatekeeper murmured, "You get used to it. I've been visiting Caine and his almost-son for 'bout two years now—I've learned to ignore the rat noises and pretend he's eating a handful of berries."

Silas said nothing. Tasha gave him a dirty look and moved in front of her son, as if to protect him from the youth's judging stare. Caine distracted himself from the ordeal by sitting in the corner, whittling some shape out of a block of wood.

"You look like a good listener," Garrick said, again claiming Silas' attention. "A story should take your mind off bloodier matters."

The youth made no remark, but looked attentive.

"Want to know how this city started?"

Even under their bizarre circumstances, the offer was intriguing. At last, the youth allowed him a nod.

"The story's as old as Larasca itself, passed from parents to kids since the Xaviers' 1st year In Reign. It's probably a lot of hearsay at this point, but you know how it is."

Garrick adjusted himself on the bed, no doubt getting comfortable before the long tale. Silas braced himself.

"Back when this country wasn't 'Larasca', the city above us was called Siobhan, home to one of the five temples of the old deity Neschume. The temple's Priestess, Hope, was blessed with peculiar powers of foresight, they say. She had a vision that all the sacred temples were going to be destroyed, including her own. To save Neschume's followers, she asked them to leave their homes and follow her into the mountain's caverns, where she would use the sacred artifact, Claiborne, to bring life to the hidden land.

"Many people didn't believe her. They thought that the Goddess would protect them as she always had, for Siobhan was her most blessed city. It was the warmest land in the Empire of Asyrias during winter, despite the snow, and the trees never shed their leaves, or the flowers their petals. The people refused to leave this paradise, not even for their Priestess. Even so, Hope did rally a small number of worthy followers and brought them into the caverns, sealing them in with large rocks.

"In the caverns, Hope helped them build a life for themselves. The ladders and bridges were constructed with her guidance, all sturdy enough to survive to this day. For sustenance, Hope performed a miracle: she planted the sacred orb into the soil, and from it sprung an orchard of citrus trees that bore fruit through the longest winters. Though the Priestess' gifts and guidance, her followers made this their home.

"However, their peaceful existence could not last forever. Only a few years passed before soldiers from above marched through Sanctuary, apprehending the cave dwellers as they found them. The brutes would have killed them, if Hope had not come forward. She offered them her life in exchange for the followers', and they accepted. The Priestess was taken deeper into Sanctuary and wasn't heard from for many years. She did return, three times, each time appearing from the deepest part of Sanctuary. After that third time, neither she nor any soldier has been seen in Citris since."

A pause.

"Except for now, I guess. Kind of ruins the story."

The tale intrigued Silas for a number of reasons. The mention of Neschume and the ancient Empire confirmed Giovanni's assertions at the temple's ruins, negating Silas' usual mistrust. The Empire, the Priestess, and the artifacts had indeed existed.

"Do you believe in that goddess?" asked the youth.

Garrick laughed, as if it were a joke.

"Does anyone? I know as much about Her as you do, but a good story is a good story. I guess an absent Priestess led to absent belief. A bit of a shame…"

It was then Silas saw movement among the headstones, some distance from the open window. He stood, going close to better understand what he had glimpsed.

"See something, boy?" Garrick asked.

He saw the green of Rina's dress in the torchlight, heard her soft laugh. There was someone with her. As they came closer, the clink of soldier's armor sent a fiery tremor through his body. Rage followed.

She's betrayed you.

Silas left in a flash, the hovel's door slamming shut behind him. However, he was followed.

"Hey!"

Caine's voice. Silas ignored it.

He stormed though the field of headstones and drew his weapon, blind with rage. The blond soldier was greeted by a blade to the throat.

"Have you lost your fawking mind, Rina?" Silas snarled, "or are you just trying to make me angry?"

The young woman seemed more furious than worried by the threat to her soldier.

"Put down your weapon," she ordered. "Alastor is no threat to you."

He growled, using the flat part of his blade to raise the soldier's chin, meeting his trembling gaze.

"Explain yourself."

The youth had a pale and uninspiring face, although there was no feature upon it that was unpleasant. The arrogance of wearing such conspicuous golden armor was not lost on Silas; however, it was something about the youth's emerald eyes that disgusted him most.

"L-look, You," the boy stammered. "I came down here to help an old friend, no need to jump me! You're the guy who has to get into the capital, right?"

Silas replied with a feral growl, which the youth must have interpreted as a 'Yes.'

"I can get you and Rina a couple of cloaks and take you up into the city—tomorrow, even. Just – just put down your sword!"

Slowly, Silas lowered his blade. Although he did not trust this 'Alastor' any more than before, he did not feel the need to anger Rina any further.

"When, tomorrow?"

"Meet me at the top of the secret passage tomorrow…morning, I think. Rina will show you where it is. But hey, if you want to take a little longer down here, be my guest! I'll bet you need time to wash or…sharpen that sword…"

His sycophantic pandering only aggravated Silas' temper, which – now suppressed – made his head throb. By the time he heard Caine's shout, all his tolerance had been spent.

"What are you doing?!"

"Leaving," Silas snarled.

He sheathed his weapon, casting a glare towards Rina—which was coolly returned. Silas had a need to say something then, feeling it necessary. Yet, he could find neither the words nor the emotion to convey.

Frustrated, he departed.

Rina introduced Alastor to Caine and the others, who seemed ordinarily wary of him—none reacting as rashly or as brutally to her friend as Silas had. Their exchange had made her cross, a feeling she was rather unaccustomed to. The sensation was like a thorn in her side, present even as Silas left and growing more irksome the longer she ignored it. By the time she had escorted Alastor back though the passage, she found that her mood had soured more than improved. She made her best effort to hide this change.

"You've got one brutish lover," Alastor said, shuddering no doubt with the thought of the violet-eyed youth.

"He's not my lover," she replied. "Only a friend."

"Like Kaish was?"

Though the words were harmless, she found herself recoiling from their bite. Yet, Alastor's cool smile could mask all hostility.

"Listen, Rina…"

He leaned towards her, forcing her to crane her neck as she always had. She realized that she had never had to strain to meet Silas' gaze, for he never seemed to be close enough – or when he was, his shouting made her sights turn elsewhere.

"I'm sorry for not protecting you better, back in the Rank," he said. "I wasn't as strong, back then. I promise, if Lance were to grab your hair again, I'd knock his nose right off his face."

Alastor flashed that charming, distracting smile, before leaning suspiciously close. Instinctively, she turned her face away. Her friend sighed, and the kiss that was clearly meant for her lips was bestowed upon her cold cheek.

"Thank you," she said, half aware of the words she uttered.

They said their goodbyes. Alastor waved once before he disappeared around a corner, his flickering shadow following soon after. Knowing she would see him in a few hours' time, Rina wasn't troubled by his quick departure. For now, things seemed to be working out as planned. Her good humor returned, she knelt and opened the trap door once again.

Silas' voice pierced the silence.

"Just like that, you leap into his arms."

She turned to find the dark youth standing over her, eyes like a hawk's, trained upon its rival.

"That's none of your concern," she snapped.

"It concerns me that a convict is so keen to ask aid of a soldier. Are you naïve, or just stupid?"

Rina was livid.

"Who are you to call *me* a convict?!"

Silas forced the shoulder of her dress down her arm, far enough to expose the slave's mark upon her white flesh.

"Did you think I didn't know the meaning of that mark? Your chopped hair? Apathy is not ignorance. Whatever foolishness gave you that X is leading us both down a dangerous path."

Red-faced at this violation of her modesty, she pulled up her sleeve, pushing his body from her.

"You're hardly one to lecture me about the choices I've made! You would have been hanged the night I met you if it weren't for that soldier!"

"It was for **your** sake that I returned to that bloody town—I could have left you on that riverbank."

"Why didn't you?!"

Rina realized too late how close he was, closer than he had been before the push. She had to look up at him, almost straining to see the intensity of his violet eyes. She had never seen them so close. There seemed to be many layers of color that gave them that hue: gold around the iris, making them rich with gleam; red glistening like fire; glacial sapphire beneath them all, smooth and changing as the stream that had guided them through the forest.

His lips parted, words resting there, waiting for a breath of life. But they would never leave their resting place. In a moment, Rina was crushed between him and the wall as his lips were thrust upon hers.

Her anger succumbed to the heat of his body. Their mouths locked, meshed, gnashed; she felt the scrape of his otherworldly fangs as he drew all breath from her, kissing her as though he wished to draw out her soul and swallow it whole. His hands possessed hers, pinning them above her head to render her helpless. And yet, she kissed him. She kissed him until the raw taste left her dizzy, her heart too present in her ears, drowning thought with the sound of its drumming—rising, pounding, pounding.

They fell into rhythm: her breasts rising, his chest falling. Hers falling, his pressing. He released her hands as his own slid down her body, caressing her with warmth. Her own tangled in his black hair, feeling each knot, as their lips locked, breath twisted together in dance—pounding, rising, falling. Wordless. No questions. No pain.

It was he who broke their kiss. He kept her against the wall as he pressed his face into her neck; she felt him inhale, like a dog taking in a new scent.

"Be still," he said.

He gave no explanation for his actions, no reason for his words. His powerful arms were wrapped gently around her, cocooning her in warmth only he could give. They were as binding as chains, yet gave her the shelter of a home. It was then she knew—it was Silas who smothered Kaish's memory.

Chapter XXIII

A cool stream bubbled past Kaish's feet as he stood amongst the trees, staring up at the sunlight as it trickled down past dense leaves. He felt spots of it warm upon his face, touching his cheeks and eyes while other parts were left in darkness. He was alone here, alone with the gentle sun and the stream, the leaves and the breeze. And then, she was there. The fair-skinned girl, her chestnut locks cropped to her ears, was there across the stream, her blue eyes bright in the trees and the sun. He felt too much joy.

A dream.

Although he realized this, he didn't want to believe it. Kaish wanted to continue staring at that beautiful girl across the stream, so near to him; so far away. He had everything to say to her, and nothing. The result was silence. It seemed an eternity before his betrothed's soft voice finally drifted through, but a whisper in this transient place.

"I can't go back into the forest," she said.

Her words baffled him. He gazed upon her for a long while, finding no answer in her soft gaze.

"I don't understand," he said.

She only smiled.

"It's time I leave it behind."

Though she smiled, he saw terrible sadness in her features. It fell like a mist about her, dampening her sights. He longed to brush away that dampness, to make her smile sincere.

"Why don't you come here?" he asked.

The girl drew back, startled away. Terror had replaced her sadness. Yet, as suddenly as it had come, the look was gone. Tears filled her gaze again, glistening like glass.

"I'll be alone," she said, tears beginning to fall. "I'll be alone on the other side."

Kaish couldn't decipher her words, as much as he longed to. His heart ached with pity—though for what, he didn't yet understand.

"Why must you be alone, here?"

She choked upon her reply, whatever it might have been. Her head was limp as a broken doll's, each tear glistening as it fell to join the stream. The sight broke his heart.

Kaish remembered his strength. The hand he offered was steady, unshaken by even his own doubt. He remembered his smile.

"Cross, Rina. I will be with you. If I'm here, you will never be alone."

Slowly, her despair melted away. Her tear-stained lips turned to smile, as she regarded him with tenderness. However, as her hand reached out to take his, she hesitated. She looked behind her, once.

"There's one more thing I must give," she said.

Behind her, almost hidden by the trees' shadow, there was a girl. Her black hair was long, waved like a flowing river, and her fair skin was virgin to the sun's rays. Upon her striking face were red lips, as dark as blood, and eyes of the purest blue. Kaish had never beheld such beauty. The mere sight of this unknown girl, but a glimpse in the shadows, stole his breath away.

"Will you wait for me?" Rina asked.

He nodded, sincere as he could be.

"I swear to you, I will be here."

The girl smiled her sweet smile, so perfect upon her alluring face. He had never noticed how womanly her features were: her cheekbones well defined, a woman's body already blossomed from a girlish shape. The eyes he had so admired were more than a startling color—they were wise.

"I'll be here," she whispered, slowly withdrawing her pale hand. "I'll cross over, and we will be together."

Plink.

Plunk.

The sound of dripping water roused him from his dreams. The scuttle of prowling rats convinced the prisoner to open his eyes, in hopes to ward the rodents off with movement. They were drawn to the scent of his shirt, so dirty now that it was rotting from his body, the Stag's insignia distorted by filth.

Plink.

He snarled at a rat as it came near, having learned that the sound terrified them. He watched the creature scurry away.

Plunk.

Kaish had heard that dripping for many days, now. It came without warning, or explanation. It was always the same.

Plink.

Plunk.

He remembered hearing it before, long ago. The sound alone conjured the memory of his tiny home in Levanche, where he and his mother, Alessia, spent their penniless existence. He remembered being six years old, lying on the floor in the front room as the rain pummeled their thin roof. There were two leaks in the roof that Alessia could never patch. They continued to let rain in, one drop at a time.

Plink.

Plunk.

All his life, he had been tormented for being Talonian. Yet, the truth was that he felt as Larascan as any of his tormentors. The time he spent in Talon had been a brief existence, when he was too young to cling to memories. His mother had never properly learned Larascan, however. The Talonian language had been the only tool of communication in their household. Thus, his accent had developed, and he had been branded a stranger.

Plunk.

A small stream ran by his childhood home, just deep enough for him to cool his feet in during hot summer months. Mistrusted by the other village children, he spent his time among the frogs in that stream, searching for rocks made perfectly smooth by the water. Kaish found only three during his time there: the first found during his first year in Larasca; the second when he was seven, while his mother was washing his only shirt in the water; the last when he was fourteen, before he had joined the Stags. He had kept those with him, reminding him of a simpler time.

Plink.

Alessia had brought only two artifacts from her home in Talon: a golden bracelet, the origin of which she kept hidden, and her wooden flute.

She could weave the most beautiful melodies with that instrument, warding away all of his darkest fears.

"Music is the remedy for all pain, my Kairos," she would say. *"There is no feeling in the world that cannot be sung away."*

Kairos. He had tried for many years to forsake his childhood name, but it continued to haunt him. Around every corner, there was someone who knew it, someone who spoke it in ignorance: Kairos, Kairos. It meant "an opportunity," his mother had said, "a time to act."

Whose opportunity? he had asked.

Plunk.

The Kyron war had ended just months before his own birth. During his childhood, the wounds from that conflict were so raw upon the Larascan people that their usual mistrust of foreigners remained amplified by wartime hatred. For many years, Alessia had taken care to ensure that her black-haired child was kept from the eyes of soldiers and Protectors alike. However, all her caution could not protect the boy from his own curiosity. It was by chance that he met General Marcus. The General was intrigued by the dirty-looking boy who kept away from others, content to patiently observe the traveling soldiers from afar. When the child asked who he was, he explained that he was a servant of the King.

"Why would you want to serve that King?" he asked.

"Because the King protects my loved ones, and by serving him, I serve them."

Then, the man had given him a single gold coin, and a smile.

"When you grow up, perhaps you can serve King Cedric along with me. We are a brotherhood, us soldiers. You will earn many of these coins, and you will never again know hunger, or loneliness."

The boy never forgot that day. He made a vow to himself that he would join the King's Ranks and serve the country that had become his home. He would earn money for Alessia, so they could fix the leaks in their roof. He would make friends, so he wouldn't have to play alone in the stream another summer.

The summer of his fourteenth year, when the Stags were still trained separately from their soldiers, a recruiting Captain arrived in Levanche. He said he would take any youth willing to leave his home and turn him into a proud soldier. The boy heard the call. In the middle of the night, he stole his mother's bracelet and her flute, and joined the Captain as they left the city. He forsook the name his mother gave him, going forevermore by a name that had no meaning.

Plink.

King Cedric died in 648 I.R., only months after Kaish began his training. Within two years, the new King, Attlas, had completed his plans to close the Stag training camps. Without a war to fight, Attlas saw no need for them. Those who wished to continue their training were instructed to join a military Rank and learn on the road, and would be advanced when their General saw fit. Feeling remorse for his selfish decision, Kaish returned to Levanche before finding a Rank. However, he found no home to return to. The townspeople said Alessia had contracted a mysterious illness shortly after his departure. To prevent it from spreading, their home was burned upon her death.

"Wouldn't want to catch any Tallk germs."

Plink.

Plunk.

General Lance had outright refused to accept him, at first. It was only after Kaish had begged his veteran soldiers to persuade him that he was given an opportunity to prove himself. After humiliating the Stag Colin in a weaponless fight, the soldiers pressed their General to recruit him. Even so, they could not pressure the General to advance him. In four years, all but two of the original Stags had been advanced: Colin, and Kaish. It had made him angry, at first. However, time had helped him accept his fate. He had no home to run to, no friends to stand up for him. His life had come to a standstill, without opportunity. Then, Rina came.

She was his beacon of hope. After four long years, she had become the only light at the end of his day—a single chance for a better life. Although he knew it had been rash to entrust his mother's bracelet to her, she had deserved it. When he closed his eyes, he could still remember the sweet taste of her pink lips, so soft and free. But it was soon tainted by the taste of river water, and the sound of her screams.

Now he was locked away, his last hope extinguished. It seemed fitting, now. He was a man with neither purpose nor means of escape. Now, there were true bars to enforce his mental state.

Plunk.

A sudden light pierced his thoughts. Kaish pressed himself into a corner, fleeing it as the rodents did. Closing his eyes, he hoped that the steps he heard were not for him. However, his hopes were in vain. When he opened his eyes, he found a vacant, sapphire gaze staring back at him, staring out through strands of very black locks.

"I've come with a warning," said the man, his voice lacking something vital.

Kaish's vision was still spotted by shadows, damaged by the light. His tongue, dry with neglect, could barely croak a remark.

"Who are you?"

The man did not respond to this, capable only of following his previous thought.

"You will die, soon."

Kaish stared forward, making no attempt to seem surprised. Yet, the affirmation of his fate chilled him to the core.

"Above, there are soldiers preparing your chains. They will come soon to take you to your execution."

The Talonian could almost hear the rattling above, each chain tested for durability. He wondered if the cuffs would grate the skin upon his wrists.

"Honor will be restored to you, in death," the man continued, no word more emphasized than any other. "By order of a guilty Queen, you will be immortalized in this city. Your life will not end in death."

Kaish heard the opening of far-off doors, not near enough to blind him. He could almost feel his time running out—the chains' rattle counting each moment.

"How do you know these things?" he asked. "Who *are* you?"

But the stranger was already gone, vanished into the dungeon halls.

The shaking chains brought the light of flickering torches. The bars were unlocked, and soldiers flooded the room. Kaish was bound and shackled, a cloak tied too tight around his throat. He fought none of it.

As the eldest soldier courteously drew the dark hood over his head, he remembered his mother's hands upon his hair, feeling his black curls.

"As compliant as your father's, twisting whichever way I bend them."

Plink.

Plunk.

Chapter XXIV

*N*ot even Silas understood why he had kissed Rina. There had been this great force building within him as they spoke, drawing him to her – a pressure growing that would not reside until he released that energy upon her, breaking the unseen barrier between them. He desired her. He wanted more than just her lips, that torturous, futile exchange of breath and water. He wanted from her all that Sh'ka had taken from him, and more.

Yet, he had let her go. Silas forced her away, as if in embarrassment, telling her to return to the hovel below. He would sleep amongst the headstones that night, away from her.

Why?

He did not trust his own intentions. Her innocence was her beauty, and he could not bring himself to take it.

Fool.

Silas didn't see her again until he ascended the ladder through the sacred passage, finding her with the blond soldier. He was surprised how angry he was to see the youth touching her, even to fasten the cloak around her neck. Still, he said nothing. When the girl noticed Silas, she seemed embarrassed, and drew her hood to hide her face. Silas understood.

Alastor made good on his promise. The soldier provided Silas a cloak as well – though a short one, meant to try his patience – and led both him and Rina to the surface, through the passage the soldiers had made for themselves. The blond youth needed only flash his sickening smile for the guards to let them pass, without questioning. Yet, the questions this raised in Silas' mind were overshadowed by the looming presence of the city beyond.

Silas' first step onto the frozen grounds of the capital awakened strange feelings within him, unclear and nauseating in their intensity. The icy warmth against his face was as natural as his skin; even so, the bright sunlight overwhelmed his unsuspecting eyes. Around him was the splendor of the city, marble bricks comprising the walls of every building, made whiter by the snow that fell like petals upon the soil.

"This is the capital?" Rina asked in awe, her hood already drawn back to expose her fair features.

"The Scholars' Square," Silas replied, "the western quarter of the city."

Both she and the soldier stared in shock, baffled by his apparent knowledge. He said nothing more, unable to justify it; it was Alastor who next spoke.

"So…what are you looking for up here?"

Silas could not answer him immediately. His eyes wandered the buildings, though his vision was unsteady—flickering, adjusting to new light. The words came before he thought them, springing from a deeper awareness.

"We have to split up," he said. "Search for the shop of the inventor Clarke Temlar."

Alastor nodded, wrapping an arm around Rina.

"Easy. We'll find it before mealtime."

Silas tensed in the face of this blatant affection, his hand twitching into a fist meant for that youth's visage. Still, for Rina's gentle glance, he held back.

"Then go," he said.

Rina allowed herself to be led away, refusing to look at Silas again. Silas turned the other direction, allowing himself to resent her.

The icy streets welcomed him like an old friend. Though the well-dressed people were strangers to him, he recognized each surrounding tree – knew the pattern of their still-green leaves, burdened by snowfall. He knew each turn in the road, the marble glint of each roof, as though he had memorized their pattern from a world above.

Ghostly recollection brought him to an abandoned street, to a shop with a long, flat roof. In his mind's eye, he could see the shadow of a black horse tied to the tree before it; beside it, a cloaked man stopping to brush snow from a mounted sign.

Temlar, it said.

The street was empty in all but Silas' thoughts. It was a creeping sort of insanity: images surfacing, flicking like a candle's glow upon the landscape.

The shadows guided him to the door, left ajar. It creaked in the warm breeze, beckoning him closer. Still, he hesitated. He sensed an intangible presence beyond that frame, threatening to overwhelm him.

His hand trembled about the handle, despite his strength. It was with great difficulty that he forced open the door to the inventor's shop.

A strange sound greeted him – a metal clicking, clicking.

Tick. Tock.

Its origin was a large, wooden creation standing on one side of the room, its flat face adorned by what seemed to be a moving sundial. It continued to make that incessant noise, with no regard for its new company.

Tick. Tock.

Wooden dragons were mounted upon the walls, some still dripping with fresh paint; amongst the floors' shavings were discarded hilts from play swords, and half-furnished figurines forgotten in the rubble. Extraordinary shields were scattered upon cluttered tables, glistening like diamonds. Yet, Silas' gaze was drawn past them, towards the darkest corner of the room. There, a covered mirror loomed behind a dusty table, veiled by shadows.

The black cloth concealed all but one corner of the mirror, which itself was speckled and grey. It was unimpressive, dull, compared to the other artifacts in the shop. But despite many layers of dust, Silas could make out a faint design upon the cloth, embroidered with violet thread—a dragon, curved like a crescent moon. The Xavier insignia.

Silas felt his fingers wrap about the cloth, sliding it to the floor. Beneath, he found a mirror framed by the most elaborate of carvings: fruits, leaves, and winged creatures were immortalized upon solid oak. Each curve was familiar to the pads of his fingers; his reflection was not. The tall, battered man who stared back at him now was little more than a stranger to his eyes.

There was a single artifact upon the table, reflected in the mirror before him – a round, metal box, a glass rose upon its lid. Although it was one of the inventor's most beautiful creations, it was as forgotten as the mirror, dust so thick upon it that it had no color.

Silas found the latch upon it, then lifted up its silver lid. Within, metal parts turned, producing the melody that haunted his dreams.

Lovely boy.

Silas grew ill. He doubled over, forced to grip the table with shaking hands as his head throbbed, acid lurching from his stomach to his throat. Vision blurred, tilting, the image in the mirror changing before his eyes. Staring back at him was a pale woman, sapphire eyes like slits upon her face, hair black as nightfall—his spitting image.

Sleep.

1st Day of 12th Month, 644 I.R.

Reja's father didn't come to dinner. His caretaker told him that his Papa had been called away to Raine, and would come home as soon as he could. His mother would tuck him in, that night.

Oh my pretty little son,
Close your eyes in gentle sleep
Feel my hand upon your throat
Pressing down until you sigh
My lovely little boy
My cursed little toy

2nd Day of 12th Month, 644 I.R.

Reja's mother told him he was sick. Each day, she would bring him a small cup of medicine, which smelled of oil and incense. It burnt his throat as it went down, and coated his stomach like mortar.

"It makes me sick. I don't want it, Mama!"

The woman ignored his cries, tucking him in each night. When he grew drowsy, she opened his music box and sang him to sleep.

Every time I see you, hatred for you only grows

Lovely boy

I never wanted you to be

So close your eyes in sleep

Disappear, my little spawn

My lovely little boy

7th Day of 12th Month, 644 I.R.

Oh my pretty little child

Close your eyes in deepened sleep

I'll be waiting for you here

Hold my hand and slip away

My lovely little boy

My pretty little shame

Reja was too sick to remember his father's name, or his mother's face.

Yet, he drank her medicine; poison coated his insides.

"Rest, child. The castle knows you are ill."

Her lips were cold upon his forehead.

"Your father is rushing home to you."

The world was growing colder, cold as the sheet she pulled over his head.

"Good night, my Prince."

The music box cracked upon the stone floor; the song ended.

Then, the door swung open.

"Hey! What are you doing in my shop?!"

A short man stood in the doorway, with the same scholarly build and fiery hair as the man who had frightened the band of thugs in Raine. His face, too, was the same—yet, Silas knew it for another reason. It was already imprinted in his memory, made in another life.

When Temlar snatched a sword from the wall, Silas' was drawn in a moment. The unpracticed assault was parried, the attacker's weapon flung across the room.

Silas had never seen such anger upon a man's face, scrunching it beyond recognition. And then, as the inventor's green eyes stared into his own, the fury melted away. Little by little, awe smoothed his countenance.

"Those eyes…"

Too quick, the red-haired man whipped a dagger from his waist, snatching Silas' hand. The blade slit his palm down its scarred center, reopening the wound Vaan had left. The cherry-red blood flowed fresh.

Silas roared.

"Fawk!"

The inventor wouldn't let him reclaim his hand. Although he dropped the dagger, he continued to watch the blood flow, as if mesmerized.

When Silas could take no more, he ripped his hand away. He had a thousand curses to impart – but when Temlar knelt before him, forehead to the ground, the youth's snarl died in his throat.

"I knew you would return to us," the man said, shoulders trembling with repressed sobs. "I-I told him…"

Silas stared at him, vacant. As Temlar rose to his feet, the youth drew away, unsettled—intimidated. Yet, the crying man smiled for him.

"Long live the Xaviers. Long live our King."

The capital was overwhelming to a rural girl like Rina. She had never seen so many fine buildings, or stumbled over such evenly-laid cobblestone paths. Although Alastor advised that she keep her hood up – her hair, though longer now, was not yet long enough for her to pass for anything but a commoner – she could not bear to have her vision impeded by its shadow. She wanted to see the towering, frosted trees with her own eyes.

"It's so incredible," she said to her friend, who now lagged behind her.

"If you like a few pretty statues and creepy leafy trees, sure," he replied.

His sarcasm aside, she enjoyed having a natural conversation. She might have become accustomed to Silas' grunts and growls, but she delighted in hearing real words in response. She had just forgotten how to hold up her end of the exchange.

"You all right, Rina?" Alastor asked, grasping her shoulder. "You seem pretty distracted."

The touch caught her off guard—she flinched from him as she had never flinched before.

"Do I?"

Her thoughts were elsewhere. Her mind remained in that dark cavern, where Silas had pinned her to the rocky wall. She could still feel his warm lips upon her, his hot breath filling her lungs.

"Where's the Rank?" she asked, attempting to alter her thoughts.

"I thought we were looking for that inventor."

"Yes, but I have a feeling that Silas already found him…"

She smiled at her friend, urgency in her eyes.

"Please? I'd love to see the Stags again."

The remark made Alastor noticeably uncomfortable. His gaze shifted past her, as it used to, as one hand tapped his golden armor. For once, she noticed just how long it took him to compose his reply.

"They're busy, I think."

"Doing what?" she asked, suspicious.

"There's a ceremony," he replied, "They're probably helping to…set it up."

Her wary look was answered by the crowds of people moving past them, congregating in the center of town. Before she could question this, Alastor took her arm.

"You want to see what's going on?"

He gave her no opportunity to protest. Alastor seemed strangely hurried, too eager to move her onward. He smirked as he led her, a sinister tilt to it.

Uncomfortable to begin with, she felt stifled by the mob about her, even when Alastor pushed to the front. There, they had full view of the stone platform in the center square. A curved dragon was etched deep into its surface—the same insignia that had once flown above the soldiers' wagon. Blood already stained the carving.

"They practice on pigs first, I heard," Alastor chuckled.

Rina's throat closed, horror whitening her face.

"What is this?" she whispered.

A tall, masked man ascended the platform, dragging a great axe with him. A smaller man then set out a wooden block, meant for cattle. It was then that a white stallion emerged from the crowd, bearing a beautiful, raven-haired woman, a golden crown upon her head. Behind her, two guards followed, their russet mares large enough to trample a man.

Rina stood still, overcome by the sight. She waited in awe to hear her Queen speak—but no words would come. The elegant woman was like a statue in the background, her sapphire gaze set upon the platform.

Too soon, the main attraction arrived. Led by three guards, a hooded youth was brought onto the platform, rusty chains shuddering with every step. The cloak seemed too heavy upon his shoulders, weighing down a starved frame; his skin was pale as the snow around them, starved for daylight. Something about his hands, strong and weathered, reminded Rina of her betrothed's touch. When she saw the dark curls spilling from beneath his hood, mangled with grime, anguished memories choked her heart.

"Rina! Where are you going?!"

She didn't know the man upon the platform, destined to be slaughtered like cattle; she didn't know why she ran. She barely felt Alastor's hand upon her wrist, gripping it as tightly as it could, trying to keep her there. His fingers wrapped about her bracelet, which could not hold. As it slid away, she was free.

She pushed past the cheering crowd, feeling sick and pale. She didn't know where she was going, or where she had come from. All she wanted was to be rid of that place.

Cruelty…

Standing there, a dark figure in a white landscape, she saw Silas. He was a pillar in the middle of the street, solemn and strong. He was there when she rushed to him, rushed into his arms.

He was there as she cried.

Kaish saw her as she left, her chestnut hair falling free of its black hood. He had thought he would never see such locks again, outside his dreams. He almost thought he was dreaming now—but then, he remembered the jeering faces about him, around her.

"Spy!"

"Traitor!"

He was surprised by the peace within him, in the face of these words; surprised by his smile as he beheld Alastor's smirking face.

Beside him, his sentence was read.

"Kairos of Talon has been charged with destruction of the Queen's property and conspiring against the Kingdom of Larascan. The punishment is death."

More cheers, scattered curses.

"Does the Talonian have any last words?"

He had none. Peace had quelled his tongue, his last memories already filled with thoughts of Rina's blue eyes. Now, he knew words would be wasted on these people, who knew nothing of his life – who stood there in pride, mocking someone they believed was less than them. They did not deserve his final words.

His silence was not enough for the crowd. The Queen's voice rang out, silencing the cries.

"The foreigner deserves no statement."

Kaish was resigned to his fate. He stood still as the executioner pulled down his hood; his knees buckled as the man forced him down. As the axe was raised, speckled by icy flakes, he recalled a word from his childhood.

La foresta.

The land of many trees: the Talonian name for Larasca. The land that would one day cast out Rina, into his waiting arms. He would be there, waiting. Waiting until she returned to him.

Wait. Please.

The axe fell.

Talonian blood spilled down over the block, staining the carved dragon. Slowly, the Xavier insignia turned crimson red.

Chapter XXV

$\mathcal{S}$omething had changed in Silas. Rina sensed it as they descended into the caverns of Citris, returning to their hideaway. He seemed oblivious to Alastor's presence, or indifferent to it – even when the soldier helped her down the ladder, Silas did not glare. His mind seemed to have been displaced.

Rina saw two scrolls tucked into his cloak, almost hidden.

"What are those?" she asked.

"A map," he said, "and a letter."

"From who?" she pressed.

Silas would not reply. He said nothing more until they arrived in the hovel, waking the inhabitants with the door's loud slam.

"Do you intend to spend the rest of your lives hiding?" the youth snarled.

Caine and Tasha snapped up from the bed, as Garrick grumbled to his feet.

"What's this racket?" the old man muttered.

Once Alastor had squeezed past the door, Silas unfurled one of the yellow scrolls across the bed, between Tasha and her lover. Upon it was an ink diagram, riddled with symbols Rina could not understand.

"Tomorrow is the Winter Ball," Silas explained. "The four Squares of Joanissia will be empty: denizens of the Peasant Square are forbidden to leave their homes, while members of the Merchant Square and the Scholars' Square will rim the castle to glimpse the nobles' gowns as they enter the ballroom. The Noble Square, of course, will be completely deserted. We can take all we need from the city, then easily infiltrate the castle."

"Have you lost your mind?!" Tasha cried.

"You're suggesting an organized break-in? Into the castle?" Alastor said, more in shock than anything. He seemed oddly unnerved, his impatience growing.

The graveskeeper seemed intrigued.

"What are you getting at?"

Silas gestured to a small place on the map, to the lower portion of what appeared to be a tower.

"Give me one night, and I can find an underground entry into the palace. After that, I'll only need six men, at most. With that small band, I guarantee we will be able to not only corner our Queen, but force her to remove each and every troop from Citris."

"And how do you propose we do that?" Tasha asked.

As Rina drew closer, she could see Silas circling a small section of the map with his finger; however, the word upon it held no meaning to her. Shock had already silenced her companions – hers did not come until he spoke again.

"We take Azalea hostage."

Caine gawked; Tasha stared.

"The Princess?" she asked.

Even Alastor sat alert, clearly bewildered—horrified.

"You're serious?"

"She won't let her guards near her room as she changes. When she emerges, our men take her, and choose one to deliver the news to the Captain of the Guard. If the Queen wants to avoid controversy, she'll agree to our terms."

A baffled silence stifled the room, his audience agape. Rina didn't understand where this new sense of leadership had come from, or the facts that now rolled off his tongue. No one seemed to know what to say. Alastor especially sat in discomforted silence, fidgeting strangely, seeming caught somewhere between anger and fear. Only Tasha found words.

"How do we know if the Queen got the message?"

Rina looked to her in shock, unable to believe that the woman was considering Silas' insane proposition. Yet, she had never looked more serious.

Silas responded with some level of surprise, not anticipating this question. Even then, he responded smoothly.

"Rina and I will attend the ball. I have a contact on the surface who will help us to make a seamless entrance; then, we can observe from within."

No one was more stunned by this revelation than Rina herself; she stared, wide-eyed with fear.

"I-I can't dance," she whispered, "please, not me."

Caine looked upon her with pity, perhaps knowing how hopeless it was to change Silas' mind. However, Tasha seemed only excited, an unusual sparkle to her gray eyes.

"Get up, Caine. We're going up the ladder."

"You can't possibly be thinking of going through with this load of hob-nob?" Garrick asked, making no secret of his doubt.

"Caine will gather the troops, and I'll get my old dancing shoes," Tasha said, a sharp smile on her face. "We have a Princess to kidnap."

Caine followed behind her, obedient, as she pushed through the crowded hovel to the door. Although he went without protest, he didn't seem as enthusiastic as she.

"Soldier, you come with us," Tasha ordered. "Silas, you watch Sen. He can only nap for so long."

Despite clear reluctance, Alastor did join the exiting party – but not without a long look towards Rina. He seemed to want something from her, still. The girl had had too little to say to him after the execution, when he had come to find them. She sensed that she had displeased him in some way by her departure; however, he had angered her just as much by taking her to such an event. As long as her anger remained, it wasn't safe to speak with him.

Garrick stood from the seat he had taken on the side of the bed, cracking his neck as he did.

"Sorry, kids, but there's no way I'm staying with that pale brat when his mom don't got him on a leash. Good luck with it."

Then, he left them alone.

Rina could see the red-haired boy still curled upon his pile of blankets, protectively clinging to his whimpering pup. It was a sweet sight, as she had always felt it was. Yet, Silas seemed deeply uncomfortable. She noticed how he kept to the other side of the room, eyes set coldly upon the sleeping child as he gripped his hand.

Suddenly, she noticed the bandage that bound it.

"What happened?" she asked.

He barely glanced to her.

"Your hand," she insisted. "Is it bleeding again?"

She knew that the wound had only just closed; she had seen him tying and retying bandages for months, only going without one during the last stretch of their journey. I worried her, knowing that the difficult injury was causing him pain once again.

"Do me a favor, Rina," he said, "don't ask questions today."

Soon, the boy sat up. Rubbing his eyes, his hair, he adjusted to his new surroundings. His gaze surveyed the room like a predator's, unusually sharp, unusually alert. Soon, it settled—locked upon Silas' bandaged hand.

No one spoke. For the first time, Rina began to understand Silas' discomfort. Though she couldn't explain why, that same unease took hold of her, stirring fear in her heart. She was not blind to his abnormal nature, his fangs or his white skin. Without his mother to tuck him away, the threatening nature of these traits was free to fully manifest. No one moved until the pup began to whine, nuzzling its furry body against the pale boy.

The spell was broken. Sen began to coddle the dog, stroking it with all but motherly affection. At once, Rina breathed a sigh of relief.

"You really love your dog, don't you?" she asked the boy, beginning to smile.

He had nothing to say to her. However, her words must have stirred some feeling within him, for he looked again towards Silas. Now, his gaze was more human.

"You know what I am," he said.

The soft voice hardly belonged to its owner, so feminine, almost ethereal; its words were for Silas alone.

Silas showed no feeling. In response, he gave only a nod.

"You're afraid of me," said the boy.

He said nothing more. His attention returned to the dog, which he stroked and coddled with the gentlest of looks. All his otherworldly traits were diminished with this action. Rina no longer saw his pale skin, or his unusual teeth – she saw only a loving child, lost without his mother.

Before long, the pup broke free from his hold. Whimpering, it bounded down from the little pile, running up to the youth who observed them. It wagged its small tail, familiarizing itself to the taste of Silas' feet and ankles until the youth finally pushed it away. Yet, it was not a harsh action. As Rina observed, Silas brought himself down to the creature's level, allowing it to rub its face in his uninjured palm. When Sen came to retrieve his pet, Silas did not flinch. He lifted the pup himself, and placed it in the boy's pale grip.

"Never let anyone tell you how to live," Silas said. "As long as people fear you, they'll want to control you. You can't let them. Live well, despite them."

His violet eyes met with the boy's emerald orbs – and though Silas did not touch him, Rina could see the unspoken bond between them.

"Do you understand?" he asked the child.

Sen nodded, saying nothing in return. Cradling his pup, he returned to the pile of blankets, curling up upon them. Very soon, the child slept again.

Tasha and Caine returned, both wearing proud looks. Caine waited by the door as the blonde woman tossed Rina a pair of fine, black shoes, far different than the kind she usually wore – they were completely hard, raised in the back by some kind of wedge. Rina examined them, perplexed.

"What are these?" she asked.

"Dancing shoes," the woman replied. "You're going to have to get used to them."

The woman looked to Silas, who seemed grateful for the delivery.

"I suppose I'll teach her how to dance; but I want you to promise something in return."

"And that is?" he asked.

"That you let me be involved with the kidnapping."

Neither Silas nor Caine appeared pleased with this request, Caine even less. Disapproval written on his brow, he stumbled over many words before he could finally form a coherent protest.

"Tasha, this is too much! Can't you be content to keep your son safe?"

"The boy can protect himself. I'm tired of twiddling my thumbs and waiting for something exciting to happen!"

"We're hiding in a graveyard because something exciting *did* happen! Be reasonable, for once in your life!"

But the woman would not be satisfied. She bickered with her lover until Rina found it painful to watch, the two unwilling to cease until Caine gave up entirely, holding his head with exhaustion. It was then that Tasha turned again on Silas.

"Well? Are we agreed?"

Silas seemed no less annoyed than Caine; however, not being the patient type, he agreed – not to please her, no doubt, but to avoid the confrontation.

"Whatever. Come if you want."

Tasha clapped her hands together with feminine excitement, rousing a groan from Caine. She ignored this.

"Get your flute, dear," she told him.

The man sighed, not resisting. When Tasha beckoned them outside, Rina obeyed. To her surprise, Silas quickly shed his cloak, following close behind.

"The trick to court dancing is simple," Tasha began, positioning the two of them near each other in the open space. "Just follow – you know how to dance, Silas?" she asked, suddenly.

Silas nodded, moving uncomfortably close to Rina. The blood rushed to her face as she tried not to breathe, afraid he would feel it on his neck.

"Tell her the basics," he said. "She can follow me."

Tasha gave her a simple set of instructions, informing her of where Silas' hand would rest upon her waist, where her own would touch his neck, and his hand. She told her of the basic step, and what each change in the music would entail. Yet, none of it meant anything when a melody again rose from Caine's Talonian flute. Rina froze instantly, those old feelings stirring within her, rendering her immobile.

It did not matter. In moments, Silas was guiding her step – as long as he held her body, she could not stumble; every step was fluid, melody entwining with dance, twirling, the melody flowing about them warmly, warm as his body. She had not realized how gracefully he maneuvered his own strong frame, entirely in control of his posture, his limbs, his strength. It was as though ghosts guided his every step.

She could not meet his gaze, no matter how hard she tried. It seemed he was hiding it from her, afraid that one shared look would reveal too much. Although they were close now, he still seemed distant from her. And yet, she was happy. The music was kindling in her soul, that his warmth had set aflame.

Once, she noticed Alastor watching them in the darkness, his visage half-shadowed by the flickering torchlight. She had never seen such a look on his face. For his lips to be so taut, his eyes so green—for a moment, she glimpsed the wickedness devouring his soul.

That night, she walked again with Alastor to the ladder, going to return him to his Rank. Her thoughts remained with Silas, who had dismissed himself to investigate the supposed underground entry from which Caine's men would enter the castle. She could not distract herself from the ghostly feeling of his hand still upon her, or the dizziness that lingered after imperfect spins. There was a smile painted upon her face as she thought of the ball they would attend the next morning, as false pretenses meant little to a young woman who would never have another chance to be nobility.

"I can't believe you, Rina."

Alastor's voice shattered her thoughts. She looked to him with a start, thrown off balance.

"Can't believe what?"

"How quickly you forgot about Kaish. I thought you were better than that."

She was struck dumb. Lifeless, staring, she beheld her friend in shocked silence.

"Can't talk? Typical."

Alastor stared down at her with an icy gaze, his countenance drawn with such contempt that it scathed her soul.

"You think I really didn't know what was going on between you two? You promised yourself to him, didn't you? You pledged to *marry* Kaish, and yet now you're fooling around with that possessive bastard while Kaish *mourns* you, thinking just like everyone else that you're feeding trees."

The soldier threw a golden bracelet to the ground, allowing it to roll through the dirt before it settled at her feet.

"I'll come down tomorrow to lead you to the surface; I'll help you with your little 'resistance.' But don't think it's because I approve of what you're doing."

The youth began to ascend the ladder, coldly turning his back on her.

"Spend the night thinking about the choices you've made."

He was gone too soon, the trap door's slam echoing above her head.

All at once, her tears fell like rain.

Kaish...

Alastor was right. Silas' presence had eclipsed her memories of Kaish – as she lifted the bracelet from the soil, feeling its familiar etchings again beneath her fingertips, she realized that she did not know when it had left her. She had lost it, and had not cared enough to know she had lost it.

I'm so sorry...

She was a traitor, and a liar. Rina had allowed her gentle companion to fade into obscurity, as she was seduced by the brutish nature of a stranger man. She had forgotten herself, as she had forgotten him.

Rina's legs could no longer hold her; they buckled, bringing her down into the soil beneath. Her tears ran like blood from her eyes, from a wound that could not be stitched. Honor dictated that she refuse Silas' feelings for her, for it was clear that he had them. However, it would hurt less to cut out her own heart.

I'm sorry...I'm sorry, I'm sorry...

The broken girl pressed the bracelet against her own face, as if to bind it to her skin. Her tears would clean its band.

To my beloved Reja,

Although you are young as I write this, I have recently come to realize the fragility of my own mortal state. My mind has been burdened with too much knowledge – such is the curse of our family. However, I feel that I must impart some of what I have come to know to you, my child, for it is your past as well as mine. True wisdom will not come to those ignorant of their own origins.

Through this quill and this ink, I will impart to you the story of the Xavier family. I use this medium so that in the event of my premature passing, the story will not be buried with me. However, you will need more than these words to understand the tale. I ask that you take the key from my study and enter the boarded tower, where the shames of our family have been locked away. Descend to the bottom level: there, our story will begin.

Silas followed a long and deserted path through Sanctuary, past the orchards and the mysterious lake, until there was only the light of his own torch to guide him. He walked and walked until, at last, there was nowhere more to go. Around him, there was only darkness.

Above.

He cast the torch's glow to the shallow ceiling above, finding a large, metal circle embedded in the stone. Upon it were ancient carvings, now indecipherable; in the center was a smooth handle.

With minimal strength, he turned the rusted handle, moving the whole of the circle until it came down—and with it, a rope ladder.

It had taken years of living in darkness, groping blindly for an identity among strangers, for him to reach this point. Foggy memories still shifting like specters through his consciousness, he stood on the cusp of reality, ready to claim the life he had lost.

Once he had made certain that he still carried the letter Temlar had given him, he ascended the rungs carefully, hearing the old wood creaking beneath his weight. His father's words fresh in his mind, he emerged in what he knew to be the lowest level of the boarded tower.

Once, there was a dark creature named Jaska. Everything about him was rotten and rank: his face was so unspeakably hideous that it had to be forever concealed in shadow. Yet, Jaska was a creature of incredible power. In his gnarled hands was the ability to grant any wish the human heart could design; and any wish he granted brought him more power. However, his gifts came at a price. Those who asked presents of him could offer no less than their soul in return, to do with as he saw fit. In death, Jaska transformed these forsaken souls into his pets: Dragons, doomed forever to embody the flaw that led to their demise.

Silas' torch lit the curved walls around him, revealing the seven long portraits mounted upon them. Although dust floated about the room, their paint was still as vibrant as the day they were created. The glow of one, in particular, called to him: a portrait of a white dragon, standing entirely still, its wings curved about it like a cloak. As Silas approached, it seemed to grow larger and larger, until it threatened to overwhelm him. Its white eyes pierced his soul.

The first Dragon, Nukpana, was called Solomon in life. He was a well-known philosopher and alchemist, guilty only of indolence. He allowed his many apprentices to do most of his work – such was his preference. He allowed life to slip him by with minimal effort, until he realized that he had squandered away his youth. To reclaim what he had lost, he sent his apprentices out on a quest to capture whatever material might be the metal essence of youth and vitality. It was one of his apprentices who brought Jaska to him. Jaska offered him a potion that would restore his vibrancy; in return, he asked only for his soul. Solomon agreed, and earned great fame for the discovery of this potion. The northern mountains of Larasha – Larasca, while it was still a part of the Empire of Asyrias – became known for many years as the Solomon Mountains, in honor of the miracle he found there. In his death, his soul was transformed into the white Dragon of sloth: a manipulative creature, never to dirty its own hands.

The next portrait portrayed a dragon with black scales, his wings spread high above him, reaching towards a cloudless sky. Beneath him was a glistening lake, his reflection upon its crystal surface – the only object in his glistening eyes.

The black Dragon, Corwin, was once the Prince of Asyrias. His given name was Micah Konstantin, a name that lives on in today's Rionan royalty. His beauty was known throughout the land; yet, his vanity was well-hidden. He was so afraid of losing his looks that he sought the ancient wishgiver to ensure they would be preserved. He asked to be kept beautiful for all his days, for he knew no other way to maintain happiness. Jaska granted his wish; however, happiness didn't come. Micah's suicide birthed the onyx Dragon, a beast who appreciates nothing but its own beauty.

The next creature displayed a massive, green-scaled dragon clutching two shadowy figures in its talons, crushing them until his nails turned red.

Adrian, the emerald Dragon, is not so harmless. He was born Davin, the simple son of a pig farmer. He so desired the love of the most beautiful woman in the village that he sold his soul to Jaska to ensure he would have her. Yet, throughout their relationship, he doubted her love. He convinced himself that she had fallen in love with another man – and to ensure that she could never leave him, he locked her inside their home until she starved to death. Soon after, the weight of his regret pushed him to fall upon his own knife.

Adrian is not a creature to be trifled with. He can transform the faintest shard of envy into a blade to pierce the strongest armor.

The third dragon had scales of the darkest red, which glowed of their own accord. It drew back onto its hind legs atop a mountain of ice, massive wings unfurled from his form—a great pillar of flames rose from his jaws. They filled the skies above him, dissolving clouds with furious power.

The story of the red Dragon, Aiden, is the most heartbreaking. He was spawned from the heartache of a man named Bourne, alive during the final days of the Empire of Asyrias. As the Empire's law-enforcing power began to wane, there was much unrest among the smaller villages. Bourne said the wrong thing to a rival village leader, through no fault of his own – less than a day later, he returned to find his wife and three children murdered in their home. Possessed by rage, his sole desire was to avenge their deaths. Jaska appeared to him and offered him a terrible, destructive power. He couldn't refuse. He massacred hundreds in his blind rage, no amount of blood capable of sating his grief, until another vengeful man finally took his life.

I ask that you be most wary of this creature, my son. You must not allow Aiden's rage to make you blind.

The fifth portrait featured a sapphire dragon, whose wing curled downward to veil her face. Above her, an apple tree reached towards a dark night, trying to escape the thorned vines that fought to strangle its trunk.

The blue-scaled Dragon, Sirena, lived the life of an inconstant woman. She was born Anna, a noblewoman of the old world. She was beautiful and greatly desired, a fact she was well aware of. Although she married young, she allowed herself to take a lover only days after her vows. All might have been well if she had left it at that; however, when a hooded stranger appeared to her, offering to remove her husband, she agreed to his price. She married her lover—yet, months later, cheated on him as well. When she was stoned for adultery, Sirena took shape, a beast who can mold herself into the most alluring of forms. She is a destroyer of men.

The following portrait was almost appealing. Great, russet wings were stretched out beneath the earth-scaled dragon as he basked in a mountain of rich fruits, great mouth open to accept the steady flow of a scarlet waterfall.

Not all of Jaska's creatures were cruel. Hale, the brown Dragon, was merely unfortunate. He was once a man named Daemon, disowned by his merchant father for being a drunkard. His only wish was to open a tavern of his own. Only Jaska trusted him with the gold it would take to begin his business venture. When Daemon drunk himself to death, Jaska took his soul as payment. Hale is the most benign of the Dragons; however, his power is no less great.

Of all of them, the final image was the most haunting. It stood larger than the others, somehow isolated from them, though close in proximity. This golden dragon bore two heads, split from its long and serpentine neck. One had eyes of saffron, cool as coins, while the other stared eternally through eyes of earthly brown.

The tale of the seventh Dragon is the beginning of our own story. It begins with a fortune-seeker named Fabian who traversed the Solomon Mountains, searching for the fabled elixir once discovered there. He had recently been disinherited from his family fortune and could not bear a life in which he had no wealth. He sought to make a fortune on the youth-restoring liquid and restore himself to the comfortable life that had been stolen from him. What he found instead was Jaska's temple – his home, for he wore a mask of piety. The hooded man did indeed offer him wealth, for the usual price.

However, Fabian would not be content with this. For his soul, he wanted no less than a kingdom with all the trappings of royalty, and a legacy that would carry on for a thousand years. Jaska said this was possible, for a higher wager. Three terms would have to be met: first, Fabian would have to pledge not only his own soul, but the soul of his every blood descendant; second, he would allow Jaska to enter his domain as he pleased, for as long as his legacy continued; last of all, Fabian would allow Jaska to purge his Kingdom of all trace of the creature's nemesis—the goddess Neschume.

Fabian agreed to these terms. Jaska loosed his Dragons upon the small region of Asyrias known as Larasha, the land most blessed of Neschume. Her five temples fell to their might, reduced to rubble, crushing the beliefs of her followers. When this was done, the powerful creatures raised mountains from the flat lands of the south and east, and flooded the land between them to create the Great River. This desolated land, now isolated from all but one side, became Fabian's kingdom: our Larasca. Jaska called him Xavier, the owner of this new world.

This is only half of our story. The other begins when Fabian, our first King, met his Queen.

There was a ladder in that room, a trap door above it. Silas stifled his own hesitation to ascend it, pushing himself into the room above.

He found himself in the main level of the tower, moonlight streaming in from long slivers of windows in the stone. The room was filled with mountains of gold and jewels, glittering in the night's glow; however, a thousand rusty objects strewn amongst them now tainted their sheen. Swords still caked with blood had settled in the piles, along with shields, bracelets, yellowed papers, and even bones.

Almost buried by the clutter, Silas spotted the remains of a marital bed – its frame broken, blankets now made thin by the feasting of insects. Above it was a portrait of a woman, whose dark hair had a silken glow, and whose deep-set eyes stared past the world, as if they had already seen all it had to offer.

Jaska had come to be aware of a small following of Neschume still thriving in caverns beneath the newly-built capital, Joanissia. Making good on his promise to rid Larasca of Her influence, Fabian stormed the hidden caverns with his soldiers. He would have killed the settlers he found there, were it not for the Priestess who stepped forward. Her name was Hope, their leader, and Neschume's most trusted prophet. She was also the most beautiful woman Fabian had ever laid eyes upon. Immediately, the King fell in love. He swore to her that he would spare her people, if she agreed to be his wife. Left with no option, Hope agreed. She was stripped of her sacred name and given a royal one; thus, she became Sabella, our first Queen.

The tower you are standing in was built for her. Fabian, seeking to please his bride, constructed it to her specifications. The lowest level, dug deep into the ground, would allow her passage to and from the city of Citris for as long as she lived. The main level would be her bedchamber, and the uppermost level would be her place of worship. Although it violated his dark deal, he could not bring himself to deny her this. However, her open worship of the deity drew Jaska's attention. He was furious to find that Fabian had taken one of Neschume's Priestesses for a wife, livid that he had allowed her to invite the Goddess into his castle. No longer content with just our souls, Jaska swore that if Fabian did not kill his beloved, his Dragons would become a plague upon him and his descendents, dooming each and every one of them to a tragic demise. Even then, Fabian refused to harm Sabella.

There was something strange about Sabella's portrait. Despite her fine clothes and royal jewelry, it seemed she wore a very primal necklace about her throat, so tight it seemed to choke her. Upon closer examination, Silas saw that it did not appear to be a necklace – rather, it was painted in broken parts, as if it had been tattooed upon her skin. It seemed unusual upon the pure skin of a pious woman.

The first Queen died in childbirth, leaving behind twins: Prince Carwyn, and a Princess, Aurora. It was with these children that our miseries began. When she came of age, Aurora was given to the leader of Kyro, one of the five nations that rose from the rubble of the broken Empire of Asyrias. After giving him a son – Amelio, the first Alexander – our last Princess succumbed to a deforming illness, dead before her twenty-first birthday. However, her soul did not go to Jaska, as was agreed. Because of Sabella's sacred blood, the hooded creature could not claim her soul. Instead, after a week of peaceful stillness, her soul simply dispersed into nothingness. This was true of Aurora's son, and Carwyn, and his son, and his grandson. No matter what we might do with this life, our end is the same: nothingness.

Shame overwhelmed the first Xavier. After his wife's death, he filled her bedchamber with the gold Jaska had given him, locking it away. Since that day, her tower has become a resting place for all the things we Xaviers are ashamed of. It provides a home for all the things we must lock away from our hearts.

When Fabian died, his soul was not spared its punishment. He was transformed into the golden Dragon, Darian: a creature that feeds upon greed. However, his regret was so strong that it split the creature's single mind in twain – and in its second head, glistening in Fabian's eyes, is the creature's ever-present guilt.

Silas moved towards the staircase that spiraled up the stone walls, ready to ascend to Sabella's place of worship. However, he was paused by the tap of an artifact against his foot, as if it had been placed decisively in his path. He saw an Akalinian bracelet at his feet, its glimmer somewhat dulled by this corrosive environment. When he lifted it, he found a name engraved upon its side, each letter very clear.

R'ja

Instinct led him to rebury the artifact, though reason could not tell him why. It was a feeling the object gave him, as though it had been stained by some ancient curse that would plague him just as readily. It was only when the bracelet was deep within a pile of gold that he breathed more like himself.

He ascended the long stairway, leaving behind the vault of disgrace. When he emerged above, he found himself in an entirely different realm. Heavy snow pattered upon the cone roof overhead, turning to rain and leaking in through cracks along its rim to pool upon the floor, then seep to the tower's outer walls, allowing water to paint the walls with dark, swirling curves. In the center of the room was a stone alter, shaped like the fullest moon, and cast in the colored glow of moonlight as it shifted through three towering mosaics.

Sabella's prophetic blood affected more than just our souls. Although there have been no more Princesses in the royal line, there have been many occurrences of identical twins. In addition to this, every third generation is gifted with some power of foresight. This has been seen both in the Alexander and Xavier family trees. My brother and I were the result of both these anomalies.

Incredible power was shared between us. I knew his mind as though it were my own, just as he knew mine. Both of us suffered vivid visions of another time – mine of this country's past, and his of its future. That is why

I know these things. In my dreams, I have seen this plight of the Dragons and Sabella's sacrifice, Aurora's death and Fabian's shame. I have seen it all, and yet, I am no wiser. It was Caden who was truly blessed. He saw things that only he understood, no matter how he tried to explain them to me. They made him very wise indeed.

I am sorry now that I could not be my brother, Reja. He was the father you deserved. When we were cut from our mother's belly, it was mere chance that the midwife's hands found me first. It was Caden who was strong and resilient, unaffected by Father's apathy. I was weakened by it. I am a flawed and inconstant man, and I deceive my people by making them believe I am anything otherwise. Larasca does not need another King trapped in the past. What it needs is someone who sees a future for it, unafraid to do what is necessary to lead his people to thrive within it. This country would have had this, if my brother had not freed me from that Kyron prison. I wish I could be grateful to him. Even now, I cannot.

I have preserved his memory in the windows of Sabella's place of worship. They now depict the last portraits Caden drew of his visions; perhaps you will understand them better than I.

The first mosaic was cast in the dullest light; shadows altered its many colors. Upon it were two men, of equal size and stature, whose swords were locked in combat. They were the same man, it seemed – their hair, their face, their eyes shaped the same. And yet, one had skin as pale as the moon, the other dark as the earth. Their swords were crossed before the image of the Xaviers' insignia, the curved Dragon witness to their quarrel.

Silas gazed upon it for a very long time, searching for some hidden meaning. The dark-skinned man resembled himself, he thought. Yet, he did not know his doppelganger. Knowing he knew nothing, he shut it from his mind.

The second was of a man and a woman, who seemed cut from the very same cloth. Their hair was black as ebony, their skin white as snow. Their backs were pressed together – the man staring forward, stiff and warrior-like, while the woman arched her curved body with shameless lust, hair spilled away from her neck in a permissive way. Though they touched, they seemed unaware of the other, and though they were so different, one seemed a mirror into the other's soul. The man's eyes were a solid black, staring too deeply into the unknown; the woman's eyes were white, seeing nothing at all.

The youth saw no meaning. His mind, he realized, rejected abstract things. Once more, he turned aside.

Caden's final work portrayed the back of a young woman knee-deep in a rushing river, with hair so red it seemed dyed with blood. She gazed upon a ridge of burning mountains, flames leaping high off their peaks. This image glowed more brightly than either one before. Moonlight brought these flames to life, bathing the room in orange and yellows. It was a terrible, beautiful sight. This, too, Silas had no answer for.

Humbled, Silas walked to a stone basin placed at the edge of the room, collecting water that drained from above until it flowed over its sides. On the wall above it was a mirror, speckled by time. He observed himself in its surface. For the first time, his fingers traced his Storma eyes, and his thin lips. Again, he felt the strange, childish smoothness of his cheeks.

I hope this letter will be unnecessary, and that I may tell you these things with my own voice. How often I have imagined such. You have so often proved yourself a brilliant mind that I have wished to have you grow swifter, to be my companion as well as my son. Yet when I find myself wishing this, you appear to me with all your childish sweetness, and I could not imagine you any other way.

You make me wish I did not have to die. You have given me the strength to be a better man, so that you may be proud to follow in my footsteps. However, I know that I will someday have to leave you behind. Should I leave this world too soon, remember all I have taught you. Do not let our history be forgotten. Most of all, never forget that of all my worldly possessions, it was you who was my greatest treasure.

I am sorry, son.

With all my love,
Cedric Raphael Xavier

Slowly, the letter crumbled in Silas' hand, until there was nothing left of it. His heart could no longer tolerate its presence. He allowed it to fall to the ground as he stared into the mirror, seeing only parts of himself—his reflection as broken as his memory.

All at once, a terrible stench filled the room, as if the very air had begun to mold and decay. Silas was overwhelmed by it, brought to his knees by coughing and gagging. His ears were soon scathed by a venomous cackle, which echoed endlessly off the tower's enclosing walls.

"It seems the little boy is all grown up."

Silas forced himself to rise again, not letting the tainted air subdue him. As he turned, he came face to face with a hooded man whose soiled beard scraped the floor, lips curled away to reveal gnarled, yellow teeth.

"Your devastation is not your fault, certainly. How can a boy with holes in his memory possibly hope to remember a father's love? Without memory, thoughtful words can never be more than words. Feelings are what stir the brew…"

His cackle came again, the sound like nails upon Silas' skull.

"Worry not, dear child. Your poor memory was only a casualty of war between your mother and her wits – that little concoction of hers was not meant to wipe it clean, as it did so well. It was merely meant to prove to the castle that you were, indeed, a very sick little boy, whose death should come as no surprise. A knife in your heart would have raised too many questions, so that job had to be left for another time, to stain another's hands."

Through a haze of fear and disgust, scattered pieces were beginning to align themselves in Silas' thoughts. Memories of this vile specter rose from the grave, stirring hatred in his heart.

"Say nothing more," he ordered, though it did not yet have its bite. He was pleading now, fear and anger fighting for control.

The man's face cracked its terrible smile.

"That wasn't the first time your mother tried to kill you. Her hatred of you began long before that, on the day your dear Papa burned her lover alive. He should have kept her from seeing the burning, at least, for she was too heavy with you to be subjected to such carnage. Yet, in his defense, he wasn't quite himself. A man changes when he sees another man in his bed, all but naked with his pregnant wife. Could he remain gentle when he saw so vividly that his wife's patience was a lie, and that an adulteress would soon birth his only son?"

Silas was racked by waves of such abhorrence that they threatened to make him ill, his body trembling as he futilely gripped his throat.

"No *more*," he said again, bestial fury overwhelmed by a child's misery. "No more words…"

"She tried to take your life, that night," the creature continued, feeding on Silas' despair. "She poisoned herself to ensure you would leave her body. You were born early, small, and in terrible pain. The Queen thought she had triumphed in robbing her vicious husband of a legacy; however, she had once again underestimated her King."

Silas could bear no more. He struck his fist against the stone wall, shrieking at him now to end it. However, no matter how he clutched his ears, clawing within them, he could not distort that creature's words.

"Your precious Papa was not so precious that night. He fought very hard to ensure what he did to you would remain a secret. It was he who locked you in the castle, away from the taint of the sun upon your tender skin. It was he who prevented strangers from looking upon you, in case they would be the ones to see something different, something that marked you as the beast you were. I thought, at least, he would disclose his dark deed in his well-crafted letter—it seems I thought too much of him."

The creature cackled once more, and the sound brought Silas to his knees. He roared now, clinging desperately to the few memories he had of that gentle man, who played a music box as he drifted into sleep.

"The night you were born, Cedric brought you to me. In this very room, he begged me to give you life, no matter what the cost. I told him – for him, I would charge only his guilt. I knew that would be enough to drive him to his grave.

"He laid you upon this altar, small and pitiful, dying upon the stone. There were many ways to save you, well within my power. However, I chose the one that would most benefit my Kingdom. On the night you were born, I drained your body of the weak liquid that sustained it, and filled your veins with the scarlet blood of my red Dragon—Aiden's blood."

All around the tower, Silas heard the howls of beasts he had never heard before. They shrieked and moaned like dying soldiers felled upon their blades. Their silhouettes flashed shadows across the moonlit mosaics, not like the glorious beasts of Cedric's paintings, but of terrible, shapeless fiends. These were the creatures of nightmares. These were Jaska's Dragons.

One shadow remained in the mosaic behind Jaska, its massive presence turning it all but black. He was the most grotesque: his head misshaped, a jaw unhinged as it roared without purpose, thin, hooked tail slicing the air about it. Silas was drawn upright, stilled by its presence, as though his soul was entangled in its twisted shape.

"Cedric did not know what would become of this boy, not human, not beast. But he allowed it to happen. He watched as that blood healed his frail body, and the child cried with new strength. He had sold that child's soul twice-over, to keep his precious heir."

"I'm sorry, son."

At last, a roar ripped from Silas' very soul.

"STOP!"

Slowly, everything dissipated. The shadows vanished from the mosaics, their roars gradually fading into the night. Yet, that hooded man remained. He stood in absolute stillness, as if turned to stone. Silas, thinking the conflict was over, allowed his breath to leave him. His body collapsed against the wall, feeling the water from the ceiling trickle down into his clothing. However, as exhaustion closed his eyes, that rasping voice came again.

"There is a reason your mother kept you alive as long as she did."

There was no mocking laugh, this time. Silas' eyes snapped open to find Jaska perfectly still, his gaze hidden by his shadowed hood.

"You were small and frail. You were slow to grow. Small for your age, all who were allowed to see you could only pity a child who they whispered would never fully be a man. This sniveling, weak child was no threat to a woman like her. That is why my prophecy at the Autumn Ball left her so shaken. All at once, she could see you for what you truly were."

Silas stared at him with vacant eyes, all his emotions spent. It was this sight that again aroused Jaska's cruel smile.

"You remember, don't you?"

His smile became laughter.

"You remember everything, don't you?"

The youth stared forward, feeling nothing. Yet, thoughts stretched on, longer than any he had ever had before. Shadows became shapes, faces merging with voices, events becoming dates. Memory possessed him, then—the eight years he had forgotten.

18th Day of 11th Month, 644 I.R.

The Autumn Ball was in chaos. The creature Jaska had appeared without warning, passing through the double doors as though he had been an invited guest. Terror drove the dancers to the walls, hiding from Jaska's devastating presence in each other's arms. Yet, his yellowed smile wasn't for them. Jaska was ascending the red path towards the royal family, who stood upon their platform.

"Get him out! Someone get Reja out of here!"

Raoul and Saito tried desperately to follow Cedric's orders, attempting to drag the stubborn boy away from his mother and father. Yet, the child clung to the chairs, crying that he would not go without them. By then, it was too late. The boy and his mother saw Jaska raise his gnarled finger towards the Prince, as his smoldering voice burned his words into their minds.

"Do not be deceived by his slow growth, for the runt will grow tall, harboring strength unmatched by any man. However, that strength will bring him grief. By that man, two women will fall: the one who bore him, and the one who succumbed to his whim."

Jaska's laughter filled the space, becoming denser and denser, until it seeped into the youth's lungs and began to choke him.

"Enjoy your identity."

The hooded man was gone. The ghostly aura about the room was lifted, the pattering water cleansing it away. Alone, Asyrias lay beneath the stone basin, allowing the spilling water to trickle over his face.

Chapter XXVI

5th Month, 643 I.R.

Czar Dmitri Konstantin must have known how poorly the Xavier Prince would take to his betrothed; no doubt Princess Natasia was as sour in her own castle as she was in Larasca's. To curb the effect of Asyrias' inevitable resentment, the Rionan Czar sent a token of peace along with his sharp-tongued child: a beautiful nightingale, with feathers of the rarest gold.

Although the young Prince did despise Natasia, he fell in love with the nightingale. He tended to her long after the Princess had gone home, paying her such doting affection that his cousin Attlas teased that the boy would sooner marry that bird than his own fiancée. The child named her Charlotte, for the name sounded as sweet to him as her song.

Cedric was thrilled that his son finally had a playmate. However, his wife complained so bitterly about the creature that the boy was forbidden to take Charlotte's cage from his room, as she loathed the smell of it. Asyrias considered it a personal banishment, and for as long as Charlotte was confined to his room, so was he.

It was a humbling thing to see that hot-tempered boy so tamed by a small creature. Whenever a servant peeked into his room, they would find him smiling, allowing the yellow creature to rest upon his pale fingers or shoulders, letting her fly free until Twyla would coax her back into her cage at night, cleaning the mess in time for Asyrias' father to tuck him into bed. The Prince's smiles became more and more frequent, until it seemed at last that he was a normal child.

Such peace could not last long. Too soon, Asyrias burst into the King's chambers unannounced, roaring as he cried.

"She's GONE!"

He collapsed in a heap on the fine rug, crying so hard that he shook.

"She left me...She LEFT me!"

At once, Cedric was there. He lifted his child from the rug, holding him tightly in his arms.

"Who left you, Reja?" he asked.

"Charlotte..."

Distraught, the child sobbed in his embrace, staining the King's silken shirt with his tears. Cedric was patient. He carried Asyrias to the window, gently rubbing the child's back until he had been soothed into silence. The Prince could feel the sun's rays warm upon his skin, shining through the glass.

"Look outside, Reja," said the King, "tell me what you see."

Eyes still red with misery, he peeked out the window. The world outside was alive with spring. The ever-blooming flowers were at the peak of their annual beauty, reds and golds bright against the greenery of Joanissia. Trees laden with leaves rose high from the landscape, allowing dozens of colorful finches to dart in and out of their shade.

"I see...birds," he murmured.

"Yes, birds. Don't you think Charlotte will be happy out there, singing with other birds?"

The Prince adamantly shook his head, declaring with childish defiance that she would be happier with him. Cedric chuckled at this display. With a kiss to his forehead, the child's anger was subdued to a pathetic whimper.

"Learn this now, my child," the King said, his fingertips brushing the tears from the boy's pale cheeks. "Sometimes, the things you love are better off away from you. When that happens, you'll have to let them go."

This made Asyrias cry even more.

"No! I don't want to!"

Cedric was calm, patiently waiting out this flow of tears. When there were none left to fall, the King tucked Asyrias' head in the crook of his neck, and rest his own cheek in the child's dark locks. There, the boy felt safe.

"Sometimes, it's not about the things you want. If you love something, you have to do what's best for them. Sometimes, that means watching them go."

The King kissed his child's forehead.

"You've done a noble thing, my Prince."

Asyrias did not feel noble. He felt sad, and angry, and heartbroken. Yet, a part of him understood his father's words. That part of him dried his tears, allowing him to feel peace in Cedric's hold. Resigned, he closed his eyes, listening to the birds' songs growing fainter as they soared further into the world, away from him.

It was a strange thing to know his own identity, yet reject it so completely. These memories of fine garments and servants, of a father's strong embrace, did not belong to Silas of Alore. To him, Prince Asyrias had died that night long ago, the day before his eighth birthday. Silas Wolfslayer did not know that sheltered, sickly boy—and so, he buried him deep within his heart.

When Silas descended into the graveyard, Caine was there, awaiting him. He noticed for the first time how similar the man was to his father – the same neat, dark hair, with gentle eyes set in a visage of strong features.

"The four men are prepared," he said. "They're reliable. They'll await your instructions tomorrow morning."

Silas nodded, dropping the rest of the way from the ladder into the soil beneath.

"I'll show them the passage tomorrow."

Although the man seemed pleased, he was clearly not satisfied. He remained there, hesitating, something caught at the tip of his tongue.

"I have something to give you," he said at last. "I know that we don't know each other very well, but I have a feeling that you'll need it more than I."

Caine led him back into the hovel, which was all but empty. Only Garrick was asleep on the bed, snoring away. Both Tasha and Rina were nowhere in sight.

"Tasha is out patrolling the grounds. She's been restless for a while, even before this mess started…"

"And Rina?" Silas asked.

Caine had no answer for him, seeming sorry that he didn't.

The man spent time digging through his drawers, soon unearthing an old key from a pile of shirts. With it, he knelt before the great black chest that had first drawn Silas' eye and opened its lock. Within lay exquisite shoulder plates, the armor black as onyx, crafted with the skill of the castle's blacksmith. Silas could not recall seeing his own father with armor so fine.

"Barons are usually descended from soldiers of some sort," Caine explained, lifting the armor up to examine it. "It's not uncommon for them to wear plates like this over their ballroom attire, to boast their honor. If you wear them, maybe you'll fit in."

Then, Caine placed the armor in the youth's arms, giving them over as easily as the last slice of bread.

"Where did you get this?" Silas asked, humbled by gratitude.

"I used to be a stable boy in the capital," the man replied. "My master promised to give me one of his black colts, Casey, when I came of riding age – but by the time I could ride, my master had forgotten our deal and traded my horse for these shoulder plates, to show off at the Autumn Ball."

His soft laugh was all that betrayed his bitterness.

"The tables turned, though. My foolish master took a fateful trip into the mountains one day, and never returned. Killed by bandits, they said. I was left unemployed, homeless, and too proud to return to a life in the Peasant's Square. However, fortune smiled upon me: his widowed wife took pity on my situation, and remembering the promise he had forgotten, offered me this armor in lieu of my Casey.

"I joined the diamond trade, soon after. It got me out of Joanissia, gave me a chance at a new life. When my group was given passage to this hidden city, I knew I had found my home. This armor is all that remains of my life in the capital."

Silas didn't know what to say. He was as grateful as he was baffled, unable to understand why Caine would offer such a gift to him. The man smiled, as though he understood his bewilderment.

"This armor needs to see the outside world again – it needs to see the finery of a ball. It certainly doesn't do me any good just sitting there, rusting in that crate."

Caine gave him a fatherly clap on the shoulder, his grin warm and light.

"Do what you will with it. I won't accept it back."

The youth was out of practice with showing gratitude. Silas stumbled over the words in his mind, trying to sort them, put them in the right order; however, he was distracted by another's gaze. He turned, finding Rina there, her eyes bloodshot, the tender skin about them rubbed raw.

"What's wrong?" he asked.

His words spilled out, unchecked. Yet, by her impassive expression, he might not have said them at all.

"Silas," she said, addressing him so curtly that it could not have been her voice. "I have to speak with you."

He and Caine exchanged a look, mutual uneasiness passing between them. Reluctantly, Silas handed the armor back to Caine, who placed them in plain view atop the crate. The youth was free to follow Rina deep into the graveyard, where the torchlight barely flickered.

When he saw her there, blue eyes cast down to the soil, glistening with dense tears, he could not help but approach. He reached out to her, a gentle hand touching her shoulder, the other her soft neck. He wished to kiss her again, and leaned down to taste her lips.

All at once, Rina pulled from his grasp.

"Don't."

Anger gripped him first, before reason. How could she reject him after their last embrace? How could she refuse the desire he saw in her very eyes?

Yet, she stayed out of his reach. Slowly, she displayed the golden bracelet that had always rest about her wrist, as if this were some sort of repellent.

"I've been deceiving you," she whispered.

She twisted the bracelet about her pale wrist in that old, nervous habit.

"This is from my betrothed, Silas. By accepting this from a Stag named Kaish, I promised that I would marry him."

Concern fled his gaze, replace by shocked dullness. His mind overwhelmed, it could provide no reaction. For what could have been an eternity, he felt nothing at all.

"I had to travel to Joanissia to meet up with his Rank," she continued, determined to drive the stake deeper into his heart. "I wasn't certain if I would get there in time, or if anyone cared. They all thought I was dead, so it wasn't likely. But…Alastor says he's still waiting for me…"

Then, the anger resurfaced. It gripped him tighter than before, tensing every fiber of him until some burst, seeping red into his vision.

"You didn't *tell* me?" he snarled, claws digging into his palm. "You bloody whore—you let me **kiss** a married woman?!"

"Whore?!"

New tears welled in her eyes, her pain leaking from her soul.

"I haven't given myself to anyone, Silas!"

"How could you do this to me?!" he bellowed, losing control. "After all we've been through, you're just going to crawl back to the scrawny coward who slapped some jewelry on your wrist?!"

He had never seen Rina cry so openly. His burning rage could not withstand her tears, her every sob dousing his fury.

"I'm so sorry…sorry…"

His regret emerged too slowly. By the time it had braved the depths of his anguish, she was already rushing from him, escaping deeper and deeper into the fields of headstones.

He could have pursued her, he realized. He could have rushed after her, trading his too-harsh words with apologies until there was nothing left for her to cry over. Yet, he watched her vanish, the damage done. All he could do the following morning was patch it, and hope things would be almost as they had been.

It was a time before he felt the small, canine nose brushing over his foot, memorizing his scent. Moving without thought, he knelt before Hero, softly touching one of the pup's long ears. Just as he had anticipated, Silas looked up to find the Demon child before him, emerald eyes seeing into his soul.

"Why didn't you follow her?" Sen asked in his strange, soft voice.

Silas looked to the soil, wading through the sea of feelings that stirred within him in hopes to find an answer to that question.

"Because…I had to let her go."

He pressed his hand over his face, protecting it with this trembling mask.

"I let her go."

Sen nodded, understanding these simple words. In silence, the child knelt down with him, bravely climbing into his lap. Laying his head against

Silas' chest, the red-haired boy closed his eyes, offering his own body as comfort. Silas, lost, sheltered him in his arms.

This is what's best for her.

Rina could not succumb to his whim. This, the Prince understood.

Chapter XXVII

*S*ilas' apology could not mend the rift between them. Although Rina understood his anger, she could find no more words to say to him. Standing by him was standing leagues apart, and she could not see him the same way again.

It seemed the plan would proceed without trouble. Silas disappeared with the four chosen men into Sanctuary early in the morning to show them the secret passageway. Then, once Garrick was comfortable watching Sen alone, Tasha and Caine departed to join them. The final step of the mission had Alastor again bring Rina and Silas to the surface, then proceed to collect supplies from the empty Squares to bring back to the rebels.

Once they set foot in the city, Silas promptly led her away from the soldier, taking her to the flat-roofed shop of the inventor he had spoken of.

"Try not to touch anything," Silas warned.

Rina nodded, and he pushed open the door.

A man of slight stature ushered them inside, fiery hair wild about him and a thin smile on his lips. His inquisitive eyes seemed haunted, shadowed by the past. Yet, he was welcoming.

"So sorry for the mess, my lady. I can never seem to keep this place in order…"

Sir Temlar guided her past trinkets and odd contraptions to a fine dress hanging in the window, loose sleeves translucent as mist, and a silken skirt that glowed like the night sky.

"This was my sister's dress," the inventor explained, sliding the gown down from a copper hook. "Amelia just hasn't had the hips to wear the thing after her third child, poor girl…"

He showed her into a cluttered back room, where a mirror with an elaborate frame had been propped against a dusty wall.

"You're all right changing alone, right?"

She nodded, amused by his flustered appearance.

"I'm old enough."

"Of course you are, of course…"

Temlar closed the door behind her, shutting her into that small space.

The gown felt unusual in her grip, so smooth against her tender skin. It was too fine a fabric to be held in hands once stained by the scent of cheap liquor. Even so, Rina soon slipped off the dress Tasha had given to her, allowing it to remain in a heap on the floor. While she dressed, she heard Silas' low growls from beyond the door as he grunted and griped about the courtly attire Temlar had found for him.

"Hold still," the inventor spat, "you're worse than my nephew."

"Don't you compare me to a kid," Silas growled.

"Ha! Matthew's six years your senior and still a pain in the ass. He's got such a violent streak that I've been charged with babysitting the grown man while his mom's under the weather, poor Amelia…"

Temlar's sigh was heavy with fatigue.

"Reminds me of you, that boy. Always has."

There was silence, for a time, aside from the occasional snarl as a garment was pulled too tight. Then, Silas' voice came again.

"How did you know Cedric?"

A hesitant pause.

"My father was the palace carpenter – an unofficial confidant of the King, they say. The royal twins, Cedric and Caden, were born just months after my brother Creed and I. Cedric told me later that it was normal for a set of common twins to be born shortly before a royal set, to serve as their earthly 'keepers' – don't ask me how he figured that, Cedric said a lot of strange things. My father was always bringing my brother and me to the castle while he worked, so the four of us grew up together.

"We were close, us four. Caden and Creed were always sparring in the garden while Cedric and I read, discussing poetry or the new artists of the time. The Princes knew we were commoners, but they never treated us as such. Cedric even financed my dream of opening this shop. When Raphael sent his boys away to that war, I knew my world would never be the same. Creed moved to Raine, unable to deal with the hatred he felt towards our King, and Caden never came home. Now, with Cedric gone, I'm the only one left."

Their conversation wasn't as audible after this; Rina could distinguish only a low murmuring now and again. She laced the last of the gown over her waist, which was still tamed by her corset. A glance in the mirror revealed how well the gown suited her body: the delicate sleeves spread from her arms like silvery wings, the dark skirt flowing as beautifully as a river at dusk. For a moment, she felt beautiful. However, before she could bring herself to leave the storage room, she felt the golden band about her wrist. It was cool to her touch, familiar – yet, it now seemed as heavy as a shackle.

When she emerged, the inventor looked upon her with pride.

"What a vision," he said.

Rina's gaze was on Silas, who stood transformed in the window's snowy light. His unkempt locks had been tamed, crowning him in their dark elegance, and his white, silken shirt softened the color of his skin. The black armor latched upon his broad shoulders, across his chest, seemed to contain his feral power, altering that raw element until it shone with noble brilliance. Entranced, Rina almost overlooked the thin chain fastened about his neck, bearing an all-too familiar ring. Before she could say anything, Silas had tucked it away.

"You two will take my place at the ball," said the inventor, already hurrying them to the door. "Give them the names of my nephew and his wife. Matthew wouldn't be caught dead at such an event, royal invitation or not, so the nobles have no idea what he looks like. For tonight, you are Matthew and Victoria Wulf."

A carriage arrived, drawn by two black horses. After passing a few coins to the pale driver, Temlar opened the door for the two conspirators.

"Good luck, you two."

The moment they were seated, they were shut in together. Soon, the wheels turned over the smooth stones of the road beneath, as the horses proceeded – *cli-clunk, cli-clunk*. For a long while, it was the only sound in the carriage. Silas kept his eyes turned from her, to a small window in one of the doors; Rina, unable to look at him, kept her gaze firmly on the one across from it.

This wasn't her usual, stupefied silence. She had nothing to say to him. Although she had forgiven him with words, she still felt too much anger to forgive him with anything more sincere. The longer the tense silence went on, the more firmly she was grounded in her own resentment.

Lost in her own toxic thoughts, she was unprepared for the moment Silas did speak.

"You're too beautiful."

She looked to him with a start, discovering foreign gentleness in his violet gaze.

"I know that I apologized before, but you can't forgive me. You shouldn't. I shouldn't have…"

Though she waited, he couldn't seem to complete his thoughts. It soon became clear that what he wanted to say was fighting the words he should have said.

"Let's forget what happened last night," he went on. "For tonight, let's pretend everything is as it was. When the time comes, I will surrender you—just not tonight."

Despite everything, this was enough.

"Just for tonight," she agreed.

A ghost of a smile flickered upon his lips.

The carriage came to a halt before a long staircase, ascending to the open doors of an overwhelming castle. The setting sun cast strange shadows across its weathered stones, touching each of the four towers with different light. Music was breathed past the open doors, luring them closer.

Silas took her arm, and aided by his warmth, she found the courage to ascend the staircase with her head held high.

A guard stopped them at the entry, bearing a scroll so long the other end threatened to roll off the staircase.

"Name?" he asked.

"Temlar," Silas replied.

When the guard gave him a suspicious look, he smoothly added, "the nephew."

The man didn't seem to be in an interrogative mood. After finding Temlar's name, he gave them a dismissive nod, sending them on their way.

Past the grand doorway was a world of finery. Baronesses with gowns of diamonds were twirled by male hands gloved with silk, moved by a melody that rose from the strings of wooden instruments Rina had never seen before. She would have remained there at the top of the staircase, stupidly staring, were it not for Silas' firm guidance. It was by his will that they stepped onto the marble floor, becoming one with the moving portrait of nobility that danced upon it.

Despite the strange chill within the castle, it all began to feel very natural. Though it was still hard to look into Silas' eyes, his touch was far from intimidating. He was patient when she forgot a step, never altering his dignified persona – and when she danced well, they were light as air, floating above the marble floor. For a moment, she forgot she was a tavern girl; for a moment, she was a Princess.

A presence shook her from her dreamlike state. She was first aware of it when Silas stiffened, familiar rage tightening his jaw as his gaze locked upon what threatened them. At first, she was confused; however, a glance in that direction stirred the same fury within her.

"Giovanni!" she whispered, breathing his name like a curse.

The man was dancing playfully with a dark-haired servant girl, laughing in an all but vulgar way. When he noticed their looks, he smiled, his joy but salt upon their wounds.

"Look away," Silas said, despite the anger in his voice. "He isn't worth acknowledging."

They returned to their dance. Yet, though the atmosphere was the same, they could not find their rhythm. Old barriers had risen between them, creating a rift that compromised their façade. Rina was almost relieved when a fair-haired man touched Silas' shoulder, stopping them.

"May I cut in?"

He was a man of very distinctive features, with skin as pale as his locks and piercing, gray eyes. He was not handsome in the way Rina judged men to be such – yet, there was an enticing aura about him, seductive as a song.

Though visibly reluctant, Silas stepped aside. The man took his place with practiced grace, holding her hand and waist before whisking her back into the flow of the dance. Rina felt lost without her partner, but Silas' face was soon lost in the crowd, as she was swept away.

"Have you attended many balls, my lady?" the man asked, his voice of a smooth timbre.

She displayed a smile.

"No, Sir. This is my first."

This answer must have sated his curiosity, for he momentarily fell silent. As they passed the platform that supported the royal throne, Rina again set eyes on the raven-haired Queen. She was as beautiful as before, like a statue carved from ice; however, her painted smile seemed too calm, firmed as if in triumph.

"I am rather surprised it is your first," the man continued. "Many Ladies of Joanissia attend their first when they are years younger than you."

""My parents thought me too young, before now," she lied.

The man seemed to accept this, humoring her with a smile.

"So it seems. Do you have a name, my lady?"

He extended her arm as Rina twirled beneath it, feeling the flowing skirt wrap about her thighs before he took her again. The action was impressively graceful for a girl who was panicking, realizing too late that she had no family name.

"Only if you have one," she replied, smoothing alarm with clever words.

He responded well to her, chuckling. It seemed he was a man charmed by wit.

"Raoul Markovich," he said. "Now, your name."

Rina had been backed into a corner. She had a peasant's name—he would know it the moment he heard it. She tried quickly to weave another lie, every moment ripping time from her grasp. Relief overwhelmed her when she heard the guard's voice from the height of the staircase, announcing the arrival of an important guest.

"Princess Azalea Xavier, wife of Attlas."

Her relief was choked by fear. She gazed up at the stairway with shock, seeing the Storma Princess standing there, garbed in a magnificent black gown, untouched—unharmed. Their plan had failed.

"Have you ever been to Citris?" Raoul asked, his grip suddenly tighter about her body.

Too late, she saw the guards closing in on Silas, backing him against the corner of the room. Too late, she realized that it was they who had been trapped.

Raoul guided his captive to the platform as though it were part of their dance, discreetly binding her wrists with his own hands as he forced her to kneel before the ruling Queen.

"I believe she is the female leader, Your Highness," he said. "She matches Sir Alastor's description. The dark-skinned youth seems to be her cohort."

Rina's blood ran cold, hearing this name.

Alastor.

Her friend. Her traitor.

The woman did not stand, her icy gaze already surveying the prey caught on her behalf. By the time Rina thought to resist, Raoul's hold was so tight his nails dug deeper with every move she made.

"Let go of me," she warned, possessed by newfound rage.

The Queen laughed, making a show out of the struggle before her.

"Feisty, for a peasant girl."

In the shadows, Rina saw four guards restraining Citris men, their crude weapons confiscated and their wrists bound by coarse rope. Apart from them was Tasha, who hissed and snarled as she fought her bald captor. Even in her disbelief, Rina noticed one man missing.

"Look what has become of all your pawns," said the Queen, knowing what Rina saw. "You should have thought harder before executing such a poor strategy."

"Where's Caine?" Rina demanded.

"If you mean your messenger, he is being dealt with—just as your partner will be."

Rina turned to see the guards fighting to drag Silas to the platform. What was surely meant to be a discreet act was quickly becoming a scene, for the youth resisted with all his feral power. She was terrified for him, forced to stifle her instinct to cry for help. She knew they had no friends here.

Her horror was far from over. She turned in time to see a new man ascend the platform from behind, he by far the tallest and most intimidating of the guard. The Xavier insignia was marked upon his heavy armor, branded with red-hot steel. In his hands was a sword that dripped with blood, which he displayed to his smiling Queen.

"Yes, Captain?" she asked.

"The messenger is finished, Your Highness."

Rina felt the chill of the castle begin to seep into her bones. She stared at the scarlet blade, watching the blood drip to the ground, drip onto white marble.

Tasha began to scream. This time, no amount of strength could restrain her—she screamed and screamed until the dancers began to take notice, as she resisted all efforts her snake-eyed captor made to contain her. Even the Princess, who had barely begun to mingle among the guests, stood noticeably still as she watched her sister begin to squirm. Soon, Queen could take no more of it.

"Someone remove her from this hall," she ordered, no doubt aware of the ill feeling that rippled through the ballroom, infecting her guests.

Tasha's guard growled curses as he tried to wrestle her through a side entry. However, just as he had begun to pry her fingers from the door's stone frame, a red blur swooped down from above. Suddenly, the red-haired boy was clinging to the arm of his mother's captor, his fangs bringing forth a fountain of blood.

"My finger! My fawking finger!"

At once, Rina recognized the General's voice. As Lance screamed and shrieked, forced to pry his own severed finger from a child's sharp teeth, she could not help the vindictive pleasure that welled within her.

Tasha, freed, rushed onto the platform, her strident voice commanding the attention of the hall.

"You are all her prisoners!" she screamed. "You're living a lie! You are not safe – you crowned a serpent as your Queen; she will see her poison ravage the land until all you love shrivels and dies at her feet!"

Two men apprehended Tasha, their combined power enough to carry her away. Her son was restrained as well, disappearing through the door with the other prisoners.

All the hall was still, smothered by silence. The Queen's satisfaction had turned to fury, her groomed nails dug deeply into the royal throne. Yet, piece by piece, her composure was soon reassembled.

"Raoul," she said, her voice strangely calm. "Leave the conspirator at my feet."

Rina was tossed to the ground like a pile of rags, her head striking hard against the marble floor. Yet, she clenched her teeth, stifling her pain. She felt nothing as the woman dragged her up by the roots of her hair, forcing her to stand.

"Pay no mind to the words of that madwoman," the Queen declared, pulling harder on her tresses. "Here is the mastermind who fed her such treasonous words—the woman who would destroy this Kingdom to take my place."

At last, she struggled. She screamed in her own defense.

"Liar!"

Rina saw Silas fighting harder against a great many guards, so many now that they formed a cage about him.

"The law states," Morana continued, "that such ambitions have one remedy, to be prescribed at the moment there is visible proof."

The Queen ordered her Captain to her side, who forced Rina back to her knees. There were screams as her hair was brushed from her neck, his bloodied sword rising high above her.

She was terrified. Her heart pumped heavily, as though it knew to savor each rush of blood.

I'm going to die.

She thought she would feel peace when she faced death, for it would mark the end of all her suffering. Yet, there was only fear—fear as she clung desperately to the life she had not fully lived.

All at once, a mighty roar shook the hall.

"Leave HER **ALONE**!"

Rina looked up to find Silas in the center of the hall, a trail of battered guards behind him. The nobles scattered when he came, no doubt as disturbed by his bedraggled state as they were by his powerful voice. Yet, the sight of him there, standing tall – his clothes ripped from the conflict, hair in its natural, wild disarray – was the most beautiful thing Rina had ever seen.

"I was the one who organized the conspirators, not her," he declared, sharp teeth flashing in warning.

The Queen regarded him with haughty indifference.

"Then you will die in her place."

"You can't touch me," Silas snarled.

Morana smiled, as if delighted by his defiance.

"And who so thinks he is above the law?"

Silas hesitated. Yet, when his gaze locked with Rina's, uncertainty melted into calm.

"Your son."

Whispers rippled through the hall, disbelieving eyes cast upon the youth. Even Rina gazed upon him in bewilderment, unable to imagine a world in which his confession could be truth. Still, he withstood the whispering. He ripped the chain from around his neck, dangling it from his fist.

"Upon this chain is the gold ring you placed upon my finger on my second birthday. Your handmaid, Twyla, will swear to its authenticity."

He tossed the ring to the feet of a dark-haired servant, identified by her modest garments. With clear hesitation, she examined the artifact, turning it over and over in her hands.

"It is real, Your Majesty," she announced, her voice quivering with sobs. "I was there the day you gave this to him…"

She approached him slowly at first. However, the careful advance soon became a rush, and she ambushed him with her tearful embrace.

"Reja…Reja, you're back from the dead…"

Silas tensed, clearly not expecting such a reunion. Even so, the handmaid's display seemed to melt the hearts of the surrounding nobles. Now, their mistrustful eyes were shifted past the youth, their whispers directed at their anxious Queen.

"Forgive me if I am not so quick to believe the testimony of a hysterical woman," said the Storma.

No one was swayed by her words. The low murmuring continued, darkening the atmosphere with doubt. Soon, the Queen's composure began to crack under the weight of their suspicion.

"Though you make an impossible claim, I am in a merciful mood. Since you truly seem to believe you are my dead son, Asyrias, then you must be willing to prove yourself worthy of his lineage."

"And how do you propose I do that?" Silas asked.

"By completing an impossible task."

Rina glanced behind her, seeing the Queen withdraw a black gem from the yoke of her gown.

"This is an Avdotian diamond. They come from the depths of Avdotia Lake, outside the city of Malldon. You have a month to travel; today being the first day of the new year, 655 I.R., I will expect your return on the 1st day of 2nd Month. If you delay your return for even a day, the prisoners will be executed as planned. That is the punishment for their crime."

Silas seemed hesitant—angry, even. But Rina knew as well as he that the situation afforded him little choice. Slowly, the youth gave his binding nod.

"Agreed."

The Queen showed no joy.

"You will be accompanied by a man of my choosing. I expect him to return in one piece. Until then, away with you."

The youth stepped back, though his violet eyes remained on Rina. She held his gaze for as long as she could, as the bloody sword above her was sheathed, as new guards bound her wrists. She stared into his eyes, unwavering, that gaze her last bond with the outside world.

'Wait,' the silent word upon his lips.

She was dragged out of the back doors, forced to break his gaze.

Chapter XXVIII

*T*he atmosphere had changed in the King's Council. The Councilmen sat stiffer in their seats, very few looking directly at their monarch. This day, Twyla observed that the Queen had assumed the King's seat, allowing her puppet Prince to sit beside her. The blond boy looked entirely out of place, eyes shifting about him as he tried futilely to escape the stifling attention.

"I think the Council understands why we are here," Gabriel spoke, his voice the first of that tense gathering.

"That young man is nothing but a fortune-seeking cur," Morana insisted. "How could you believe such an impossible claim? My son is *dead*!"

"But your handmaid suggests otherwise," remarked the powerful man.

Gabriel turned to the Kyron then, causing her to recoil. She was not used to being addressed in such meetings, especially in the midst of such heated discourse.

"The ring he presented to you – do you know without a shadow of a doubt that the object was our Queen's gift to Asyrias?"

All eyes were on her, imploring her reply. Stiffening further, Twyla almost broke under the burden the Kingdom had placed on her shoulders. The confession fell from her lips.

"I swear to it. The ring belonged to Asyrias."

Gabriel bowed his head, processing this information in silence. This revelation struck each Councilman individually – casting shadows over Raoul's face, draining the color from Saito's skin. Even Reade and Reginald were bewildered, unable to decide between them whether to be angry or terrified. It was Antonio, the youngest of them, who seemed the most hurt by it.

"What does this mean, Your Highness?" he asked, his gentle eyes grown so dark.

Morana was stoic. Jaw taut, back straight, she replied with a shewolf's dignity.

"I do not have to defend myself from a liar's words."

Whether her Queen meant Asyrias' claim or Twyla's defense of him, the handmaid began to understand the precariousness of the position she found herself in. Indeed, she had never been on the receiving end of Morana's icy stares, her sapphire eyes appearing to crystallize with hatred. For the first time since childhood, Twyla felt fear.

Gabriel spoke again, his calm voice betraying no emotion.

"Although you claim there is no truth to the young man's claim, you agreed to acknowledge it, should he return upon completion of his quest. Logic asks why you would do such a thing, if you did not believe him."

The Queen said nothing. She had the look of a peevish child caught in a lie, and nothing could conceal it.

"Well, didn't you see him?!" exclaimed her puppet-Prince, too juvenile to know when to hold his tongue. "The bloke's too brown to be her kid, and he's freakishly tall. Besides, there's no way he'll come back in a month, so why shouldn't she get him to run an errand for her? Either way, the cave-people are all gonna get the axe."

Twyla felt some pride when the collective anger of the Councilmen stilled his tongue, and he folded beneath their gaze. Alastor looked back down, tugging anxiously at his silk collar to stop it from choking him.

"The matter is simple enough to be put to a vote," said Gabriel, ignoring the youth's unthinking words. "An Xavier must be placed on the throne. If the young man does return, who will deem him worthy enough to wear the crown?"

Despite the Queen's fury, Twyla watched three hands rise. Reade and Reginald, following the dictates of Fabian's law, had no choice but to support a legitimate heir. Gabriel, honest and principled, naturally supported the boy he no doubt sensed was Cedric's child—his own great-nephew. Antonio, Saito, and Raoul remained still, supporting their Queen for reasons all their own.

Three supported, three did not. Gabriel turned his gaze to the Captain of the Guard, who stood so silently by the door.

"Art, you must tip the scale."

Twyla watched with bated breath as Art's soldier stance grew lax, shaken by hesitation. Although it was his duty to attend the King's Council, it was not often the Captain was asked to speak. It must have been difficult for a man of few words to be handed such an important decision.

"I..."

Gradually, he reaffirmed his solid stance.

"I am sworn to serve the Xavier line. If Prince Asyrias returns, my allegiance lies with him."

Twyla had never seen her Queen so consumed by rage—her elegant features contorted into the most hideous of sneers, body tight and trembling as it tried to contain it. No doubt, the Queen understood her position. With Art now a pawn of the opposition, Morana could not easily remove Gabriel and the lawmakers, lest Art's men "accidentally" let a disgruntled assassin into her chambers. However, Twyla remained defenseless. She, who had never been good friends with the soldier, was at the mercy of the undermined Queen.

Wary of Morana's calculating look, Twyla fled the Council room. She took shelter in her own modest chambers, which now seemed as chilled as the rest of the stone palace. For once, she felt no comfort as she closed her doors and lay upon her downy sheets, staring up at the moon as it shone through her arching window. She had made a powerful enemy, this night. Although it was not her way to regret speaking truth, she now wished she had better taught herself how to lie.

Some time passed before there was a knock on her door; yet, she jumped all the same.

"It's Antonio," came a voice, "I'm alone."

She relaxed, calling to welcome him in. Soon, the handsome Lesser Advisor had seated himself by her vanity, comforting her with his familiar smile.

"What did I miss?" she asked, sitting more properly.

"The Queen ignored yet another letter from the Duke of Lucadia, Gabriel lectured us all on the art of subtlety, and Her Majesty left in a huff. More or less the same routine."

Twyla sighed with relief, grateful for her friend's attempt to make light of the day's events. Still, not even he could stray far from them. Soon, his gentle look faded to a somber one, hesitation all that prolonged the almost peaceful silence.

"Are you so certain of that young man's identity?"

The handmaid nodded, kneading her hands over her fine skirt.

"Even if it weren't for that ring, how could anyone ignore those eyes? They were Storma, too narrow to be anything but—widened though they might have been by Larascan blood, which only proves further that he is the grown boy Cedric sired. It was him. It could only be him."

"Dark as he was?" Antonio asked, understandably skeptical.

"Cedric never let him set foot outside the castle. He even sealed Reja's window shut those last couple of years, lest the boy get the idea to open it and lean too far into the outside world. No one knows what the sun might have done to that fair skin…"

Antonio fell into silence, holding his head, as was his fashion when he was overwhelmed. Twyla didn't blame him. She allowed her gaze to drift back towards the window, observing the everlasting moonlight.

"I fear for him, Antony," she said, softer now. "They'll kill him in Malldon. It's been a horror since the war, and Morana knows it. They've turned Kyro's terrible religion into an even more horrifying one, one our Prince cannot fight. They'll see him dead…"

She was mortified to hear the Kyron laugh; however, seeing his distant, grim gaze, she began to forgive him.

"Nothing could be worse than our Catsavionism," he said. "A cult that parades about as a religion, preaching words stolen from a genuine faith to justify the slaughtering of innocent people—nothing could be worse than that. It has enslaved our people for half a century, yet no one will come to their aid."

Though she tried to feign indifference, her words were lost somewhere in the dark memories of her childhood: her mother and father taken away from her, priests in golden robes telling her that she was worth nothing unless she bowed before them.

"I would have been an altar girl, if Giovanni had not saved me," she admitted, despite herself.

"And if Baldric had not come, I would have been a Catsavion Priest."

Antonio laughed again, the memories so terrible that they seemed to displace all other emotions.

"Give it a year, and we would have become what we despised. In that way, the bloody Kyron War was a blessing."

They did not often talk of their origins. They were both people who preferred to cherish the present moment, taking long strides to leave their shadows behind them. Yet, it was somehow cleansing to speak of them now. In time, Antonio smiled, as did she, as she cherished the all-but-familial bond their past had forged between them.

"I didn't mean to depress you," said Antonio.

She shook her head, already feeling her good spirits return.

"After a day like today, it's hard to avoid. Your company is enough."

They spoke for a time in their native language, avoiding any further mention of their troubles. Before long, Twyla began to breathe easier. Thoughts of Morana, of Reja, and her own well being simply began to fade away. The peace might have continued the rest of the evening, were it not for the second knock on her door.

"Who is it?" she called, rightfully wary.

Then came his familiar chuckle.

"A visitor."

Giovanni sauntered into the room as if he owned it, still dressed in his ballroom attire. His handsome face lifted her spirits, has it had for many weeks, and the opening in his silken shirt made her crave the warmth of nights before, of his clever words and kisses. Yet, his knowing smirk now had a sinister tint to it, cool enough to make her uncomfortable in her skin.

"How do you fare, my dear?" he asked, standing near her, his back entirely to Antonio.

"Not well," she replied.

"Well, that's not what you said last night."

She was accustomed to his lack of subtlety, though she was conscious of Antonio's disgust. Her appreciation for her lover's presence began to subside. She gave the ex-Commander no encouragement, turning her head so he could not mistake her exhaustion for neediness. Yet, he remained there, either oblivious or indifferent.

"No doubt, you're still wondering how Reja lived. I did promise I would tell you, but I've had little opportunity. One must tread lightly in enemy territory."

"I might wonder," she said, her voice taut with caution, "but I've decided it would be best if I didn't know."

"But you do know, don't you?"

In the halls, Twyla thought she heard the sound of the guard's rattling armor, too many to be the ordinary patrol. As she grew more anxious, the night air seemed heavier about her, stifling her.

"We're in no mood for your mind games, Giovanni," said Antonio, bristling as he rose from his seat.

His protest was unusual to her, for of the Councilmen, he was always the most tolerant of the ex-Commander. However, it seemed that he was as aware of the atmosphere as she, and somehow sensed Giovanni's ability to aggravate bad situations.

The man laughed, stroking the heavy mustache that still divided his face. Their discomfort only fueled his apparent amusement; he remained there in a stubborn way, planting himself like a poison weed. Twyla's usual desire had faded, irritated by his coldness—yet, he smiled at her.

"Think back, Twyla," he began. "It's night, the 7th Day of 12th Month, 646 I.R. What were you doing that night?"

"I don't know," she snapped. "It's been ten years."

"You don't remember what you were doing the night Reja 'died'? Seems like a night that would stay with you."

He smiled, a smile that made her feel sick.

"You came to me, but not with your usual, physical demands. You were holding our little Prince, who was cold as death, and a fine, silver dagger. You were crying, 'Her spell is broken, her spell is broken,' and you could no longer complete her demands. It seemed our Queen had altered your state of mind so that you would carry out her one request: that you stab the heart of her fair child."

Twyla was mortified. She stared up at Giovanni in utter disbelief, left unable to speak.

"How can you claim something so treasonous?" Antonio cried, as furious as she was frightened.

"I claim nothing. It is truth."

The ex-Commander knelt before her then, grasping her shoulders, as if to keep her in that place.

"I saved you. I took the boy, as you asked. I promised to raise him as best I could. To satisfy the Queen's bloodlust, I allowed you to draw blood from the cross upon my own hand and smear it upon the blade. You were to return with a child's body from the Peasant Square's open grave, to lay beneath the Prince's shroud. Before you fled to the grave, I gave you a potion of my own creation—liquor, mostly. Once you had finished your task, you could drink the concoction and wipe your mind clean of that night. I gave it to you out of pity, you see. I knew you could not live knowing what a terrible thing your Queen had asked of you."

The blood fled her face, leaving it icy to his touch.

"You remember now, don't you?"

Too soon, the memories flooded back.

The sky had been very dark when Morana had placed the boy in her arms—her boy, in truth, for she had cherished him far more than the heartless Queen. It was Twyla, not Morana, who had been there as he said his first word, took his first steps, read his first book.

"He has troubled me long enough."

Then, there was the cold diamond against her neck, the strange, ethereal whisper of her Queen.

Then, darkness.

She was brought back by the sound of wood slamming against stone, her door kicked open by powerful guards.

"We're here for the maid," they said.

Twyla didn't realize she was sobbing until the men forced her salt-streaked palms away from her eyes, forcing them behind her back.

"Twyla?! You can't take Twyla!" Antonio cried, foolishly trying to pry their hands from her wrists, "She hasn't done anything wrong!"

"The Queen has named her a conspirator. We have no choice."

"The Queen has lost her mind!"

The handmaid was too broken to speak in her own defense. She could only look helplessly at her fellow Kyron, who was trying to desperately to save her from her fate—and her lover, who stood so very still, apart from her.

One of the guards spoke to her as they forced her from her room, away from them.

"I'm sorry, my lady. I wish it did not have to be this way."

For reasons beyond her power, his words transformed her. Her tears grew hot, vengeful rage giving life to a once-obedient tongue.

She breathed harsh words.

"I hope she burns."

Chapter XXIX

1ˢᵗ Day of 1ˢᵗ Month, 655 I.R.

*R*ina hit the ground hard when the guards threw her into her cell, twisting her ankle in an impossible way. She bit back her cries of anguish until they were gone, refusing to give them any more reason to taunt her. However, once the men's shadows had drifted from the flickering torchlight, nothing could dam her welling tears.

It hurts…

Her wrists were bound tight by coarse rope, wispy pieces carving lines into her skin. Hands secure behind her back, she could not reach down to her swelling ankle.

It…hurts…

The black world around her still seemed a blur, more nightmarish than real. Her mind could not absorb the memories of that day. They were twisted like dreams, barely a part of her. It was impossible to think that the dangerous, wolfish man who had brought her there was born of royal blood. Yet, if royalty were responsible for the dark place around her – colder than the rest of the palace, where black moss clung to damp stone like a parasite, filling the confined space with such rank air it choked her – then spawning beasts was a natural thing.

Her ankle began to pulse like her heart, already full and red. Her silent tears could not soothe it. She pressed her back against the cool wall; with its support, she relinquished control of her misery. She succumbed to sobs.

"Your ankle?"

The small voice seemed to rise from the shadows. Shocked, Rina was silent, her gaze falling on the small, red-haired boy who knelt before her.

"Too much blood in your ankle," Sen said, sitting comfortably on the stone ground as he examined her injury, "needs pressure."

To her surprise, the strange child tore a strip from his own soiled shirt, beginning to selflessly bind her wound. As he worked, she noticed the red marks upon his wrists, too similar to her own.

"How did you free yourself?" she asked, despite her shock.

"Gnaw," he replied. "Small ropes. Sharp teeth. But…Mama's too thick…"

At last, she realized she wasn't alone. Across the cell, half-concealed by shadows, she saw the golden-haired woman staring past the iron bars. She sat still against the wall, knees pressed against her chest defensively. Despair was a cloud about her, concealing her beautiful features with absolute vacancy.

"Mama looks like Hero did," the child said, ripping another strip from his shirt. "Hero, sad before he died."

Stunned, she noticed at last that Sen was without the brown puppy he had not once let out of his sight.

"Hero…died?"

Sen nodded, eyes falling as he began to secure the strip around her ankle.

"Soldiers came. Took Garrick. Hid with Hero, but they would've found me. Would've hurt Hero. I drained him…no blood…no hurt…"

She stared at him, uncertain what to say or think. The child had killed his own pet. Yet, he didn't seem monstrous. The way he sat in solemn silence, devoted to his task, made him seem all but honorable.

Rina sighed, her thoughts returning to more immediate problems. Soon, she became more aware of the cool metal still pressed against her chest, concealed by her corset as it had been since Pem had laced it upon her. The guards had not thought to search her, since she was a woman. For once, her sex had been to her advantage.

"There's a dagger…in my breast," she managed, hesitant as she was. "If you can remove it, do you think you could use it to cut my ropes?"

She realized the instructions were too complicated for a young boy; yet, he seemed to understand. Ignoring her modesty, he peered down her gown, then reached down and gripped the curved handle. Despite the circumstances, she had to blush when he revealed the sheathed weapon.

"Oh..." he murmured, curious.

"Please," she urged, though gently. "Free me, and I'll free your mother."

Sen nodded with new resolve. Separating the weapon from its sheath, he gestured for her to part from the wall, his cool confidence more befitting a soldier than a child. It took only minutes of careful cutting before the rough ropes fell away, freeing her.

She thanked Sen as she dried her tears, more than grateful. Ready to make good on her promise, Rina reclaimed her dagger and made her way to the other side of the cell, ignoring the pain of her wounded ankle. The woman barely lifted her head when she neared, as though Rina's presence was little more than a shift in the air.

"Can you move?" Rina asked.

Tasha nodded, moving just enough from the wall to reveal her binds. They were thicker than Rina's, and older. They seemed to grind rust into the wounds they inflicted.

"Hold still…"

Rina had to work diligently to free the woman, for there were many knots in the ropes. Both women were mostly silent during the process, with Tasha only flinching when the blade came too close. However, when the dagger was almost through the last threads, the woman began to tremble. She whispered curses, most foreign and unfamiliar, until at last she was reduced to sobs.

"*Bozhe…*"

Though overwhelmed, Rina's comforting instincts took over.

"We'll be out soon," she soothed, finally freeing her from the binds, "Silas will be back before we know it, you'll see."

But Tasha scowled, her sobs no less frequent.

"Shut up. This isn't about that!"

Tasha used her newfound freedom to grip her blonde locks, pulling at them so hard they threatened to tear.

"I'm…with child," she whispered, trembling all the more, "I'm carrying his child, and I never got to tell him…I never…"

Rina gaped, this revelation but a new weight on her guilty consciousness. She drew back, stupidly fumbling for some sort of reply.

"I thought you weren't married," she said.

"I'm not."

She saw Tasha's hold on her golden tresses begin to lessen, her trembling fingers slowly gliding down her neck.

"I would have married him," she said, her voice much softer now. "But I couldn't. Princesses can't marry commoners."

Rina stared, staggered. Slowly, she lowered her dagger.

"Princesses?"

Tasha would not look at her. The woman's emerald gaze remained on her red-haired child, who finally approached. She was silent as she guided him into her hold, sheltering him with her warmth. She was still, regaining her composure, until at last she spoke.

"Caine didn't know my real name. No one did. Except…Silas, I assume. I never did ask him. That's what you called him, right?"

"How would Silas know?" Rina stammered, mind spinning.

Tasha's smile seemed more like a grimace.

"My name was Natasia Elena Konstantin, second-born Princess of Riona. The only thing that gave my life any worth was that I was similar in age to the spoiled Prince of Larasca, whom Father promptly engaged me to the day after my sixth birthday. Your Silas was a different creature, then. A pale, sickly boy with the namesake of a broken country…"

The woman must have misread Rina's overwhelmed look, for she laughed at the sight of it.

"Relax. Your boy-toy and I despised each other."

"You knew?" she managed.

"Who he was?"

The woman shrugged, her attention on the boy who clung to her.

"I suspected, I think. I didn't think much about him after they told Father he was dead, but it felt somehow anticlimactic. He still has those strange eyes, though they've changed colors—shaped like his mother's. How I hate that snake of a woman…"

She closed her eyes as if to dream, gently stroking the boy's crimson locks. In return, the child pressed into her hold.

"Do you really want to hear my story?" she asked. "It might be nice to tell it, after all these years. It's not like you're going to go squeal to anyone."

Faintly, Rina nodded, already sinking onto the cold floor beneath her. It was too much to take in, for one day. Her head ached from it. Still, she nodded, ready to accept the burden of another's secret.

"I was always running away," Tasha began, strangely calm. "I was never content with the life I was born in. To be a second-born Princess is bad enough – a firstborn has some claim to the kingdom, if a male heir cannot be produced – but to be a second-born Princess with an ever-increasing number of sisters makes for a pathetic life. The "Great" Czar Dmitri was always trading out wives, killing one, exiling another, hoping that the next woman would give him the heir he so deserved. My mother was lucky, I guess. She was one of the few to die in childbirth."

A vacant smile; still, she continued.

"I don't know why Father was so determined to keep me at home. He wasn't fond of me, as far as I could tell, and after Asyrias 'died' there was no political reason to keep me around. Yet every time I escaped that frozen palace, Father sent his guards after me, and they dragged me home kicking and screaming. The last time, though, I got away. Maybe he knew what a scandal it would be, if he did find me."

She paused, tensing some. Her hold on the boy seemed to tighten, trying to shield him from some unseen power.

"I'll tell you more after he sleeps."

The child appeared disturbed by the sudden silence, squirming some. However, the silence was soon filled by his mother's gentle voice as she breathed a beautiful, foreign lullaby. Rina sat transfixed, entranced by the mysterious song. She had never had a mother to sing her to sleep, and could compare it to no song she had heard before. She had never imagined someone's voice could weave such feelings of security, of love.

The song ended too soon, the child rested, contented. Tasha relaxed, watching him with affectionate eyes.

"People assume he has no feelings, but he does. He feels everything, perhaps more than we do. I…admire him, at times. He has a strong soul."

"He doesn't act like a normal child," Rina said, fascinated.

"He isn't."

Tasha hesitated again, eyes set on the girl who shared her space. Rina could not help but feel she was being tested.

"What do you know about Demons?" the Princess asked, suddenly.

"Demons?"

"Nothing, then."

Tasha sighed, exhausted.

"That used to surprise me. Demons are a plague upon Riona, and I assumed it was the same everywhere. It seems those mountains keep them from venturing outside my country."

"Then, is Sen a Demon?" Rina asked.

The woman grimaced, hesitating once again.

"…Let me start from the beginning."

Her sigh, chilled by the air, came as a soft, white cloud.

"Demons are animals. They look like people, but they aren't. They are born with nails to shred skin, muscle to break bones, and teeth to puncture veins. They attacked our livestock, our horses, our pets, and often, our people. They do not distinguish between humans and animals, but find one as good a meal as another. It is not their muscle they are after, but their life source – their blood. However, I believe their favorite is human blood. It is just the more difficult to obtain.

"No one taught me this, but I've learned there are two types of Demons. The first type is speechless, more beastlike than human. They walk about in tattered garments stolen from their defenseless victims, blood staining their faces and hands. There is no art to the way they attack, just screaming and clawing until they can wrestle their victim into submission. Those are the ones we are taught to protect ourselves from. We can avoid them by staying away from the forest, and staying in well-lit areas. Those creatures hate sunlight, afraid of their own shadow.

"The second type is considerably more dangerous. They walk among humans, disguised as nobility. They conceal their fangs with mysterious, closed smiles, and plan each meal according to their taste. Unlike their cousins, these are more than thoughtless killing machines. These can scheme. They have also learned the art of...reproduction."

Even Rina shuddered, the word strangely sinister in context.

"You mean, the other type doesn't?"

"That's the strange thing about Demons," Tasha replied. "There are no females. All Demons are born male, to human mothers. There are fewer of the bestial type, since they are less likely to rape what they eat. With the second type, it might not always be rape. Some make a woman truly believe that she is loved, before they harvest her for the child and drain her when she is no more use to them. Others simply plant their seed and leave her, allowing the offspring to be born and later consume the naïve vessel."

Rina choked on her own tongue, mortified. She looked at Sen with new horror, only to receive a chilling look from Tasha.

"I'm not finished," she warned.

The girl nodded, forcing herself to look elsewhere. It was not her nature to judge; she would try very hard not to do so now.

"Father didn't believe the latter type existed. He believed we were safe in our walled capital, away from the forests and caves were the bestial blood-suckers dwelled. One day, though, my little sister Sasha went missing. Sasha was only ten, and my father's clear favorite. We expected it was the work of some disgruntled lord, but the ransom note we found explained very clearly what had been done. The Demon instructed my father to leave one of our capital's most beautiful maidens in the square at the beginning of each month; failure to do so would result in Sasha's quick demise.

"At last, my father understood that he was dealing with a breed that could think, plan, and out-wit him. Terrified, he obeyed the Demon's wishes. I watched many girls no older than I sent out into the main square at the beginning of each month, and saw their pale, shrunken bodies left at our doorstep each morning. No matter who watched the square the night before, no one could spot the Demon commit the act. I knew all along that this thing was toying with us, but Father is not quick to act under pressure. It was two years before he finally decided to fight back."

"But how could he fight something like that?" Rina asked.

"With other Demons."

Once again, a distant smile flickered upon Tasha's face.

"All of Riona had heard of the *Schyaest* – the Six, you would say. They were something of a legend: Demons, ageless as the rest of their kind, who had sworn off human blood and taken on different personas to integrate themselves into human society. We knew nothing more of them than their names: Petya, the Faithful; Demyan, the Just; Koldan, the Strong; Afanas, the Beautiful; Savin, the Wise; and Isaak, the Merciful. Although they seemed more myth than anything, Father decided they were the answer to his prayers. He used all of his forces to seek them, until at last they came to him.

"I'm not entirely sure why they decided to come. I had run away again that morning, and Father's men had only just dragged me back home when they arrived in the Main Hall. They were unlike anything I had ever seen before. They had a timeless air about them, all of them very solemn and sincere—all...beautiful, in their own way. Isaak spoke for them, the tallest and physically the most impressive. I remember...his hair. It was thick, vibrant, very long and...red. Red like blood..."

Rina's gaze drifted back to the sleeping child, noticing again the unusually crimson hue of his locks. Tasha must have noticed, for she swiftly covered them with her own hands.

"Merciful, they called him," she said, her laughter bitter as poison. "Leader of the Six, Isaak – the Gentle, the Merciful, all the legends said. They claimed he had once pulled a thorn from a snake's side after it had bitten him, even freed a bird from a cougar's jaws. But he was not so merciful to me. He came to me that night, injected me with his venom so I couldn't fight. Being bitten by a Demon is not an experience you can forget. Their poison renders you entirely still, robbing you of both the physical and emotional ability to fight them. I thought he would kill me then, but apparently that wasn't his goal. He didn't even undress me entirely, hid his face in my neck like he was ashamed, but he took me just the same. He stole my innocence, my worth, my body away from me, and gave no reason why.

"He apologized before he left, as if that made it any better. He said I would understand, one day. But I don't. I don't fawking know why he did that to me. Then, he was just gone. *Gone*, like it didn't matter to him at all. Like I was just another scrap of meat!"

Though anger rose in her like the tide, labored breath soon seemed to suppress it. Rina wished she knew better how to ease such suffering; however, it seemed she was as powerless to help this wounded Princess as she had been to heal a damaged Prince.

"I conceived. Somehow, I knew I would. I fled the castle as fast as I could, and this time, Father didn't pursue me. I found refuge in an abandoned temple – at least, I thought it was abandoned. During the beginning months of my pregnancy, I was able to support myself there, harvesting the berries that grew in the gardens behind it, catching a rabbit here and there. I had always been a good hunter, though Father didn't particularly support that 'manly' habit. For months, there was no one there to disturb me, and I became comfortable there. Yet, one day, I met a man dressed in ancient religious robes, with a gnarled beard and this…terrible odor about him, like death. He claimed that the temple was his, but he didn't ask me to leave. The next day, he was gone.

"When I saw him next, he began to offer me things. First, he asked what I would trade to have never conceived my child and forget that I was raped, to return home to my family a virgin again. He said he could do this for me, for a price. At first, I thought I would trade anything. But…then I realized that I had begun to look forward to meeting my son. Demon or not, his presence within me had become a comfort. I rejected the man's offer and I thought I was done with him. Yet, he returned again, this time offering to rid my son of his Demon heritage, so that I might birth a normal child.

"I don't know why I turned him away, that time. Life might have been easier for me if Sen was born human. Still, it didn't feel right for me to deny him his heritage. Again, I thought I was finished with that rancid man, but he returned once more before I gave birth. He asked me if I wanted to alter my son's fate."

"His fate?" Rina asked, somehow unnerved.

Tasha nodded, a dark shadow crossing her features.

"That man claimed that Sen was destined to walk a dark path. He said…it was a prophecy, he said. I'll never forget what he said to me."

Again, a faint hesitation, the words catching in her throat. Still, they rose again, a soft whisper in the cell.

"The blood-stained child, born by sin, will succumb to hatred and lust. Blinded by anguish, he will bring ruin to all who are tied to him."

Rina's heart ached for the both of them. She wondered how much of Tasha's brave nature was just a façade, carefully constructed to protect both her and that boy from a world that had already doomed them.

"I turned him down again," she whispered. "I didn't believe him. Even now, I don't want to believe him. After that, he never bothered me again.

"Sen was born in that temple. He was…beautiful, from the moment he was born. They say all Demons are beautiful babies, since their mothers are more likely to keep them alive if they are. Yet, he seemed different. He was never demanding, as they say the other cursed offspring are. He always had the gentlest cry, and never once nicked me with his claws or his fangs. He was kinder to me than anyone had ever been, more than my own Father. I've loved him ever since."

Sen stirred a little, as if hearing that he was being spoken of. Still, he pressed closer to his mother, his pale hands clinging gently to his mother's tattered garments. Tasha's eyes glistened with tears.

"I'm not sure how I ended up in Citris. I just...wandered there, somehow. Sen lives on the blood of rats, and the only place he could eat them without drawing attention was the graveyard of that crowded city. That's where we met Caine. He was strong, patient, more handsome than any noble I had seen. Most of all, he accepted Sen. He wasn't afraid of him, and he didn't judge me for having him. For just a moment, I thought...we could be a family, all three of us. Now...now he's gone..."

Sobs choked her, halting each breath.

"It's just...me, again...and a baby...and Sen..."

Rina could only be silent, allowing her to mourn. Before long, the air was still once more, the tears subsiding.

"Thanks for listening," Tasha whispered.

The girl nodded, wiping water from her own eyes.

"That's what I'm good for."

Tasha laughed. The air between them had settled, allowing them to smile.

"Silas will come back soon," Rina said, trying to believe it herself.

The woman rolled her eyes, leaning back against the cool wall.

"I don't trust him as far as I can throw him. Skinny little brat or possessive, burly bastard, he's the same to me. Still, maybe your faith will be enough."

She closed her eyes, then, breathing more deeply. Before long, the Princess had fallen into exhausted slumber.

Rina envied how quickly she could sleep. She felt off balance in this place, disturbed by the sounds and the shadows. As the mother and child rested, Rina rubbed her sore wrists, staring out the cell doors. She achieved a sense of serenity in watching them, her eyes watching the torchlight dance over the iron bars. She kept herself calm.

Peaceful. I am peaceful.

However, this fabricated peace soon came to an abrupt halt. A visitor came, her black hair spilling from the hood of a dark cloak. Rina shrunk back as the woman knelt before the bars, revealing a small tray of dried food.

"What is your name?" came a gentle voice.

Although wary, Rina was not threatened by the woman. She stiffened, but replied.

"Rina."

"Ah…"

A smile haunted her features.

"It fits you, somehow. I can imagine Azzy falling for a 'Rina'."

At last, the visitor pulled down her hood. Rina immediately recognized her Storma eyes and her curious smile, even having glimpsed them from across the room.

"Princess Azalea," she said, stunned.

The woman nodded, though she didn't smile again.

"I don't have much time with you. Sister has the guards watching my room very closely; it won't be long before they realize I'm gone."

Again, she offered her the food.

"Take it. It's twice your ration for the week. Morana plans to keep you alive, not healthy."

Rina knew she had little choice, yet she hesitated. She regarded the food with caution, not yet brave enough to accept the stranger's offer.

"At what price?"

At last, the Princess smiled again.

"Clever girl. Nothing ever comes for free."

She moved the plate just away from the bars, just out of her reach.

"I have a deal to make with you," she said. "I'm in a mood to make my sister's life hell, but in no position to act on it. You can, though. Since you are Asyrias' lover, Morana will be less inclined to kill you if she catches you. That would be bad news for her when he comes back. She underestimates me, and she can't do anything about you. It's a perfect partnership."

"Wait…"

Rina was almost frightened by the Azalea's coy tone.

"What exactly are you asking me to do?"

"Pull a few pranks, I suppose."

The Princess laughed, daintily covering her mouth as she did so.

"Juvenile, right? But it will be so pleasing. My sister has no sense of humor, and I'm tired of seeing her scowling all around the palace. Besides, there's nothing else I can do. Nothing else. There's nothing else I can really do, because she is Queen, and I am nothing."

Coolly, Azalea pushed the meal a little closer.

"What do you say, Rina? Extra food in return for a few errands. It might be just enough to keep the three of you alive."

Already, Rina knew she had no choice. Tasha would lose her child living in these conditions, and should she refuse this bargain, the guilt would fall on Rina. She was treading dangerous waters, but there was no other way to shore.

Slowly, she nodded.

"I'll do whatever you ask of me."

The Princess was pleased, smiling victoriously as she slid the food back towards her. She rose again, drawing her hood to darken her face.

"Thank you, Precious Rina."

She laughed airily, the sound as chilling as the air.

"Thank you. The fun starts soon, Rina."

Her laughter seemed to trail her like a shadow, lingering after her as she vanished into the halls, into the flickering torchlight.

Chapter XXX

Mirrors surrounded Silas, reflecting his image a thousand times around him, each reflecting the other into eternity. He had no way of knowing the limits of his space, how wide or how deep it was. He was confined, yet stretched to the brink, each reflection of him pulling at him, pulling him in all directions.

The image just before him began to fluctuate, ripples distorting it like water. When he reached out to it, a pulse changed his own face into another's. Emerald eyes stared back at him, more Larascan than any. This man was of his own height, though of a slender mold, his power not in the physical realm. His auburn hair was a hue of sunset, and his skin had a whitish glow. His mournful smile revealed his identity.

Father.

Behind Silas, a mirror shattered. He turned suddenly to see it mending, changing into another sight. It now displayed Cedric with his young son, who was paler than he. The small, frail boy was staring out the window, watching men ride horses through the courtyard.

"Can I do that, Papa?" asked the boy.

Cedric hesitated.

"No, my son. I promise, you would not like horses very much."

"But you ride a horse," he said, disappointed.

"I have been riding horses for a very long time," the man replied, using a comforting hold to turn the child from the window, "but I am me, and you are you. You shouldn't strive to do things just because I do."

The scene melted away, ripples changing it to another. This time, the Prince sat on the sidelines as he watched his father and Lesser Advisor Antonio battle with wooden swords, graceful as dancers. Though there was a warrior's look upon the King's face, he laughed with delight with every fine parry, as did Antonio.

There was such longing upon the child's face. When the battle was done, Antonio smiled and brought his sword to the boy.

"Would you like to learn?"

His pale eyes came alive with delight. He leapt with joy—but just as he tried to take the weapon, Cedric gave Antonio a slow, disapproving shake of his head.

"I'm sorry, Antonio. You know that sort of thing isn't for Reja."

Despite the remorse on the Kyron's face, he brought the weapon out of his Prince's reach.

This image faded, replaced by hundreds of others. Day by day, the child reached out to explore, only to have his father hold him back. No matter how he strove to follow in his father's footsteps, Cedric would block the path, telling him as gently as he could, "You can't."

"But why, Papa?"

From afar, Silas could see the dull look in Cedric's eyes. Each time he held his son's hand, the look would flicker, his gaze turning ever so briefly from the sight. Asyrias had never understood that look. He saw only Cedric's loving smile.

Silas understood. Cedric's smile was a mask, hiding his shame.

"I disappointed you."

Silas bristled with anger, staring into the King's vacant eyes.

"What did you expect? What did you expect me to be?!"

Cedric could give no answer. He was silent as death.

"I was YOUR fault!"

His fist shattered the mirror, littering the ground with glass and blood. Yet even as his hand bled, the mirror reassembled, again trapping him in a room of a thousand faces.

"Am I what you wanted, now?"

He stared into his own face, now. He saw his inhuman eyes, his fangs, his powerful arms and legs. He was strong, now. He was dangerous.

"Father...Father, look at me..."

His father was gone. He saw tears streaming down his cheeks, spilling to the ground to dilute the blood.

"Father...don't leave me..."

He was alone.

Silas held his head, his roar echoing in the chamber. The glass was crushing him, trapping him in a thousand images.

Is this what you wanted?

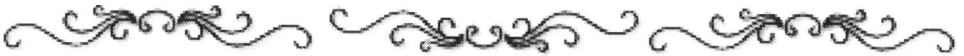

15th Day of 1st Month, 655 I.R.

He awoke heaving, a nightmarish feeling still choking him. Yet, the night air was still. It was quiet enough for him to pretend he was alone with his thoughts – however, a pair of empty eyes soon disturbed this illusion.

"Can't sleep?" came Ariel's flat voice.

Silas grunted, rolling onto his back.

"No."

His travel partner's perpetual stare had once been unnerving to Silas. Many things about Ariel were unnerving: his expressionless face, the way he never seemed to sleep, and the uncanny resemblance he shared with Silas himself. When Morana had first presented his escort, Silas had thought he was staring into his own reflection. Their face was the same, – though Ariel's was whiter – all except the color of their eyes and the length of their locks. Silas could think of no reason for this resemblance. He had entertained the thought that Cedric had fathered an illegitimate child, but Ariel had a Storma's eyes—and Morana had certainly not conceived again.

Even so, Silas had become accustomed to Ariel's peculiar nature. He did not speak unnecessarily, and posed no discernable threat. However, Silas would continue to keep a wary eye on the sword the Queen had given the youth, as though it alone could act on her behalf.

Ariel stood without a word, stretching his arms up, then to each side, his body acting on some old instinct.

"We are near Malldon," he said, moving towards his gray horse. "If you cannot sleep, we might as well move forward."

Though annoyed initially, Silas agreed. He forced himself up, his bones cracking as he did so, before proceeding to his own horse.

Morana had given him Cedric's stallion, Aldrich. He could not think of why, except maybe she hoped it would die making the journey. His black splendor was greatly diminished since his days as the King's steed, his thin frame showing clear signs of neglect. He gnashed his teeth bitterly at Silas whenever he drew near and protested resentfully whenever his rider demanded to go anywhere. Silas, less than patient, was swift to return his steed's foul disposition.

"You going to behave for me today, porker?" Silas growled, giving a less-than-pleasant tug on the reins.

Aldrich grit his teeth and reared back, a puff of air billowing from his nostrils like steam.

Ariel turned his dull gaze towards them from atop his own stallion, who seemed as vacant as he.

"He would be kinder if you did not whip him with snarls."

Silas scowled, and Ariel turned away. With that, they rode forward.

A worn bag of gold thumped against Silas' side as they went, each metallic chink reminding him of his goal. Guards had taken his pouch from him at the castle, and all his possessions with it—including Caine's beautiful armor. The coin they gave him was barely enough to survive a few nights in Malldon, which they claimed was long enough to complete his task. When he returned, his things would be returned to him.

Without the journal Vaan had stolen, the pouch they had taken contained only a few items: a pawn from his old chess set, the dried foot of the first rabbit he had killed, and some Alore coins he had managed to win in gambling some years before. Not long ago, those few possessions had meant the world to him. Yet, they meant nothing to him now. The only thing he wanted returned to him was Rina, unharmed.

Soon, the city of Malldon rose from the icy ground. Small, stone buildings stood meekly in the fog, separated by jagged paths that ended nowhere. The town itself could be easily overlooked, for the trees grew as thickly there as the forest could allow, and shamelessly stretched their barren branches over the gray structures.

"Avdotia Lake should be beyond the city," said Ariel, already dismounting his steed.

"How far beyond it?" Silas asked.

For the first time, Ariel hesitated. The longer the silence stretched, the more irritated Silas became.

"You have no idea, do you?"

"Did you expect me to?"

"You're my bloody escort, of course I did! Do you even know what direction it is?!"

Still, all of Silas' fury could not have coerced an answer from that blank face. He let the feeling leave him in a hot sigh, deep breathing slowly quelling his rage.

"Fine," he growled, "I'll find it myself."

He dismounted behind Ariel, who was already leading his horse further down a jagged path. Silas thought he felt hateful eyes upon his back, boring holes through him. Yet when he turned, there was no one. There was only the gray fog creeping over the winding road.

The youth won the battle of determination with his stallion, who eventually resigned himself to be dragged forward. As he went, Silas observed the city, trying to find some sign of life in Malldon's deserted streets. However, there was not even a candle in a window to aid the early-morning light.

Cozy place.

Suddenly, something knocked into him from behind. He turned in a muddle, a hand instinctively gripping his hilt when he saw the perpetrator: a woman, smiling like a temptress.

"It's not very honorable to draw your weapon on a lady," she said, fondling the strings that secured her cloak. "We have no way of defending ourselves from it."

He found her appearance distracting. Her hair was as black as his, and spilled with royal ringlets down her slender shoulders, just touching her womanly curves before they settled about her waist. She wore her corset tighter than most, forcing her shape into its most pleasing of forms. An entrancing aroma rose from her, filling his senses—pine, like the forest.

"Go, then."

He lowered the weapon that had barely left its sheath, allowing her to sweetly depart from him. Despite his better sense, he found his eyes following her as she left, still transfixed by her appearance.

"You're attracted to her," said Ariel.

Silas didn't deny it.

"Just keep going," he said.

Ariel nodded, though held his gaze a moment longer than usual. Silas ignored this, again taking hold of Aldrich's reins to follow his escort. However, he felt suddenly that something was absent. His clothes were where they should have been, as was his sword. Yet, when he reached down to the worn bag that decorated his side, he found nothing but air.

Gone.

He clutched at the air, as if that would prompt the bag to materialize. When it would not, his nails dug deep into his palms.

"Bitch," he snarled.

Ariel was pointing down the street, answering him before he even knew what question to ask.

"She went down the back alley into that building, there. Try not to make a scene."

"Watch the horse," Silas ordered.

Silas rushed to the building in a blind fury, all but possessed by bloodlust when he threw open the double doors. All at once, he was attacked. A sudden flurry of brown fur came upon him in a screeching tumult; his pain came from a frenzy of teeth and claws. The thing itself was impossible to describe—small and fur-covered, it used the grip of both hands and feet to cling to him, wielding its long tail with the agility of a third limb. Cursing loudly, Silas barely managed to toss the creature to the ground.

"Hey! What do you think you're doing to my Keane?"

The source of the shout was a short, burly man standing behind a bar, glaring daggers as he dried an old mug. All around, people were gathered about tables with mugs filled with liquor, dim light allowing them to hide their drunken stupor.

A tavern.

The thief was sitting at the bar, a coy smile on her face as the furry creature clamored up onto the arm of the man behind it.

"Where's my gold?" Silas demanded, his patience spent.

The tavern keeper shook his head in apparent disapproval, though of *what* was a mystery.

"I give him a week," he muttered, only to the girl. "I'm surprised the Priests haven't nabbed him already."

"With those eyes? I give him three days," she replied, haughtily sipping a mug.

Silas did not take kindly to being ignored. Fury overwhelming him, he slammed his fist on the bar—the wood cracked.

"The gold," he snarled. "*Give* it."

The two were silenced, staring with rapt attention. Even the furry creature that climbed the tavern keeper was stilled, great brown eyes fixed upon Silas.

"…I've got it," said the keeper, finally setting down the mug.

"Arlen!"

The girl's pretty face was fixed in a scowl, her body stiff.

"I promised to watch your savings," the man snapped, "but it ain't yours if you stole it."

"So hand it over," Silas warned, thrusting out his hand.

"Hold your horses, pal. I'm not just going to let you walk out with it – for all I know, you stole it first."

Arlen smiled, though he retreated out of Silas' reach.

"How about the two of you face off in a little drinking game? The last one standing takes the gold, fair and square."

Frustrated as he was, Silas was ready to kill the man to get his money back. Yet, inexplicably, he was willing to compromise. He didn't need another death on his hands. Although he had never had liquor before, the task seemed simple enough. After all, his heart pumped Dragon's blood. There was no doubt in his mind that this would be to his advantage.

"Just fill the glass," he said.

Arlen looked to the girl, waiting for her approval. Naturally, she gave it with a smile.

"I'll bet he's a lightweight."

As he was filling the mugs, the creature – Keane – scrambled down Arlen's arm to the girl's abandoned drink, greedily burying its furry face in the foamy liquid. Though clearly disgusted, she did not try to reclaim it.

Soon, two tall beakers were placed before them, filled to the brim with a bitter-smelling substance. He could see his own scowl reflected in the glass, as if he could taste it by scent alone. Still, he lifted his glass, as did the thief.

"Can I have the name of my opponent?" she asked, smiling in her enticing way.

Though he tried to regard her with contempt, even now, he found her beauty too distracting.

"Silas," he conceded.

She smiled again, the beaker almost to her lips.

"Raven," she said.

Their game began. They both drained the first cup; Silas found the taste as nauseating as its stench, but stomached it. The same was true of the second, and the third. As Raven seemed to giggle more, he felt fine – he thought he was fine. However, at some point, the room began to tilt. Everything was muffled, his limbs not quite a part of him.

He thought he saw Keane clutching his glass as he drank from it, the creature smiling a big, yellow smile down at him, brown eyes staring into his.

The room was spinning, threads of thought unraveling, turning into nothing.

Morning greeted him with gray sunlight, its meager beams just enough to pierce the fog and touch his face.

His head ached. He held it, eyes still closed as he remembered to breathe.

Vague images stirred his consciousness. He thought he remembered Rina, her skin and body warm against his. He could taste her sweet lips, feel her gentle hands upon his body as he ravaged her form, taking from her all that he had ever wanted.

The feelings were vivid. Yet, his consciousness rejected it completely.

Wake.

Slowly, he opened his eyes. Above him was a wooden ceiling he had never seen before; around him were unknown walls, oak furniture he had never laid eyes upon. He sat up, holding his aching head, and saw his clothes strewn across an unfamiliar floor.

Horror's icy hand crept down his spine. He remained frozen on a stranger's cot, staring at his own clothing.

Too soon, he heard a woman's breath from beside him, felt a stirring in the quilt that half-covered him. Too soon, he saw that woman upon the cot—her black locks tangled upon the pillow, the blanket fallen away from her to reveal the rise and fall of her soft, pale breasts.

"*Fawk*!"

He half-whispered the curse, stumbling over his own feet as he escaped her bed. The ruckus woke her; Raven yawned as she sat up, pushing her fingers through the knots in her hair. She made no move to cover herself.

"What's wrong with you?" she asked, the words distorted in a yawn.

"What did we *do*?!" he bellowed.

She raised a brow, seeming more surprised than anything.

"You don't remember?"

"Fawk, NO!"

His anger had little effect on her. If anything, the thief was amused by it. Raven held her head, *laughing* at his ferocity.

"Amazing! You were perfectly lucid while it was happening…"

Mortified, repulsed, he snatched his clothes off the floor and stormed outside, barely stopping to secure his pants. If he didn't see her, he wouldn't think of her; he wanted to wipe the stain of her from his memory.

Outside, Morana's servant was waiting in the shallow snow, the bag of gold in his hand. His gaze was set on a black cat that rolled in dirt sheltered by a tree's spindly branches, the creature's jaws locked on a struggling, yellow bird.

"It's time to go, Ariel," Silas growled, pulling his long shirt over his head.

The man nodded, tossing him the old bag.

"The horses are tied around back. You told me to stay outside with them while you took advantage of a willing woman."

"Shut up," he snarled.

He made a vow to himself that he would never touch another glass of liquor. Ever. Not a force in the world could pour it down his throat.

"Just turn around and get moving," he warned, "I'm not in the mood for your corpse stare."

Silas' patience was but thin ice across a fiery pit. They would have left then—however, Raven's sudden call froze him to the spot.

"You're not leaving, are you?"

He turned to see her standing in the doorway, little more than a blanket to cover her. She was smiling again, despite his scowl. She had an entrancing smile.

"We made a deal," she said. "You wanted to find Avdotia Lake; I wanted you in my bed. You held up your end of it, so it's time for me to do the same."

The youth was becoming more and more frustrated with his own forgotten behavior. It seemed another person had taken hold of him the night before, sharing with people memories he had never lived.

"I'll find it alone," he said, each word wound tight.

She rolled her eyes, smiling even then.

"It's half a day's journey from here, and the forest only gets denser. It could be weeks before you find your way through it alone. Unless…you have weeks to spare?"

As repulsed and angry as he was, he knew when he had been backed into a corner. A glance to Ariel showed that his escort was already resigned to follow her, for his vacant gaze was drawn to her like moss to sunlight.

Weeks…

Rina didn't have weeks.

Despite his feelings, he was playing Morana's game. To win, logic, not feeling, would dictate his decisions.

"…last night never happened," he said.

She placed a finger to her lips.

"If we don't talk about it, then it didn't."

The girl knelt gracefully on her doorstep, her blanket slipping inches down her body as she held her arms out to the black cat behind them.

"Diana~" she called.

The feline made its way to her, allowing herself to be swept up into her slender arms.

"Wait here," said Raven, fondly stroking her pet. "We'll need supplies where we're going. I don't plan to let you die so easily, Reja."

He could taste his own disgust. Now, he wanted nothing more than to rip that night from the fabric of time, to cast it and his other self into the darkness of oblivion. Yet he was distracted from this loathing by another sight—for as the cat opened her great eyes, licking yellow feathers from her lips, he saw the blue of her stare. Those orbs glowed like sapphire, tempting as diamonds. He had never been so transfixed by something inhuman.

"You see her beauty," said Ariel.

Raven smiled, no doubt believing the words were for her. Cradling the feline like a babe, she brought it into the house with her, closing the door.

Chapter XXXI

8ᵗʰ Day of 1ˢᵗ Month, 655 I.R.

The days wore into each other, the dungeon's perpetual darkness making an outcast of Time. Rina wasn't sure how many days she spent staring at the cracked ceiling, watching spiders weave in and out of the jagged lines. At times, she forgot Tasha's presence; then, the Princess' calm voice would break the silence.

"How's your sanity?" she would ask.

No matter what strange things had previously occupied her thoughts, she would always reply, "Well."

Such was their existence. Silence. Sanity.

Though never less than well behaved, Sen did not do as well in captivity. It wasn't long before he began waking in the middle of the night, plagued by chills and shakes. His already pale skin had turned a chalky color, and day by day, it seemed his pink gums were receding from his fangs, turning gray. Tasha would never acknowledge it, but Rina suspected that these were all signs of starvation.

That day, the child was curled in his mother's lap, her warmth helping his shakes to lessen. Rina could hear him speaking softly, no doubt trying to distract himself from his pain.

"What are you gonna name him?"

The woman smiled, however weakly.

"And how do you know it's a boy?"

"I just do."

Tasha didn't seem all that surprised.

"…James, then."

Despite his trembling body, the boy smiled.

"Like Caine's Papa? The one that died?"

The Princess nodded, soothing him with a kiss. The gentleness of the sight was almost painful for Rina, who had known no mother. The only time she had ever been offered such closeness was now a foggy memory of frozen winds, and Silas' warm embrace.

Silence returned to their cell. Rina again laid on the floor, staring up at the cracked ceiling. The dull sight gave her some peace.

Too soon, the stillness was broken by the rattle of a key in the lock.

"Who's there?" Tasha cried, solitude turning bravery to skittishness.

A hooded woman pushed open the cell door.

"A visitor," she replied. "I have business with your friend. Don't worry—I plan to bring her back."

Tasha sneered, hissing like a cat. The act made Azalea pause, though Rina couldn't tell if she was offended or amused.

"I would watch the way you look at people, prisoner. It would be a shame if the guards stopped bringing you extra rations."

Although Rina had been expecting this day, she had not expected it to come so soon. Ashamed by Tasha's accusing look, she quickly followed Azalea out of her cell, proceeding through the dark halls of the dungeon.

"What will I have to do?" she asked, her neglected voice cracking.

"Something easy," the Storma replied.

The Princess stopped her at the bottom of a long staircase, handing her a key and a map.

"This is a diagram of the palace. Today, you're going *here*," she pointed to a section in the upper portion of the map, "to get a key from my sister's vanity."

Rina grew very pale, uncertain what heinous act she had committed in life to lead her here—ready to steal from a Queen.

"What about this key?" she asked, meekly displaying the rusty, skeletal object.

"Silly girl, that's for *you*, when you come back. I know you'll kindly lock yourself in again without trying to escape; anything like that would cause much unneeded trouble for dear Asyrias."

The madness of her smile made Rina shiver.

"Take the key from Morana's second drawer, on the right side. After that, you're going to avoid guards and take this back route," she trailed her finger down the diagram, "to the stables. There, you're going to free my sister's horse."

"W-what?" Rina choked.

"Just a little practical joke, remember? It's all in good fun. Good fun, that's all…"

Azalea ascended the steps alone, leaving behind the bewildered prisoner.

"After I leave, wait a few minutes. If you don't hear footsteps, then the path is clear."

She opened the great doors, blinding Rina with white light.

"Good luck," the Princess giggled, a demented sound.

All at once, she was gone.

Rina remained at the bottom of the staircase, fighting her last will to remain. She wasn't ready to commit this act, not alone. She longed to have Silas there, calmly walking ahead of her, carving a path. But he wasn't there now. A wild world lay ahead of her, no paths to be seen. All she could do, now, was hold her breath and push forward.

The palace was a gray, dark place. The stone walls above were the same as the stone walls of the dungeon, without the decay. Above, however, she had to search for shadows to cling to, hiding from not only the few guards on her path, but from the surreal stares of the mosaic dragons that decorated every hall, letting in icy light.

It was a great relief when she came to the Queen's room. It was in the westernmost tower of the palace, which was populated only by scattered guards and lost bats. Reaching for the golden handle, she half-hoped to find it locked; however, the slightest pressure released the door from its frame, the old hinges creaking as it swung ajar. Nothing stood between her and her goal.

Within, the Queen's private self was on display. Twisted by a sleepless night, silk sheets had slipped down under the drapes of a linen canopy, catching the wintry light that came through her cracked window. A dying fire fought the air's chill, proving as futile as the thick robe discarded upon its hearth. Though not in extraordinary disarray, the room had a restless feel to it, containment fighting chaos—a soul at war with itself.

Focused on her goal, Rina quickly knelt before the vanity, counting drawers until she came to the one Azalea had specified. She expected to shift through diamonds and brooches to find the key. Yet, the vanity had contents of a different sort. In the drawer were two letters—one folded, and the one beneath it facing downward. Despite her reluctance, Rina couldn't help her curiosity. Unwilling to unfold the first letter, the girl carefully pulled the second form underneath it, and turned it over to read the text.

Upon the yellowed parchment were strange markings. They appeared not as Larascan letters, but as small images. Each character was unique, made up of curved and deliberate shapes and placed below the figure atop it. Rather than lining up side to side, like she was accustomed to, the strange text made sparse lines down the paper. Though she was unable to read even Larascan text, Rina somehow understood this was a letter written in Morana's native language, one she had had no reason to speak in eighteen years. Yet, she had kept it.

Unwilling to further infringe upon the Queen's privacy, she put down the letter. Beneath the papers, she found the key Azalea had spoken of. She quickly closed the drawer and stood, more than ready to flee that place. However, the Queen's mirror caught her eye. She saw herself in it, dirty and thin from captivity, but expected nothing more. Raised an orphan, she had become accustomed to this reflection. She wondered now what Morana saw when she beheld her reflection. Was she as content with the image?

She knew she could spare no time to ponder. Key in hand, she rushed from the room, forgetting to close the door as she departed.

It took less time to navigate to the stables. Once outside, she was more at ease with the situation. The guards who patrolled the outside were a lazy sort, and the few she did see were preoccupied taking their afternoon nap. Having been trapped in the icy castle for so long, she couldn't help but notice how warm the outside air was, though the ground was encased in ice. It was a phenomenon without explanation, so pleasant she found no reason to dwell on it.

The horses paid little attention to her when she entered the stables, most just resting, enjoying the warm air. At first, Rina found herself overwhelmed by her task, for there were many fine horses of different sizes and colors, any one of them beautiful enough to belong to the Queen. However, one stood out from the rest. In a stall with a golden gate stood a magnificent mare, its coat of the same shimmering white as the snow upon the ground.

Rina approached it slowly, wary of its alert gaze. As she examined the creature, she realized that this was not their first meeting. The girl had seen her once before, at the cloaked prisoner's execution.

"Hello," she whispered, now close enough to touch the gate. "Do you want to go play?"

The creature's black eyes regarded her haughtily, as the Queen had regarded the doomed man. Anger began to rise within Rina, beyond her control. Even now, she hated being reminded of that day – being reminded what people could do to one another.

"You should go for a little walk," Rina said, the key clicking in the golden lock.

The door swung open, freeing the horse's path. The white mare seemed to hesitate. She took one step forward, as if testing the intentions of her liberator. Rina was still.

"Go on," she said.

This was her rebellion against the world. If she could not fight against all the hatred, cruelty, and vindictive pleasure of others, then she could cause chaos in their lives. All at once, she came to understand a small portion of Princess Azalea's madness.

It's all in good fun.

At last, the creature fled, throwing her head back as she indulged in a joyous whinny. Rina watched as she disappeared into the gardens, her hoof prints revealing weeds beneath the snow.

Safe in the shadowy half-light of the hour, Rina enjoyed a more leisurely viewing of the steeds. She had always loved horses, though she was too low-born to be taught to ride one. One mare, in particular, brought her pause. She was white, like the Queen's, but of a softer hue. Her snout was shaped more elegantly than the rest of the horses, and her brown eyes were filled with warmth.

"A Kyron steed. Well cared for, it seems."

The sudden voice made her heart stop. She spun on her heels, shocked to find Valten – a soldier of Rank 12 – standing across the way.

"Relax," he said. "The Rank is leaving. I don't much feel like going back to report your escape."

She had almost forgotten Valten's strange nature. Although he had always been particular about his appearance, he was now particularly well groomed. His brown hair was cut precisely about his face, just below his very Larascan jaw, and his sallow skin was mostly concealed by long sleeves and pant legs. He never held her gaze long; his eyes always shifted towards more important things.

"I'm going back to Malldon," he said, opening a stall to retrieve his brown stallion. "I kept my horse here so I wouldn't have to explain to Lance that I was deserting. He's been downright unbearable since the little freak bit off his finger. I'll tolerate him no longer."

Rina tried not to smile at the report of the General's misfortune. Even so, she touched her tattered sleeve, recalling the scar beneath.

"What's Malldon like?" she asked, quietly.

Silas had been sent there; she hoped it was at least hospitable.

"The same, I expect," Valten shrugged. "Always the same."

Once he had prepared his steed, he mounted it, taking the reins in his pale hands. No doubt he planned to leave without another word; however, Rina stopped him.

"Did Kaish already leave?" she asked.

Her words must have disturbed him. Despite his nature, he held her gaze for a long while, his green eyes indecipherable.

"Kaish is dead, Rina. They executed him before the ball."

She stared, uncomprehending.

"…dead?"

Alastor had taken her to that execution. He had smiled as he watched the Talonian ascend the platform; he had tried to keep her there.

"I don't know how you survived that fall," Valten continued, his horse already carrying him past her, "but the Tallk might've liked to know that you did. The other soldiers and I were quite surprised to see you at the ball—you looked quite nice, by the way. I could hardly tell you were foreign."

He sighed grandly, finally turning from her. Rina watched the horse's tail swing behind them as Valten rode into the white gardens.

"I guess some people are harder to kill," he said.

When he was gone, there was nothing more to hold her up. She sank to her knees, sharp hay piercing her skin.

Desperate, she gripped the bracelet about her wrist.

Kaish…

The cool metal had absorbed the chill of the castle. Beneath her fingertips, it was cold as death.

She remained there, miserable, silent. She was suspended somewhere between anguish and anger – anger at Alastor for his betrayal, at the Queen for taking his life, and at Kaish for letting himself be destroyed. They had been so close to meeting again, to embarking upon a life together. Now, she was alone.

Time passed slowly, allowing her to remain frozen. However, too soon, she heard the creaky doors open.

Panicked, she rushed into the stall Valten had left open, and crouched in the shadows. From there, she could see a tall, dark-haired man approach the white mare across the way. He appeared foreign, for his skin was of an almond hue. When he spoke, the words sounded like music.

"Ah, Aina…"

He stroked the mare's soft snout, summoning a huff from the beast.

"You are my most loyal friend. Eighteen years since you carried me and Baldric from Kyro, yet here you stand, strong as ever."

He sighed, the sound like tears.

"Baldric told me to remain loyal to the crown. So long as I remain loyal, I'll never need a place to sleep. But how can I, after what Morana did to Twyla? The Queen could not have asked for a dearer friend. Twyla has carried out her every demand, from clothing her to caring for her child. Yet, she repays her with chains and solitude."

The Kyron rest his head against his mare's, hanging from her neck.

"I'm lost, Aina. It feels like I'm falling, trapped in a world unraveling at its seams…"

Rina felt the tears trailing down her cheeks. She swallowed her sobs, knowing with certainty that they would have her caught.

The walls of the stall were not solid: only two wooden railings kept the horses from escaping. Unable to remain there, she swung under the railing, silently making her way to the open door. If she was seen, she did not care.

Kaish's bracelet, loosened by her own hand, slid from her arm and into the hay—abandoned.

⁂

Rina closed the cell door behind her, hiding the key within her corset. She saw Sen alone, this time. Tasha slept against the other wall, arms wrapped as though he were in them; however, he was very awake, pacing, shaking, by the opposite wall.

"Why do you let yourself starve?" she asked. "There are rats."

Sen stopped his pacing, turning his hungry gaze on her.

"They never…come close. Stupid…s-stupid…rats…"

Rina nodded. She was half aware of herself, now. Her tears dried upon her face, it seemed her mind had left with them. She felt only a dark void within her, seeking to absorb the few hopes that lingered there.

Why dream?

She knelt before the boy, drawing her sleeve from her wrist.

Why feel?

"A child shouldn't starve," she said.

The boy hesitated, his trembling gaze surveying her bare wrist. The bracelet had left a mark upon it: it was white where the metal had been, preserved from time and the altering heat of the sun. It was this part that the boy touched, his cold skin sending shivers through her body.

When he bit down, she was overwhelmed by an indescribable sensation. She could feel it rising up her arm, down her neck, taking hold of her beating heart. It was terror; it was euphoria. She surrendered, and he drank.

Suddenly, something ripped Sen's fangs from her.

"What are you doing?!" Tasha shrieked.

Rina was too weak to hold herself upright. She fell, knowing there was no one there to catch her. Vision faltering, the shadows shifted, turning into shapes. A black wolf rushed across the wall, snarling at her, shame in its violet eyes.

I'm sorry.

She heard her own tears falling, in the distance.

Plink.

Plunk.

Chapter XXXII

16th Day of 1st Month, 655 I.R.

They left Malldon in the early morning hours, when the sun had not had a chance to disperse the city's heavy fog. Yet, despite its presence, Silas caught sight of a stone structure towering just beyond the city, the peaks of its rooftop rising above the mist. It was not large enough to be a palace, yet was larger than any commoner's estate and built with only the finest of stones.

"Is that the castle of your Duke?" Silas asked, for he had never seen such a strange structure.

Raven rode her horse only a short distance in front of Silas and his escort, close enough to peek behind her and see what he asked of.

"Psh, that? It's too fancy for the useless Duke Marcellus. He's just a figurehead, really. Something we use to keep the King out of our hair."

"You have a Queen," Ariel reminded, in his flat tone.

"Whatever."

Silas glanced back to the structure, seeing the colorful glint of stained glass catch the sun's faint light.

"Wasn't there some ancient temple in Malldon?" he asked, recalling something Giovanni had told him.

Raven didn't turn back, this time. Silas could see her body stiffen, tightened by either irritation or fear. Neither could be deciphered from her voice.

"I don't know about ancient. That temple's only been standing since after Raphael's Draft. It's the headquarters of Catsavionism, where the Priests live and receive offerings."

"Priests?" Silas asked.

In all his travels, he had never come across a religious city in Larasca. It seemed Larascans wanted nothing to do with a higher power, or had never considered the idea. To hear of one here was somehow unsettling.

"I guess you wouldn't know. You're an outsider." Raven paused, glimpsing them for only a moment. "The Priests run our city. Whatever they decide the 'Great Goddess' has dictated, they dictate to us. I'm not sure just how much everyone believes in their Goddess, but the Priests, they're…persuasive."

"How so?" Silas pressed.

"They cleanse impurity."

Although not quite satisfied, Silas would not pry further. She seemed to have said all she wanted to say, which was more than enough for him. He expected he would soon learn more than he wanted to know, with or without her help.

A time passed in uncomfortable silence, their steeds guiding them though the dense forestry, over uneven ground. No longer needing to lead, Ariel soon fell behind the group, without explanation. Silas rolled his eyes, seeing no more reason to linger back. No sooner had he caught up to Raven than she addressed him again.

"What is up with your brother?"

"Brother?" he asked, startled.

"Blank-face looks just like you. Are you honestly saying you're not related?"

Silas glared, almost insulted by the assumption. He didn't waste his breath trying to correct her, assuming his disgust was enough.

"Fine," she said coolly, reading his look. "Related or not, do you know what's wrong with him? Is he blind? Stupid? What is up with that vacant stare?"

The youth shrugged, his gaze returning to their path.

"Just the way he is. He's quiet; I prefer him such."

Raven's laughter was light, mocking in the gentlest of ways.

"I see. You're just that strong, silent type."

"I speak when I have something to say," he snapped. "I see no point wasting time with mindless chatter."

"Interesting…"

She was quiet after that, though he could feel her eyes on him for an unsettling period of time. He could tell when he was being tested. Irked, he held his tongue, suppressing his natural urge to growl.

The ride was uneventful after that, the three of them venturing deeper into the woods without further conversation. The icy forest was as gray as the city they had left behind, the trees doing little to fight the fog that settled over the white ground—like a rain cloud descended from the heavens to rest.

Before long, they came to a break in the trees, where the snow evenly coated the ground. There, in the clearing, was a glistening lake, which stretched as far as the eye could see. However, they were not alone there. A large, fearsome wolf, its gray fur matted with twigs and blood, stood like a sentinel upon the water bank. It displayed its fangs in a low snarl; its eyes glowed crimson red.

"Shit," Raven cursed.

Her horse reared back, alerting the wolf with its terrified cry. Silas knew they had little time to react. Despite Aldrich's protest, he dismounted, brandishing his sword.

"Fawk! What are you doing?!" the girl shrieked.

Silas came to a halt before the beast, sword held high. He should have attacked. His body screamed for him to fight. However, the creature's crimson eyes held him transfixed, staring into him, through him.

Leave...

He held the sword in a trembling grip, fury summoning his bestial roar.

"LEAVE!"

The wolf pounced, claws and teeth ready to shred his skin. Silas was faster. His blade impaled the beast as both fell back, blood spilling, staining Silas' clothing.

The wolf shook, trembling, fighting to regain control of the failing body. However, its crimson eyes began to dim. Soon, Silas saw his own gaze reflected in lifeless orbs.

He heard Raven close by, though not close enough to be of any help.

"Is it dead?" she asked.

Silas pushed the corpse off his body. His sword had penetrated deep into the beast; it took force to jerk it loose. A new mess gushed forth, slicking his trousers with a soup-like mixture of blood and gore. Though the smell revolted him, his upbringing allowed him to clean the sword in the snow with little more than a grimace.

"It's dead," he reported.

Raven knelt beside him, turning the animal on its back to examine the injury.

"I guess we'll be eating wolf tonight," she said.

"We're not staying the night."

"Oh?"

The girl gave him an infuriating smile.

"We'll see."

The youth saw Ariel riding into the clearing, regarding the gory scene with his usual stoicism. Unsurprised, Silas allowed his gaze to drift back out over the water, which glistened like a diamond against its gray surroundings.

"Is this the lake?" he asked.

Raven nodded, already using a dagger – he hadn't noticed she was armed – to skin the creature.

"That's Avdotia Lake. They say it's cursed, so this place doesn't have a lot of visitors. What did you want to do here, exactly?"

He had no intention of responding. Once he had shed his soiled shirt, he dropped a rock in the clear water, testing its depth. It fell for a long while, drifting this way and that, before it finally settled amongst the smooth stones of the deep.

As he dived in, he heard Raven's shout.

"What?! You crazy son of a bitch!!"

Avdotia Lake was barren. Nothing of substance grew beneath its murky waters—not a stem. Its floor was entirely covered by smooth, onyx stones, some covered by thin algae. The parasite's green tinge provided the lake's only color, for not a creature stirred its depths. He turned over stone after stone, searching for some sign of the diamonds the Queen had demanded of him.

Nothing.

His stomach knotted itself in his fury, which could be directed at no one. He knew it was not beyond his twisted mother to send him on futile quest, but it enraged him just the same. Even so, he would keep looking. He would look until he suffocated.

Fool.

He was losing air fast. Despite his resolve, he knew he would soon have to abandon his search. Although the wintry chill of the water had no effect on his warm skin, a growing pressure on his ears further urged his ascent. Yet before he could surface, he caught sight of a large boulder in the depths. It was massive enough to break the surface of the water, where dim sunlight, exaggerated by the water's ripple, illuminated deep carvings etched into its flat face.

Before he could investigate, his desperate body forced him to breech the surface. The sudden sting of cold air eased the fire in his lungs. Useless, he could only float there, heaving in an attempt to re-inflate them.

Behind him, he glimpsed the girl and his escort on the shore, one unsaddling his horse while the former cast a large canvas over a tree branch. She truly meant to stay the night.

Despite his annoyance, he would confront her another time. He dove again, this time approaching the mysterious rock.

He was surprised to find that the surface he had first thought was smooth was actually covered with thin algae, like the green-tinged rocks at the bottom of the lake. However, this algae was gray, so transparent it only changed the texture of the stone.

Upon the face of the rock he found a strange inscription, written in what seemed to be plain Larascan text. Yet there was no order to it. Lines would crisscross each other aimlessly, forcing him to follow each line with increasing diligence. In total, there were seven. Three lines began with a calligraphic letter; four did not.

"*Last we spoke is long past...*"

"*..as no waters can bind us...*"

Once more, his lungs had begun to scream for air. He reread the engraving with new haste, trying to burn the image of it into his thought. Then, he was forced to abandon his task. Silas again breeched the cold surface and swam back to shore.

Water dripped from his hair and skin when he lifted himself onto the bank; he tried to ignore the ice melting beneath his hands. Despite the words that filled his head, he made time to address the girl nearby who so blatantly decided to go against his wishes.

"I told you, we're not staying the night," he growled.

Raven looked at him from the canvas, which she had been staking into the ground with broken branches.

"The day's almost over," she replied, infuriatingly calm. "I don't plan to travel when it's dark. I know traveling at night is probably no problem for a crazy man who swims in a half-frozen lake, but your lackey agrees with me."

Silas grit his teeth when he saw Ariel nod, sitting comfortably beside a fresh fire.

"It is most logical to set up camp," said the man. "We are fortunate Raven decided to prepare her saddlebags with overnight equipment."

No one was obeying him. As deeply annoyed as he was, he knew he had more pressing matters to deal with. The words of the inscription still swirled about in his head, more likely to vanish with every neglectful moment. As if possessed, he took hold of a stick buried beneath the snow, beginning to carve the lines into the frozen ground.

Focus.

Giovanni had tortured him with puzzles, growing up. A riddle in the middle of the day meant either real steak that night, or another week sleeping in the street. He had become so adept at solving puzzles that they became his preferred form of punishment. Now, his trained thought would not cease until he ordered every line. He searched for their pattern, their length, anything he thought might help him decipher the text. Any letter with a special shape, he underlined, knowing they had the most meaning. At last, he discovered their riddle.

> *Last we spoke is long past*
>
> *and still we await the next man of worth.*
>
> *Remember our names. We honor every summon*
>
> *as no waters can bind us.*
>
> *Scream not, we hear your call*
>
> *here, we await your coming.*
>
> *arise, our fallen Savior*

The words left him only a new puzzle. He read and reread it, hoping this alone could help him understand.

Remember our names.

Whose names?

"What are you doing?"

Raven's voice was as unwelcome as her presence. He shot her a scathing look in hopes to deter her advance, to no avail. Now wrapped in a fur jacket, she knelt down beside him, openly reading all he had carved.

"Nothing that concerns you," he snapped, brushing snow over part of the words. "Go back to your tent."

Raven was not discouraged. She smiled, brushing the snow away from the carving as she continued her inspection. For a time, she was silent. Unable to decode the words himself, he watched her, secretly hoping she failed as miserably as he.

"Larasha," she murmured.

He raised a brow, baffled by the sound.

"What?"

She looked up, clearly surprised he had heard.

"That's the old name for this country, isn't it? I heard it somewhere."

Silas looked back to the lines, trying to understand where the word had come from. Then, he saw it. He had written the lines straight down, allowing the first letters to line up in that distinguishable word. However, he noticed more than that. If it truly was one name, three of the letters should not have been capitalized. By ornamenting the L, R, and S, three new words had been created.

La, Ra, Sha.

He smiled, always pleased when he solved a new puzzle. Still, as much as he would have preferred not to acknowledge her assistance, Raven's wit had been the key. He could not help but be impressed.

"…thank you."

The youth had not realized before how rarely he said those words. Raven, who had not known him long enough to understand her fortune, regarded them without a bit of surprise.

"It just needed a woman's touch," she teased.

She went on her way, humming in a pleasant way. Silas found his eyes watching her movement, again observing the womanly curves beneath her fur-lined dress. He didn't understand why she still intrigued him, after the mistake he had already made with her. Perhaps it was his body, more than his mind, that desired her so.

He shook off these feelings. Now that he understood a piece of the inscription, he returned to the words.

Giovanni had taught him a handy method to understanding long poems. The key, he said, was to remove what did not matter. It is only when the words are reduced to their barest meaning that they can be easily understood. Remembering this, he smoothed over the parts he felt were unnecessary, until three lines remained.

We await a man of worth.

We honor every summon.

No waters can bind us.

The meaning was clear, strange a meaning as it was. He looked back out over the water, seeing the clear lake glistening with new light. It seemed to beckon to him now, the fog parting before him, creating a path to the shore.

Against his better judgment, he decided to attempt something half-sane. Silas removed his soaking boots to stand at the edge of the lake, the only place where the water was slightly shallow. The chilly water seeped between his toes as he stared before him, into the close depths.

"I deciphered your riddle," he said, watching the clear water begin to swirl. "Your wait is over: La…Ra…Sha."

For a moment, the waters were still. Not a ripple graced its surface. However, he remained, patiently watching the deep waters beginning to turn, slowly swirling. The depth became a great void, black as the night sky.

Six hands dragged him down.

Raven hummed to herself at she prepared her tent for the night, rather focused on her task. She was surprised to see that Reja had again dived into the freezing water, but she had decided that he was wrong in the head, and he could do what he well pleased. It made him amusing to her. He was attractive, besides, which made it easier to ignore his obvious insanity.

"Does Reja always swim in frozen lakes?" she asked Ariel, who still warmed himself by the fire.

"He does not want you to call him that," he said.

"Maybe," she said, smiling, "but that is his name."

The young man shrugged, holding his hands towards the open flame.

"He has many names. I do not believe he is ready to acknowledge that one."

Raven rolled her eyes, amused by his reply. Even so, she was intrigued. Everything about the two men was strangely intriguing, from Reja's dark skin to Ariel's lifeless eyes. They were foreign, definitely, but she had never seen foreigners of their sort. She risked a lot by being with them; however, her interest in them outweighed her anxiety.

She returned to her task, humming again while she put the finishing touches on her sleeping place. The canvas was stretched over two branches, which allowed her more space within, and a large, thin blanket covered the snow beneath. It would be comfortable enough, with a couple more blankets. Though she had no intention of inviting Ariel in, she would offer a place to Reja. After all, they had shared a bed once before. His warmth would be of good use.

Too late, she noticed Ariel's alert gaze. He stood now, staring deep into the forest.

"Intruder," he said.

The girl shuddered, swallowing fear.

"Don't be ridiculous, no one comes here."

Even so, she followed his gaze into the woods, her heart pounding hard in her chest. Barely concealed by the fog, she saw a Priest's golden robes, stitched so finely with the riches they took from their followers.

"…excuse me," she said, forcing a smile. "I should go look for more firewood."

She knew already what she would find, and that she needed no excuse with a man as emotionless as Ariel. Yet, she uttered the words in fear, as if afraid no one would look for her unless she did.

Calm as she could make herself, she left camp. She wandered into the dense forest, knowing already that he would be at the end of her path, waiting for her.

"Sister," said the Priest, rising up haughtily when she arrived, "why are you helping Impure Ones?"

Hector was as cold as ever, his green eyes no longer like hers, so chilled by ice that she could not look into them. His golden robes cast a long shadow over the ground, darkening her path. One would have never known he was handsome, once. His features were so transformed by power that his face was terrible to behold, deep lines set like serpents across his brow, from his eyes.

"Because I felt like it," Raven replied, her own voice taut. "It's none of your concern."

"Neschume does not look kindly upon those who help Impurities."

"Shut up," she hissed. "How would *you* know? Why would She ever talk to the likes of you?"

This seemed to strike a nerve in him. His scowl deepened, his false piety wavering in the face of her insolence. Yet, when he relaxed, his smile was enough to disturb Raven from within.

"I know about your little effort to leave Malldon. You know we Priests don't take kindly to letting people go."

Raven paled, choking on her own tongue.

"You're giving your money to that heathen bartender, so it can't be traced to you," Hector continued, amused by her horror. "Clever, really. You should have picked a better man to put your faith in, one who does not take bribes so easily."

"Snake," she spat.

"Do not act so low, sister. I have decided to take pity on you. Should you hand over the two Impure men, then I will gladly finance your little escape."

His words caught her off guard. Raven could not help but hesitate, always so repulsed by the sight of her own brother in a Priest's robes. He was toying with her, as he and the others toyed with the fears of the townspeople. She had to leave that place, if she were going to do anything worthwhile with her life. If Hector was all that stood in her way now, then she had little choice than to meet his demands.

"Give me a few days," she said.

Reja and Ariel were strangers to her. Though she pitied them, in the end, they were just in the wrong place at the wrong time.

"So you show your true colors," Hector said, making no secret of his pleasure. "I expected no better from a lowly whore."

"Don't smile like you're better than me."

Her brother bowed low, as though to mock her. For a moment, Raven felt shame churning within her, tightening her throat.

"My fellow Priests and I will arrive on the third sunset," he said, calmly. "Do your best to keep them here until then. Use your…talents."

"Just get lost," she snapped.

Hector smiled his sickening smile, trying to be pleasant. Still, too soon, he was gone. She was alone there, alone with her own treachery.

Silas awoke sputtering, coughing water from his lungs. His body ached from the force of a great fall. When he opened his eyes, he expected darkness – instead, the world around him was illuminated by a strange, blue glow, which rose from the waters beneath him, lapping at his heels. He had never seen such a color. Around him were the crumbling pillars of a once-grand structure, now broken, stone and glass piled in the shallow pool. Here, hidden in the depths of Malldon's lake, was Neschume's vanished temple.

The Temple of Avdotia.

Looking down, his breath caught in his throat. Within the blue water was a field of black diamonds, stretching as far as he could see. He couldn't believe his eyes. Here was the end of his journey, his key to Rina's cell. Disbelieving, he reached down to take what was his.

"Do not touch those, if you ever want to leave."

The woman's voice was ethereal, low and smooth as the water. Silas fell back, stunned to see three figures appear like shadows in the ruins. They were women, sharing the same beautiful face; however, reptilian scales clothed their naked forms, only their necks and faces allowed the supple flesh that came with humanity. Each woman had a prevailing color in her scales, matched by piercing eyes. One was blue, her hair a vibrant gold and a pretty smile set on soft lips; green had a fierce stare, her hair black as regret; the last was red, with fiery hair of the same hue. Yet, her gaze was the most serene.

"Who are you?" Silas managed.

The crimson-scaled creature stepped forward, though the others regarded him just as intensely.

"We were holy, once. Our names were—"

"Prudence," said the blonde.

"Faith," said the dark-haired woman.

"—and Justice."

The woman closed her scarlet eyes, lost in another time.

"We were the Priestesses of this temple, chosen by Neschume herself. Our family had known it since the day the three of us came from our mother's womb, this mark upon our skin."

Prudence raised her right arm, while Faith raised her left. Silas could barely make out the outline of an unusual shape, beginning with half the hilt of a sword, then swirling to almost indistinguishable figures, resembling a flower, or a blade, or a mirror. A similar marking was etched onto Justice's chest, beneath her crimson scales.

"All who are chosen by Her will bear a similar marking. Thus, we were raised to serve her. We knew of no other life. We wanted nothing more than our life in the Avdotian Temple, until—"

"He came," said Faith. "The foul creature with a shadowed face. He told me that Neschume did not exist. I did not believe him, at first, but he returned to me again and again, with more and more proof that what he said was true. How could She exist when there was famine, poverty, illness, deformities, war? If she did exist, she had forsaken us. When I lost faith, so did my sisters."

"But we still cared very much for the people who followed Her, and sought solace in our temple," came Prudence. "We did not want them to lose their faith, like we had. So, we asked the Dark One for the power to watch over them, enough power that we could pretend to be their Neschume."

"He gave us a large black diamond," Faith continued, "filled with power. So long as this diamond was hidden in the depths of our temple, we could cure the sick, raise crops from barren soil, even bring a soul back from the dead. However, not even this was the limit of the diamond's power. Jaska's gift was capable of such terrible things that there were times we feared it would destroy us."

At last, the woman reopened her crimson eyes.

"The world began to fall apart. We heard of the other temples falling to ruin, one by one. At once, we knew it was Jaska's doing. When he and his Dragons came to the Temple of Avdotia, we were prepared to fight. We used the power of the diamond to fight against him—a violation of his terms. Because we had broken our promise, the diamond shattered into a thousand pieces, and we were at his mercy.

"Jaska tried to do away with us. The Dragons destroyed our temple, but as hard as Jaska tried, he could not lay a finger on its Priestesses. The holy mark upon our skin created a protective seal, shielding us from his evil. However, in the end, it could not save us. Because we had offered our soul in exchange for his diamond, Jaska was free to exact his revenge in another way. He cast the shattered diamond and our ruined temple into the depths of Avdotia Lake, and transformed us into one of his creatures."

"Our scales are his gift," said Prudence.

"As was an eternity to live in the shadow of our mistake," said Faith.

"We are cursed," said Justice, "cursed forever to live in this lake, unless someone calls our name."

Silas managed to stand, his head reeling as he tried to absorb the flurry of information.

"But I didn't call your names," he said.

"You did," said the blonde.

"Those are our new names," said the black-haired woman.

"New names?"

The woman with crimson hair stepped forward again, scales glinting as water dripped down her body.

"When one becomes Jaska's creature, you abandon your mortal name, so that person can be rightfully mourned by those who knew them. We are someone else."

"La," said the blonde.

"Ra," said her sister.

The crimson-haired woman smiled, regally bowing her head.

"Sha," she finished. "We are separate only physically; we see and feel as one."

Silas was overwhelmed. He stared at the creatures, his logical mind furiously attempting to reconcile their existence.

"…water nymphs," he said, finally.

La smiled playfully, seeming amused.

"You can call us that."

"Or naiads, or sprites," said Ra. "Doesn't matter what we are to you."

"Whatever you are, I *need* one of those diamonds," he demanded.

The nymphs smiled in unison, the sight chilling him.

"You are wrong," said La.

"A diamond won't save her," said Ra.

"A diamond alone won't save Rina," said Sha.

Silas stared, rigid as ice. It felt as though his soul had been laid out before him, wholly exposed.

"How do you know her name?"

"Because you are like us," said Ra, slowly sitting, sliding her emerald-scaled feet into the blue water. "You are a creature of Jaska's creation. We share a bond: us, his Dragons, you."

"We do not usually wish to help Jaska's chosen," said La, "after what he did to us."

"But we have decided to offer you our aid," said Sha, "for in helping you, Xavier, our own goals will be that much closer."

"Then let me take a diamond," Silas growled.

The nymphs regarded each other with their ethereal gaze, never less than calm. Without speaking, it seemed they divided amongst themselves the weight of a celestial gamble—to trust him.

"It was our duty as Priestesses to guard three of Neschume's seven sacred artifacts," said Ra.

"During the time we lost faith, they were useless to us," continued La, childlike pride in her sapphire eyes. "But now that we remember Neschume's love, they've been returned to their former glory."

"What does this have to do with me?" Silas snapped.

If any of them were surprised by his impatience, they did not show it. All at once, they came together, speaking to each other in soft breaths. Then, they began a slow descent into what he had thought was shallow water, until they had disappeared beneath the field of diamonds.

Suddenly, La rose up from the water before him. In her scaled hands was a silver hand mirror, reflecting his shocked visage back at him.

"This is Vera," she said. "It will show you all that truly threatens you, so you can hope to guard yourself from misfortune."

La vanished, swallowed again by the shifting waters. Unsettled, Silas spun about in time to see Ra rise from the depths, clutching the hilt of a strange dagger. It was strangely large, and unusually shaped, formed like the wedge of a sundial.

"This is Hasan," she said. "It is the most unreliable of the sacred artifacts. It draws not blood from its victims, but time. Perhaps that person will lose years of their life, or gain them, or be wholly misplaced—lost forever in a time that is not their own."

Intrigued by this weapon's supposed power, he tried to take hold of it, just to see its anatomy for himself. However, Ra soon vanished into the pool beneath him; the weapon slipped through his fingers.

When he turned again, Sha stood before him. In her scaled hands was the most impressive artifact of them all: a sword whose blade glowed crimson, feathers etched into the metal guard, transforming it into a pair of golden wings. Between these wings was a hole, perfectly round, that seemed strangely out of place—as though a clever thief had stolen its most precious gem.

"This is Corliss," said the nymph. "In its natural form, it is an unbeatable weapon. The poison blade proves lethal to all who cross its path. However, should the wielder hold the blade with his own hand as he cuts another, whoever receives the blow will be cured of all ailments, physical or otherwise. The wielder, in turn, will absorb the poison and perish."

Sha held the weapon towards him, grasping each of its golden wings.

"It is this weapon that will set her free."

Silas didn't understand why he would need such a dangerous weapon. Yet, the longer he beheld the glorious artifact, so majestic that it shed its own light, the more his resolve melted away.

"…what do I have to do?"

"You must prove yourself worthy of Neschume's sword," she said.

"How?"

"By completing three trials."

Corliss slipped from her hands in pieces, dissolving into the pool beneath like ash. In its place, she held the silver mirror.

"Each will be designed to test a separate part of you. Upon completion of each test, you will be given a conciliatory reward. Should you pass all three, Corliss is yours, as well as the diamond you seek."

"And if I fail?"

Sha breathed a great sigh.

"You will lose whatever you decide is dearest to you."

The stakes were steep. Silas hesitated, uncertain if he was strong enough to make this decision. However, his feelings were shaken by an image, forming on the mirror's surface. For an instant, he saw Rina. Her hair was matted, beautiful skin bruised and pale, and her eyes—lifeless.

His doing. His fault. And yet, it was she who suffered for it, she who deserved it the least. If there was any way to save her, he had to see it through.

"I accept your challenge."

Sha smiled. As she lowered the looking glass, her sisters appeared on either side of him, water trickling down their scales. Slowly, their slick hands slid over his face, blackening his sight.

As they pulled him into the abyss, Sha's whisper filled the air about him.

"Your journey begins at dawn."

Chapter XXXIII

18th Day of 1st Month, 655 I.R.

A soft song roused Rina from her shallow sleep, the sound now familiar to her. It was soothing, despite its foreign timbre. The longer it filled that small space, the more she forgot the dull ache in her wrist, healing beneath bandages borrowed from her recovered ankle.

"Where did you learn that song?" Rina asked, seeing Sen already asleep in his mother's arms.

"Why should I tell you?" the Princess hissed. "I'm still angry, you know."

As it turned out, Sen had never tasted human blood before. Tasha wasn't as angry as she was worried he would develop a taste for it; however, it appeared that wasn't the case. He had not asked to drink from Rina again, or his mother. Yet his shaking had ceased, and some color had returned to his milky skin. He smiled again, though as rarely as before. For now, it seemed Rina had saved his life.

"You don't have to tell me," said the girl, "but I'll listen, if you do."

Tasha's stories gave her some solace, grim as they were. It was better to explore Tasha's past than the darkness of their cell, or memories of her own.

The Princess sighed, no doubt ready to give in. She was stubborn, but she was also bored.

"I told you I had all sisters, but that's not true," she began. "I had a brother, once. His name was Nikolai – Niki, we called him. His mom was just five years older than me, the same age as my eldest sister. I wasn't usually fond of my father's wives or their spawn, but I did love those two. She was always kind to me, and the baby was…very sweet. He was sickly, though. Father wouldn't acknowledge that his son was feeble, so it was up to Niki's mom to take care of him. I felt terrible for her, so I started helping. She would sing this song to him every night, no matter how sick he was. I don't know how she could stand it, seeing him that way…"

Rina smiled, though it hurt. She began to understand that seeing Nikolai's illness had been as painful for Tasha as Sen's state was to her now.

"What happened?"

"He died," said Tasha. "He was only three. We expected it, but it didn't make it any better. I thought Father would take pity on a grieving mother, but he's not that kind of man. He had her executed for her 'failure', just like the rest of them."

Tasha shrugged in the face of Rina's horror.

"Sometimes I wonder what sort of man Nikolai would have become, with the parents he had. Would he have been a gentle Czar? Or a tyrant, like Father?"

She sighed.

"A mystery, I guess. Children are a gamble."

Rina nodded, lacking the experience to form a thoughtful response. Both of her own parents were a mystery to her: she had no way of knowing which she resembled.

"Can I ask you something?" said the woman.

Halfheartedly, Rina nodded.

"Have you ever thought about what it would be like, to be Queen?"

The girl coughed, startled.

"Me? Queen?"

"You have the attention of a Prince. It's more than a possibility."

"I..."

It was too much to comprehend. She couldn't imagine herself having that much power, for any reason. Even as a child, she had never dreamt of having anything more than a happy home.

"I'm sorry. I've never even considered it," she said, finally. "Even if I had, there would be no point. He hates me now."

Tasha rolled her eyes.

"What'd you do? Smooch him too hard?"

Rina's face turned red, despite her grimace.

"We...had a fight. He thinks I'm with someone else, but...I'm not..."

Anymore.

"He called me terrible things," she said, weakly. "I don't think he wants anything to do with me, anymore."

"That's why he's risking his ass traveling in the middle of winter to save you."

"Not me, you and all those men—"

"Oh, shut up."

Tasha scowled, more irritated than she had been in a long while.

"Either you can keep feeling sorry for yourself, or you can be glad there's someone in this screwed up world that bloody cares whether you live or die."

Rina cringed, regretting her words. She still felt a measure of guilt for what happened to Caine, as if Silas' actions were just as much her own.

Unfortunately, there was no time to console Tasha. Too soon, there was a jingle in the lock, and a hooded visitor outside the door.

"I'm here to borrow your blue-eyed friend," she said.

Tasha sneered, her eyes following Rina as she was led away.

Princess Azalea accompanied her to her destination, this time. They ascended through many wings, avoiding the occasional guard, until they came to the entrance of an eastern tower. She said nothing of the horse Rina had set free, nor did she seem to think of that previous task. The prisoner couldn't help but wonder *why* she was so quiet—her eyes seemed far away, her senseless smile so fixed it might have been painted. Azalea didn't speak until they approached the great door, drawing out a rusty key.

"This is the castle aviary," she said, fiddling the key in a large lock. "This is where they keep all the messenger birds. I don't know how the whole messaging system works, really; they just fly back and forth all on their own. Tahn's not here, so we can do as we please."

"What are we doing here?" Rina asked.

"Freeing the birds, of course."

"*What?*"

Rina stared in utter horror, appalled by Azalea's smile.

"Relax," she said. "It's not like we're letting them *outside*. We're just letting them fly free, inside the castle."

Rina could have died of terror.

"I can't do this. I won't—"

"You won't, hm? What about your precious girlfriend?"

The girl was silenced, her opposition drawn inward. Satisfied by her silence, the Princess again began to fiddle with the lock.

"On their own, the birds won't leave the tower," she explained. "You're going to have to lure out their leader."

"Their leader?"

"Pretty Tobias," said the Princess. "He has an interesting story, if you want to hear it."

She wasn't in the mood, but that made no difference to the Princess.

"Tobias was Dayu's bird; the sorcerer snuck him into the aviary when he arrived with Morana and me. I was just a little girl, then, so I didn't realize that it was bad for my sister to bring her secret boyfriend to her marital home. Dayu called him Toshiro, then. Cedric was so sweet that he let Toshiro stay with the other birds because he thought Toshi was my sister's, not knowing she and Dayu were using him to exchange secret love letters. Isn't that sweet?"

Rina felt sick, but said nothing.

"I'm really not sure why Cedric let her keep Toshi, after Dayu burned. He made her change his name, like that made it a different bird, but he still let her keep him. I think Tobias is her only friend left in all the world. Still, he's become a greedy thing, as of late…"

At last, Azalea opened the lock. She pushed open the double doors, revealing the palace aviary.

Light streamed down from high above, momentarily blinding Rina. When her sight returned, she could see hundreds of magnificent birds soaring past the barred glass, the curved walls, rising up into the beautiful domed ceiling.

"There," said Azalea, pointing to an iron rafter, "do you see him?"

Upon that rafter sat a large, black hawk, whose majestic eyes were transfixed by the Princess' fine clothes.

"Ever since Dayu brought him to the aviary, the other birds have followed his lead. Wherever he goes, they try to follow."

She reached into her bosom, drawing out a broken, white brooch.

"Morana never really wanted this, but she wanted it less after she broke it. I think it's safe to give this to her pet."

The Princess handed the jewelry to Rina.

"After I'm long gone, get his attention, then throw this out of the room. The greedy little pest won't be able to resist, and all the other birds will fly out after him. Understand?"

Rina nodded, reluctantly taking the offered brooch. Still, she found herself eyeing the beautiful necklace Azalea proudly wore about her neck, each of its blue beads crafted with obvious care.

"Why not use your necklace?"

Azalea laughed, fondly touching its glass pendant.

"I wouldn't dream of flinging this at a bird. This was Father's only gift to me..."

The Princess smiled, curtsying to Rina as though they were of similar importance.

"Wait until I'm quite gone."

Rina sighed, giving a dull, consenting nod. Soon, the cunning woman had disappeared down the hall, humming too strangely as she abandoned her toy.

The aviary was as peaceful as before, the birds enjoying the calm freedom of that place. The girl wished she did not have to disturb such harmony. Still, it seemed her wishes mattered as little now as they had before.

Why try.

It did not take much to reclaim the attention of the black hawk. As soon as Rina lifted the brooch, Tobias stood erect, ruffling its feathers as he eyed the trinket. She found it curious that his eyes did not match—one brown, one gold.

"Hello," she said.

She did not know why she spoke to him; even so, he stretched his wings in acknowledgement.

"You want this, don't you?"

The creature made no sound, but it craned its neck down to better see her. All around, other birds began to watch him, sensing the shift in his interest.

Rina felt herself smile, despite her emotions. She felt twisted inside, hopelessness entwined with apathy, disgust turned to amusement.

"Fetch."

She felt power when she tossed the brooch. She smiled as Tobias rushed past her, shrieking with joy or irritation when he snatched up his prize. The other birds whipped her hair as they escaped, a whirlwind of air and sound. Rina found herself laughing, the mad sound masked by their cries, by her own hands. She laughed, crying.

Suddenly, she felt she was being watched. Standing at the other end of the hall, dark eyes wide with shock, was the owner of the white horse.

"You're…that girl, from the stables…"

Panic.

Rina tried to escape, but he was faster than her. He snatched her bandaged wrist, forcing her to face him.

"You have Kyron eyes," he said, shocked.

For the first time, she managed to free herself from a man's grip. Yet, she didn't run. Rubbing her throbbing wrist, she was still, without the will to escape.

"Go ahead and report me, or whatever you have to do," she said, quietly. "I'm finished. All I ask is that my cellmate is taken care of, if something happens to me."

The man was speechless. He stared at her, clearly bewildered. However, the sound of footsteps froze them both.

This is it.

She stared only at her wrist, prepared to meet her fate.

His push came so suddenly that she lost her balance, stumbling back into the tower. All at once, she was locked behind the great doors.

"Hey!"

But her cry met no reply. Overwhelmed, she could only press her ear against the wooden door, trying to hear what was on the other side.

"Antonio?" came a low voice.

"Yes, Gabriel?"

"There are birds in the castle."

Two strident voices followed, frantic.

"Madness! Chaos!"

"Anarchy! ANARCHY!"

Gabriel's voice came again, fatigue to its tone.

"Forgive their hysteria. Reade and Reginald were attacked by falcons on their way to the Queen's study. As you're standing in front of the aviary, I assume you know the cause of this…debacle?"

Rina's heart was in her throat. Her previous bravery was forgotten as new fears sprung within her.

"Actually, it was my fault. I needed to send a message to one of my Wall-Patrol, and I didn't notice the birds were riled up. I just opened the doors and off they went."

Rina choked, stunned beyond belief.

"Pigshit!" cried Reade (she assumed).

"Kyron brat!" Reginald shrieked, "what are you hiding?!"

"There's no need for that, you two," said Gabriel. "Panic is no excuse for foolishness."

There was a pause.

"Are you sticking to that story?"

"It's truth."

Another long, agonizing pause.

"Well, try not to let it happen again."

Heavy footsteps followed, almost enough to cover the others' protests.

"That's it?!"

"What about all these bloody birds?!"

"This is a job for our Queen," said Gabriel, his voice tinged with amusement, fading away. "I wouldn't want to meddle in her affairs."

Little by little, the strident protests faded into the halls. Soon, the only sound left was the pounding of her heart.

The doors opened, the foreign man smiling down at her. For a long time, she was speechless.

"Why?" she managed.

When the Kyron bowed, it seemed the most noble act she had ever beheld.

"There has been much talk of you in these halls—Asyrias' blue-eyed lover."

He smiled at her, the gentle sight so welcome she could not correct him.

"It's time this family embraced such a kind spirit."

Then, like a dream in morning light, he was gone.

The air felt lighter when she returned to her cell; its darkness, now, seemed less oppressive. Yet when Rina saw Tasha curled against a wall, pain on her face, her own spirits began to dim once more.

"Is it the baby?" she asked, gently.

The Princess looked up, fatigue in her eyes. Slowly, she managed a nod.

"Never wish for children. They're a pain from the beginning."

Even so, despite her discomfort, Tasha managed a smile.

Rina couldn't help but admire her strength. The Rionan had endured more hardships than the girl could imagine, yet did not succumb to indifference. Even now, she hoped, smiled, and sang.

"Can I...ask you something?"

Tasha sat up, regarding her with mild curiosity.

"...can you teach me your song?"

The Princess seemed startled, at first; but when she saw Rina's sincerity, she gave in. She smiled again, and for a moment, Rina felt the world was new.

Chapter XXXIV

17th Day of 1st Month, 655 I.R.

*I*t felt like a dynasty was sitting on his chest. Silas groaned as he awoke, body aching, water in his ears. He didn't recognize his surroundings. A flickering lantern cast some light on the surrounding walls of fabric, which shifted in a cool breeze. Soon, he saw Raven sitting near him, back against an exposed tree trunk as she watched him wake.

"What *are* you?" she asked.

He scowled, though he wasn't yet conscious enough to be annoyed.

"Whatever you are."

"Clearly not. *I* would never survive hours of being underwater without coming up to breathe."

She clearly expected an explanation; she would be disappointed.

"What am I doing in your tent?" he growled.

"I found you unconscious on the shore last night. Ariel dried you off and helped carry you in here, to keep you out of the snow. Please, forgive us for being considerate."

"And where is he?"

"Outside. He said he wanted to sleep outdoors, for whatever reason. Both of you are so odd when it comes to the elements."

Silas tried to get up, but found his muscles heavy with fatigue. He fell back, giving in to temporary helplessness.

"Hn," he grunted.

It was difficult to think. Every time he closed his eyes, he saw the nymphs' glowing scales. He still couldn't understand what he had experienced in Avdotia Lake. Here, on the surface, his memories were too much like dreams.

His company was distracting enough, he found. Raven had decided to lace her corset over her dress, binding her waist and adding to the prominence of her breasts, which rose and fell so slowly.

"Why do you wear your corset so outwardly? It's…"

"Mystifying?" she asked, with her clever smile.

"Indecent."

She laughed, apparently amused. All she needed to be closer to him was to lean over, bringing her eyes and breasts stiflingly close.

" 'Indecent' is a word for married women and bitter hags. By the direction of your gaze, I'd say you like it."

He didn't appreciate her closeness – though her scent was overwhelmingly appealing – nor her assumption. Yet, when she touched his still-bare chest, an involuntary shudder ran through him.

"You really don't remember the other night?" she asked.

"If you mean that mistake, then no."

Despite his icy words, she smiled.

"That's a shame…"

She touched his face, leaning over him once more.

"Well, any man with assets like yours is free to share my bed whenever he pleases."

Consciously, he was disgusted. However, it seemed his body was intrigued—he could not bring himself to move from beneath her, where her chest was in plain view, and her pine scent filled his senses.

The sun had begun to rise, soft light touching the tent's walls. Seeing this, Silas broke free of Raven's spell. He pushed her off, swift to stumble out of the small space.

"Where are you going?" she called, holding open the tent's flap.

He snarled.

"It's none of your concern."

Silas passed Ariel, asleep by the smoldering fire, as he returned to the lake. For some reason, he could not help but feel concern for his emotionless escort, who had slept without a blanket.

Focus.

He approached the lake as the sun rose on the horizon, stretching golden rays across the shivering surface. When he looked into the water, it was La's face that stared back at him, blue eyes shining. The breeze carried her unearthly whisper.

"Are you prepared, Xavier?"

Slowly, he nodded.

"Yes."

Her hands rose from the water, dragging him down.

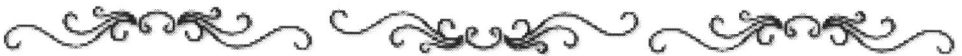

Darkness surrounded him, shifting, seeping into his every crevice. It was a place of nothingness, where air seemed hardly present, and he stood without support. Everything was tilting, or it was still.

"Where am I?"

His own voice seemed detached from him, echoing above or below.

All at once, she was there. The blonde nymph stood before him, sapphire scales shimmering in the darkness, eyes glistening as she smiled.

"This place does not exist," she said. "Whatever happens here occurs only in the context of your mind; you must not allow yourself to be fooled."

"Is this my test?" he asked.

She shook her head. As he watched, she reached behind her with dripping hands. Soon, the nymph revealed a stone-framed hourglass, its yellow sands still pooled in the bottom of translucent glass.

"I sustain you, yet I am your pain. Why do you seek me?"

Silas stared at her in confusion.

"What?"

"A true King must withstand a thousand diversions to solve his Kingdom's problems."

A mysterious smile possessed her features; slowly, she lifted the hourglass into the still air.

"All I ask is for you to disregard your environment to consider my question. When the last grain falls, you must have an answer."

"But what was your question?!" he cried.

The hourglass was turned, the grains beginning to fall. Bit by bit, they tumbled into a single stream—its sound a whisper of his fate.

"I am a man's sustenance and his poison.

I am ruin to those I inflict,

yet many do seek me.

What am I?"

The grains fell faster and faster, until they were a whirlwind of sand. They surrounded him, whipping him with hot air, the dust filling his lungs until he toppled over, choking. Eyes closed tight, he felt the world around him change.

"Thus begins your challenge, Xavier."

He opened his eyes.

Silas found himself standing in a large tent, its taupe flaps trembling with a gust of a hot wind. His feet were bare upon a crimson rug, which was embroidered with foreign symbols and colorful animals. Although he remained shirtless, his trousers were shapeless and dry. Around his wrist was a golden bracelet, coins dangling from its chain in an Akalinian fashion. He could not remember having worn such a thing since his days with Sh'ka.

Behind him, he glimpsed a young woman kneeling on a plum cushion, her back to him. Somehow, he knew the chestnut hue of her loose curls, though their length brushed the floor. Her every move held soft elegance, even as she so simply removed beads from around her slender neck, dangling them over the short table before her like a charm.

"Reja, will you help me?"

Her soft voice caught him by surprise. He refused to believe his ears; yet when she turned around, her blue eyes dark and gentle, he could doubt no longer.

"Rina?" he whispered.

He had missed her sweet smile.

"R'na," she corrected. "You sound like a Larascan…"

She turned back towards the small table, slowly gathering her hair and allowing it to fall over her shoulder. Her back was all but bare, covered only by two black ties: one around her mid-back, the other loose about her neck.

"Can you fix this for me?" she asked, blushing like she always did. "I can't get it right."

He still didn't fully understand what he was experiencing. They were both speaking the Akalinian language, fluently, and Rina was asking to be addressed by a Kala name.

It's only in your mind.

Despite his reluctance, he went to her. He was hesitant to touch her, as though her body were made of glass. Yet when he took hold of the loose tie, barely brushing her warm skin, he was tempted by the notion of untying the ribbon, allowing her scanty top to fall free.

I am sustenance and poison.

"What's wrong?" she asked, glancing over her pale shoulder.

He reconsidered. He tied the tie properly, even checking to be sure it was secure. However, when he stood, she seemed disappointed.

"Is that all the attention you give your wife?"

His heart stopped beating. He stared down at her, his tongue lodged in his throat.

What?

R'na smiled up at him, half coy, half teasing. Almost hesitantly, she reached up to touch the bracelet about his wrist, her own sliding down her tattooed arm like a shackle.

"I know it's still new to you. It's new to me too. But...you should know, I like it when we're alone..."

She tugged his bracelet, the one that matched hers, until he came down to her level. Suddenly, she embraced him, her warm face buried in his neck. At first, he didn't know how to react. Still, the longer she held him, her body so close to his, the more his defenses began to wane. He noticed how the candlelight illuminated her soft skin, so much of it exposed by the scandalous Kala attire. Her long hair was like spools of silk, unwinding down her curved back.

Returning her embrace, it seemed that her body was made for his, fitting so perfectly against his chest. He realized he was free to touch her silken hair, her soft skin, for it almost belonged to him.

"Why did we marry?" he asked, quietly.

Her laughter was warm against his neck, her embrace loosening as her hands trailed around him, at last resting on his chest.

"Because you said you couldn't be without me."

He watched her lips as she spoke, reddened by the way she always nipped at them. He longed to kiss them again, and keep her body beneath his until he was done with them. His hands sliding down her back, he leaned down to take what he so wanted.

The pounding of drums interrupted his plans. Suddenly, R'na was gone from his hold, rushing to the flaps of their tent.

"The ritual is about to start," she laughed, smiling back at him. "Don't be long, all right?"

Too soon, he was alone with his frustration.

"Are you distracted, my Prince?"

Silas tensed at the sound of the nymph's voice, almost angry for her intrusion. Even so, she was right. Already, he had lost sight of his task.

I am ruin to those I inflict.

He ran the words over and over in his mind, now trying to focus on what he had come there for.

"How much time is left?" he asked the air.

"Enough, perhaps. Perhaps not."

He was angry with himself for this lapse of judgment. However, even then, he couldn't justify remaining in the tent. Illusion or not, Rina was with him in this world. Silas was not willing to give her up so easily.

A large fire roared outside the tent, encircled by the young women of the troupe. As the drums pounded, all moved in the same rhythm, hips swaying, curving like snakes, captivating the ring of men who patiently watched. He saw R'na among them, smiling her perfect smile. The coins of her marital bracelet shivered with her every movement, adding an entrancing chime to the music.

Silas tried not to stare, to no avail. He saw her, only her, beside the flames. He could see the slight curve to her long arms in a spin, the tight flex of her abdomen when she moved her hips, and the swell of her breasts, barely hidden beneath her scarce top.

You seek me.

He could think of nothing but her beauty. No matter how he tried to piece together the riddle, it all came apart when she smiled at him, her eyes longing for him.

The women were reaching out to the men, this time drawing them into the dance. R'na reached out to him as well, dark curls falling about her face like a noble wreath.

"Reja," she whispered.

He joined her without a glimmer of thought. Though he consciously knew only dances of the palace, somehow, he understood how to move. Her every step was matched by one of his, balancing each other. He was predator, she was prey—she was the sky, he the earth. He felt her heat every moment their bodies touched; he became intoxicated by her scent.

What am I?

Somewhere beyond them, the sands of time continued to fall. Silas could almost see that cascading stream, and the growing dune that had sprung up beneath. Yet, he was distracted by R'na's skin glowing in the fire's glare, the heat of which caused her short breath. Again she returned to his arms, her back pressed against him for what was meant to be a moment. He wrapped his arms about her waist, holding her there, as he breathed hotly against her neck.

What am I?

R'na stayed there with him, her fingertips digging deeply into his arm. She knew his desire. His mouth was moist in want of her taste.

All at once, the pieces came together. One by one, they interlinked, his mind whirling as the sands fell, everything falling into place.

Their lips were a breath apart when the answer surfaced.

"Lust."

The last grain fell.

Everything dissipated. Slowly, his wife turned to dust, disintegrating in his hold. He fell to his knees, trying to cling to her, until there was nothing left but darkness.

"You make easy prey for such poisonous desire."

Silas stared at the ground, feeling nothing. Even when the nymph appeared before him, he could not bring himself to lift his head.

"What's wrong, dear Prince?" La asked, kneeling before him. "There's a heaviness about you."

He bristled, anger springing from deep within him.

"Leave me alone," he warned.

"Did I show you something you did not wish to see?"

He held his head, fighting his heavy breathing. This time, he would not give in to rage. Anger would change nothing. Even if he were to roar and bellow, it would not bring Rina back to him.

"I am sorry for your pain. It was not my intention," she said, sincere remorse in her sapphire gaze. "Regardless, you passed your trial beautifully. You have earned a small prize for your achievement."

At last, he heaved away the last of his anger. Stillness washed over him, masking pain with a dull sort of acceptance.

"What have I earned?"

"A story of your past."

The abandoned ruins emerged from the darkness. The two of them stood in the blue water, diamonds beneath their feet. Slowly, the nymph knelt down to the dark waters, her golden tresses slipping over her shoulders as she gazed into their depths. Her scaled fingertips touched its surface, bringing forth a flicker of light.

"Look into the pool," she said.

He stared down at the water, watching as the bright ripple disturbed his likeness. Gradually, its surface began to change. His reflection trembled, overcome by another sight. Soon, he saw the shifting image of a young Storma man emerging from a lake, dragging himself to the shoreline where he could cough the water from his lungs.

"Who is he?"

Silas glimpsed La's sad smile, nearly hidden by her dripping locks.

"Mazaki Dayu," she said. "His very name means 'to rip'."

In the water, the reflection of Dayu lifted something black from the shoreline. Though dark, its color gleamed in the moonlight.

"There are those blessed of Neschume, who are granted special power by Her. Each of those blessed by Her are born with black markings on their skin, such as those worn by my sisters and I."

Silas' gaze drifted to the faded marking on her arm, almost hidden by the blue scales Jaska had cursed her with.

"Although Neschume's markings have been seen on both men and women, the men have always been descended from a woman bearing such markings. In the past, all women blessed of Neschume were trained to be Priestesses, and Priestesses so rarely married that there was little chance for such a lineage to be created. That is why blessed men are so rare. Yet, Dayu was born with one of Her markings, curving very plainly around his right eye, betraying his inherited power.

"Since the fall of the Empire of Asyrias and the destruction of our temples, there has been very little talk of Blessed Ones in Larasca. Knowing this, you can imagine our surprise when Dayu appeared in our abode. He said he had searched far and wide for others like him, born marked, with such strange abilities; his search had ended him in Avdotia

Lake. He was a lonely soul, outcast because of his strangeness. We pitied him, my sisters and I, and told him our story.

"When he learned of how Jaska had imprisoned us, Dayu was so moved that he vowed to undo this curse. He would be our champion, he said. We, lonely, trusting creatures, thought it wise to put our faith in him. We entrusted him with seven of Jaska's diamonds, in hopes that he could use their power to overcome our enemy."

The image in the water flickered. Within it, Dayu's hand curled about the diamond, possessing it.

"We did not realize the diamonds were a corrupting force. They brought out the darkness in him, and altered his blessed gifts. His natural arrogance became self-obsession. No longer was his goal to destroy Jaska—he wished to become him.

"To further his own power was his first priority. He returned to Storm, his home country, in hopes to use the power of the diamonds to gain control of the Emperor, Shioya Ryuu. However, once he had infiltrated the Emperor's inner circle, he became…distracted."

The water rippled, one image changing to another. A young Storma woman leaned against the frame of an open door, dressed in the colorful, silken robes of her native land. Her black hair, brilliant in the moonlight, hung loose about her waist, some strands gracing her pale cheeks in a sudden gust. Brightest of all was her sapphire gaze, filled with tears.

"Shioya Miyuki was the eldest Princess of Storm. She was a neglected child, shamed by her mother's exile. Her father made no secret of his scorn for her, and openly showed preference towards her infant sister, Arisa, born by his young, hand-chosen bride. Were it not for her sharp tongue, Miyuki would have had a great many suitors, for her unusually blue eyes captivated all who gazed upon her. Sadly, she was often alone."

The black-haired woman closed her eyes, the tears trailing down her porcelain cheeks. Yet, they were soon kissed away by a young man, whose right eye was marked by dark, curving lines.

"Dayu did not love her. The diamonds would not allow that. He must have seen her weakness as an opportunity, and exploited it to its fullest. First, he made her love him. Then, he used the diamonds to weave a spell about her, so that love would never die.

"Emperor Ryuu made a terrible mistake when he tried to build a bridge across the Great River. Larasca's vicious King, Raphael, took the act as a declaration of war, and sent his organized armies across the river to destroy what they found. Storm was not prepared for the brutality of Larasca's forces. The Emperor had no choice but to make peace with the Larascan King, and offered his two daughters to prove his goodwill. Miyuki and Arisa had no choice but to leave their homeland. Even so, Dayu would not be left behind. He followed Miyuki back into Larasca, into the heart of Jaska's power."

Again, a ripple shifted the image. Miyuki stood upon the steps of the great hall, dressed in white; gazing down at her, gentleness in his emerald eyes, was the young face of Silas' father.

"She changed her name when she arrived in Larasca. Do you know her name, Xavier?"

Slowly, Silas nodded.

"Morana."

In the pool beneath, Cedric leaned down to kiss his bride, who stood like stone upon the steps.

"Dayu had now been placed in a position to face Jaska, as he had planned. However, he saw an opportunity to do more than just that. With the Princess of Larasca firmly under his control, he could easily dismantle the Xavier dynasty. Destroying them, he would have the crown—destroying Jaska, he would rule over the very fabric of the land, able to bend the mountains and the seas at his whim. Larasca would bow to him.

"He was quick to set his plans in motion. Using all seven diamonds, he could have taken control of Jaska's Dragons and turned them against him, easily destroying his greatest threat. Unfortunately, there was a problem. After leaving Larasca, Dayu could not return with all seven at one time, as to do so would bring him excruciating pain. Jaska must have realized the threat Dayu posed to him, and created a 'barrier' around his precious lands to make the man's life difficult. Because of it, Dayu was forced to bring the diamonds at scattered times, slowly transporting his collection from Storm, hidden in the Princess' jewelry box, to the castle in Larasca.

"When it seemed he would succeed, his arrogance got the better of him. Only months after Morana's marriage, Dayu poisoned King Raphael, allowing his lover to ascend from Princess to Queen of the lands. She was an impressive actress. She made her dear husband believe that she cared about him, though all along she was using his bed to entertain her Dayu. They might have succeeded in this great charade, if the young King had not caught them in a terrible deed."

A new scene formed in the blue water. Silas shuddered to see the pregnant Queen pinned down by her Storma lover on the royal bed, his hands beneath her dress as they shared in a heated kiss.

All at once, the door swung open. Armored guards snatched Dayu from the bed, dragging him from the screaming woman. As he was hauled away, Cedric entered his chambers. His eyes had never been so cold.

"Is this how much you think of me?"

He grabbed her dark locks, his powerful grip causing her shrieks as he forced her up, ripping her hair back.

"Whore! I'll make you scream!"

The sight flickered into nothingness, the screams fading into silence.

"Your father was not a cruel man, Asyrias. He loved your mother, more than his life. But he was not the sort of man that could bear to be betrayed. After that day, I don't believe Cedric was ever the same."

La touched the water, summoning the image of a raging fire beneath her hand.

"After Dayu burned, Morana was not free. The lingering spell prevented her from ever caring for her brokenhearted husband, or the child born of their forced union. Even now, Dayu's influence has turned her love of him to obsession, and leads her to the mad goal of bringing his soul back from the dead. This cannot be allowed to happen."

When she lifted her hand from the water, the fire disappeared. She stood, gazing down at the miserable youth with her unearthly eyes.

"...why did you show me this?" he asked.

She smiled, slowly extending her hand towards him.

"You are not the only one who has known suffering. You must understand that everything is connected."

Silas would not take her hand. He stared down into the water, seeing again the glimmer of the Storma woman's face. She was serene, all except for the tears in her sapphire eyes.

Mother.

As La touched his hair, the Storma's face vanished. Everything around him began to blacken as cool water streamed down his face.

Chapter XXXV

 rincess Azalea was restless, that night. When tossing and turning in her bed proved futile, she began to wander the corridors, distracted by the transformative power of darkness. Once familiar rooms were strange to her now, shadowed with mystery.

The scent of incense drew her to Saito's chamber; the aroma was alluringly unusual, familiar only in a vague childhood memory. She was usually quite bold when it came to entering another's space—yet though the door was ajar, she hesitated. She had not been alone with her tutor since her marriage. Somehow, she sensed the danger of approaching him now.

At last, she disregarded her caution. She pushed open the door as she would any other, inviting herself in.

Inside, Saito knelt at a small wooden table, blowing out the end of an incense stick. Smoke rose up as he placed it beside another in a dish at the base of a small, stone statue. Azalea was intrigued. Although it seemed human, the statue had no face, nor any other markers to betray its sexuality.

"I expect you're having a hard time sleeping," he said suddenly, apparently aware of her presence. "We caught most of the birds, but those that are left make quite a racket in the corridors."

She smiled with silent pride.

"What are you doing?" she asked.

Saito did not turn to her, calm though he was. He gazed only at the statue, as two smoke streams twisted about its body.

"I'm paying tribute to my goddess," he explained. "Just because Morana chose to leave her faith in Storm does not mean I had to."

For some reason, this made her uncomfortable. No one in the castle ever spoke of the religion. She became self-conscious, afraid of seeming ignorant.

"Do you remember Her?" he asked.

Hesitantly, she shook her head.

"I was just a little girl, Saito. I don't remember much of anything."

At last, he turned around. She saw sadness in his dark eyes, unchanged by the smile on his face.

"We call Her Megami-sama," he said, calmly. "Would you like to hear a story about Her?"

She nodded without thinking. Saito had always told wonderful stories to her; she had missed them when he went away.

"Many years ago, before the Great River rushed forth from the Griffon Sea, a terrible creature ruled Storm. This creature was called Oni – an ogre, you might say. He was twice the size of a man, with gray skin and teeth like knives. He commanded the Storma people to pay him tribute, forcing them to part with crops, livestock, and even their own children to satisfy his monstrous appetite.

"His demands wreaked havoc upon the land. There was destruction, chaos—until she came. Unbeknownst to the suppressed people, Megami-sama descended from the heavens in the form of a beautiful maiden. Of all the things Oni had a taste for, his favorite was the blood of attractive women. He allowed her into his abode—but when Oni tried to claim his prize, Megami-sama reached into his chest and ripped out his black heart.

"Our Goddess had freed the people of Storm. For many years she remained, ruling as their Empress. In time, she chose an honorable man to become her spouse, and gave him a son. That boy would become our first Emperor."

Azalea laughed, though she didn't mean to.

"How far-fetched," she said, "why would you have a woman save the day? We can't even hold knives."

By his look, she knew she had hurt him. Yet, he gave her only kind words.

"Women are capable of extraordinary deeds."

She wished he wouldn't look at her so gently. The Princess turned with a huff, wishing to leave; however, his voice gave her pause.

"You're doing a very foolish thing, Azalea."

"Hmm?"

"These petty deeds. They have to stop."

She shrugged, concealing her smile.

"I don't know what you're talking about."

"Don't play dumb," he said, unusually stiff. "I'm deeply concerned, Princess. I see a glint of madness in your eyes, and I fear it threatens to overtake you. You're only putting yourself in danger."

"That's really none of your concern."

"Of course it is!"

He stood so suddenly that it seemed a gust came with it, hot with the fury of his soul. She had never seen him so overcome by emotion, allowing it to contort his perfect face. But as she stared, shocked, his visage changed. Frustration melted into sadness, as longing welled like tears in his eyes.

"Can't you see how I feel about you?" he asked. "The day you became a woman, I realized how deeply I longed for your happiness. With every passing day I have seen you become more beautiful, your wit more and more refined. You are more than any man would deserve, me least of all."

She stood stunned. All these years, she had told herself to forget her childhood adoration of him—a child's dreams never came to pass.

"Be quiet," she said. "He is gone, but Attlas is still my love."

"You never loved Attlas," he said, more firm than she. "You always tried, but you were from two different worlds. Your marriage was destined for heartbreak."

He hesitated, his body shaking.

"There is a belief in Storm that two people can be bound together by an invisible thread, their fates forever entwined. No matter how they might strive for life with another, their true happiness lies with the one at the end of that thread."

He gazed at her with such conviction, though it seemed he was ready to collapse.

"I do not believe it was accident that your father chose me to follow you here. Since the day you came into my life, I have felt this pull towards you, this terrible need to ensure your happiness. I am…bound to you, Arisa."

The Princess was overwhelmed. A thousand feelings overcame her, twisting until they formed a knot around her heart.

He approached her, too brave for a man of common blood. The traditions of both Storm and Larasca forbade his approach—yet she was still, rooted to the floor. He gazed into her eyes, bravely running his soft fingers down her cheek.

"I—"

Her hand was on his mouth. Whatever he was going to say died behind it. Whatever it was, she wouldn't hear it.

"Get away," she whispered.

The Princess ran from him, back into the blackened corridors of the palace. Saito was left alone, his sensible heart retreating to its shelter.

Chapter XXXVI

18th Day of 1st Month, 655 I.R.

*S*ilas awoke when he resurfaced, that night. Unwilling to chance another encounter with Raven, he dried himself off with the stained shirt he had left on shore, and chose to spend the evening beside the silent escort and his fire. When he sat, Ariel didn't acknowledge his presence. The man continued to stare into the flickering flames, his eyes reflecting them like mirrors.

Though the ground was uncomfortably damp beneath him, Silas was exhausted enough to doze there. He awoke before sunrise, groggy, but rested. Even then, Ariel was exactly where he had been before, staring vacantly into the fire he tended.

"Who is Rina?" asked the man, speaking suddenly.

Silas tensed, his suspicion returned.

"Where did you hear that name?"

"You," Ariel replied. "You said it in your sleep again. It happens on occasion. Is it a woman?"

The youth scowled, irritated as much with Ariel as he was with himself. It disturbed him that he seemed to have no control over what he disclosed to others, private as he was in waking hours.

"Maybe she is," he muttered.

"Do you love her?"

Silas hesitated. He had never thought of 'love' in the context of Rina. Her safety was his priority, he felt, and perhaps her comfort. It displeased him when she was unhappy, though her happiness really had nothing to do with him. But love had never crossed his mind.

"I doubt it," he said.

"Why? You think of her."

"That's not the same as loving her."

Ariel shrugged, never once turning from the flickering fire. It was dim now, little more than embers clinging to blackened wood.

"Why do you think of her?"

Normally, Silas wouldn't answer such a question. However, Ariel's interest was intriguing to him. The escort normally said very little, and it seemed he didn't care to know anything at all about Silas. His inquiries now showed he was indeed capable of a deeper level of thought; if the youth cooperated, perhaps he would learn something about the expressionless man.

"She intrigues me," he replied. "She's beautiful, yet it doesn't make her vain. She's sincere, kind. She is…quiet, content to observe her surroundings, able to adjust when things get bad…"

It was hard to describe her so bluntly. To Silas, she was an elusive entity, something that couldn't be captured in so few words.

"She's everything I'm not," he continued, his voice softer as he drew into himself. "I didn't realize how much I looked forward to seeing her every morning. Even when nothing makes sense, she's there, constant. She doesn't expect me to be anything but the way I am, even though I'm…"

Awful.

He grew quiet, trying not to remember the pain she was in now, caused by his own arrogance. Yet, to his surprise, Ariel filled the silence on his own.

"My sister was like that," he said. "She was…accepting. Beautiful. I…miss her…miss her so…"

His flat voice had begun to falter, trembling on the cusp of emotion. Silas sat up, shocked to see tears streaming down the young man's blank face. After that, Ariel would say no more. He just sat there, staring vacantly at the dying fire as water stained his cheeks.

Silas could not help but pity him. Clearly, Ariel was powerless against the malicious force that made him as impassive as he was; his tears proved that beneath that mask, there was a real man, who hoped and felt just like any other. Still, even if Silas knew how to help him, he had no time. The sun had begun to rise on the horizon.

"I have to go," he said.

Ariel did not reply. Motionless, he stared at the fire.

Thoughtfully, Silas left his presence. He descended to the riverbank, removing his boots to stand upon the shallow ridge in the water. This day, Ra stared up at him, her black hair swaying with the current.

"Are you ready, my Prince?"

He nodded, entranced by her emerald gaze.

"I am."

Once more, watery hands rose from the lake, pulling him to the depths.

Silas woke to find himself again in that dark realm, space and time suspended around him. He was dizzy, uncertain even of the dimensions of his own body. Though he waited and waited, the green-scaled nymph did not appear before him. This time, he was alone in a black world.

"Ra!" he bellowed. "Show yourself!"

He heard her laugh, somewhere in the shadows.

"Don't be so quick to panic. We heal best when we are alone."

He grit his teeth, chilled by the emptiness of the space.

"What is my test?"

"Today you face a test of strength. You must seek to overcome the sickness within you; otherwise, you will surely succumb to it."

"Sickness?"

Gradually, shapes began to materialize from the shadows. Tall, stone walls solidified in a gray mist, followed by red ivy that climbed their heights, a breeze rustling their dying leaves.

Four walls surrounded Silas. Behind him, a broad opening revealed the further corridors of the walled maze. His only company was the short pedestal before him, cracked and disfigured by time—and protruding from it, the brass hilt of a sword.

"Seize your weapon. Your opponent lies within the origin of the maze."

This time, he didn't hesitate. He stepped forward, grasping the cold hilt in his unyielding grip. The sword slipped effortlessly from the stone, as though it were water. Reflected in its blade, Ra's emerald gaze flickered, observing him.

"How long do I have?" he asked.

"As long as you find necessary."

Her voice began to dissipate, fading into the solemn breeze.

"Persevere."

At last, he was alone.

The hilt of the blade still felt cool against his hand, reminding him of its existence. As he slipped it into the ring of his belt, he could hear the wind whispering through its halls, awaiting his first step.

Seek your opponent.

He closed his eyes, savoring his last moments of peace. When he exited the small passage, the maze welcomed his search.

The path stretched on. Silas tried not to focus on how long his steps took, their echo disturbing the quiet plane. All around him, invisible, prying eyes bored holes through his soul. All the while, he heard a slow, faint trickling, red water venturing down the cracks of the walls to rest in the vines' damp soil. The musty scent that arose reminded him of the palace's black dungeons, where the fears of his childhood had dwelt.

Turn after turn, he traveled the endless passages. The same darkened vines choked every wall, hiding any differences under a blanket of uniformity. Before long, he could no longer remember which way he had come, or where he had meant to go. Everything was the same.

So soon a failure.

Silas continued onward, cursing when a dead vine cracked beneath his boot. For a moment, the sound disrupted the quiet air. But before it could settle, the breeze carried another whisper across the walls—the echo of a young woman's voice, somewhere far ahead of him.

"I will not go."

The voice was familiar to him, distant though it was. Its echo drew him closer, guiding him through the maze.

"Why should this year be any different? I have not gone before, and I will not go now. You know I have better things to do with my time."

As he neared its source, Silas could hear the low voice that responded to the woman, as soft as it was desperate.

"I beg of you, give him this one year. A child deserves to see his mother on his birthday."

"That spoiled brat needs nothing from me; you coddle him enough to fill the role of three mothers."

A faint light shone through a crack in the wall beside him: there, at last, was the source of their voices. Silas was drawn to that light, like moth to the flame. He pushed the vines away from the wall, allowing the crackling branches to fall to his feet. Through that crack, he glimpsed a dark-haired man reaching out to an exotic Princess.

"He's only a child, Miyuki. Please, come. Make him happy," he urged. "Don't let our past ruin his innocence."

The woman smacked his hand away, her beautiful face disfigured by fury.

"Don't call me by that name," she rasped.

Though momentarily deterred, Cedric's cause had not yet been abandoned. He moved towards her again, eyes begging for her acquiescence.

"He's your son, too."

"A son I never wanted."

Silas could remember this day. The day of his sixth birthday, he had stood on his toes to see into his mother's keyhole, to know why she had not come to the celebration. He remembered this. Yet, his damaged heart still pounded strongly at the sight of it, the grief no less severe. To glimpse Morana wrenching her hand from his father's grip, even as the man pleaded for her mercy, awakened the pain of wounds never healed.

"You gave him life," Cedric said. "Do you see nothing of yourself in his eyes?"

The Queen spat her words.

"All I see is a doomed child. Just like the Empire of Asyrias, his Kingdom will divide and burn, and his ashes will be no greater than his peasants'."

When Cedric stepped towards her again, there echoed a great strike—Morana's hand met his cheek.

"He will fall, you will fall, just like the Kingdom he is named for!"

Then came his father's anger. He saw that gentle man transformed before his eyes: his gaze narrowed to hot slits, jaw tight, his powerful grip snatching Morana's wrist, subduing her with a warrior's hold.

"Perhaps, Morana. Perhaps your curse may come to pass," said the King, his voice falling to a lower, darker place. "But when that happens, you will be more alone than us. When that happens, you won't be able to hold yourself up."

Silas wrenched himself away from the sight. At once, the sounds began to fade, as if they had never existed. Yet his breath was still heavy from their weight, memories dancing across his eyes, giving him no escape.

That was the last day Cedric called you Asyrias.

Suddenly, another voice gripped his attention. There was more this time, bellowing with the intent to be heard.

"He's gone into the alleys! Someone cut him off!"

Protectors.

Gripped by instinct, he ran. The footsteps kept close behind him, resonating throughout the cold maze. He rushed through the winding halls, trying to ignore his fear, the pounding in his chest.

Silas could remember this sensation. The night Sh'ka had betrayed him, the Protectors began their endless pursuit. Whether summoned by his recollection or by the labyrinth's cruel power, he heard her voice again. Sh'ka's presence enveloped his spirit, whispering to ignite his fury.

"How strange, to love a beast."

He saw a figure behind him, adorned by the glint of Akalinian jewels. Blinded by fury, he forgot his escape. Silas gripped his sword, swinging at the shadow, only to find branches felled by his blade. Their dead leaves fluttered after them, disturbed by the sudden gust.

"I think I saw him, Chief!"

Edmund's voice reminded him to run, instinct ruling him once more. He heard the familiar thudding steps behind him, threatening capture. He kept running.

A dead end was all that stopped him. Somewhere, among all the twists and turns of the stone walls, he had chosen the single path that allowed no protection. However, at the end of the corridor lay something unnerving. Where the last wall should have been, the one that prevented further passage, were the red bricks of Giovanni's home.

All at once, his Alore home loomed before him, its torn curtains fluttering behind broken windows. At the doorway was a fifteen-year-old boy, banging his brown fist against the strong, oak door.

"Giovanni! Giovanni, I'm begging you! Let me in this once!"

But though the boy continued to pound the door, slamming his fist again and again until it began to chafe his hand, no response would come. Soon, his pounding began to loosen the flowering vines clinging to the frame, releasing their poison powder into the air.

"I'll solve anything you ask! Any puzzle, any duel, I'll do it! Please, Vaan! Help me! Help your son!"

Footsteps grew louder behind him, accompanied by the frantic exchanges of the armored men. The boy didn't hear him. He collapsed to his knees, powerlessly hanging on the door's silver handle. His other fingers tangled in his raven locks.

"GIOVANNI!"

Silas could see his adoptive father sitting before one of the broken windows, watching the adolescent scream. He would not help him.

Soldiers rushed past Silas and surrounded the boy. They dragged him away, screaming and snarling like a beast.

Giovanni pulled the curtain closed.

Slowly, the apparition vanished. Silas was left staring into an empty clearing, alone with his rage. His hand gripped his sword, grip tightening, trying to smother his anger until it burst from within him. He rushed into the clearing, swiping blindly at the clinging vines, screaming as he unleashed his wrath.

"Show yourself!" he roared. "**GIVE ME MY OPPONENT!**"

Nothing would answer him. Here, he was alone.

Trembling, he managed to place his sword back into his belt. He returned to the labyrinth with a deadened gaze, necessity moving his heavy body. By now, the endless walls gave him neither comfort nor pain.

Weak.

The maze offered him thousands of routes, each bending to a different path. He followed them all, searching tirelessly for the center of the maze. And yet, he became only more lost amongst the vines. Every sound was a threat, every creak an assault. Adrift in this misty world, Silas fast became anxious, uncomfortable, suspicious.

Then, he heard laughter.

"Maybe I'm not afraid of him."

He knew her voice as well as he knew his own. He knew the sweet chime of her laughter, and the soft sound of her gasp. Overcome by emotion, he began a frantic search of the halls. He rushed forth, pursuing what he was afraid were the last remnants of his gentle friend, until he saw the glint of her brown locks.

"Do you think I should be?"

Silas chased the sight. He caught glimpses of her - a flick of her wrist, a flash of her gaze – but she could not be found. Her gentle laugh became torturous to bear as she evaded him, her presence entwined with shadows.

He tried calling for her, angered by the futility of his pursuit. Yet just as he was about to give in to exhaustion, she turned around a wall just before him, followed by the happy wag of Ride's mangy tail.

He remembered the smile she always gave that creature. During their travels, when he had remained in camp to rest, he had seen her lie down with the mongrel at night, whispering to him when she thought her comrades were asleep. She spoke more then than she had during all their day-lit hours. She didn't know that he lay awake while she spoke, intrigued by her wishes, her fears.

"Maybe I should be," she whispered to the creature. *"He is built like a beast. He talks like a beast, growls like a beast, and is about as understanding as a beast might be. But if he was going to hurt me, he would have done it by now, wouldn't he?"*

She laughed softly, her ghostly hand touching Ride's gray fur.

"There's something beautiful about him. I don't know what it is yet, but there's something truly remarkable inside him. That's why he saved my life. I want to know that part of him. Someday, I'm going to know it for myself."

Again, he tried to rush forward, trying to see her. As he did, he began to realize the selfish reason for his pursuit. He tried to see her now only because their journey together was coming to an end; the day she was released from prison would be the last time he saw her face.

His search brought him to small enclosure within the maze. In that place, her ghostly presence was joined by another: a man who towered over her, with skin darkened by the elements, and a sharp, violet gaze—himself.

Tears stained Rina's cheeks, her hair unkempt; gray dust coated his own skin. He saw the man reach for her, only to be knocked away.

"Don't," she whispered.

This was the moment he had ceased to feel. Silas was forced to watch every action played out again, this time subjected to the feral cruelty on his own face.

"Whore," he had called her.

Her face was overcome with such anguish. He knew it now, too late to heal it: the pain of her heart being torn to pieces.

"I'm so sorry," she sobbed. *"Sorry..."*

She ran past him, so close he could almost feel her warmth. But his other self only watched, impassive and unmoving.

"Go after her!" he bellowed to the man, furious with frustration. "You bastard, **move**!"

But though the man reached out, anger dying in his eyes, he did nothing more. Soon, he withdrew his hand, fading into the gray mist.

Alone, Silas forced himself to turn about, rushing again down the labyrinth's passage to find the heartbroken girl. He ran long and far, until he came to a pool of rusty water, dripping down from the walls and into the shallow dip. He recognized the pool as the spring outside Caine's shack, where they had drawn their water during hiding.

There, he saw her. Rina was hunched over the spring, clutching at her face as her shoulders shook. When her hands slowly parted, tears trickled down her arms, dripping into the brown pool.

"*I'll break,*" she whispered, again and again. "*I'll break...I'll break...*"

Her sobs choked his heart. He fell to his knees, only able to watch her sobbing form.

"I didn't mean to hurt you, Rina," he said.

She cried, slumping further over the tainted pool.

"What could I do?" he asked. "How could you tell me that the one good thing in my life belonged to someone else? Did you really think I wouldn't be upset? That I wouldn't say things I didn't mean?"

The trembling girl couldn't hear him. His every word slipped off her, like rain falling from glass.

"I couldn't help it, Rina," he said, almost choking on the words. "I'm not like you, Rina. I don't think things through…"

Each time he said her name, he could feel regret tighten its hold on his heart. Slowly, the dark-haired girl faded away from him, out of reach. Only her tears remained, mixing with the swirling water of the tainted pool.

He couldn't take it. His head, his eyes, his heart hurt too much to bear.

With a sudden cry, he struck his sword into the spring, kneeling in the water to press his forehead against the hilt. He tried to fight his misery, but didn't have the power. He lacked even the strength to stand.

"No more," he whispered.

He clutched to the hilt—a child a mother couldn't love; a boy abandoned by his caretaker; a man forsaken by his love.

Red began to seep from the clinging vines, tingeing the water like rust. All around, the mysterious breeze toyed with the leaves, mocking his grief.

She was right to choose him.

Silas tightened his grip around the hilt, forced to bear the sting of his own thoughts.

You're a cursed beast, man neither inside nor out. Beasts do not love.

"Stop," he snarled, nails like claws digging into his scalp.

A curse to all who surround you.

"STOP!"

But it would not stop. His own thoughts ripped him to pieces, claws dragged down the fabric of his soul.

Roaring like a beast.

Silas thrust his fist into the reddened water, his terrible howl shaking the walls. As the water settled, its surface revealed another shadow looming over him. Though the visage was without feature, he felt from it a cold smirk, as though his pain fueled its satisfaction.

You were born to suffer.

The shadow drew a sword from the air, allowing the brilliance of its blade to reflect in the rusty pool. At once, Silas knew its identity. The origin of the maze swung its weapon—the creature of his consciousness attacked.

With a great clash, his own blade met that of his attacker. His gaze met with another of violet, a man whose fangs gleamed in his cruel scowl: a perfect replica of himself, armed to destroy.

"Why won't you die?" it snarled. "Persistent pest."

Silas was pushed back without effort, sprawled backwards in the red pool. At first, his weakness came from shock. He used his sword to hoist himself up. As rage overcame him, he swung blindly at his opponent; yet when their swords met, he did not see his reflection. Giovanni held the sword.

"I'm afraid you're never going to win, my boy; not while clinging to your emotion like that."

All his strength went into parrying Vaan's sword; but no matter the swiftness of his swing, the soldier would evade. The man moved without effort in their lethal dance, smirking all the while, knowing he would prevail. However, as they fought, the face of his adversary again began to shift. When next their swords clashed, he was the object of Sh'ka's smile.

"I don't see why you're trying so hard. Life is a game."

He forgot his sword then. Silas put all his force behind his fist, aiming to silence her.

She proved too quick. Sh'ka sidestepped his assault; her foot slammed into his stomach. He doubled over, his sword clattering to the ground before him.

"You always were an easy target," she said.

He grabbed for his sword, coughing blood from his lungs. Another kick ended his futile reaching, as a heel of much firmer material dented his side. As he snarled, he saw Morana's icy glare set upon him, her beautiful hair tangled by a wicked gust.

"Pathetic."

New rage ignited his power. With a sudden burst of strength, he snatched his sword from the rusty water, which was now darkened by his own blood. When he brandished his weapon, it was not Morana that parried his assault—it was Rina's dagger.

"You?" he whispered.

Her blue eyes glowed with anger much different from his own. It was a cool, collected sort of rage, fueled by a vast reserve of resentment rather than inflamed ire. It burned through him, slowly, agonizingly.

His sword slipped out of his grasp, splashing back into the rusty water as he stared at his opponent. Rina was not so hesitant. Her dagger's point soon met his forehead, and with it, she guided him to his knees. Silas was forced to stare into her eyes, object of their dark hatred.

"You left me caged like an animal," she said, her voice too calm. "What sort of noble man would leave a woman to rot?"

The dagger's point came to his throat, lifting his chin.

"You sicken me. There's nothing inside you but a cold, black soul."

Her words drained his strength. The moment her weapon was pulled away, his head fell limp. Water touched his forehead, soaking into the hair that fell to shroud it.

You can't fight what's truth.

Her dagger trailed along his exposed neck, as if testing the thickness of his skin. He sat motionless, subdued by the executioner's axe.

You can't survive this.

Even in the shadow, he could make out his features in the stilling water. His violet eyes were bloodshot, sunken and shadowed. It was like staring into the face of his own corpse.

You can't fight.

The blade swung above him, sighing as it made a last descent.

He would die, here.

You can't.

Yet as he retreated into himself, savoring his final thoughts, he heard his own beating heart. It pulsed strongly in his chest, defiantly pumping his unnatural blood. All these years, he had survived on borrowed time, by the desperate wish of his loving father. What right had he to surrender that blood to anyone, to make little of the King's love?

Silas was his father's last wish. Silas was a powerful man.

His sword still dripped with red water when it clashed against Rina's—water ran down his face and arms, allowing him to taste the pool's rust. With the slightest flick of his blade, her dagger was ripped from her hands, clattering onto the stone beyond them. He stood without hindrance, arm extended, sword pointed at his foe.

"You have no right to say those words."

I will survive.

"You will not stand in my path."

I will succeed.

"You are not Rina," he said, forcing her to kneel beneath his blade. "I will not stand here and endure your presence. Leave."

Slowly, the woman's countenance began to blacken. She became but a shadow among the walls, without face or name. He maintained his posture, silently witnessing the transformation. His last word was but a snarl.

"Leave."

The creature faded into the mist, no more than a gray memory.

All around him, the labyrinth began to disappear. Soon, Silas stood alone beside the pool of water, whose color had only grown redder.

Ra's voice came from behind him, without introduction.

"Beautiful, Xavier."

The green nymph walked around him, her eyes observing him like a solemn predator. Though he was stiff, silent, he was not threatened by her.

"Would you like your prize, my Prince?"

"That depends on what it is," said Silas, watching her as sharply as she watched him.

The creature smiled, though hers was more grim than her blue sister's. Wordlessly, she knelt beside the pool, stirring the water with a stroke of her fingertip. The crimson liquid shuddered, glistening with otherworldly power.

"I possess the ability to show you the present," she said. "Name whoever it is you most wish to see. No matter how far away they might be, I can show you them and their present circumstances."

No thought was necessary for a reply.

"Show me Rina," he said. "The real one."

She nodded, no emotion crossing her lovely face. He watched warily as she swirled the water, seeing its crimson hue gradually shift and darken, creating a black surface. His reflection disappeared from the trembling waves, replaced by the flickering of a dungeon torch.

He heard the most beautiful voice echoing on the dungeon walls, weaving melodies in a foreign tongue. The gentle song left him breathless, bringing tears to his tired eyes.

"Who's singing?" he asked, quietly.

"Rina," Ra replied. "Her cellmate has taught her a lullaby."

Soon, he saw her behind iron bars—her hair tangled from neglect, her fair skin coated with filth. Yet, her voice filled those bleak chambers with beauty.

The sound of footsteps caused her to cease her song. As she sat up, alert, Silas saw what she did: the golden-haired soldier from Citris, who had betrayed them.

"Ri," said the youth, touching a bar of her cell, "you look…awful."

The girl hardly moved. Desperate, the blond soldier grabbed the bars of her cell, no doubt hoping to reclaim her attention.

"Listen, Ri...I haven't been all that honest with you."

At last, Rina slowly lifted her gaze towards him. She betrayed little more than the vaguest interest.

"When I came here, to Joanissia, I caught the Queen's eye," he said, smiling anxiously. "She needed an heir, and...she chose me. I'm the Prince of Larasca, Rina."

Silas grew cold, all of him trembling with rage. Yet, Rina showed no response to her friend's confession. She continued to stare plainly forward, as though his words meant nothing at all.

Alastor scrambled in a sudden search, hastily revealing a key from his silken pocket. With a quiet click, the gate creaked open.

"I appealed on your behalf. You can live free now, with me. You could even be a Princess."

He smiled again, infuriating the man who watched them.

"What do you say?"

Rina didn't move. Alastor stood at the open gate, waiting eagerly, though his tenseness betrayed some anxiety. All at once, she rose to her feet. She moved like a phantom, torn dress floating over the ground, eyes nearly hidden by her disheveled tresses. Yet, when she looked towards her savior, Silas saw a sudden spark of life.

Suddenly, Rina smashed her lips against the soldier's, instigating a long, passionate kiss.

Silas could feel his blood cooling, turning to ice. The image faded from the black surface, allowing him to see a feral snarl distort his face. Red rimmed his eyes. Across from him, the dark-haired nymph looked into her own, somber reflection.

"You have many senses, Xavier," said Ra, lifting her hand from the black water, "sight is only one of them. You must not trust your eyes alone."

Her words fell on deaf ears. Rage possessed him, shredding his sensibility.

"Fawking BITCH!"

His roar altered the black world around him. The sky trembled, turning to water. It fell like rain over them, filling the void, until he drowned in his own despair.

Raven found herself rather unamused that day. She had no choice but to remain by that dull lake, able only to engage Ariel in lifeless conversation while Reja spent his day in the water. Honestly, she had been disappointed that he had not chosen to share her tent the night before. She had missed his warmth in that small space.

By the time the sun set, she had no more excuse not to rest. She laid down in her thinner gown, protecting from the chilly air with a fur blanket, quite prepared to endure another night alone. She amused herself with the thought that she might wake later to drag the violet-eyed man back out of the river. Yet, no sooner had she fallen asleep than she was woken again, an unusually warm hand upon her neck.

"I changed my mind," came Reja's voice.

His breath was hot as he kissed her ear, showing the same spine-tingling expertise he had the night of their contest. When she opened her eyes, the lantern's dimming light illuminated his regal features, casting orange shadows over his soaked pants, his strong, damp chest.

She pretended not to hear him, merely yawning behind her hand as she again curled beneath her blanket—he didn't buy it. He grasped her shoulder, flinging her over as his lips took hers. Aroused by his forcefulness, Raven accepted his kiss, tangling her fingers in his black locks.

"Why the change of heart?" she whispered, laughing into his mouth.

It was his turn to ignore her. He kissed her again, a hand loosening the string that secured the back of her gown.

"Keep quiet."

Raven smiled, allowing the dress to fall away from her shoulders. For once, the air's chill did not hinder her, for something about his warmth prevented its bite. As they undressed, he seemed unconcerned with where their clothing fell, or even dimming the lantern light. She nearly melted at the heat of his skin.

As she surrendered to his power, she forgot all her cares. For moments, their lost souls became entwined.

Ariel could see black shadows against the tent's wall, their immoral act illuminated by strength of a dying lantern. He didn't want to see. Yet, Ariel watched as the Prince ravaged the shameless girl, listened to their selfish sounds of folly.

"So this was his mistake," he said.

Fur brushed against his brown boots, accompanied by a smooth, patient purr. He looked down to see a black cat wrapping herself about his leg, tail swaying with pleasure. Her sapphire eyes were unmistakable.

He knelt down, lifting the cat from the snow and into his arms. Even then, her hum did not cease.

"Don't purr," he said. "He'll never speak of this again."

Her rough tongue caressed his neck, fur bristling against his smooth skin. He shivered; he did not like her. Yet, she was inescapable. He would not fight her.

"You have not won."

His gaze flickered back towards the tent, seeing the shadows dim. The lantern had given up its fight.

Chapter XXXVII

30th Day of 1st Month, 655 I.R.

The floor was cold against Rina's back, damp as it had always been. The ceiling held no more mysteries for her; yet, she watched it, observing its every crack. Her hand ached, though its injury was long past.

She thought of Silas. She thought of him a lot. She thought of his irritated sort of patience, his rare, reluctant smile—she thought of their kiss. It had been so different from any other she had had; it lacked Alastor's fumbling awkwardness, or Kaish's reserved, careful pressure. Silas had swept her away with his intensity, baring all of himself before her to accept.

Thoughts of Silas involved a great deal of uncertainty. She was ashamed of her sudden yearning for him, which had not been prevalent until recent days of her captivity. She was afraid it had surfaced because of her awareness of her betrothed's death—that she cared for Silas because there was no one else to care for. Yet, she remembered sensations she had experienced long before her captivity: a lightness in her chest when he spoke to her, an aching in her heart when wrapped in his embrace. She had felt those things even when Kaish was alive.

She was fickle, or she was immoral; either way, she was ashamed.

Her head ached, though the pain was half imagined. She touched her lips, still remembering the heat of Silas' breath. He tasted like fire—she longed for its singe.

Footsteps disturbed the quiet corridor, approaching her cell. Trained, Rina rose to her feet, awaiting the Princess' arrival.

Suddenly, a small hand gripped her own.

"Don't go."

The maturity of the soft voice startled her. Although Sen spoke in his usual whisper, so not to wake his mother, its tone had become somehow richer, the childish hesitancy vanished. When she turned, she noticed that the boy stood taller than he had even a few weeks prior, and the crimson locks had lengthened past his ears to grace his shoulders.

"I have a bad feeling," said the child. "Don't go with her today."

His words made her wary.

"Why?"

His emerald gaze fell, crimson locks shrouding his eyes.

"I had a bad feeling before the soldiers came to Citris. I had a bad feeling before Sir Caine died."

He squeezed her hand with urgency.

"I have a bad feeling now. Don't go."

As ominous as his words were, she knew she had no choice in leaving. Still, she couldn't help but be intrigued by the child's unusual growth.

"How old are you, Sen?" she asked, curious.

He seemed surprised, though he replied promptly.

"Three years."

His physical and mental maturity far exceeded three years. She was fascinated by him, almost wishing she could stay and uncover more mysteries of his Demonic heritage. Unfortunately, no sooner had he spoken than Azalea's key turned in the lock, signaling her imminent departure.

"I'm sorry, Sen," she said, as gently as she could. "I have to go."

She pulled from his hold, trying not to see the hurt in his eyes.

"Take care of your mother, all right?"

Azalea smiled when Rina went to her, and pleasantly locked the cell door when she came out. The Princess waved to the child who came to the iron bars, staring out with a broken look.

Rina, ignoring her own anxiousness, followed Azalea to the surface.

The training room was one of the most impressive sights in Joanissia Castle. It spanned the length of the Grand Hall, with oak floors polished to such a gleam that the painted ceiling could be seen in its surface, its thousand glorious warriors and weaponry shimmering above and beneath. All the room was rimmed by a sturdy balcony, from which women could observe their lovers as they sparred.

Azalea could not remember being in this room since Attlas had been learning swordsmanship, back when the two of them were little more than adolescents. She would have never thought the next time she would enter that space would be to observe her sister furiously attempting to coax her black hawk down from the chandelier. Already, it was clear her minute patience was wearing to nonexistence.

The Queen was flanked by two Councilmen: pale-faced Raoul, who always seemed to hover about her, and Saito.

"It seems wise to give up your fight, your Majesty," said the Storma. "Tobias rarely changes his mind, once he's settled."

Azalea could not help but feel uncomfortable around her former tutor; though some time had passed, she had yet to come to terms with his confession. Still, she would not allow her discomfort to impede her approach.

"How long as he been up there, Ana?" she asked her sister, smiling sweetly.

"Too long," she snapped.

The Princess smiled, amused. Her eyes traced the rope that held the chandelier, following it along the wall to the darkness of the balcony above, and the servants' entry just beyond it. Today, the prisoner's task would be simple: use the servants' door to gain access to the ropes, then send the chandelier crashing down.

Azalea understood the dangers of such an act, especially since the Queen was so close to the lighting fixture. Even if she were not, the fallen candles would surely set the wooden floor aflame. Yet, with the Princess' mind suspended somewhere between madness and despair, these consequences seemed delightfully thrilling.

"He is indeed a stubborn creature," said Raoul, watching the bird arrogantly ruffle his black feathers.

"He has his rebellious moments," the Queen remarked. "Much like my horse did."

"She has yet to return?" asked the Grand Advisor.

The Queen shook her head, releasing a slow, hot breath.

"Do you at least know where she might be?" Saito asked, earnest.

Morana turned her head, her sapphire gaze boring through her younger sister.

"No," she replied. "But I believe Azalea does."

The longer the Princess was forced to endure that icy stare, the more her defenses began to falter. Even so, she managed to feign indifference.

"I don't know what you're talking about."

"I see."

The woman pointed towards the black hawk, who still sat obstinately between two flickering candles.

"And why does Tobias gnaw on my white brooch?" she asked. "Surely, you had nothing to do with that."

As Azalea observed the white gleam in Tobias' dark beak, she began to be aware of the sinister air in the room. It seemed to emanate from the Queen, falling from her in slow, chilling waves.

"I know you did this, Azalea."

The Princess stiffened, her stomach twisting into a knot. Only Saito seemed concerned—but as he tried to calm the Queen, a terrible scream shook the hall, sending Tobias into flight.

The doors opened, allowing passage to Art and two of his men. In the Captain's powerful hold was a young woman, dirtied by imprisonment—Rina.

"Shall we take her back to the dungeons?" Art asked.

Azalea was horrified. She stood still, watching in terror as her cold-blooded sister approached the struggling girl.

"I do not usually tolerate escaped prisoners, but I am in a merciful mood," said the Queen, gazing down at her opponent. "Tell me who let you out, and I will allow you to leave my presence unharmed."

The Princess could hear her own heart pounding in her ears, her anxiety beginning to overwhelm her. She knew she was going to be betrayed. Yet, as the prisoner stopped struggling, returning the Queen's cool stare, she said nothing at all.

"Well, Girl?" the Queen pressed, voice trembling with suppressed anger. "Who let you out?"

The girl remained perfectly still, defying her with silence.

The Queen grew tense with rage, drawing back as if in revulsion.

"Twist her arm," she ordered. "If she continues to be uncooperative, snap it in two."

Rina cried out as the Captain twisted her arm behind her, bending and bending it until it approached nature's limit. But despite all that pain, even then, she would say nothing.

The Princess couldn't believe her eyes. Had she been in Rina's place, she would have betrayed her accomplice in a heartbeat. She couldn't imagine having the sort of strength that prisoner displayed, able to silence her tongue in the face of such agony.

Before the bone could break, Azalea heard her own voice echo off the walls.

"I did it!"

All eyes turned towards her. Ashamed, her confession spilled forth.

"I set her free. I've been bribing her to do my bidding. Please," she hesitated, unable to lift her gaze from the floor. "She had no choice. Please, let her go."

When Azalea could finally look up, the Queen's face had become unreadable. Morana stared past her, up towards the hawk that roamed the high ceiling.

Saito moved towards her, anxious to diffuse the volatile situation.

"Your Majesty—"

"Take the girl to the vacant room of the east tower," she commanded her Captain.

"And the Princess?" Art asked.

A sinister smile overcame the Storma.

"I want her isolated."

Even the guards stood shocked, staring at their Queen. But the woman would not retract her words; her chilling gaze graced them all, as her order came with more austerity.

"Isolate the traitor."

Everything moved too quickly. By the time Azalea thought to run, the guards were upon her, restraining her without regard to her modesty. She screamed, writhed, but they would not release her.

"Morana, what are you doing?!" Saito cried.

"Nothing more than what is dictated by law."

"She is your **sister**!"

Instinct overwhelmed the Princess. She found herself reaching towards her Storma tutor, as if he alone could wake her from this nightmare.

Although he never took her hand, she saw his features transformed as she was pulled away, his body overcome by visible rage.

"You would do well not to question your Queen's decision, Saito," said Raoul.

Something broke within the Storma. Azalea saw him snap about, pointing a trembling, accusing finger at the Grand Advisor.

"You!" he bellowed. "*You*, bow alone to your heartless Queen!"

Chapter XXXVIII

19th Day of 1st Month, 655 I.R.

$\mathcal{I}$n the blackest hours of morning, a breeze rustled the leafless branches of Malldon's trees. Their sticks rubbed against one another, shivering in the sudden chill. Silas, recovering from a sleepless night, allowed the sound to fill his thoughtless mind.

"What's wrong, Reja?"

Though it was dark inside their tent, Silas could almost make out Raven's curious eyes from where she lay beside him.

Irritated, he said nothing. He turned away, shedding the blanket from his naked body so she would have no excuse to come closer.

"Funny," said the woman, laughing. "You'll screw me, but you won't talk to me."

"I told you not to call me Reja," he said.

"Maybe, but you won't tell me why. It's just too interesting: why would you have told me your name was Reja if that's not what you wanted to be called?"

"I wasn't myself."

"And you are now?"

He growled, his habit when he felt threatened. Yet, the sound only served to amuse her.

"I'll tell you something about me, if you'll tell me something about you."

Despite his mood, the notion was somewhat intriguing. He still knew little to nothing about the woman beside him, which seemed foolish now. Abandoning his reluctance, he gave a prompt reply.

"You start."

Raven rolled onto her back, then, staring up at the branches that supported their tent. He could see a glimmer of her smile, though there was distance to it.

"I should tell you about Catsavionism, then. You're an outsider, so you wouldn't know. It didn't even come here until Raphael's Draft…"

The words sparked something in Silas' memory, surfacing from the days of Giovanni's tutoring.

"Raphael needed more troops in Kyro," he said, unable to help spouting what he knew, "and the men in Malldon weren't volunteering."

Raven nodded, visibly surprised.

"I guess people in Malldon were religious back then, too. It was the last city in Larasca to still believe in a Goddess. The men were choosing not to join the Ranks because it was against their beliefs to kill another human being. When the King got fed up with their pacifism, he began enlisting them by force.

"Most of Malldon's men were sent to Kyro during the draft. When they returned, they were different. Not only were they filled with hatred towards their Xavier King, they were changed by the belief they had observed in their Kyron enemies. The Larascan Ranks were there to destroy Catsavionism, which had dethroned the Alexanders and reduced a nation to anarchy—the Malldon men sympathized with it.

"I'm not sure how much Kyron's Catsavionism was altered by misunderstanding; whatever the men brought home was not the same religion. They ordained Priests to run the temple, replacing the Priestesses who had run it for years. Then, the Priests began to purge the city of anyone who would not comply with their laws; after that, they targeted anyone who they considered immoral beings; when that did not satisfy them, they began to remove anyone who did not look Larascan. Should you fit into any one of these categories, you're deemed Impure, and must be eliminated."

She smiled dully.

"That's how my parents died. Mother was an adulterer, Father was a skeptic. It was sad, but inevitable."

Silas cringed, painfully sympathetic. He knew was it was like to lose one's parents, to live without familial comfort.

"I'm sorry," he said.

"You know what? That's not even the screwed up part," she snapped, anger finally seeping into her tone. "The screwed up part is that my own brother was so *inspired* by our parents' murder that he decided to become a Priest himself. Self-righteous Hector claims that Father should have known not to defame Catsavionism in public, and that Mother got what was coming to her. Now he's part of that bloody cult, keeping all of us captive here until they either throw us on a pyre or give us the privilege of living to dementia!"

She was breathing hard, holding her head as it all came out. Somehow, Silas understood her. He knew the agony that came with holding all his hatred inside until it overwhelmed him, leaking out when he wanted it least.

Almost gently, he touched her arm.

"My turn," he said.

She relaxed. Raven looked up at him, her smile returning as the stress seeped back inside.

"I…used to care for someone," he admitted. "But she betrayed me, and now…I'm lost."

He knew it wasn't much, compared to her confession. Yet, she seemed satisfied.

"Did you let her call you Reja?"

He rolled his eyes.

"No."

She had never had the chance.

Raven laid her head on his chest, fondly running her fingers over his firm muscles. She was quiet, apparently thinking to herself.

"What's it like in the outside world?" she asked.

"Dark. Cold," he replied. "Protectors instead of Priests."

"Protectors sound much nicer."

"I'll let you think that."

The young woman smiled.

"I've been saving money to leave this place," she said. "I'm not sure how much it'll take to start a new life somewhere, but I have to try."

Silas watched her, admittedly fond of the way her fingers felt against his skin. For the first time in a long while, he was calm.

"Then I'll take you with me when I'm done here," he said. "Be ready by tomorrow morning. Don't worry about money."

Raven looked up at him, shocked.

"You would do that? For me?"

"You need help," he replied. "I have no reason not to."

The knowledge of Rina's betrayal had left a gaping hole in his heart, which hurt too much to leave vacant. He would allow himself to care for this girl, Raven. She beautiful, clever, and somehow like him. Perhaps she would be enough to fill the void.

His words seemed to overpower her. She looked at him with blank, trembling eyes, her sharp tongue dulled to silence. Though he didn't understand her look, he felt no reason to pry.

Golden rays had begun to illuminate the thin walls of their tent, heralding a new day. Unable to think of Rina, his purpose was diminished; yet even so, he rose up, solemnly dressing as he remembered the other prisoners.

"Where are you going?" Raven asked, strangely frantic.

"I'll explain later."

He pushed open the tent's flaps, shuddering in the light that glared from the lake's surface. Vaguely, he could see a woman's silhouette against the dawn, her crimson locks rising with the breeze.

"Wait," she said, "I need to tell you something!"

He had no time for it. The cloth fell shut behind him as he abandoned the tent, blindly approaching the glistening waters.

Unlike her sisters, who had hidden in the depths, Sha stood tall in the shallow ridge of the waters, allowing him to see her unearthly splendor.

"You have changed, my Prince," came her ethereal voice.

He returned her gaze in silence, feeling nothing.

"This will be your final test," she said. "Are you prepared to endure it?"

Slowly, he nodded.

"I am."

She came to him when he stepped into the water, its chill seeping into his boots. When she embraced him, the water climbed up his legs and to his torso, ensnaring him in a liquid web that dragged him down.

Sounds of a forest filled the world around him. Overhead, he heard the soft flutter of birds' wings and the rustling of leaves in the warm wind. They seemed so high above him; the forest's canopy was not usually so far away.

Where am I?

Malldon's snow was gone, replaced by dark earth and green sprouts that squished between his toes. He looked down, flexing the small, pale hands of a child.

A new voice filled his consciousness, neither his nor Sha's.

"Papa...I'm lost..."

He almost recognized it. The voice had followed him through a thousand dreams, so familiar it might have been his own.

"Papa..."

A bird of vibrant, yellow feathers soared past him, tousling his hair with a gust. Yet, he was too distracted to think of it twice. As its shadow passed over his palms, he listened intently, waiting for the sound to come again.

Who are you?

"I'm scared, Papa..."

Black fur brushed over his legs, a soft purr grabbing his attention. At his feet he saw a cat, its fur matted by pine from the forest floor, and its gaze as green as the leaves above.

The moment their eyes met, she lost interest in him. Her tail swished behind her as she wandered away.

"Wait!" he cried.

His voice was startling. Devoid of its deep tremor, it was small and timid, no more powerful than an infant's whine. Yet despite its weakness, the sound startled the feline; swiftly, she fled.

"Come back!"

He chased her deep into the forest, confronting every bend with his usual vigor. However, this became more and more difficult for the child's body to endure. Every breath grew shallower, his legs burning from the demand he placed on them.

"Help me..."

A brilliant light began to break through the dense canopy, guiding his pursuit. The radiance gave him comfort in the shadows. Bathed in its light, he began to run faster, swallowing every pain with his shallow breath. The black cat leapt over a bend, disappearing into the brightest glow. He followed her there, into the light.

The forest vanished. Silas was standing at the base of a stone staircase, stretching up to the massive doors of a castle. There, at the foot of the steps, was a tall, regal man wearing a golden cloak. He appeared fretful, gripping his auburn hair as he paced the length of the steps. But when he saw the child, warmth filled his emerald eyes, his unease melting away.

Tears clouded Silas' young gaze. He stumbled to the man, throwing his arms around his sturdy legs.

"Papa," he whispered, choking on his tears.

It was only when Cedric began to lead him up the steps that he noticed the cat's disappearance. He looked all about him, but the creature was nowhere to be found.

His curiosity was forgotten when he felt his father's hand around his, guiding him forward.

"Where are we going?" he asked, in his new, soft voice.

Cedric smiled down at him, squeezing his pale hand.

"To a place you've never been."

The castle walls loomed above the child, he the object of the glass Dragons' hungry gaze. Afraid, he clutched his father's hand, trying to hide in his shadow. His father was quiet, solemn, until they stood before the largest door in all the palace.

"Reja," said the King, looking down at his son, "I'm going to give you something very important. Do you promise to be careful with it?"

He nodded, unable to take his eyes from the grand entry. Smiling at the boy's amazement, Cedric soon parted the doors.

Sounds of screeching animals filled the corridor, their foul scent overwhelming the unsuspecting boy. Yet despite these unpleasant sensations, the long room was alive with color, furs and feathers of every shade caged within an assortment of iron bars.

His father knelt beside the boy, extending to him a slender key.

"Take this. With it, you may release one creature from my menagerie."

The key was pressed into his hand without further instruction. Though Silas looked to his father for guidance, Cedric only pushed him forward.

"Go on."

All around him, the animals shrieked and barked and hissed from their cages. He tried to pass through without fear, but their madness overwhelmed his small heart. When his gaze met with that of a great, fanged creature, he cried in lieu of screaming.

Focus!

All the animals were too manic, or too pitiful. When he passed a yellow nightingale, sitting still in its cage, he would not give it another glance—the creature seemed too dead to free. He passed it by, and many others, until he came to that black cat.

She sat at the edge of the hall, her tail still swishing proudly along the floor as she stared bravely into his eyes. Her binds were different than the others. No cage about her, her only restraint was a long chain, burdened by a heavy lock about her neck.

He smiled, soothed by her familiar presence. He knelt before her, key in hand.

"Kitty..."

As his key hovered by the lock, he heard his father's voice.

"Are you sure you want to help her?"

The child nodded, content.

"I do."

He was pleased with his decision. As the key clicked in the lock, he heard her steady purr.

Everything began to disappear. He reached for the cat's soft fur, only to have it vanish beneath his fingertips, the creature turned to naught. Silas saw his hand darken, his grown shape returned to him—in exchange, his Father faded into darkness.

Sha materialized before him, her eyes as black as his surroundings. Their gaze afforded him neither comfort nor answer.

"Did I pass?" he asked.

The red nymph said nothing. Silently, she lifted La's silver mirror, reflecting his anxious visage back at him.

"In the right hands, this mirror shows more than just what threatens you," she said. "It will also show you absolute truth."

His reflection vanished, replaced by the horror he had seen before: Rina kissing the blonde soldier. Yet just as Alastor had begun to ease into the sensation, closing his eyes and kissing her in return, the young woman pulled back.

Suddenly, his handsome nose cracked beneath Rina's fist.

"Fawking **porker**!" she spat, his blood dripping from her hand. "Conceited **bastard**! What makes you think I would ever want you?!"

The soldier gripped his broken nose, stumbling when she spat at his feet.

"You will *never* be my Prince."

Rina locked herself back in her cell, returning to their shadows. Alastor was left to remain there, shocked—blood dripping down his ruined face.

The imaged flickered to black.

"She never betrayed you," said Sha. "Her betrothed has perished. She thinks of you even now, anxiously awaiting your return."

Every word dried in his throat, withered in the presence of his shame.

"Your judgment has been clouded by illusion and doubt. Misled, you chose to save the selfish cat from her chains, at the expense of the nightingale she had chosen to follow."

The mirror vanished from her hands, leaving him face-to-face with the crimson-haired nymph. In her eyes, he saw the familiar gleam of disappointment.

"The object of your illusion will be taken from you," she said. "The object you most care for, as agreed."

He was stricken with terror. In her eyes, he saw the chosen victim: her black hair floating in icy water, green eyes growing cold and dim.

"Don't bring her into this," he pleaded. "She had nothing to do with my mistake!"

Sha scoffed, seeming almost angered by his protests.

"We are holding you true to your word. We have taken what you claimed to care for—count yourself fortunate that your fickle affections changed this outcome."

Dark water licked at his heels, slowly constricting as it pulled him deeper, deeper into the lake.

"Your misery changes nothing," said Sha, her scarlet gaze observing his descent. "The woman will be struck down by the serpent of your creation."

He sputtered, his furious cries only bringing more water into his lungs. Soon, there was only darkness.

Silas surfaced coughing, trying to regain his bearings. All around him was the orange light of dusk, touching the landscape like fire.

By the time he could stand, he saw Raven standing farther along the shore, staring forward. She was paler than she had ever been, the color gone from even her lips. All too soon, she crumpled.

"Raven!"

He managed to catch her failing body, supporting her in his shaking arms. Blood seeped from her ankle, mixing with the clear water. As he watched, a snake slithered back into the depths—its scales glistening like black diamonds.

How could I be such a fool?

Silas held onto her as tightly as he could, his body trembling. He had never felt so heavy.

"This shouldn't have happened," he said, his voice as unsteady as his hold. "I'm so…so sorry…"

Tensing, the woman shook her head.

"Don't…"

It was hard for her to speak. Her every breath caught in her throat, sharp as knives.

"I betrayed you. I don't deserve your pity."

She looked up at him, tears sprung from either pain or regret.

"Hector is coming to kill you. He told me to…stall. I tried to tell you…"

Raven smiled, the tears spilling down cold cheeks.

"Guess I'm no better than your last lover."

He wanted to be angry. He wanted to scream at the woman who abused his trust, as he would have any other. Yet, his passion was gone. Looking into her sad, lonely eyes, he felt nothing but remorse.

"You did what you had to," he said, the words gentle.

She stared up at him, shocked by his kindness. Then, new tears welled in her eyes. All at once, she began to cry.

"Hold me tight," she whispered. "Just until…"

Silas would do so. He held her in his arms, watching the blood seep into the pool around them. His eyes felt hot, water in their depths, filled with loss.

I'm so sorry.

She was a kindred spirit, as lost in her world as he had been in his own. It hurt knowing he had been the one to cut her journey short, to stop her from finding her way.

"You have a voice like my father's," she said, trying to smile. "I hope…I can hear it again, someday."

"Your father's?"

She shook her head, laughing softly.

"No," she whispered. "Yours."

Suddenly, she lifted his sword from the water, forgotten since the day he had arrived. She pressed it against his chest.

"Here. Take this to Hector…and run him through."

Raven's voice cracked bitterly, her eyes closing. As he took his weapon in one hand, her hold on it grew lax. Her arms fell, her skin turning to ice.

He felt her weight in his arms, a solemn reminder of his own shortcomings. His heart aching, he leaned over the water with her, past the shallow ridge he knelt upon.

"Rest, Raven."

Silas allowed her body to drift into the depths, forever a part of the nymphs' watery realm.

The youth remained there—still, lifeless. With one decision, he had lost the key to Rina's freedom, and taken a woman's life.

Forgive me.

He covered his face, his mind beginning to crumble.

Forgive me…

Silas did not stir again, too lost in his own misery. However, his senses returned when the edge of a blade chilled the back of his neck.

"You've outlived your use. Speak your last."

Though unnerved, Silas was not afraid. He heard his mother's words through Ariel's expressionless voice, and found them calming.

Resigned, he lowered his head.

"I should have fought harder for her."

He closed his eyes, listening to the sound the sword made as it sliced the air. Every moment seemed more precious to him, as each slowly slipped away.

The blow never came. Instead, water dripped over his neck, cool as the weapon's blade. He looked up to see Ariel standing over him, holding the hilt of a melting sword, which turned to clear water upon Silas' skin.

Silas stared, disbelieving, until he saw the red nymph standing before him. She stood with Ariel, her scaled hand wrapped about his as the sword succumbed to her power.

"This is not his wish," she said.

At once, he saw tears falling from Ariel's dull eyes, dripping like the remnants of his weapon.

"He is paying the price for a terrible crime he committed, the day he held the time-stealing dagger to his own throat."

Sha gazed at the emotionless man, showing pity.

"Do you wish to know his identity, Xavier? To know the youth who turned Hasan's power into his curse?"

Natural hesitancy gripped him, for he sensed the solemn nature of Sha's inquiry. Yet, he could not deny her. He had to know this man—a man with a face like his own reflection.

"Who is he?"

A smile graced her red lips. As he watched, she pushed Ariel's black hair from his ear, whispering soft words to him. When she touched his hand, life filled his sapphire eyes.

"He was born Ariel Baldric Xavier, Prince of Larasca. His mistake has removed him from his own time, into yours."

Sha looked towards the youth she spoke of, strangely calm.

"You gaze upon your own son."

For a long time, Silas could only stare at the man. It felt as though he were seeing him for the very first time. He saw the young man's strong stature, his handsome face—his eyes, so like the Storma Queen's.

Silas was overcome. Suddenly, he had doubled over again, unable to speak for his own sobs.

"Father?"

Ariel's true voice was gentle, lacking Silas' unnatural growl. He couldn't have been more relieved.

"Why do you weep, Xavier?" Sha asked.

"Because…"

He raised his head, his eyes stinging, his throat raw from laughter and sobs.

"I have a son," he said. "And…he's perfect."

Ariel winced when he heard this.

"You can't say that. If you knew why I was here—"

"It wouldn't make a bloody difference."

Silas' mouth ached, unaccustomed to such a smile.

"No matter what you've done, you're my son. My…my blood," Surviving, despite all the terrible things he had done. "Your existence alone brings me hope."

He gazed into his son's sapphire eyes, seeing their relief. For the first time since childhood, Silas felt the strength of unquestioning, familial love.

When Sha released Ariel's hand, his eyes dimmed to vacancy.

"He remains under Morana's spell. Should you break the curse on her, his will also fade."

She knelt before him, extending a black diamond to the shaking youth.

"Perhaps we misjudged you."

He took the diamond, dazed.

"I have seen the goodness in your heart," she said, wading past him. "You have the makings of a glorious King."

Silas turned in time to see her descend into the lake, the glint of her red scales slowly disappearing into the deep waters. At last, Avdotia Lake was still.

Crunching ice announced the arrival of unwelcome visitors, who emerged from the surrounding forest with torches and blades. Their leader, whose golden robes gleamed brightest, had Raven's face.

"You must be Hector," said Silas, rising from the lake.

"You are Impurities," said the man, drawing his sword. "Impurities must be cleansed."

"I see."

Silas handed the diamond to Ariel, who passively accepted the gift. Hands free, he moved in front of the expressionless youth, protecting him.

"What makes me Impure, exactly? Is it my skin? My eyes? These fangs?"

He stared defiantly into the visage of every Priest, seeing their fear.

"I am the result of 655 years of royal breeding. I am a creature born of this country, shaped by this country, molded into something capable of possessing this country."

The weapon he drew was not Edmund's sword. It transformed in his hands, the blade glowing crimson, the golden hilt rippling with etched feathers. When the Priests saw its glow, they trembled, falling away in terror.

"I am Asyrias Xavier," he declared, raising Corliss to the twilit sky. "Cross me, and I will see Malldon burnt to the ground."

Chapter XXXIX

30th Day of 1st Month, 655 I.R.

As the sun set behind the white horizon, the Queen gazed into her candle-lit vanity, gliding a fine brush through her raven locks. Her sapphire eyes gazed back at her, pleasure flickering in their cool depths. Azalea's necklace rest against her breast, its cerulean beads glistening in the firelight. At last, she had claimed the gift that rightfully belonged to her. The meddlesome Princess was locked away, as was her haughty accomplice—yet, Morana was restless. Despite the darkness outside, she remained at her vanity, knowing sleep would not come to her that night.

A simple chain hung from the edge of her mirror, a golden ring swaying at the end of it, disturbed by a sourceless breeze. Morana stiffened at the sight of it, seeing her own eyes harden, throat clench. She remembered the violet hue of those Storma eyes, their very shape mocking her.

Her son's eyes had not been that color. They had been her own color when they closed, his poisoned breath slowing for the last time.

He's dead.

Yet, the ring continued to sway, filling her with doubt.

She should have questioned Twyla when the ring was confiscated. No doubt, the treacherous handmaid was the only one who knew the truth of this situation. However, to question her would have been to admit guilt, and she was not in a position to raise suspicion. Her subjects, her servants, even her Councilmen had all begun to doubt her. She could feel her power over them slipping like sand through her fingers.

The Queen reached into her vanity drawer, feeling Dayu's letter beneath her fingertips. She often reached for it in times of uncertainty, to remind her of days when she had known love; his mention of the ring that hung before her now was but ominous coincidence.

Shioya Miyuki

汐泰 美雪

The child within you is not of my seed, as we had hoped. Its energy is of Cedric's nature, soulless and corrupt. However, though you hate the man who has done this to you, do not be foolish enough to kill the child outright. Though he hides behind a naïve smile, the man you have married is one of great cunning. Deceive him for as long as you are able, if you value your life and mine.

Within the envelope, I have enclosed an enchanted ring. Place this upon your heir when he is old enough to walk, and you will ensure that he does not reach manhood. In this way, you may doom this cursed Kingdom.

The presence of the child may prove beneficial to our plans. While his father is distracted by the task of raising him, our own activity will be overlooked. I will transport the seventh diamond to the castle before he has reached adolescence—then, the Creature and all his Kingdom will kneel at our feet.

I will soon arrive in the castle with the fifth jewel. Remember your patience. Even from afar, I can sense your quivering form as you try to smother all that rage. You must look forward to the day when I will cleanse the world of all you despise. Together, we will rule Paradise.

Mazaki Dayu

魔裂 蛇柳

Two days remained—soon, the prisoners' fates would be decided. Even so, she halfheartedly hoped that the youth would return, bearing the final diamond. Her dreams would become reality; at last, she would know joy again.

As she placed the letter back in the drawer, she noticed another tucked beneath it, the royal seal upon the envelope cracked open.

She always avoided the sight of this letter. She knew its contents, and the knowledge alone filled her with such contempt that she could not bear to acknowledge its existence. Yet, tonight, she was drawn to it. Morana lifted the dusty envelope from the drawer, tracing the red seal with her smooth nail. When removed, the parchment crackled, thinned by time. Cedric's words remained, his beautiful handwriting immortalized by his black pen.

My Dear Genevieve,

Do not frown so deeply, my love. I know your secret. You are with child, and you have gone to great lengths to keep this from me. The maids have loose lips, you see; I would not entrust any more of your secrets to them.

Smile, love. I will not deny this child. Although it cannot fill the hole left by my Reja's passing, I will cherish it no less. Morana has rejected me with both her body and soul—she cannot sway me to turn you away. Your

condition is my doing, and I do not regret it.

Meet me in my chambers tomorrow, when the moon is high. I will

prove to you then that my love is sincere.

Yours,

Cedric

Her anger burned anew. She trembled as she held the letter, her fingers turning white, her head throbbing with the intensity of this emotion. It was inexplicable—she had not cared for Cedric. Everything about him made her blood curl: his smile, his laugh, the smell of mortar that clung to his hair when he finished piecing together that colored glass.

Love, he had called her, sickeningly sweet.

Yours.

Cedric and Genevieve had made no attempt to hide their affair. Since the day the King had met the clever peasant, he had made no secret of their rendezvous in town as he treated her to the finery of the Noble Square, buying her dresses, jewelry, even pets. The young woman was only as old as Morana had been when she was first married, no more than seventeen, and surprisingly beautiful. Whenever she appeared at the palace gates, the gatekeepers would whistle at her, and the pages would rush down for the privilege of leading her through the castle.

Morana was sickened by her existence, but turned a blind eye to it—until Cedric brought her to live in the castle. Then, she was forced to see him take that girl into his room every night, as he smiled like a conqueror. No one but her seemed to be opposed to it, servants and even the

Councilmen actually pleased by the young woman's 'refreshing' nature. She smiled too often, laughed like a twit.

Before Genevieve, Cedric had often tried to convince his wife to lie with him. Though she scorned his presence, he would touch her gently, his eyes begging for her submission. But the girl changed that. No longer would Cedric tap on her door late at night, whispering through it that he was sorry for whatever he had done—say that he needed her there. These futile attempts dwindled to naught, as all his affection was wasted on that young, frivolous prize.

Morana's anger infected every part of her, possessing her with thoughts of such foul intentions that she could not bear to look at her husband. She was reminded of Dayu's warning: that the Xaviers were unnatural, soulless beings, weeds sucking the life source of mankind; every one of them must be removed.

She suppressed her murderous sentiments for as long as she was able. They were forced deep within her, festering like an infection. There they remained, until Twyla brought her that letter, confiscated from one of Cedric's maids.

The Queen could not allow a bastard child to exist. The very thought of it churned her insides, sickening her. She could not allow another Xavier to be brought into the world.

When night fell, Morana stole the Xavier sword from the armory. She intercepted Genevieve before she could reach the King's chambers, and deadened her mind with the spell of Dayu's diamond. The girl willingly took the sword in her hands.

The Queen waited outside Cedric's door until it was finished. She heard his confused whisper, the cot creaking as he rose from bed. Then, there was the beautiful sound of his choking, sputtering. His strong body hit the ground, his head striking the stone with a crack.

Very soon after, another body fell, the woman's sobs turning to silence.

Every image of that day was engrained in her consciousness. Morana could remember the bloody sight when she opened that door, blood seeping from Genevieve's impaled abdomen onto the body beneath her, staining his silken garments. The very smell of it had given the Queen great pleasure. She felt herself smile at the mere memory—yet, her reflection showed no joy. There was sadness in that sapphire gaze.

Did he have to die?

He had to die. She knew that, and was thrilled by her decision. But her reflection did not change, haunted by misery she did not feel.

Alone, again. His death brought loneliness.

There was a knock on the door. Startled, she shoved the letter back in the drawer, slamming it shut.

"Enter," she said.

Raoul entered her chambers, seeming as calm as he always was. However, she could see through the deception. His body was tense, his gray eyes watching her like a wanting predator.

"You seem upset," he said.

She wasn't prepared to endure him. She turned away from him, choosing instead to gaze upon her own reflection.

"I am tired, Raoul. Don't pressure me tonight."

Despite her warning, he approached her. She knew him well enough to know that her wishes were lost on him when he was in this mood. The

Queen shuddered as his cool hands slid beneath her sleeves, grasping her shoulders.

"You've refused me many days this month, my Queen," he said, boldly leaning down to kiss her neck. "I hope you understand how patient I've been. It's been difficult to diffuse all the allegations against you; people even believe that you staged your own son's death, hoping you could one day rule alone. Though I know you are guilty of no wrongdoing, being constantly turned out of your chambers is giving me doubts."

His grip on her shoulders tightened.

"I do not enjoy being toyed with."

She shook herself out of his hold, standing.

"I will not suffer this insolence," she said.

Raoul hesitated, clearly seeing her hostility. He changed his approach. Calmly, he touched her face, a touch upon her back pulling her closer to him.

"I have always admired your spirit, Morana," he said, his fair hand trailing down her skin, "but I must be given some demonstration of your loyalty to me. For years now I have kept my vow of silence, disclosing nothing about our acts, in hopes that you would one day realize that the time had come to marry anew. I once staked my very life in want of your company, and feel I am doing so even now, with the way the Councilmen whisper behind my back."

"I am *tired*, Raoul," she said, more forcefully now. "I bid you goodnight."

This time, he wouldn't hear it. He held her tighter, forcing his lips on hers.

A relationship with the Grand Advisor was advantageous. Larasca was not kind to its women; to remain in power, she needed certain pieces positioned about her, shielding her from rebellion. By giving into his wishes, she had enduring protection against the suspicion of the other advisors, as well as an advocate in every political circumstance. Even if the others all turned their backs, she could have Raoul to keep her from the axe.

However, that night was different. Even with these thoughts in her mind, she could not endure him. She was sickened to have his bony hands about her, his thin lips twisted with hers. He lacked the substance of her former lovers. It angered her now that he thought he possessed her—she, who had been wife to an Xavier.

A great strike turned his face. Raoul stared at her, shocked, as he touched his red cheek.

"Get out," she hissed, her hand still shaking. "Get **out**."

Despite his anger, he would remain there no longer. Soon, the doors closed behind him, leaving her alone.

She slumped against her vanity, holding her aching head. The air seemed too thin around her, unable to fill her lungs. She heaved, feeling sick.

What's happening?

Morana gazed over her shoulder, seeing the woman in the mirror. Though anger burned in her breast, the face she saw was stained by tears, spilling powerlessly down her face. It was the face that had stared back at her once before, staring back from Cedric's mirror as he lay dead upon the floor.

She breathed harder, trembling, ripping at her hair. Rage filled her, controlling her. She gripped the blue beads about her neck, pulling until the back of the band snapped beneath her hair.

"Stop," she whispered. "Stop crying."

But that woman could not stop the tears streaming down, mourning the life she had destroyed.

"Stop," she said. "**STOP!**"

The beads shattered against the mirror, cracking the surface with their force. The ring perched upon the edge slipped off, clattering onto the wooden vanity, rolling until it came to rest upon the center of the wood. There it laid, glistening in the moonlight like a foul omen.

The Queen slumped back into the chair, staring into the shattered mirror. Countless eyes gazed back at her, broken.

Chapter XL

31ˢᵗ Day of 1ˢᵗ Month, 655 I.R.

The eastern tower was a haunted place. Ghoul-eyed statues leaned out from the walls to watch the staircases, smirking towards any soul brave enough to enter their domain. However, the worst fiends had been carved into the pillars of the highest room. There, stone dragons stared past the tattered curtains to the open balcony beyond, their lips curled in devilish smirks. They had no pity for Rina's broken spirit, her throbbing wrists bound by heavy ropes. In all her life, she had never felt so alone.

She endured the night there, lying still upon the dusty ground. Nothing stirred until morning, when a warm breeze blew in from the open balcony, bringing with it flakes of Joanissia's snowfall. The flakes glistened in the dawn, floating high above her, their beauty making that dark place bearable. As long as she watched them, there was no pain. There was no loneliness.

Too soon, the doors opened. The Captain of the Guard entered, donning his heavy armor; behind him, Morana stood in unsettling silence.

"The Queen has come to see you," said the Captain.

Rina stared, not reacting to the news. Shortly after, a few words from the Queen dismissed her Captain, and the man left the room. The girl was left alone, defenseless.

Morana approached her, no emotion on her pale face.

"Sit up, girl."

Rina sat up, seeing no reason to defy her. She returned the Storma's cold stare, feeling no dread. She was already imprisoned, sentenced to execution. What more did she have to fear?

The silence stretched on and on, the Storma growing visibly angrier. Rina said nothing—until the Queen's hand struck her cheek.

"Who do you think you are?" she hissed. "Are you his lover, is that it? Do you feel stronger because a Prince is coming to save you?"

Her face stung, but she did not show her pain. Rina looked back at the Queen, seeing her trembling gaze, her sunken, shadowed eyes. Signs of her tortured soul were written upon her face, present despite all the finery she wore.

"Why are you so miserable?" Rina asked her Queen.

These words incensed her to fury. Morana struck her again, harder, before snatching Rina's tangled locks.

"You will learn your place," she rasped.

The Queen dragged her onto the stone balcony, chestnut strands ripping from the girl's scalp. Before she could scream, Morana had her head shoved beneath the wooden railing, forcing her to stare down into the depths.

"Sir Alastor tells me this is your greatest fear," said Morana, her sharp nails tightening in Rina's locks. "Think of it: I could easily drop you from here, and no one would know nor care that you were dead."

Rina watched with terror as icicles cracked from the balcony, plummeting down like stone. The ground was a thousand leagues away, so far down that she would surely die before it snapped her bones.

"It doesn't really matter whether I drop you or not. At sunrise tomorrow, you will know that your Prince has forsaken you. Your head will roll, and no one will be there to cry for you."

Even stricken by fear, Rina could not accept her words. Tears in her eyes, she managed a whisper.

"You're wrong."

Morana's nails dug deeper.

"Child," she spat. "I was not unlike you, once. I invested all of myself in petty hopes and dreams, believing in the goodness of life. That was before I knew the true nature of the world—hideous, and unforgiving."

The Queen shoved her further over the ledge, forcing her to confront the white abyss.

"You are nothing. You were born nothing, and you will die nothing."

Despite all her fear, Rina could feel new resolve rising within her. Her body grew still, the shaking ceased. All she could think of was her frustration, her anger.

"He's coming back," she said again, forcefully now.

"Don't make me laugh."

Rina spun about, sending the startled Queen backwards in surprise.

"He's coming **back**!"

The older woman toppled over as the girl wrenched back from her grip, forcing her off balance. As she fell, Rina managed to stand again, her heart pumping too hard for her to realize her shock. The Queen stared up at her, enraged—but as she rose up, the Captain pushed open the doors.

"Your Majesty, there is a visitor in the throne room."

"Send him away, Art," she snapped.

"I can't," he said. "Baldric Alexander will not be ignored."

Morana's anger turned to bewilderment. She glanced towards the prisoner, jaw tight with suppressed hatred, but could look no longer.

"Stay put until I return," she threatened.

Soon, the doors closed. Rina, drained of her strength, collapsed to her knees. She leaned back against the wood railing, feeling the warm wind lace ice into her hair.

He's coming.

Rina closed her eyes, feeling her pulse begin to slow. She felt certainty set into her bones, bringing a smile to her face. Though the world was far beneath her, something in her heart told her not to worry; something in her told her at dawn, she would be free.

Baldric Alexander was the last person the Queen wanted to see. One of the members of Cedric's former Rank, the Duke of Lucadia had been a close friend of Morana's husband for many years, even allowed to sit front row at their wedding. Unfortunately, he and the Queen had not had such a healthy relationship. Their mutual distaste came from the traits they shared: both too stubborn, hotheaded, and uncompromising to care for the other.

Still recovering from the peasant's assault, she was already tense by the time she opened the doors to the throne room, preparing herself for emotional warfare; however, the sight beyond them jolted her consciousness. She was shocked to see the intimidating man embracing

Lesser Advisor Antonio, laughing like a juvenile. They prattled on in Kyron, the conversation too jubilant—never ceasing.

Morana did not care to endure a conversation she could not understand. Already irritated, she sat upon her throne, hardly waiting until Art took his place beside her before she interrupted the foreigners' reunion.

"Why have you come to Joanissia, Duke Baldric?"

The man turned his blue gaze on her, making no secret of his impatience.

"Perhaps you would know, if you had bothered to read a single one of my letters. You have some nerve, ignoring me like that."

"Do you forget whom you're speaking to, Baldric?"

"No," said the visitor, scowling in nauseating insolence. "It's you who underestimates your opponent, Morana."

She knew it was to her advantage to remain calm. Yet, something about the Duke's haughty gaze put her on edge, tensing every part of her until she felt she would snap. He had always been that way. He walked with a stride that demanded attention, and spoke as though he owned everything in the room.

"What is it you want?" she said, forcing the words through tight teeth.

"My daughter."

Startled, the Queen's irritation gave way to curiosity.

"And who is this 'daughter' of yours?"

"Her name is Rina."

Her shock became laughter. She laughed and laughed, unable to accept his words. It was impossible to believe that that silent, dirty girl belonged to the arrogant Duke of Lucadia.

"That prisoner?" she laughed. "What proof do you have that she's even yours?"

"I'm here. That should be enough for you."

The Queen leaned forward, still more amused than threatened.

"That girl is imprisoned for treason. Do you think I can set her free just because some man with an expensive coat demands I release her?"

"Listen to me very closely, Morana," he said, not a semblance of gentleness on his face. "If you do not release my daughter, I will lead Lucadia, Oyban, Pandore, and Siette in another revolt. All will break from your country and again call itself West Larasca. Whom do you suppose East Larasca will blame?"

Morana was clever enough to realize when she had been cornered. She looked to Art and to Antonio, halfheartedly hoping for assistance; however, Antonio's face was glazed, offering nothing, and Art could provide no more than useless brute force. There were no moves left to her.

"Antonio..." she hesitated, angered by her powerlessness. "Take him to Raphael's abandoned chambers. That is where that girl is kept."

Her advisor bowed to her, smiling too broadly. She had a bitter taste in her mouth as she watched them leave, but she convinced herself it was for the best. If the girl were removed now, then perhaps Asyrias would have no reason to remain.

<hr>

When the doors of that cheerless room opened again, Rina was alert. Her back pressed against the wall, the wind of the balcony gracing her side, she stared silently at her newest visitors. She expected the Queen and her

Captain—instead, there was the Kyron who had helped her in the aviary, and a tall, blue-eyed man.

She didn't recognize him, at first. His figure seemed but a shadow in her memory. However, as he drew closer, she began to piece together his identity. When he knelt to meet her wary look, suddenly, she knew him— Baldric Alexander, the Duke of Lucadia.

"I'm so sorry, Baldric," said Antonio, lingering by the door, "I should have warned you of the state she's in. She's been imprisoned for almost a month now."

"It's fine," the Duke replied. "I want you to guard the hall. Understand?"

Antonio nodded, respectfully bowing to the man. Soon, the doors had closed behind him.

"You must be wondering why I am here," said the man, patience in his gaze.

Though her neck ached, she managed one, slow nod. The Duke took this as reply enough. He seemed to hesitate, almost reaching out to touch her. Yet, he paused, and quickly withdrew his hand.

"I've come to take you home, Rina."

She cringed, drawing back in terrible confusion.

"I don't understand," she said.

"I've come to right my wrongs," he replied, solemn. "I should have been here sooner. Forgive me…"

Rina could only stare at him, uncomprehending. What could bring the Duke of Lucadia here, to free her? What made him take pity on an insignificant peasant?

He leaned over her, taking out a short dagger to cut the ropes about her wrists. As they fell away, he began his tale.

"It was seventeen years ago when I arrived in Lucadia. Commander Giovanni and I were sent to bring Western Larasca into submission. We decided to split our task: Giovanni would subdue Pandore and Siette, and I would conquer Oyban and Lucadia. After my forces had destroyed Oyban's resistance, we continued on to Lucadia, the so-called capital of the West. There, Duke Alasdair Talbot had crowned himself King, and had already readied forces to fight against me. When the fighting was over, I decided I would claim the Duke's crown for myself."

He hesitated, shame darkening his features.

"I ordered the deaths of Alasdair and his wife. Their daughter, Raquel, was of marrying age, and I took advantage of her self-absorbed nature. Although I had killed her parents, she was willing to be my wife, so long as I shared the power over the city equally with her. She had a brother, however, a child hardly old enough to walk. The boy was a problem. I could not hope to maintain power over Lucadia if Alasdair's son was still alive—yet, I could not bring myself to kill a child. I took Alastor Talbot to an orphanage, where he lived in ignorance of his heritage."

Rina sat stunned. Her body trembled, her spirit doused in ice.

"Alastor…is…"

Her whole perception of the world began to tilt. All this time, the smiling boy who had shared her bedroom, who had betrayed her twice in cold blood, had been the true heir to the Lucadian throne.

"There is a reason I asked you to be my Pillar in the ceremony, and he to be your Defender," he said. "Raquel could not produce a male heir for me, and the girls she bore are selfish, senseless things. After the ceremony, it was my plan to announced your marriage to Alastor, the man I would name my heir."

The girl felt short of breath, so bewildered by his words.

"Why me?" she choked.

"Because you are my child."

All at once, everything hurt. Her head throbbed, her throat ached. She could feel stinging in her eyes from tears of disbelief, which welled without her power.

"Liar," she whispered.

All her life, she had lived without a father. She could not make herself believe that she had one now.

"Your mother and I met only one night, in Alore. A'vra was a Kala, half-Larascan herself, and extraordinarily beautiful. I had my way with her, and was satisfied. I left the next day, continuing my journey with Giovanni to West Larasca; I thought of her no more. However, three years later, when Raquel had already borne me Heather and Hanna, I found a little girl on my doorstep. There was nothing about her that said she was mine, and I was ready to have her taken away—until she opened her blue eyes, and called me 'Papa'."

He reached into his pocket, withdrawing a small, Akalinian bracelet. Three coins dangled from it, each etched with a different letter.

R-n-a

Rina took the bracelet in her trembling hands, unable to stop her falling tears.

"I couldn't keep her," said Baldric, his voice losing its strength. "I had two daughters already. Raquel still had the support of many Lucadians, and causing tumult with her was risking my own position. I had no choice but to leave the child in an orphanage, where she might be cared for. All I could do was watch from afar, seeing her grow into the beautiful, kind young woman that neither Heather nor Hanna could ever hope to be."

Her tears trickled down the bracelet, which she clutched tightly to her breast. She remembered, now. She remembered a fuzzy memory of the tall man kneeling before her, staring in absolute disbelief. She knew then who he was.

"Papa," she whispered.

She sobbed, letting the bracelet fall.

"Papa!"

Rina embraced him, finally feeling her father's warmth. She cried into his body, forgetting the rest of the world.

At last, she felt his strong arms around her, protecting her as a father should.

"Come," he said, gently. "Let's go home."

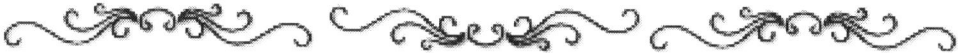

Baldric took his daughter to a washing room, where he paid a small sum to a maid to have her cleaned and properly dressed. While this happened, he waited patiently outside the door, alert to his surroundings.

He had never been fond of Joanissia castle. Even before Cedric had constructed his mosaics, Baldric could feel eyes following him in every hall, chilling him more deeply than the palace's frigid air. Merciless, angry spirits possessed these stone walls; Baldric felt it in his bones.

It wasn't difficult to occupy his thoughts as he waited. He thought of his wife's inevitable fury when he returned home with his bastard child, and of the screeching tirade his eldest daughter would force him to endure. It seemed Heather had already discovered Rina's relationship to her, and made no secret of her jealous hatred towards her half-sister. However, even this dread was soon overshadowed by another. He tensed when he heard steps in the stone hall, approaching with a too-familiar gait. All too soon, that smirking man rounded the corner, ready to greet the Duke with a mocking bow.

"Giovanni," Baldric cursed.

"Did you miss me?" he chuckled.

"I hoped you were dead. Clearly, too much to hope for."

"You must be here to claim that dear girl," Giovanni said, ignoring Baldric's ill will with a grin. "I thought she might be yours. She looks very much like that woman you fancied back in the Kala camp—in fact, I believe I was the one to introduce you, wasn't I? She was in such an awful state after that catfight with her Master, I thought she might need someone familiar with good bandaging to help her clean up."

Giovanni chuckled, utterly ignoring Baldric's scowl. Too affectionately, he clapped a hand on the Duke's shoulder.

"We're two of a kind, you know: two opportunistic men, maneuvering territory others won't tread. What you did was only natural."

"And what exactly are you blathering about?"

"That pretty Kala girl," the ex-Commander laughed. "Some would have been too repulsed by her foreign look to allow her aid, but you did much better than that. Not only did you stitch up those outer wounds, but you made sure to drill those pesky inner ones as wel—"

Baldric's fist cracked his jaw; Giovanni toppled over, hitting the stone beneath.

"There's virtue in knowing when to shut your mouth," the Duke sneered, "learn it."

The man reacted as he always had. He laughed and laughed, even as he wiped blood from his lips.

"You've worked on your aim."

At last, the door to the washing room opened. Baldric turned to see his daughter emerge, freed from the grime of captivity. She was clothed in an enchanting white dress, with dark, damp curls framing her soft face. She was as beautiful then as she had been the day of the ceremony, not so long ago.

Giovanni rose up, bowing to the young woman.

"You are radiant, Princess."

The moment she saw that cunning smile, her lovely face was changed by scorn.

"Bastard," she spat.

Baldric smiled, proud of his child.

In the distance, the rumble of commotion began to disturb the halls. Very soon, guards rushed past them, murmuring to each other.

"He's here."

"The Prince has returned."

The Duke couldn't understand the excitement, nor did he care to. However, Rina was transformed by their words. Color returned to her fair skin as she smiled, coming alive.

Suddenly, she rushed from them, pursuing the guards down the halls.

"Rina!"

He called her name in shock, moving to chase her; however, Giovanni swiftly stood in his path.

"Come," he said, "let us take a stroll to the training room. There is much to explain."

Chapter XLI

The whole of Joanissia awaited their arrival. As the Prince's horse galloped over the cobblestones, he could feel the eyes of every peasant, scholar, merchant, and nobleman upon him, observing his return. They imposed their grand expectations upon him, though he did not want them. Silas had only one purpose in this city.

Upon arriving at the castle, he and Ariel were escorted to the throne room. There the Queen sat upon the Xavier throne, unaccompanied by any Councilman or servant.

"You have the diamond?" she asked, rising expectantly.

Silas nodded, displaying the gem.

"More trouble than it's worth."

The woman seemed surprised, likely more so by his survival than the diamond he held. She came down the red rug that extended from the throne, and reached out to take the diamond—but he snatched it away.

"The prisoners will go free?" he asked.

She scowled.

"Of course. I have no more use for them."

Suspicious as he was, he again offered the Queen her prize. Her smile was strange as she reached for it, as if her lips were twisted by a puppeteer's strings; however, no sooner had her hand touched the gem that she pulled back, howling as she gripped her scorched fingers.

"What did you *do*?" she hissed.

For once, he had done nothing. He stared at the black diamond in awe and frustration, he feeling little more than a slight warmth where it lay. He glanced to Ariel, hoping for answers, but received only the usual blank stare.

Naturally.

There was a slight shift in the air about him. He was surrounded by a heavy presence, swirling about him like the mist of Malldon. Soon, untraceable whispers caressed his cheek.

"Show her."

"Show her your strength."

"Prove your worth."

Morana watched him still, dangerous fury in her sapphire gaze. Those eyes had haunted him all his childhood years, burdening him with her resentment. Day by day, they had dismantled a boy's spirit, until he was reduced to self-loathing.

"Bring an end to this sad tale."

Silas pocketed the diamond, defiantly meeting her stare.

"The gem will only change hands after a conflict," he said. "You'll have to fight me for it."

Though he couldn't call it truth, his words didn't feel like lies. The Queen pondered them for a time, cautiously observing her strong adversary. Then, she nodded in consent.

"Ariel."

"Yes, Your Majesty?" the vacant man replied.

"Proceed to the armory. You will be my champion in this fight."

Silas' blood ran cold. He watched in horror as Ariel turned and left him, thinking nothing but to obey.

"Not him," he said.

"Do you think I would waste my Captain in this fight? A guard?" the Queen laughed. "A prisoner without identity is the perfect choice."

"I won't fight him," Silas insisted, "choose someone else."

"Scared, boy?"

She proceeded to the doorway, paying no mind to his protest.

"Come to the training room when you are ready. You may also procure armor for yourself; I would not want people to think this an unfair fight."

The massive doors closed behind her, trapping him with his misery, and his doubt.

He couldn't yet bring himself to leave that place. Shadows of his past were cast upon the walls, capturing his inner turmoil. He walked the crimson path to the Xavier throne, which sat agelessly upon the raised platform.

In days past, he had knelt beside the curved arms of that chair, so small then that he could not see the swirling etchings that adorned the wood. The Prince knelt there now, remembering the warm hand upon his head, tousling his dark locks.

"Someday, you will bear this crown."

He trembled, touching the great throne. His words were a child's plea.

"I don't want it."

"The crown is not something you should want for yourself."

Energy pulsed from the golden hilt at his side, sending tremors through his body. He rose, compelled to draw the sacred sword. The metal rang as it left its sheath, echoing as he held the weapon high above him. Reflected in its crimson blade, he saw his violet eyes: the twisted combination of Morana's sapphire, and Aiden's scarlet.

The youth would never see anything of Cedric in his reflection. Fate had robbed him of that. However, that could not prevent him from emulating his father's courage.

My own son...

How could he fight Ariel? No matter the outcome of the fight, his opponent's existence would come to an end. Either he would be killed by his father's hand, or his own—for he could not live if his sire had perished.

The blade took on another hue in the torchlight, a triumphant gold shimmering across its surface. The cool air sighed about him, stilling his uncertain thoughts. As peace washed over him, he realized what he had to do.

Rina's chase brought her back to the training room, the site of her last arrest. The sight of the room made her anxious now; even so, she was caught by a wave of people flooding into the space. Moved by the urgency of eager peasants and nobles alike, she found herself on the balcony, barely able to squeeze forward to see. Although the distance from the railing to the ground was somewhat daunting, she was forced to swallow her fear. Her fellow prisoners were also brought onto the balcony, along the other rim: four Citris men stood bedraggled along the rail, and beside them, Tasha and her son.

On the ground floor, the Queen sat upon a large chair pushed against one of the far walls, giving her an intimate view of the action. Upon her head was the Xavier crown, which glowed with its timeless magnificence. It seemed at first that Silas stood before her, but such was not the case. The armored man was pale, and stood too calmly to be the youth's likeness. In his hand was a glorious sword, with a hilt of pale gold etched with black lines, and a blade that gleamed like a predator's fang.

Beneath, the Queen's Captain opened a new set of doors. All eyes went to it as Silas emerged, nothing but plain clothing and his sword to protect him.

"No armor?" asked the Queen.

"I have never fought in it," Silas replied, his voice enough to fill the hall. "I don't believe in hiding behind metal when I fight."

Rina could see the change in Silas. He held himself with great pride, his natural strength intensified by kingly assurance. He seemed entirely different from the beast she had known.

"As my champion, Sir Ariel wields the Xavier sword," the Queen announced. "Does your weapon have a title?"

The sword Silas drew was not Edmund's, as Rina had expected. The weapon he held rivaled the royal sword in beauty, with a crimson blade that glistened in the chandelier's flickering light.

"My weapon is Corliss, forged in the depths of Avdotia Lake."

The Queen was unimpressed.

"Charming."

She looked past him, speaking to all who had gathered to observe.

"These men will fight to the death. Should the challenger win, I will release the prisoners. If not, they will die at dawn tomorrow, as planned."

Rina was overcome by worry. She found it hard to watch Silas and the armored man position themselves in the center of the room, preparing to draw blood.

Morana spoke at last.

"Begin."

Ariel struck his opponent like lightning, the clash of their weapons knocking Silas to the ground. No sooner had he leapt up than Ariel came again, brandishing his sword with frightening speed. There wasn't a flicker of emotion upon the man's face, no hesitation to dull his lethal precision. Silas barely managed to block again, but a firm grip on his hilt forced the challenger back.

Every attack was Ariel's. Each came with more and more determination, but Silas would not lose his footing. Each was parried as Silas led their fatal dance.

This was not the same man Rina had seen fighting in the forest, roaring as he wildly clashed with Giovanni's blade. Though Silas was on the defensive, he was entirely in control—powerful.

Everything moved too fast. Rina choked, terrified when Silas' knee finally buckled. He went down, sword raised above his head to hold off another attack. Ariel did not hesitate. His blade flashed cruelly, coming to finish their battle.

Suddenly, his sword clattered to the ground. Silas stood behind Ariel, vibrant blood running down the scarlet weapon. The servant fell to his knees, eyes wide, mouth agape. Yet, he was uninjured. The blood came from beneath the hilt, where Silas' own hand was wrapped around the blade.

Rina couldn't understand what she had witnessed. All around her, people looked about with the same disbelief, as astonished as she. Just as she thought the battle was over, Silas moved again, his target shifted. All the room watched with horror as he rushed past his opponent, plunging his sword into the Queen's heart.

As the blade was removed, no blood came with it. Rina was stunned to see Morana perfectly unmarked, the only sign of the attack a perfect cut in her dress. The woman stared up her attacker, speechless.

"You…"

Rina could barely make out the words on the Queen's lips, spoken in but a breath. Her face began to change. Hardness melted from her, falling away with her tears. Watery trails stained her cheeks as her careful composure fell, stone walls crumbling down. For the first time in many years, her vulnerability was on display—true, human misery.

She rose like a ghost, seeming only half present in her own body. Suddenly, she embraced the man before her, clinging to him with a faltering hold.

"This man is my son," she said.

Her arms fell away as she gazed up at him, her hands trembling as she touched his face. Rina had not thought her capable of such heartbreaking intimacy. As the Storma lifted the crown from her head, the world was still, holding its breath until the golden circlet was placed upon the youth's black locks.

"Captain," said the Queen, "Bow to your King."

Without question, the Captain of the Guard approached the man. He fell to one knee, bowing his head before his new master.

Morana raised her voice, giving her final proclamation.

"Joanissia, hail King Asyrias."

All around Rina, people began to bow. They fell to their knees, some weeping as their cry rang out.

"All hail King Xavier!"

Rina stood longer than the rest, watching sadly as the Queen removed herself from the room, alone. Too late, the girl remembered the rule: no one stands as an Xavier King is standing.

She moved to kneel, but stopped when Silas came to stand beneath her, his bloody sword clattered to the ground behind him. He gazed at her for so long that she could not deny his attention.

"Here, Rina," he said.

He held his arms out to her, expectant. He was asking her to jump from that height, down to him.

"Trust me."

Too many emotions overtook her at once, from fear to joy. Despite her overwhelming terror of jumping from that height, it was enough that his arms awaited her down below. She swallowed her uncertainty, her doubt and her dread. Rina jumped down into his waiting embrace.

He was as strong as she remembered. He set her down with ease, pausing only a moment to smile at her. However, his attention soon turned up above.

"You bow not for me, but for my Queen."

He placed the crown upon her head.

"Long live Queen Nasaria."

Rina stared up at him, too stunned to think. Too soon, a new cry began to ripple through the joyous observers.

"Long live the Queen!"

"Now go forth and spread the news," he demanded. "Tell all of Joanissia the miracle you witnessed today."

In a rumble of sound, the spectators began to file out. Fewer and fewer remained, until only Baldric, Giovanni, and Tasha gazed down from the balcony.

As soon as she felt they were alone, Rina gazed up at the youth she had once called Silas. So different was he now, it was hard to know him by that name.

"Why?" she whispered.

"Nasaria is your Kala name," he explained, not answering her question. "The Kala man you stabbed knew your mother; I've known your real name for a while now."

"No…"

She touched his hand, wondering why it was closed so tightly.

"Why have you named me your Queen?"

The young man watched her, gentleness in his once harsh eyes.

"This country doesn't need another Raphael," he said. "It needs a benevolent leader, who might work to mend the wounds left by that tyrant's war. I know there is no one more capable of that than you."

Although she was touched, she sensed too much distance in his words. He stood right before her, yet seemed to be fading from her sight.

"You could do that alone," she said.

Slowly, he shook his head.

"Not me."

His hand at last opened to her touch—spilling blackened blood. It trickled to the ground in streams, staining his hand with serpentine trails. Rina could feel her own pulse slow as she watched the red pool beneath begin to grow.

"I'm sorry," he said, his voice devoid of its strength. "I won't be here much longer."

These were his last words. Once spoken, his body gave out—he collapsed into her, his feverish warmth turning cold in her arms.

Rina fell to her knees, her unsteady legs unable to support his weight.

No...

She clutched him tight, unwilling to believe he was gone. She wanted to open her eyes and wake, be it in the tower or her cell. But this was reality, crashing down around her. Though the chilled skin she felt belonged to her friend, the tears on his cheek had fallen not from his eyes, but from her own.

Tasha and Baldric leapt down from the balcony, as Giovanni hollered orders down at them.

"Careful when you pick him up," he said. "It's best we take him elsewhere."

The Rionan Princess tried to get Rina's attention, but found the girl lifeless, staring at Silas' cold body.

"Rina! Wake up!"

Rina was powerless to keep him there. Though gently, her father and friend stole Silas away from her. Supporting his arms on their shoulders, Tasha and Baldric looked back up at Giovanni.

"Where do we take him?" Baldric asked.

"His bedroom, of course," he replied.

Silas was taken, almost dragged through the doors the Captain held open. Rina wanted to follow, longing to be with him. She could not. Her legs were heavy as stone, held fast to the floor. It seemed no better to move, run after her dying love, than to stay perfectly still, allowing the memory of him to slip away.

Suddenly, she felt a hand upon her shoulder. She looked up to see Silas' opponent looking down at her. He was changed. His once vacant gaze was touched by grief, glistening tears in his bright eyes.

"Come with me," he said. "I know how to save him."

She stared, too numb to comprehend.

"Please, we don't have much time."

She had no reason to trust him. Yet, the longer she gazed into those sapphire orbs, shaped so like the Prince's, the more her defenses fell. He was the last ray of light in a collapsing tunnel.

Silently, she allowed him to lead her from that place, towards the white world beyond the palace gates.

Chapter XLII

syrias' room had not been touched in years. Dust billowed from the silken sheets as they laid him down, his weight distorting the other, smaller impression that had been in the quilt. Around them, toys were still strewn about, some chained to the floor by spiders' webs. For all these years, the room had been kept just as the Prince had left it, as if that was the charm to bring him home.

The cloud of dust filled Tasha's nose, making her cough.

"Can't we open a window or something?" she complained, seeing that even her son sneezed as he entered the room.

The younger man replied to her, smirking as he relaxed into a dusty chair. There was a red mark on his jaw, though it seemed to give him no pain.

"I'm afraid you can't, my dear. The window is sealed shut."

She looked up, noticing the edges of the window were filled with gray mortar, the same substance that ran between the cracks of the colorful mosaics.

"Of all the obnoxious things…"

She sighed, watching her son climb onto the occupied bed. The boy didn't seem to notice Asyrias' cold skin, or his stiff body. It didn't hurt Sen to see him this way, as it did her. Although she and her betrothed had never been close, it was painful to see him reduced to the sickly state he had been before, when she had first known him.

The older man, with sharp blue eyes and a warrior's build, knelt beside the injured Prince. Using bandages he found in a nearby drawer, he began to bind the ghastly wound on Asyrias' hand.

"Where do you think his sword is?" that man asked the other.

"Art probably fetched it. He's a very good watchdog."

"And how did you know where to find this man's room?"

The question inspired the other's laughter.

"It's just one of the things you learn when you're screwing his nursemaid."

The blue-eyed man rolled his eyes. Soon, his gaze shifted to her.

"Tell me, my lady: what is a Rionan doing in Larasca?"

She shrugged, preparing her usual excuse; however, the smirking man spoke before she had the chance.

"That's none other than the Princess Natasia Konstantin, no doubt fleeing her home country because of her bastard child."

Tasha had never been so furious in all her life—yet, the man laughed in the face of her rage.

"I knew you wouldn't tell, so I thought I would save you the trouble of lying."

His comrade stood, having finished bandaging the Prince's hand.

"Forgive his tactlessness."

He bowed as nobly as any royal.

"I am Baldric Alexander, Duke of Lucadia. The imbecile is called Giovanni."

The insulted man grinned.

"*I* am Giovanni Wolfslayer, legend of Larasca," he said.

Baldric scowled.

"Perhaps in your mind."

Soon, Baldric's searching eyes had returned to her, strange familiarity in their depths.

"Cedric spoke of you in his letters," he mused. "You had quite the spirit, for a little girl. He was looking forward to the day you would marry his son. I suppose if things hadn't become so complicated, you would be his wife right now."

"Maybe."

She sighed, feeling remorse as she gazed upon the Prince's lifeless body.

"That idiot," she whispered.

Asyrias' condition was strange. Though he was lifeless, his skin cold as ice, she could still see his chest move in faint, shallow breaths.

"What's wrong with him?" she asked.

"It's his Grace Period," said Giovanni.

"Grace Period?"

Baldric nodded, affirming the other man's statement.

"Cedric once spoke of it to me. He said it was the time an Xavier's soul remained in his body after his death, until it finally came time to move on. They breathe, though their heart has stopped; my family told me the same thing happened to my grandfather, when he died."

Tasha was intrigued.

"What does your grandfather have to do with dying Xaviers?"

"He was an Alexander," he explained. "They have the same ancestor. That was the real reason he was driven from the throne, though the Catsavion Priests claimed it was because he had a 'witch' for a wife. Carmen had strange markings on her skin, and she did know healing spells—but she was harmless. It was she who taught me how to make protection charms, to ward off hungry spirits…"

He shook his head, starting again.

"I never did know Draco very well. His wife died not long after I was adopted, and once she was gone, he went mad. He spent his time holed up in a hovel in Eastern Kyro, spouting prophecies. He would rave that my little sister Isabella had only dungeons in her future, and though Draco's premonitions had saved my father, Clemente, and his mother from the Catsavion coup, my father refused to believe him. Clemente shunned him as though he were a common drunk, until the day he died—but Draco was right. My family might have saved Isabella, if they had listened."

Baldric paused, something fresh in his memory.

"Draco said something strange to me, the last time I saw him. My father was about to send me into the Larascan Ranks to fight Catsavion power in Kyro, which meant I would probably never see my family again. My grandfather was an old man by then, and blind, I thought; yet he looked right at me when I saw him, and said in this strange voice, 'your blood will burn Larasca'."

As unusual as his tale was, it was not any supernatural detail that Tasha was curious about.

"You're Kyron?" she asked.

Giovanni began to laugh.

"Indeed he is—one very pale Kyron. He tried to pass as Larascan in the Ranks, but he would spew all sorts of foreign curses when you got him worked up. It made people quite suspicious. Only Cedric really trusted him."

Baldric glared, but it had no effect.

"That reminds me," Giovanni mused, "that boy Alastor wanted me to pass a message to your little girl."

"Alastor?"

Suddenly, the Duke stood alert, intrigued.

"Is he in the palace?" he asked.

"He was," Giovanni replied, "but he's gone now. Self-exiled himself to Kyro some weeks ago, poor boy."

"Fawk…"

Baldric sneered as he cursed, beginning to pace.

"I'll have to look for the idiot, at least. I'd rather make him my heir than Heather, though I might be stuck with her after all…"

"So you're going to Kyro?" Tasha asked.

"I don't have much choice."

The Princess smiled, recognizing opportunity when she saw it.

"Then take me with you."

At once, the Duke stopped his pacing. He stared at her in utter disbelief, so taken aback that his eloquence was compromised.

"*Take* you? Why?"

"I tire of Larasca," she said. "Nothing but bad weather and terrible people. And since Sen and I can't go back to Riona, I think a change in scenery will do us both some good."

"You don't understand," warned Baldric. "I left Kyro for a reason. It is a terrible place, ruled by ignorance and fear. That aside, you don't even know the language."

"Then teach my son on the way. He's a fast learner."

Sen sat up on the bed, alert as he always was when people spoke about him. He gazed at the Duke, his visage softening sweetly. It seemed Sen already understood his mother's wishes.

"Please, Sir," he said in his soft voice, "let us start new."

The hesitation never left Baldric's expression. However, confronted by the stubbornness of both mother and child, he consented.

"Fine," he said, sighing. "It seems I can't refuse a Princess in good conscience."

"Speaking of Princesses," Giovanni interrupted, "I believe I was telling you of Alastor's last words to your daughter."

The Duke scowled, irritated.

"And why not tell her directly?"

"I lack the motivation."

Giovanni smiled anew, amusement glistening in his every cunning feature. Though Tasha found him unnerving, she listened.

"Simple message, really," he said. "Sir Alastor asked that she keep him in her heart, and understand that the life she'll lead now is the result of his mistakes."

Ariel gazed upon the river that flowed behind Joanissia castle, carrying ice along its curving path, accepting more when a breeze caused the trees above to cast off their white lacing. A pale shroud concealed the garden's beauty, its red roses and emerald leaves. The brown-haired girl he had led here now seemed the only color upon the landscape, her blue eyes brighter than the sky above.

"It must be beautiful here, when the snow thaws," she said.

He managed a smile.

"In a way."

The crown upon her head seemed unusually bright, the dragons carved upon it gazing out through the gems that colored their eyes. He tried to ignore their stare.

Ariel brought her to the edge of the icy water, hoping she truly understood all he had told her about Avdotia Lake.

"Step into the water," he said. "That's what Asyrias did, before he said that spell."

"What did he say?"

He cringed, cursing a hazy memory.

"I only remember…names," he replied. "Girls' names, I think. He called them La, Ra, and Sha."

She didn't question him further. She knelt to remove her shoes, placing them in the snow beside her. When she entered the icy water, she didn't flinch. As her white skirt wrapped about her feet, she spoke soft words of summoning.

"Come out: La, Ra, and Sha."

Ariel's lingering skepticism ran dry when the water around her began to glow, light of a thousand suns casting their rays from beneath her, growing brighter as the water rippled and splashed. The youth shielded his eyes, overwhelmed by the light—yet soon, it vanished. His eyes opened to behold three unearthly women, scaled from their bosom to their thighs.

"She has already been crowned," said the first, a blonde whose scales shined blue as the sea.

"Then her Prince has fallen," said the second, with dark hair and scales of an emerald gleam.

The brown-haired girl held her heart, as though the very mention of that tragedy could pierce it.

"Silas is dying because of the sword you gave him," she said, her voice faltering. "Please, give me some way to save him!"

"Nasaria does not understand what she is asking," said the blonde.

"She will sacrifice much for his life," said her emerald sister.

The crimson-scaled woman came forward, gazing remorsefully upon the girl they called Nasaria.

"Should he die, you will be a fine Queen," she said. "You will live many years, and use them to bring peace and prosperity to your lands."

"It isn't worth his death," Nasaria sobbed. "I couldn't bear to be alone, knowing what he sacrificed for me."

The crimson creature closed her eyes, seeming resigned. Slowly, she revealed a silver hand mirror to their sight. At first, Nasaria's face was reflected in its surface, reddened by tears—but it changed. Soon, a little girl emerged from the haze, black curls spilling down her lacy gown, red lips quivering with sobs.

Tears welled in Ariel's eyes when he saw that child. His heart ached as he saw her pale hands reach towards the dark-skinned man who stood over her, ready to lift her into his strong embrace. He knew Nasaria would be won over by Asyrias' doting eyes, and the child's sweet kisses. She couldn't see the deep loss that had scarred both their hearts, scarcely concealed by broken smiles.

"Although the future you see has love, it comes at a price," said the creature. "Are you prepared to compromise your own life for the sake of this family?"

Nasaria's hesitation was fleeting. Ariel's aching heart knew, without doubt, that she would make the wrong choice.

"I will give anything for Silas' life."

The mirror vanished from the creature's hands, leaving behind a gray mist. The crimson woman looked to her sisters, who approached her in solemn silence.

"We have a liquid that will conquer Corliss' lethal poison. We will give it to you, if you do something in return."

"What must I do?" Nasaria asked.

"Offer your soul to the Goddess, Neschume."

The girl drew back, as bewildered as the youth who stood on shore.

"A…goddess?"

"She is a powerful entity, maker of all you see," said the blonde.

"But She was forced from these lands long ago," said the dark-haired creature. "Now, She is unjustly forgotten."

"Become an instrument for Her wishes," the crimson one continued, raising Nasaria's chin with a scaled finger. "With your selfless spirit in her service, some faith in Her restored, perhaps we as well can break from the shackles that bind us to Larasca's shadowed depths."

This was one part of the story Ariel had not known. He watched in awe and horror, unable to understand Nasaria's blind faith—for she did not hesitate. The slowness of her response came not from reluctance, but from the shock of icy water when she knelt before them.

"I offer my soul to Her," she said, shivering. "So long as Silas lives, all of myself belongs to Her, to do with as She sees fit."

Although her actions were naïve, careless, Ariel was touched by the sight of it. She loved so strongly that her own soul came second to that emotion. He had never witnessed such devotion to another human being. Even he indulged in only halfhearted relationships, taking pleasure in inconstancy. What he witnessed now was enough to choke him with shame.

No wonder he loved her.

The scaled women surrounded Nasaria, each placing a hand on her golden crown. All at once, they were engulfed in a great glow. Their silhouettes melded in that white light, forming a single entity. As the light faded, they had taken on a new shape—the likeness of the kneeling woman.

"Your job is half over," she said, her voice the blending of three whispers.

Nasaria rose, looking into her own countenance.

"What more do you want?"

The woman reached behind her, this time withdrawing a strange dagger, its hilt the wedge of a sundial. Ariel flinched, appalled by the sight of the weapon that had brought him so much grief.

"You must plunge this weapon into that youth's heart."

At last, Nasaria recoiled. She drew back when the weapon was offered to her, still shaking in the water's chill.

"I can't," she said. "I can't kill an innocent man."

"He is not innocent."

Once more, the enchanted dagger was offered to her.

"Neschume asks that this be done. Now is the time to prove your devotion to Her."

Although she took the dagger, she did no more than hold it in her faltering hands, staring at the blade.

"Take heart," said the holy woman, "his story will not end with this wound."

This must have been comfort enough. Soon, Nasaria approached him. Her blue eyes were filled with uncertainty, brimming with tears he did not deserve.

"Don't cry," he soothed. "This is just the way it has to be."

He unfastened the latch between his breastplates, splitting the Xavier insignia to expose his chest. The sight made her sob. As she grasped the hilt, she gazed at him through her remorse.

"I-I've already forgotten your name," she said.

"Ariel," he said.

"Ariel…"

Silent sobs clenched her chest, though she smiled just the same.

"Thank you," she whispered.

The dagger pierced his chest.

All at once, he could feel the weight of familiar shadows twisting about him, above him, within him. His vision clouded with light, everything around him beginning to dissipate.

His hand felt detached from him, reaching out to the crying woman. He focused on her blue eyes, remembering them—watching himself fade from their depths.

I'm sorry.

With a last, unraveling breath, he bid goodbye to his mother.

Chapter XLIII

*I*solation slit the last thread of the Princess' sanity. Her wounded mind peopled the darkness with shadows of her loss; ghostly Kings whispered in her ear, making her laugh, laughter echoing off the walls.

Betrayal…

Her own voice surrounded her, embraced her with the sound of laughter.

Shame, shame…

The floor beneath her was cold and dark, the same as the sky: not a star, not a soul around her but her own black one, black as the room.

Black, black…

That woman had taken everything from her. That woman whose shadow hovered there, a sister who could not bleed, bleed like anyone— like Attlas, like her womb.

Black, black, black as death.

Light flooded the room, scorching her altered eyes. She screamed like a babe, curling away from it.

"Azalea, the Queen has ordered your release."

Raoul's fair hair was lit by the unbearable light, glowing like flames. The sight of his white face hurt her now, but she stared at it, feeling her eyes burn. As she watched, he knelt before her, offering to her a glorious dagger. Its onyx hilt gleamed, washed of its misdeeds, familiar— Caden's dagger.

"I think you know what to do."

The dagger squealed as it dragged across stone walls, marking the Princess' winding path. The hilt trembled in her hands as she smiled, her smile making her feet unsteady. She could think only of its perfect blade, already sharpened by vengeance. Her smile grew, laughter welling until she at last opened the doors of her sister's chambers.

The Queen was turned from her, gazing out the open window at the white world below. Frost drifted in the room, carried by a sigh to rest in her raven locks. Though the door slammed loudly, Morana would not turn; she remained still, staring into an icy night.

"He used to stand by me here," she said suddenly, her voice somehow softened. "Before Asyrias was born, Cedric would put his arm around me here and say, 'you are my snow…beautiful, and mysterious'…"

When Morana laughed, it was not the cruel sound it had once been. It was quiet, gentle as falling tears.

"If I was snow, he was the brown earth, which nurtures and cherishes all life. You could see it in his drawings, hear it in his laughter."

She reached out into the swirling mist, her fingers trembling.

"I loved those drawings. I loved his smile. I loved the way he smelled…mortar, and glass…"

Then, came a soft, broken sob.

"I betrayed him. I betrayed him, like I betrayed you."

At last, the Queen faced her sister. Her eyes were altered, sapphire glistening like water; her strong stance was stripped away, leaving only the grace of a child.

"I wanted you to come now, so I could ask for forgiveness. I wish to repent for the horrendous wrongs I've done you…"

She fell to her knees, low as a servant.

"Forgive me, sister."

Her head fell, completing the image of martyrdom. She was poised with such innocence, frost anointing her raven locks like sinless diamonds. Azalea's sickness churned within her, creeping into her every vein. She would not stomach this perfect submission, this thought that suffering should be forgiven. The suffering would not end. This suffering was eternal.

The blade pierced Morana's throat, silencing her every poisonous word. Blood gurgled around the blade; the stunned woman could not beg, could do no more than grasp at Azalea's unyielding fingers. They held fast to the black hilt. Azalea could feel her face twist into a smile, as the Queen bled—bled like Attlas' child.

Her laughter spurt forth, same as the Queen's blood. As those sapphire orbs dulled, Azalea shrieked with joy.

"**Live,** Sister! Long live the Queen!"

The body fell lifeless at her feet, color leaving its skin. Azalea was not finished. Her blind pleasure led her to brandish her knife, carving away at its perfect skin, its breast, seeking to desecrate the hollow core of the soulless creature.

The knock came too quickly.

"Morana…"

Too soon, Saito parted the heavy doors. The color fled his skin as he saw the Princess standing before him, her black dress soiled with foul carnage—in her hand, a dripping, human heart.

"Look, Saito…look, love…"

She smiled, holding towards him her terrible trophy.

"This black heart bleeds red."

He stared as the organ fell from her hand, staining the stone beneath. So great was his fear that he did not see her raise her dagger again, grasping it with solemn pleasure.

"Arisa, what have you done?"

Too late, he saw her intent.

"**Arisa**!"

The red blade pierced her heart.

Chapter XLIV

*S*ilas was immersed in a gray world. Fog sighed at his feet, wallowing at the roots of tall, lifeless trees. It filled the air, so thick it made a chore of every breath; it concealed the black earth beneath him, and the sky above. The trees stretched on and on, offering no escape. No amount of wandering could bring their end, for every step brought him deeper into the mist, where hopes gave way to nothingness.

What is this?

He realized how his body trembled. He looked down at shivering arms, seeing the frost upon his skin, refusing to melt. For the first time in his life, he felt the cold.

"Hey!"

He called just to hear his voice echo off the trees, dying in the mist.

"Anyone!"

At first, there came only the remnants of his own call. Again, he was alone.

His body heavy, he slid down a nearby tree, finding no more reason to move forward. He watched the fog swirl around him, claiming its newest prize. However, it shifted when a dog's bark pierced the silence. He stiffened, but not before a black-eyed mongrel leapt from the forest, rolling clumsily before him.

Fawk...

He jumped to his feet, trying to escape what he thought was an assault. Yet, he paused, recognizing the creature's matted gray fur—the selfish smile on its dirty face.

"Ride?"

The mutt grinned, shaking frost from its coat. Before his eyes, the creature began to change. His limbs stretched and shifted, fur falling away until a young man knelt before him: hair falling in golden curls, a Princely thinness about him.

"Who are you?" Silas asked, repulsed.

He pouted like a child, as though the words were harsh.

"Corwin," he whined. "Why don't you know me?"

Silas drew back, too stunned to fully comprehend. Another's words came to him, the voice faint as someone else's dream.

The onyx Dragon: a beast who appreciates nothing but its own beauty.

The youth spun about, only to see another unwelcome entity. Rina's blond soldier scowled at him there, still in the royal, golden armor. His green eyes glowed.

"What are you looking at?" he spat.

He, too, began to change. His golden locks darkened to a common brown, as his young face hardened, marks of a sneer engraved in once-handsome features. All along, those green eyes remained the same, too vibrant in the dull fog.

Adrian is not a creature to be trifled with. He can transform the faintest shard of envy into a blade to pierce the strongest armor.

A sudden screech echoed in the treetops, disrupting Silas' gaze. Before he could move, a vicious mass of claws and fur came down upon him, tearing at his shirt as it shrieked. Cursing, he fought to snatch its long tail, using this to fling the creature from Malldon away from his body.

He, too, changed upon landing. A plain, tall man scrambled to his feet, tottering about as he grabbed a wineskin from around his waist. If the fall had disturbed him, it was already forgotten. The brown-eyed man toppled over once more as he gulped the liquid, mead shamelessly trickling down his face and neck.

Hale is the most benign of the Dragons; however, his power is no less great.

Repulsed, Silas tried to remove himself from their presence. It was then he felt the brush of black fur against his leg. He heard a low purr as the creature wrapped behind him, tail twisting about his legs. When this slid away, a new touch startled him; fingertips brushed up his spine, moving with a woman's sigh of laughter.

"What a strong, sturdy form…"

His disgust could not deter her advance. The woman's shapely form wrapped about him, her dark locks falling from her breasts as she leaned up, sapphire gaze locked with his as her lips came to steal his breath.

Sirena is a destroyer of men.

A hawk's screech broke her power over him. As he wrenched himself from her, he saw a great bird fly overhead, black wings spread wide as it made its final descent. No sooner had it touched the ground than it changed, taking on the form of an intimidating man. His face, handsome and angular, was reminiscent of Cedric's soft visage. Yet, he was the most unusual of the Dragons. There were moments he seemed transparent, when his body would jerk and shake, as if trying to break from the realm of existence. His eyes were the strangest of all: one of soft brown, the other a piercing gold.

Darian's regret was so strong that it split the creature's single mind in twain—and in its second head, glistening in Fabian's eyes, is the creature's ever-present guilt.

For a moment, this anguished creature seemed to smile. He extended his hand, trying to be gentle. However, his smile was soon transformed into the most monstrous of snarls, and he jerked back with revulsion.

"Just another failed Xavier," he said.

He turned from Silas and said nothing more.

Suddenly, the shape-shifting Dragons about him all stood still, their glowing eyes drawn towards a single place. The fog seemed thickest there, the frost condensing to a thin layer upon the dark soil. When Silas followed their gaze, he saw a shadowy creature emerge from the forest. Its white coat shimmered in the haze, gleaming as intensely as his blind eyes. As the great wolf sat there, head held high, Silas remembered the last time he had seen him—those white eyes staring at him as he held Rina, the wolf pack dead at his feet.

The creature changed, as the youth knew he would. Standing before him now was a man of youth, blonde locks fair enough to be white, his beard but snow upon his cheek. Though his youthful body was unmarked by labor, his gaze held the depth of age.

The philosopher's soul was transformed into the white Dragon of sloth: a manipulative creature, never to dirty its own hands.

Nukpana stood a mere foot from him, the shadow of the trees just darkening his visage. He said nothing—he only watched, waiting. Silas was frozen by his stare.

"What do you want from me?" he demanded.

Then, the Dragon gazed past him, eyes settling on each of his followers. One by one they came to him, forming a crescent before the Prince. Nukpana stood at its center, not a tremor of emotion upon his face.

"We have come to honor our King."

The creatures knelt before him, one by one, oblivious to his shock. He was no King. He did not want to be a King.

"Stand," he ordered. "I'm not who you think I am."

"You are an Xavier," Sirena purred.

"An Xavier must have the throne," said Nukpana.

Before he could think, a terrible growl shook the forest behind him. He spun about, poised to attack when the creature revealed itself. At first, it stood as a great, black dog, one he couldn't recognize. Its eyes were bloodshot, turned crimson by its rage. But as it bore its teeth, it was transformed into something familiar. Silas was staring into the scarlet eyes of the wolf he had slain, who had stood between him and Avdotia Lake.

The creature snarled and snapped at him in challenge, but Silas was unmoved. He stood his ground, returning the feral gaze with one of contempt. Only then did it change its form. The beast lifted itself from the forest floor, becoming a man. His skin shone like white ash, blood-red eyes in a pale face. He had once been handsome: his body was muscular beneath his loose garments, his striking face reminiscent of the mythical heroes. However, his wild hair had since become a fiery crown atop his head, as terrifying as the fangs that pierced his lip.

You must not allow Aiden's rage to make you blind.

"I will not bow," the beast snarled.

Silas stood silent, watching as Aiden reached for the jagged dagger at his side. He moved swiftly, grasping the weapon to slit his white palm. Fresh blood poured from the wound, more vibrant than any human's—Silas' blood.

"You are my equal."

Aiden extended his hand towards him, the Dragon's blood still dripping from his palm. This was a testament to the bond between them. All Silas was, all he had ever been, was because of this Dragon's crimson blood.

The creature waited, hand extended, for him to grasp it. This would be the pact between the King and Jaska, renewed. This King would have his Dragons, just as every King before him had had. By them, he lived and breathed. By them, he had a Kingdom to rule.

Silas' hesitancy began to melt away. Slowly, he reached out to Aiden, ready to accept this pact. Yet, just as he went to grasp the bloody hand, he saw his own scar across his palm, bestowed upon him when he had given in to the wrath in his heart—opened anew when he had discovered his true identity. Then, above that, the white mark about his finger, where the cursed ring had bound him. Someone kind had removed it. Someone beautiful, and soft, and loving; someone he wanted bound to him, so that he could always protect her, as she had protected him. Someone these creatures would own, if he took that hand.

"No."

He smacked Aiden's palm away, justified anger in his heart.

"Leave me **alone**."

There was new weight upon his belt. Corliss' golden hilt pulsed against his waist, possessed by his new strength. Silas hesitated no longer. He drew the sacred weapon, pointing the scarlet blade at his blood brother.

"I will **NOT** be your puppet," he snarled.

His words brought Aiden's fury. Smoke leaked between his sharp teeth as the man stared at him, anger narrowing his crimson eyes. All at once, a new transformation had begun. His eyes darkened and changed, as his body stretched and twisted; flames spurt from his mouth as the scaled beast emerged. He towered above the dead forest, massive wings beating the icy fog as his roar commanded the skies. This was the creature of Cedric's mosaics—Aiden's true soul.

Roars echoed all around him when the rest changed, the fiends towering all around him as they bayed to a colorless sky. Their scales gleamed in the gray world: black, green, brown, blue, gold, white, and red. Darian's heads twisted about each other, grotesque; venom dripped from Adrian's great teeth. Although Silas felt fear, he stood his ground. So long as Corliss pulsed within his grip, he would not give in to them.

"I will do as Cedric could not," he said, staring defiantly into the white eyes of their leader. "I forbid you to come into my home. As long as I live, I will fight you, until Larasca itself casts you into oblivion."

Nukpana lowered his great head, forcing Silas to confront his expressionless face.

"The Xaviers cannot resist our power. Though you may fight our influence, your children will not."

The Prince would not acknowledge him. He turned his back on Nukpana, again raising his blade against the crimson Dragon.

"Get out."

Aiden's rage flared anew. A piercing roar rang through the forest as the Dragon breathed his flames. They spread through the air, engulfing every tree in orange, and red, and black. Everything began to burn, leaving Silas without escape. As the fire engulfed him, smoke filling his lungs, he felt the power of the Dragons' possessive stare.

Chapter XLV

The light was too bright when Silas opened his eyes, reminding him of his headache. A bitter taste had settled into his mouth, generally unpleasant, and his hand felt stiff and numb. At once, he expected to be in a foul mood—then, he saw her. Her head on his chest, clutching a glass vial to her breast, Rina laid against his body. He could feel her unsteady breath, hear her gentle sobs. She was real to him. She was here.

When he stirred, she sat up, staring at him with reddened eyes.

"Silas?"

His name had never sounded so sweet. When Rina embraced him, his body felt light, yet strong enough to move monuments.

He was possessed by joy. The vial fell from her hand as he pushed her beneath him, pinning her there as he stole a long, fervent kiss. Her lips were as sweet as they had been before, nourishing his soul. This time, she didn't hesitate. Rina returned his kiss no less strongly, even reaching up to touch his face. However, no sooner had her hands touched him than she pulled back, wonder in her bright eyes.

"They're rough," she whispered. "Your cheeks…"

Silas pulled away, touching where her fingers had been. Indeed, there was the scratch of stubble upon his face, present for the first time in all his life.

He didn't know whether or not to call this a miracle. It was miraculous, perhaps, but brought him no more joy than the presence of the young woman who lay beneath him. She seemed so perfect now: dark locks fanned out upon his pillow, her warming smile set upon her innocent face. He didn't know what to say to her, anymore. Nothing seemed worthy enough for her blush.

At last, he saw the golden crown that lay beside them. It called to him, gleaming until he at last grasped its rim. All at once, he knew what to say.

"Marry me, Rina."

She seemed confused.

"You already asked me to be your Queen."

"That's not the same," he said. "I thought I was going to die. Now, I'm asking you to…stay. Stay, beside me."

He could tell she understood. She sighed, biting her soft lip, hesitating.

"Why?" she asked.

He could have told her a thousand reasons, all practical, unquestionable. Yet, as he pressed the crown into her hand, it was none of these that passed his lips.

"Because I love you."

Her eyes filled with tears, and he was gripped by fear. The words had spilled out, summoned by the agony of separation and the lingering chill of his own death. They were too much, too startling—he knew he had said the wrong thing. He was going to lose her again, because of his own stupidity. However, before he could retract his words, she was kissing him again, more tenderly than he had ever been kissed before.

"Then, yes," she whispered. "I'll marry you."

Silas had never felt such happiness. He touched her cheek, her neck, her breast, before he bravely kissed her waiting lips. Never again would he have to endure a life of loneliness, for she was there—she, who would never betray him.

The doors opened, forcing Silas to pull away. An unfamiliar man stood at the door, surprise on his venerable face. His eyes were blue, unusually so.

"Who are you?" Silas snapped.

Rina touched his hand, calming him.

"This is my father."

Suddenly, he was ashamed. Though he knew nothing about the man, he could not help but feel he had done something wrong. He hesitated, looking to Rina, then to the strong man who stood in the doorway.

"Then I should probably ask your permission before marrying her," he admitted, "but she already said yes."

The man paused, clearly astonished. However, there was no trace of anger about him. An indecisive silence was soon filled by a sigh, as the man shook his head.

"It's not really for me to say yes. She's done well enough on her own."

He paused; Silas glimpsed a flickering smile on his face.

"It seems I looked away, and she caught the eye of a King."

Rina placed the crown upon Silas' head, adoration in her eyes. As the ornament settled in his locks, she embraced him, enveloping him in her warmth. He could not help but hold her, protecting her from the castle's chill.

Asyrias smiled, knowing he was home.

The wedding was extravagant. It seemed all of Joanissia was there to see their King joined with this beautiful stranger; the Great Hall was filled with spectators, from peasants in their homespun rags to the overdressed Barons and their pretty daughters. Even the six Councilmen came to kneel before the platform, demonstrating their allegiance to their young leaders.

Giovanni watched from afar as the Captain of the Guard held a flickering candle between the man and the woman, both dressed as royalty: Asyrias in black garments of the finest silk, Nasaria's white dress glistening like diamonds. Both said the binding words of the ceremony.

"I vow to protect the light of our days," said the King. "You will never know want or woe."

"I vow to nurture the light of our love," said his Queen. "I will shoulder your burdens, and give rest to your soul."

Together, they took Art's candle, bringing it to a golden bowl filled with oil. With its fire, they lit the liquid aflame, filling the room with new light. When Art removed the candle, the two of them kissed more passionately than any King or Queen before them. All of Joanissia erupted in applause, and their leaders kissed, oblivious to the sounds of the world. Such was the nature of their love.

Giovanni stole away when the music began, the celebration proceeding. He didn't much feel like dancing again. He had had his fill of such light-hearted festivities.

He had made his place among the frost of the stairs' bottom steps, far away from the light of palace torches. From there, he could see the dark houses of the loyal nobility, stretched out as far as he could see. Above him, the celebration went on; his part in it was done.

The soldier stood, taking a moment to brush the ice from his trousers. With a final adjustment of his sword, he was prepared to depart. However, a familiar sensation halted his exit. He turned, seeing his adopted son standing at the top of the steps, staring down at him. Silas was dressed for his role, now donning even the heavy Xavier crown. Giovanni found it amusing, for even Cedric had despised that adornment.

"You look sharp, boy," he called.

The young King made no secret of his irritation. Even so, he descended the steps to join him.

"You're leaving, aren't you?" he asked.

"Perhaps," Giovanni replied.

"Where?"

The ex-Commander shrugged, chuckling to himself.

"I'll know when I get there."

"Why not stay?" Silas asked, judging the man with his eyes. "Twyla's been released from the dungeons. You should see her."

Once more, Giovanni shrugged.

"Antonio will see to her."

His gaze wandered to the strange sword hung at Silas' hip. It seemed a majestic weapon: golden hilt carved like wings, making a great contrast to its plain sheath. He could not help his intrigue.

"How about one last duel for your old man?" he asked.

The youth looked at him warily.

"This isn't Edmund's blade," he said, as if in warning.

In response, Giovanni drew his own sword.

"Do I see a hesitant King?"

This inspired a familiar scowl. Even then, his decision took time. His son looked to the weapon, then back to Giovanni, contemplating something. The man merely waited. Sure enough, the young man soon descended the last of the icy steps. He took his place across from his opponent, drawing a great, scarlet blade.

"Give me something to remember," said Giovanni.

Silas sneered.

"I ought to give you more than that."

They stood facing each other, weapons poised for battle. This time, Giovanni decided to give his son the first strike.

The youth attacked as he always did: stepping forward, random swing from the side. Giovanni evaded smoothly. He spun about, allowing his opponent to recover from tangled footing. His blade swung to counter, for he already knew where Silas would be.

This time, he was wrong. The youth had ducked to the opposite side, too swift to anticipate. Only speed saved the ex-Commander from his miscalculation. Their blades crashed, sparks flying as both countered the others' attacks. Giovanni could no longer predict his movements. For the first time, they fought on equal ground.

He could hear the crunch of ice beneath their feet. His boots nearly slid from underneath him as he reconciled the man's advances. Each came swifter than the last, forcing him to re-evaluate his own ability in order to meet them. The thrill of it brought his laughter. No longer was Silas possessed by anger, swinging mindlessly in hopes to overwhelm him. Every movement was precise, aimed to throw him off balance.

No longer was Silas the crying child he had taken in. The man who fought him now was the King his country so needed.

Giovanni's own sword was knocked from his hands, disappearing into the fresh snow. He saw the crimson blade pointed at his throat.

"Match."

The soldier's smirk only grew; before long, he felt stifled laughter shake his body.

"Well, what do you know," Giovanni chuckled. "I suppose you're right."

He stood when the sword was removed, again having to brush ice from his trousers. As he went to retrieve his own weapon, something else landed in the snow beside him—a smooth, black diamond.

"Take it," said the youth. "Do something useful."

Giovanni lifted it up, examining it curiously.

"Are you certain?"

"I want nothing to do with it."

The man chuckled, sliding the gem into his pocket. At last, he lifted his own weapon from the snow, finding its blade already cold to his touch.

"I always knew I would see this day," he said.

When he turned, he could see Asyrias' intense gaze. Yet, for once, he didn't only see their strange color. These were Cedric's eyes, masked by an amethyst glow.

"I'm proud of you, son."

He had nothing left to say.

Again he turned, beginning the long walk down Joanissia's cobblestone path. Soon, the soldier went to return his sword to its scabbard, only to find the snow had not yet fallen from the blade. He lifted it to the moonlit sky, wiping the frost away with his own palm. For an instant, he saw the King reflected in its surface, watching his departure. Giovanni grinned, knowing this was the last he would see of his Silas.

The End

It has been five years since I began my rule. I had no interest in beginning this record, but Reade and Reginald hounded me about it so mercilessly that giving in was the only way to shut them up.

I shall provide a summary of my reign to this date:

Shortly after my coronation, Raoul Markovich resigned from his position. He would not give a reason. I authorized Saito to fill his place, and he has since become an admirable Grand Advisor. To fill the vacancy left by this promotion, I saw fit to release Edmund from the Alore prison, allowing him to assume the position of my second Lesser Advisor. He brought Madeleine when he came, which was expected. It hasn't been a problem, as she seems too shocked by my title to give me any lip. Even so, it is nice to have my sister home with me.

I found Caine's armor in the back of the armory, where the guards must have taken it when they confiscated my belongings. I tried to give it to Tasha, but she was nowhere to be found. To honor Caine's sacrifice, I now have it on display in Raphael's abandoned room, which has since been restored to a remotely livable state. Even so, Rina and I chose to move into my father's old chambers—neither one of us much likes the feel of that tyrant's room.

Rina asked to have a plot in the graveyard to house the remains of her Talonian lover. Hearing of his miserable end, I consented. It was too late to salvage his bones from the Peasant Square's open grave, so all she could bury in the plot was the bracelet he had given her, recovered from the hay in the palace stables. Still, she seems content with this. His headstone will stand alongside the Xaviers', where she can go and pay homage as she pleases.

It turns out Twyla conceived by Giovanni before his departure. Some months later, she birthed twin sons, whom she named Jovan and

Gianni. Antonio has had to help raise them—how ironic that Giovanni isn't there to raise his own children.

I speak often with Clarke Temlar; he gives sound advice. I can see now why my father confided in him. At the time Twyla gave birth, Rina was also heavy with child. Temlar reminded me again of Cedric's theory of commoner twins being born as 'keepers' for coming royal twins, and the birth of Jovan and Gianni was surely a sign that Rina would bear two Princes. I denied this, of course, already concerned for my wife's safety. He was right, though. On the 11th Day of 10th Month, 655 I.R., my sons were born. The eldest is Nikolai Antonio Xavier, a bright child, quiet as he is; the second-born is my Ariel. Rina herself named him: Ariel Baldric Xavier.

My life changed when Niki and Ari came into the world. My worries all melt to nothing when one of them toddles up to me, smiling their mother's smile. They've gotten so big. Their infant plumpness has already gone away, and they fight constantly over their wooden swords and toy soldiers. Their growth gives me such pride. They're identical, outwardly, but couldn't behave with more difference. In Niki, I see the makings of an uncompromising leader; in Ari, I see a clever scholar, whose cunning will topple empires.

Rina is expecting again. We became rather lazy about preventing it, so it came as no surprise. The child is already prominent and amusingly active within her. Rina insists it's a girl, and I allow her delusion. She doesn't understand that there are no girls born into the Xavier family, not since Fabian's twins. Even so, the thought of a daughter pleases her; I won't take that away.

A situation in Malldon has been brought to my attention. There have been reports of an illness rising from the lake itself, which has infected the townspeople at an alarming rate. Saito and Gabriel believe it would be best for me to assess the situation in person—if it threatens to spread, drastic measures must be taken.

I do not wish to leave Rina at this delicate stage of her pregnancy, but I have little choice. She will have to celebrate the twins' fifth birthday without me. All I can do is travel quickly and hope for her safety.

I leave tomorrow. The twins have been told. Soon, I will go to my wife, and hope I will not have to wake her.

~Asyrias Reja Xavier

Epilogue

25th Day of 11th Month, 660 I.R.

*N*ikolai dragged his brother down to the gardens late that night, ignoring all of Ariel's sleepy protests. He had seen his mother out the window, sitting on the steps as snow began to fall. He didn't want her to be outside alone.

"Niki, you're dumb…"

Ariel tugged back as he whined, trying futilely to escape his brother's strong grip.

"I wanna go to bed!"

Nikolai grabbed his brother's nose with his little fingers, chastising him.

"Don't whine," he said. "Mama will hear."

"But she tucked us in, we gotta stay in bed…"

The elder twin squeezed his nose harder, making Ari whimper.

"We gotta watch her. Papa said so."

The Prince dragged Ariel down to the castle's gardens, sneaking out through the servants' passageway. Soon, he saw his mother sitting on the edge of the steps where he had glimpsed her, leaning against a tall, stone pillar. She seemed tired, still heavily burdened by the child within her; yet, Niki could see her smile as she stared up into the falling snow.

Gripping Ari's hand tighter, Nikolai tried to go out to her—however, he stopped, glimpsing a tall figure at the bottom of the steps. He and Ariel ducked behind a pillar as the King ascended the stairway, still wearing his golden armor, his dark hair loosened from his helmet by the persistent wind.

Ari began to tug against his brother's hold again, giddy with excitement.

"Papa! Papa's ho—"

Niki smothered him with his hand, hushing him. He didn't want to be seen yet.

Soon, Asyrias knelt before his Queen, removing his helmet to reveal his unshaven face. He smiled up at her, closing his eyes when Nasaria touched his cheek.

"You look ragged," she teased.

"It's been a long journey," he said.

He touched her hand, keeping it there.

"I came directly from the stables," said the King. "I don't feel like debriefing Gabriel just yet. I don't have the energy for it."

Nasaria kissed his forehead, as sweetly as she might have kissed Niki. In return, he touched her swollen belly.

"How's the child?" he asked.

"Missing her father," she replied. "You were gone for too long."

He sighed.

"She'll come next month, probably. I'll apologize to her myself."

The Queen laughed, the sound more vibrant than it had been since her husband's absence. Blushing, Nikolai began to smile, he and his brother more than happy to hear it again.

"I know what I want to name her," Nasaria said.

"Oh?"

"Siria," she said. "Princess Siria."

The King raised a brow, clearly surprised.

"You want to name a girl after her father?"

"Yes..."

Asyrias chuckled to himself, rising up to sit beside her. Nikolai watched as his father wrapped an arm around her, using his free hand to brush delicate flakes from her dark locks. She looked up at him, admiring him, seeming eased by his presence. Yet, Nikolai felt uneasy. He could sense something strange about them, a dark cloud, one that grew denser as the two of them came together.

His father leaned down, ready to kiss his blushing wife. It would have been a perfect reunion: the snow falling all around them, its faint chill bringing them closer. However, Nikolai's uneasiness would not let it be.

"Stop!"

The boy rushed out from behind the pillars, jumping to wedge himself between their bodies. He almost knocked his father over in the process, who gave him a shocked, heated look. Niki flinched away, always frightened by the King's angry eyes; he was fortunate that his mother sheltered him with her arms.

"What's wrong, child?" she asked.

He wiped away inexplicable tears, whimpering.

"I don't...know..."

He couldn't understand why he feared for his mother, why he wanted to keep the two of them apart. Even now, this feeling was strong in him, so much so that he feared his own father.

Ariel ran out next from behind the pillars, laughing like an idiot.

"Papa!"

When Ariel embraced Asyrias, the man's irritation left in a sigh. He relaxed, wrapping his arms around his favorite son. Niki couldn't help but feel a twinge of jealousy, for it was his younger brother who received all of the King's smiles. It seemed that would never change.

Nikolai relaxed when his mother touched his hair, soothing away his worry.

"You can listen to Siria, if you want," the woman said.

The child nodded, pressing his ear against her belly. Within, he could hear a small heartbeat, whose fluttering pulse came like a soft melody. He smiled, as he always did. He wanted very much to meet his baby sister, who would play with him when he was sad, and love the toys he gave her.

"You look tired, Niki," said the Queen, keeping him close. "Go ahead and sleep."

The Prince looked over at his brother, who already seemed to sleep in his father's embrace. His black hair covered his eyes, and he clung to the King, content. Despite his uneasiness, Niki began to feel the same fatigue wash over him.

Only for a moment...

He closed his eyes, feeling the soft flakes of winter begin to frost his dark locks. Lulled by his sister's heartbeat, he soon fell asleep.

As soon as their children were asleep, Asyrias moved nearer to his love. He was careful of the boy he held, as well as the one against her body, but he soon came close enough to kiss her neck.

"They're beautiful," he murmured, his voice muffled by her skin.

"They look like you," Nasaria replied.

"Is that bad?"

The woman shook her head, still stroking Nikolai's dark locks.

"What happened in Malldon?" she asked, gently.

At this, the King hesitated. In his mind's eye, he saw the flames rising from the cursed city, himself and his men far removed from the massacre.

"The situation has been resolved."

"And you?"

He looked at her curiously, not understanding.

"Did you get sick?" she asked, laughing.

Asyrias relaxed, calmly shaking his head.

"No."

He had checked all of his men when they left Malldon. No one showed any symptoms of the strange disease, and he had felt none himself. For now, the epidemic was over.

"Maybe you just can't tell you have it," his wife teased.

"Hn."

Nasaria gazed out over the landscape, watching the falling snow beginning to cover the green trees, lush flowers, even the river in the same blanket of whiteness.

"I love the first snowfall," she said, distance in her eyes. "I thought I would like spring the most, but there's only so long that all those colors can seem new. There's nothing like the first day when all the world starts to turn white…"

The King watched her as she spoke, bewitched by her soft features. It was hard to remain so far from her, after that long absence.

"Don't you agree, Silas?"

He nodded, though he hadn't really listened. He touched her chin, raising her gaze to meet his.

"Nothing interests me more than you."

At last, he took her lips in his, feeling her succumb to him once more. All was perfect—the snow about them, her long-missed sweetness. The King didn't yet know he had killed her with his kiss.

The Xavier Mosaic II
Princess Siria

Once upon a time, in an isolated land,

there lived a beautiful Princess.

She was beloved of all, but most of all by the King,

in whose eyes she could do no wrong.

The King is killed, her brothers fight,

and her young heart is broken.

In the dark of night, she runs away,

into the arms of a monster.

About the Author

Emma Austen is eighteen years old, studying English at University of
California Irvine. She has lived most of her life with one foot in reality and the
other in a fantasy land. She hopes that one day, the rest of the world will know
Larasca the way she does.

Join the Dynasty

www.xaviermosaic.com

16167755R00363

Made in the USA
Lexington, KY
09 July 2012